Reviews for *The President's Gardens*

"Though firmly rooted in its context, *The President's Gardens'* concerns are universal. It is a profoundly moving investigation of love, death and injustice, and an affirmation of the importance of dignity, friendship and meaning amid oppression. the novel is undoubtedly a tragedy, but its light touch and persistent humour make it an enormous pleasure to read"

ROBIN YASSIN-KASSAB, *Guardian*

"A story buffeted by the wider tides of history: the bloody churn of dictatorship, invasion and occupation . . . *The President's Gardens* evokes the fantastical, small-town feel of *One Hundred Years of Solitude* . . . shocks and enchants" TOM GORDON, *Financial Times*

A beautiful novel . . . Consistently compelling . . . In writing about ordinary Iraqis who pay the cost of wars waged by autocratic leaders, Al-Ramli touches on deep and timeless themes"

ALASTAIR MABBOTT, *Glasgow Herald*

"Like Gabriel García Márquez, with whom he is often compared, Al-Ramli has created a specific village that manages to be universal and a story that is rooted in history while reaching forward into the present day" KATHY WATSON, *Tablet*

"A tour de force" RACHEL HALLIBURTON, *Prospect*

"A stunning achievement" BEN EAST, *The National*

Also by Muhsin Al-Ramli in English translation

Scattered Crumbs

Dates On My Fingers

The President's Gardens

Muhsin Al-Ramli

DAUGHTER OF THE TIGRIS

Translated from the Arabic by
Luke Leafgren

MACLEHOSE PRESS
QUERCUS · LONDON

First published in Great Britain in 2019 by MacLehose Press
This paperback edition published in 2020 by

MacLehose Press
An imprint of Quercus Publishing Ltd
Carmelite House
50 Victoria Embankment
London EC4Y 0DZ

An Hachette UK company

A CIP catalogue record for this book is available from the British Library.

ISBN (MMP) 978 0 85705 684 9
ISBN (Ebook) 978 0 85705 683 2

10 9 8 7 6 5 4 3 2 1

Designed and typeset in Collis by Libanus Press

Printed and bound in Great Britain by Clays Ltd, Elcograf S.p.A.

MIX
Paper from
responsible sources
FSC® C104740

Papers used by Quercus are from well-managed forests and other
responsible sources.

To everyone wounded in his body, his soul, his memory . . .
or in his homeland.

CHAPTER 1

Qisma Decides to Eat Iraq

After vomiting by the side of the road on the way to Baghdad, Qisma felt hungry and decided to eat Iraq.

That was what she resolved after the farcical scene with the Americans. When Tariq the Befuddled, who had become her husband the day before, stopped his car on the side of the road, she had leaped out quickly, leaving her infant child in the back seat. Qisma knelt on the ground and disgorged her breakfast onto the rocks. That was when she saw a thicket of military boots crowding her on all sides. She lifted her head and found herself surrounded by American soldiers, their rifles trained upon her.

Qisma turned towards the car before trying to stand up, and even before she had wiped the last traces of vomit from around her mouth. She saw other soldiers pointing their guns at Tariq, who was still sitting in the driver's seat with his hands above his head. The soldiers had blocked him off with two Hummer jeeps, while an intimidating military column continued down the highway. When she saw one of them point his gun at her child too, she made a sudden, terrified motion to rise, but the heavy hands of the soldiers on her shoulders prevented her from doing so, and she screamed at the top of her voice, "I'm just throwing up. You pigs!"

The circle of boots around her took a step back, but the hands of the two soldiers on either side of her were still pressing her into the ground. She heard one of them speaking into his radio above her, and among what she could understand with her basic English was the question "What should we do with them?" and a curt "O.K." Her neck remained twisted uncomfortably, and her heart was breaking at the sight of her child crying silently while he looked at her in terror. Two other soldiers forced Tariq roughly out of the car and brought him round to the boot. He opened it, took out some of the things and put them back. Then they led him forward. He opened the bonnet, and they looked inside before closing it and ordering Tariq to bend over with his arms braced against it. He tried to resist, but they forced him to comply. He looked at Qisma, utterly humiliated, hoping that she might forget this scene and never once recall it, especially during the nights of passion to come when he would ask her to assume this same position for him.

The child's cries rose up when he saw one of the soldiers put his head and shoulders through the window to continue the inspection. This time Qisma screamed, "Let me go!" Such was the power of her cry that she felt as though she were in the middle of a square full of pigeons that had suddenly taken flight. It seemed to her that the entire column of armoured military vehicles flew up into the air, recoiling in panic. What actually happened was that her scream coincided with the passage of a flight of helicopters above the military column, even as one of the jeeps detached itself and braked to a halt only a few metres from where she knelt. Three solders got out and came directly towards her.

She knew one of them was the commanding officer because, when he directed his words at the others, they let her go at once. She stood up and hurled herself towards the car, snatching an abaya that she draped over her head. Then she picked up her child and raised him to her bosom. She turned to face the group of soldiers, or, to be more precise, their commanding officer. She stood directly in front of him, and, although he was a tall man, she somehow felt she was taller. She looked him hard in the eyes, as though to bore twin holes into them with her gaze. In clear English – for even if she had forgotten everything else she had learned of the language at the institute, she would never forget how to swear – she yelled, "What is this fucking shit? Why are you doing this? What right do you have?"

She spat the words out of her mouth as if they were flying nails that would tear at his ears. But something changed in an instant when the commanding officer replied in clear, eloquent Arabic. "I beg your pardon, sister," he said. "Peace be upon you. I am General Adam."

The tone of his voice was like cool water that doused the fire within. Her sight returned, and she saw that he was blond, with captivating green eyes. He was wearing an elegant military uniform and gave off a pleasing scent of cologne. He held himself upright in a way that she liked. For a moment she felt the desire to throw herself against his chest and wrap her arms around him. Their eyes remained locked, and he added in a kind voice, "Everyone knows the instructions – they're written on all our vehicles: 'Caution: Stay 100 metres back or you will be shot.' Didn't you see them? But it's O.K. Thank God the matter turned out this way. Is this the first time you've seen us?"

"Yes," she said calmly. "You only passed briefly through our village."

"Where are you going?"

"To Baghdad."

"O.K. Go in peace. But please, remember these instructions! One hundred metres, at least." Then he reached out his hand to caress the child's head with a smile. "Don't be afraid," he said. "What is your name, little one?"

The child turned its face away, and, after a moment's thought, Qisma replied, "Ibrahim."

This was the first time she had called her son by that name, her father's name, which she had decided to bestow upon her son in place of the name of the deposed president, the name given by the child's executed father.

"He is your son?"

"Yes."

"O.K., Umm Ibrahim. Do you need anything from us?"

"No. Just stay away and leave us in peace."

"Fine," he said with a smile. "Go in peace."

The soldiers turned away, but Qisma stood watching the general as he strode towards his vehicle. He waved at her and got inside, and the jeep swung around to rejoin the column, which immediately drove away. Qisma remembered what she had heard about the gang rape inflicted by four American soldiers on a young woman, Abeer al-Janabi, in the village of Mahmudiyah. They had killed her father – who worked as a guard at a vegetable warehouse – her mother, and her five-year-old sister. Then they raped Abeer and killed her. Afterwards, they burned the bodies. Qisma spat in disgust in the direction of the departing convoy. She returned to the car, where she found Tariq opening a case of water bottles. He took one out, opened it, and offered it to her, saying in a subdued voice, "These are from them."

All three drank from the bottle. They washed their hands and faces with the cold water, feeling a measure of calm and composure return to them. Qisma settled Ibrahim in the back seat, and the three of them continued their journey in despondent silence.

After about ten minutes, Tariq said, "Thank God it turned out like that and nothing worse! I've heard about them killing people on the road on the pretext that they'd got too close."

Qisma did not reply. In the renewed quiet that followed, both she and Tariq wondered what Abdullah Kafka would have done in that situation had he continued with them on this journey instead of changing his mind and asking to get out of the car shortly after leaving the village.

At that moment, Abdullah was alone, as usual, smoking a cigarette in the cemetery, uncertain and angry. He walked back and forth between the grave of the severed head of Ibrahim, Qisma's father, and the grave of Zaynab, his own grandmother, asking them what he ought to do with the man who had fathered him by raping his poor mother.

He addressed the grave of the old lady. "Your son, Jalal the runaway, has come back bearing the name of Sayyid Jalal al-Din. Here he is, Zaynab, one of the new rulers and rapists of Iraq. What am I to do, Grandmother?"

Then Abdullah went over to the grave of Ibrahim's head and said, "Your daughter, my dear Ibrahim, has married our oldest friend. She has gone with him to seek your body with the help of the man who raped my mother. What am I to do, my friend?"

He stood between the two graves, asking himself, "What if he comes with them to the village?" He turned in a circle, scratching his dishevelled hair with a hand that still held a cigarette, nearly setting it on fire. Then he had the answer: "I will kill him. I will tear him into small pieces and feed him to the dogs so that he won't have a grave for people to remember him by. I will kill him. I will kill him. I have endured nearly twenty years of torture in Iranian prison camps in defence of this country, and then this runaway, this man who raped my mother, returns to become master over it. I will kill him."

Abdullah squatted down. He got back up. He turned in a circle. He wandered between the two graves, smoking as he repeated, "I'll kill him. I'll kill him." Then he passed by all the other graves, one by one, informing each: "I'll kill him. I'll kill him." He carried on in this way until he grew tired of addressing the graves, and decided he would go and talk to Anwar, the young man who worked in his field, or Hamid the Snorer, his friend who spent his days dozing in the village café.

After another half-hour of silence, Tariq said to Qisma, "I'm thinking we shouldn't go straight to Baghdad today, but rather we should pass by one of the villages on the outskirts of Samarra. The village sheikh has been a friend of mine since childhood, and his father was a friend of my father's. You could say he is more like a brother to me than a friend. We could spend the night there, hear their news, and ask whether they've heard of anyone around here coming across any decapitated corpses."

When Tariq did not receive a reply, he turned to look at Qisma. She indicated her agreement with a nod. Tariq went on speaking, eager to demonstrate his importance and his connections after the humiliation he had suffered at the hands of the Americans, and to introduce her to people who were in a position to help them. "The sheikh's name is Tafir al-Shakhabiti. He is the head of the famous Shakhabit tribe. It is said that this tribe numbers more than a million people, spread throughout almost every corner of Iraq. His father was my father's friend, and they would visit each other once a year. When my mother was pregnant with me, Tafir's father asked mine what name he would give me, and my father said, 'Tariq.' The old sheikh decided to give his next son the same name, but when he returned to his village, he couldn't remember what it was, just that it began with the letter 'T'. So he called his son Tafir. We were born in the same year, just a month apart, and our fathers would bring us along on all the visits they paid one another, so we became friends from a young age. Of course, stories of strange names are nothing new in this family – they go back a century, to the days of the Ottoman empire.

"The first sheikh of the Shakhabit worked as a groom in the stables of a pasha who sometimes entrusted him to prepare coffee and serve it to his guests. The pasha was very fond of this groom. After the Ottoman empire was defeated in the First World War and the British occupation began, he chose to give all his lands to his beloved servant. He departed for Istanbul, and the groom became a feudal lord, taking the place of his master by ruling over the peasants and giving positions of power to his brothers, nephews and other relatives. Now, when the British occupied Iraq, they were different from the Ottomans in one crucial respect: they were far more eager to document, demarcate, organise and record, and they required agencies to be set up in the cities to record births, marriages, divorces and other administrative matters that the Ottomans had not cared about in the slightest. This servant-who-had-become-a-sheikh did not know how to read or write. When his first son was born and he wanted to enter the boy's name in the registry of births at one of the new government offices, he was too ashamed to admit before the British officials or his new subjects that he was illiterate, so he scribbled a few messy lines on a piece of paper and gave it to one of his servants, together with gifts of food and money. He ordered him to go to the city to register the infant and acquire an identity card for him. When the official in the registry office saw the paper he stood up angrily. 'What is this scibble?' he asked. The servant was at a loss – he had not presumed to read the name on the paper till then, and it seemed it was up to him to interpret the sheikh's impenetrable scrawl. He set the bag of gifts down on the official's desk, and thought hard about how to record the name without incurring the sheikh's displeasure. Then, at last, it struck him, and he solemnly wrote in the official ledger the word *Shakhbata* – 'Scribble'!"

Qisma laughed. Tariq was delighted and laughed along with her. He felt a sudden frisson of desire when he saw in the rear-view mirror how her breasts shook when she laughed. He thought about taking the car off-road to drive down through the trees and fields. There, by means of Qisma's body, he would regain his wounded male dignity, which the American soldiers had taken from him before her very eyes. He would repair his manhood by inscribing it on her body. But he put aside this audacious idea; far better for now to keep calming her down and making her laugh – and watching the movement of her breasts.

"But there's more to the story than that!" he announced once their laughter had subsided. "The sheikh kept calling his son by the name of his Ottoman master, Dawud Pasha, a name he had given him orally, out of gratitude and affection for his former master. And so it was that everyone knew him by this name. But when the boy grew up and went to enrol in school, carrying his official papers, he discovered that his real name was entirely different, and he was known legally as Shakhbata. He could not have been more upset. He returned to his father in tears, for his name ended in the feminine letter 'A', just like all the girls' names. The father was surprised, then angry and finally enraged, to the point that he decided to kill the servant he had sent to register the birth. But fortunately the imam of the village was present in the sheikh's reception hall at that very moment and, using his tact and intelligence, he was able to cool the man's blood and turn the situation around. He announced to them that this was a beautiful name, rare and special, and that no-one apart from his son possessed it. It was not to be supposed that he would have a normal name like the sons of servants and peasants. What's more, many of the preeminent companions of the Prophet and the first heroes of Islamic history had names along these lines.

He began to rattle them off, recounting the stories he knew from his historical and religious studies: Talha, Ikrima, Hanzala, Abu Abida and the Prophet's uncle Hamza, among others.

"After that, the boy and his father grew to like the name very much, and they ordered everyone to use it whenever they addressed him. As for the son, he liked it even more when he grew up, and after he finished his education he renounced the name Dawud Pasha, as a way of rejecting the period of Ottoman occupation and accepting the yoke of the British – their civilised enemies, as he referred to them. And so, when he became sheikh upon the death of his father, he decided that the name of the tribe would be tied to his own, and they became the Shakhabit. Actually, it was he who secured for the tribe its power and standing, thanks to his close relationship with the British. He opened the first school in the village, and he spoke English. Over the years, his own status grew in the region, since he resolved many of the difficulties that arose between the native population and the British, and he collected money from both sides. Many of his relatives and members of his tribe named their children, both male and female, with variations on his name: Shakbut, Shakbuta, Mushakhbat, Mushakhbata, Shakhabit, Shakhabita, Shakhbat, Shakhbata, and so on. And thus, the tribe began to take pride in being known as the Shakhabit."

Tariq had reached the place where he had to take a left turn for the familiar dirt road that would bring him to the village of his friend, Sheikh Tafir al-Shakhbati, on the banks of the river, after passing by a number of small villages and scattered houses belonging to the tribe. But he was surprised to find, for the first time, a checkpoint set up at the junction. Several armed young men, some in military uniforms and others in city clothes or traditional peasant robes, all wearing ammunition belts, called for him to stop. They asked who he was and where he was going and why. He told them he was Sheikh Tariq, a friend of Sheikh Tafir, who had come to visit him. They asked for his I.D. card, and those of the people with him, and he handed them over. They asked about the woman and the child, and he told them, "My wife," adding, after a brief pause, "And my son." The young man stared at their I.D. cards, and it seemed as though he did not understand or could not read well, for he kept looking back and forth from the pictures on the cards to the faces of the owners. Tariq feared they would demand to see a document confirming that the woman was his wife, for their marriage had not been officially confirmed and was sanctified only by a verbal contract, announced before guests at a small banquet in his village the previous night.

The young guard did not say anything. He just went inside the guardhouse and came out with another young man, who was apparently in charge. He recognised Tariq immediately, and Tariq him. He was the son of one of Sheikh Tafir's brothers, someone Tariq had seen a number of times in Tafir's reception hall during his previous visits. Tariq got out of the car and embraced him. After the initial greetings, the young man invited Tariq to come sit and drink tea with them.

They had a corpse with them, one of the corpses that people had become accustomed to discovering in the fields beside main roads. Qisma insisted on getting out to examine it despite

Tariq's attempts to prevent her. How could she not, when she had resolved to search for the corpse of her father and had married Tariq and set off on this journey precisely for that reason?

Even though the corpse by the road was intact, including its head, and could not be supposed to be the body of her father, of which nothing but its head had been discovered and buried, Qisma nevertheless stood staring at it for a long time, studying the holes in its chest and neck, and the patches of dried blood on its clothes. She would actually have touched it had Tariq not pulled her away. Then he thanked the young man for his invitation, explaining that they were tired from the journey, and that the child was hungry. They wanted to reach Sheikh Tafir's home before nightfall.

As they resumed their journey, Tariq was surprised to find workmen with tools and machines labouring to pave the old farming road and set up electrical poles alongside it, something that would further delay their arrival, however much it might shorten the journey in the future. When Qisma asked him how long it would take, he estimated an hour and a half. "Are you hungry?" he asked.

"Yes."

"What do you want to eat?"

"Iraq."

"Excuse me?"

"Iraq."

Confused, he fell silent and did not ask for an explanation, preferring not to reveal that he did not know what she meant. He guessed that something had annoyed her early on, and that he would be wise to avoid provoking her further. Nonetheless, she did, after a pause, enlarge on her declaration, saying that she would eat this country that was eating its children, that had eaten her father, her husband, her childhood and her future, that had eaten all her dreams. She had decided, therefore, that she would take it as fodder for a new dream. She had no idea how, but she would search for a way. Many were now gnawing at it, now that the era of the president, who had had it all to himself, was no more, that man who had raped her, though she still did not know, and did not wish to know, whether this child of hers was the product of that rape, or if he was the son of her late husband, who had disappeared after taking part in an attempted coup. In any case, she would do whatever was possible – and more – to protect her son from everything that had happened to her and to her relatives, and from everything that was going to come their way.

The silence between them stretched out. Tariq did not dare to break it until she surprised him by asking, "Then what happened?"

"What happened when?"

"What happened next in the story of your friends, the Shakhabit tribe?"

Her interest delighted him, and he thought how she was not all that different from other women and children, for she too liked stories, and that could only work to his advantage given that he was full of stories he had experienced himself or heard from others or read in books. Indeed, he was even prepared to make them up, if they served his purpose. Stories would be one of his means of winning her heart and mind so he might get from her what would make her forget the sight of him bent over the bonnet of his car, humiliated in front of her by the foreign troops, submitting without a fight or a word. Likewise, he would make her forget the stark difference in their ages, and he would tame with his tongue, not his hand, her notorious recalcitrance. He would tame her as he had tamed his first wife, and she would become putty in his hands, obedient to him in all things.

CHAPTER 2

The Great Reception

I t was not just a surprise to Tariq but a true shock when he arrived at the gates of his friend Sheikh Tafir's compound and found an armed checkpoint whose guards prevented his car from entering.

"Have you informed the sheikh that it's his friend Sheikh Tariq?" he asked them.

"Yes," they said. "And it was he who ordered us not to open the gates to you."

His distress, indeed his agony, was only increased by Qisma's comment: "Didn't you say that he was your friend and brother?"

"Yes, of course. I don't know what has come over him! What has happened? There is no power nor strength but with God alone!"

Agitated, he began getting out of the car and climbing back in. He spoke with the guards and sat back down, clapping one hand into the other. He got out and then back in yet again. Surrounding the sheikh's house was a high concrete wall that had not been there before, with its flags and guards by the entrance and at each distant corner. The house had not been an imposing, colourful palace like this before, with three flags fluttering above it – the flag of the tribe, being the largest, with the Iraqi and American flags alongside it. A quarter of an hour passed as Tariq climbed in and out of the car, confused, at a loss. He asked the guard for perhaps the tenth time, "Are you sure you told the sheikh who I am?"

"Yes."

"What did he say?"

"He ordered us not to open the gate to you."

"Fine, don't open the gate for my car, but open it for me alone, so that I may go inside to talk with him. Or else tell him to come himself so I can talk to him in person. For I don't believe what you're saying. I don't believe it! It's impossible!"

"Forgive us, but we cannot go against our orders. If you want, sir, take a seat and have a rest. Would you like coffee or tea?"

"I don't want anything. I just want to be sure of what you're saying and know what's happening. To understand."

Tariq went back to the car. He sat behind the wheel and continued clapping his palms together, invoking God's protection against the evil one, and repeating the formula about God's power and strength. After another ten minutes had passed, Qisma said, "We have to leave now if we want to make it to Baghdad before nightfall."

Tariq resisted at first, saying he would never leave that place, even if he were forced to take up residence there, until he had seen his friend. But after thinking it through, he sighed, whistled and said, "Glory to God! God decides and we abide."

He turned the key in the ignition and started to turn the car in order to leave. The guards ran over to stop them. "The sheikh also ordered us not to permit you to leave."

At that, Tariq lost what little composure he had left. "Why?" he yelled. "And what do we do in that case?"

"Please, sheikh, calm down. Just wait a few more minutes. Do you want tea or coffee?"

"I told you I want nothing from you! I want to be done with this whole affair!"

At that moment the large gates swung open and Sheikh Tafir came out to greet them in all his traditional finery: a dark gilded cloak over a gleaming white robe, the agal placed meticulously upon his head. He was flanked by a group of men, and behind them came the women and children. Tafir approached Tariq with a wide smile and opened his arms, calling out the most elaborate words of greeting, and Tariq at last relaxed. He tried to get out of the car, but the guards prevented him from opening his door until Sheikh Tafir arrived to open it himself. Then Tariq got out, and they folded into a long, hard embrace. Each one kissed the nose and beard of the other. Sheikh Tafir apologised for the delay, explaining that he could not possibly have been satisfied to receive his dear friend like any other guest, but rather had wanted to prepare for him the most sublime demonstration of welcome, one that would match Tariq's position in his eyes. "You are my brother, O sheikh. I love you like my own self."

Finely dressed women, both young and old, opened the passenger door for Qisma and carried her bag and her child for her. The wide-open gates revealed a red carpet spread as far as the palace-like house, a distance of some two hundred metres, and each side of the rug was lined by men, women and children. The sheikh led his friend courteously by the arm towards the entrance, and as soon as their feet touched the rug the women broke out in trills and the sound of automatic weapons fired in celebratory abandon roared through the air. When they had covered half the distance, a group of children presented them with bouquets of flowers and silver dishes of water, dates and milk.

Tariq turned back, seeking the eyes of Qisma to know how she saw him now. He found her smiling at him, an astonished, almost befuddled look on her face, and he said to himself with an inward laugh of delight, "Now she is ready to be the wife of Sheikh Tariq the Befuddled."

The children drew back on either side to allow the sheikhs to pass, and the two of them walked forward, continuing the journey hand in hand, sometimes shooing away with their feet the wandering ducks and chickens that passed in front of them on the carpet.

"What is all this munificence, my sheikh?" Tariq asked Tafir. "What is all this beneficence, all these blessings? Now I truly am befuddled." They both laughed.

"It is the blessing of democracy, which our Marian brothers have brought."

"Our Marian brothers? Who are they?"

"The Christian foreigners – the Americans. I'll tell you all about it, for you too need to take your share of these blessings."

As they approached the reception hall, Tariq saw, off to one side, two bulls that had been brought down upon the grass of the garden, restrained by a knot of young men, no doubt in the process of being slaughtered. After the first bull was dispatched, a powerfully built dwarf directed one of the youths to carry over to Tariq a vessel filled with blood, which he smeared with his palms onto the shoes of the guest in a gesture of honour. As soon as they entered the hall, Tariq was brought up short in surprise at the changes that had been made to this spacious room, which he had known well since childhood. It had been enlarged, and its furnishings were no longer limited to a few carpets and cushions on the floor, with a stove to brew coffee in the middle. Now there were luxurious couches and chairs and tapestries embroidered with gold thread running along the walls. Each of the couches had a low marble table in front of it with flower vases and microphones set on top. The floor was covered with a soft velvet carpet, and huge chandeliers of gilded glass hung from the ceiling. In pride of place on the far wall was a large photograph of Sheikh Tafir surrounded by smaller photographs of the rest of the line of Shakhabit sheikhs. The tribe's flag was displayed above it, framed by two swords. On the other walls there were massive paintings depicting sword fights or riders on horseback, or framed examples of the finest Arabic calligraphy – poetry, verses from the Qur'an and phrases such as "All this from the grace of our Lord", "The eye that envies goes blind", "God holds all", "Councils are schools", "Our tribe is our security", and so on.

The two sheikhs sat side by side beneath the portrait of Tafir, with the men of the tribe spread out before them down the sides of the room. Glasses of milk and tea, as well as cups of coffee, were circulated to everyone, and one of Sheikh Tafir's small sons, just nine years old, came up and whispered to him, "Mr Rahib the cook asks how he should distribute the two hearts and four testicles from the bulls."

According to the traditions of the Shakhabit, the guest and host would split the heart and the testicles whenever a bull was slaughtered. But since the honours had been doubled that day, each sheikh would have an entire testicle and could choose who would get the second. Each would also receive half a heart while choosing who would have the second half. Tariq chose Qisma for the other half of his heart, and the second testicle went to her son, while Tafir decided that the second half of his heart would be divided equally between his three wives, and that the remaining testicle would go to this young son of his, who was, as he explained to his friend, the most beloved among all his children and who had been given the name of their ancestor, Shakhbata. While the preparations were underway – for the hearts and testicles would be boiled in water and then fried in oil with onions, garlic and spices – and while the bulls were being butchered and dinner was being prepared, the two sheikhs had plenty of time to exchange their news.

Tariq informed his companion of the reasons behind his expedition to Baghdad, in spite of the terrible conditions and the chaos of occupation and civil war. It was for the sake of Qisma and the soul of her father Ibrahim, his lifelong friend, for, after coming across his severed head along with eight other heads belonging to the village's sons in banana crates, and after they had finished burying the heads, Qisma had insisted on searching for her father's body, no matter what the cost. And because she was a widow, alone with a small child, unable to search on her own, and it was necessary to have a respectable man to accompany her, she had presented the matter to him, and he had presented the idea of marriage to her, for it was not possible for him, on the grounds of religious propriety, to accompany a woman, just the two of them, night and day, with no concept of how long the search would take. She had agreed, and they had been married the previous day according to the law of God and his prophet. They had announced it to the village without putting on a wedding, just a simple family dinner, "out of respect for her sorrow and our sorrow at how we lost our dear Ibrahim, and the sorrow of the people over the nine sons they had lost".

Tafir patted the knee of his companion and said, "That is wisdom itself, the best way the two of you could have gone about it. And by God, I am at a loss as to whether I should console you for the loss of Ibrahim, or congratulate you on your marriage. But such is life! A surfeit of contradictions. And I swear by the tomb of Abu al-Anwar that I have known hundreds of people in my life, and I never saw one more good-natured than Ibrahim, nor does my love for any other match the love I have for you."

They embraced each other where they sat, with a heartfelt affection that brought tears to their eyes, and each of them kissed the nose and beard of the other. And in order to get quickly past an emotional moment that might appear as weakness before the eyes of their followers, Tafir whispered in his guest's ear, "How old is she?"

"She has just turned twenty-five."

Tafir gave Tariq a nudge and a wink as he whispered, "What luck you have! Still so youthful! The youngest of my women has ten years on her. They are three Shakhbutas, cousins on my father's side, and for that reason there will not be a fourth unless it's some young woman not of our tribe, so that I might renew my bed, my line and my youth with her, finishing up with her what remains of my life."

"God grant you long life, my sheikh. You are still young!"

"Yes, and in my opinion, according to my experience and the experience of my ancestors, a man is not judged in the eyes of a woman by his age, his shape, his height, his girth, nor by any other thing except these two: his pockets and his dick. And I, thanks be to God, am well founded in both, as you can see and as you know. As for you, I have been a witness to your virility and your burning desire for women ever since our teenage adventures in the days when we studied at the sharia school in Mosul!"

They laughed aloud and gave each other's hand a powerful squeeze.

"And now you have married again!" Tafir continued. "And you may yet take a third wife if you are to equal me, or equal your father, so that his soul will rejoice in its grave. But what about your pockets?"

"Things are going well, thanks be to God! I receive my two salaries: one from the Ministry of Education, as a school teacher, and the other from the Ministry of Religious Endowment, as an imam in the village mosque. This is in addition to what farming brings in for me, which my sons and my family take care of."

"No, no! That is not enough, my friend! We are living through a historic opportunity. It is the dawn of democracy, and anyone can do what he wants and attain the riches he desires. Don't you see how many nobodies and scoundrels have suddenly become rich and are now men of power and influence? Even the foreigners! Why have they appeared from every nook and cranny if not to plunder our wealth? It is certainly not to liberate us, as they claim, but rather for the sake of oil. They take it and throw us some of the leftover crumbs, we who have never got anything from it except agony – yesterday and today – and won't get anything from it tomorrow. Don't you see how they have destroyed everything so they can claim to have rebuilt it all afterwards, even as the Ministry of Oil – and its pipelines and oilfields – are left unscathed? They have worked to protect those seriously and professionally, even as they have left the borders open to all and sundry to smuggle and traffic anything they wish – goods, antiquities, weapons, human organs, and so on. No guards, no accounting, no taxes, no customs – and no watermelons!"

"But–"

"Listen!" Tafir interrupted, and continued, "Don't tell me this is not permitted, it is forbidden, or it is illegal. The riches of this country have never been for its people, the heedless, naive, good people, who believe in laws that were created only to sub-jugate and rob them. It is our right to take anything from our own fields, by any means. Iraq has been passed from one tyrant to another ever since God created the earth, the sun, the moon and this country itself, and the clever man is the one who knows how to seize an opportunity and to care for himself and for his children after him."

"So what do you want me to do? Should I take up arms like the others? Should I kill and plunder too?"

"No, for what you have in your power to do is much easier and more effective than taking up arms. Then again, why shouldn't you take up arms, if that's what is required, just as men have done the world over throughout history! Listen. Your father was a sound counsellor and supporter of my father, and in these matters I will do the same for you. The path to success, the ropes that stretch out to it, are many, and it is therefore incumbent on us to travel these various paths and pull on each rope. When the Americans arrived in our region, some of the nationalists in our tribe – or the insane or the despairing – fought against them. They killed seven of us, and we killed one of them. Then they made haste to negotiate with us and record our demands. At the same time, some of us were participating in the political process in Baghdad. We had one foot here and one foot there, and we leaned wherever the profits were greater. We were able to put many of our sons to work in the army, the police and government institutions, and whoever they refused to employ – on the grounds that he was an employee or soldier of the former regime – would do as they must and join the opposition. And that is their right, for whoever has spent his life as a soldier and does not know any other way to feed his family will agree to do the only thing he knows how to do. He blows up a tank for five thousand dollars, he kills a foreign soldier for three thousand, or an Iraqi for one, and so on."

"No! No, my sheikh! That's not how things are done. I shall never agree with you on that."

"Listen! I'm telling you how things are. I'm not saying that this is right or wrong, and I personally don't get involved in bloodshed. Besides, there is another way, and from it I have amassed all you see here. A source of profit that is easy and reliable, and which I counsel you to pursue."

"And what is that?"

"Right now there is a fund for the reconstruction of Iraq. But the truth of it is that it's a lie within a lie, for it will not restore to its former place one brick that has been torn down. Nevertheless it's a great swamp from which billions are ladled out. Countries, companies, political groups and individuals take from it such plunder as has never been seen in the history of the world. Every region has an American general overseeing it, and every general divides up his region and assigns responsibilities to his officers. And these officers are the ones responsible for granting contracts. Things like repairing a bridge, paving a street, building a school, outfitting a hospital, restoring the water works, buying agricultural machines – an infinite number of projects. And the majority of these officers accept bribes. They record that you have received the funds for a project, but actually they put half the money in their pocket, and of the remaining half, you give half to the contractor, while the rest goes into your own pocket. And so on. On top of that, no-one calls anyone to account because everyone participates in the plundering, so a project to build a school, for example, results in just two mud rooms. A project to outfit a hospital, just a lick of paint and a few chairs. A project to repair and restore a street, just two ditches filled with two bags of cement. And so on. Should you prefer to do nothing at all, it's enough to pile up some bricks and bags of cement, and then blow it all up when the deadline approaches, blaming terrorism and the lack of security."

"Indeed, that is what we hear, for how many projects have they promised in our region, and yet we have seen nothing? It is all millstone and no tahini!"

"Exactly, my friend. Millstone and no tahini, because the tahini makers eat all the tahini, and all that's left for everyone else is the millstone. So, do you want the tahini or the millstone?"

"The tahini, of course!"

The two men slapped each other's hand in delighted agreement, and Sheikh Tafir called to one of his men, "Zaidan! Call General Adam, and invite him to join us for dinner." Then he turned back to his friend. "This General Adam is the one chiefly responsible for this district, which also includes your village, and he is the one who appoints the officers. I'll introduce you. I'll advise him to ask his officers to grant you some of his contracts, just as I'll ask his permission to give you his private number, which he only gives out to a select few, among them sheikhs like myself." He fell silent for a moment and added, "Like us."

"But I'm not the sheikh of a tribe. I'm just a religious sheikh in a small village mosque."

"Brother, don't make things so complicated! What's the difference? And what keeps you from being the sheikh of a clan as well? In these times, it's within our power to call ourselves whatever we wish: sheikh, politician, businessman, artist, poet – anything. And no-one will oppose us. For we live in the age of speed and moral chaos, and people have no time to investigate and put things to the test, but only to accept at face value what they see."

"The big difference between our village and yours is that

you're all from one tribe, but we have different origins. Indeed, among us are those who do not know their exact origin, like my dear friend whom you know, Abdullah Kafka."

"Abdullah Kafka. Of course! How is he? Has he not got married yet?"

"No, and he's still the same Kafka he always was. I've been thinking of some way to persuade him to marry, but he's a stubborn fellow."

"Listen, the titles that people give themselves are what they choose, their choice alone, other than the names that derive from a grandfather, a place, or a profession. After that, they ascribe to them a venerable aspect or even holiness, as they wish. I know the story of your village, how it was founded by a group of Bedouins and farmers around some palm trees on the banks of the Tigris. That's why its name was Nakhila, the Village of Palms. The village expanded further as other Bedouins settled there, along with gypsies who were passing through, and labourers gathering the harvest. It went on like that until it became several villages: Nakhila the Greater, Nakhila the Lesser, Second, Third, North and South Nakhilas, Between-Two-Nakhilas, and so on. The solution is to call yourself Sheikh Tariq al-Nakhili. Over time, you draw in those who believe they belong to the Nakhili tribe, and you condemn and reject those who do not take pride in their association with it. In that way, belonging to the Nakhili will become the essential principle and measure. And after you've amassed money, relationships and authority, you use the tried-and-tested principle of carrot and stick, for most people are still like beasts in their dealings with others."

Tariq the Befuddled stared into the face of his friend, truly astonished. Then he put his arm around the other's shoulder and pulled him in, saying, "I always thought I was cleverer than you, but once again you have proved me wrong."

Tafir smiled and replied, "No, not always, for here embodied before us is your cleverness triumphing over mine." Tafir gestured with his eyes to the far end of the guest hall where the women were gathered, Qisma among them, and went on: "You have married a young, beautiful, civilised, educated woman, while I have nothing but a few old backward cousins!"

They laughed together for a long while until they were interrupted by one of Tafir's guards, one of those who had stopped Tariq at the gate. He approached Sheikh Tafir and whispered, "They have sent word from the first checkpoint that the Americans have killed the son of Hajj Ta'ih al-Shakhabiti on the grounds that they caught him planting explosives along their road."

The sheikh stiffened and sat up straight. Then he said to the guard, "Damn it! Fine. Do what has to be done."

CHAPTER 3

The Snore of the Resistance

General Adam sent four of his soldiers to Sheikh Tafir to deliver his thanks for his invitation and to convey, with regret, that he could not be present for dinner on account of an urgent task, but would come the moment he had finished, and he asked that they hold off on the evening prayer until he arrived. Their message delivered, the soldiers joined the rest of the guests, whose number exceeded a hundred, drawn from among the high-ranking Shakhabit and the sheikh's relatives and friends, some of whom were members of the district's governing council. The sheikh recognised the general's precautions and fully understood them. The general was wise to avoid eating and drinking anything offered to him by the people of the land his soldiers occupied in case he were poisoned. As it happened, the general arrived in the company of additional soldiers just as the guests were finishing dinner, the men in the main hall, the women and children in a room on the far side of the palatial house.

Tariq the Befuddled was surprised to see that General Adam was the very same officer who had got out of his jeep and spoken with Qisma a few hours earlier, and who had ordered the soldiers to set them free and give them bottles of water. Tariq was relieved that the general did not recognise him, but not surprised, for

Tariq's face had been obscured while he was bent over the bonnet of his car. Tariq hoped that Qisma would not see the general because the two of them would certainly recognise each other, and he could not guess what her reaction might be.

Sheikh Tafir sat the general between him and his friend Tariq in the place of honour. Some of the general's soldiers stood guard at each side of the room. One stood just inside the door and another outside it. Others were stationed with the check-point guards in front of the main gate. Doubtless there were yet more soldiers posted at the corners of the perimeter wall and on the dirt road that connected the village to the highway. The two sheikhs switched from their dialect into Modern Standard Arabic, which they had learned through years of study at the religious institute, because the general himself spoke it well.

After the initial pleasantries, Tafir began commending his companion to the general in the highest terms, sometimes to the point of outright lies, saying, "This is Sheikh Tariq al-Nakhili, whose father before him was both a religious sheikh and a tribal sheikh. He is lord of all the villages of the Nakhil region, and he has been my friend – nay, my brother – since childhood. I trust him more than myself, and you have my guarantee that you, sir, can work with him in any matter whatsoever, you or your officer in charge there."

The general asked Tariq about the way the coalition forces had entered his region and his village, for he had not been involved with the invasion forces. Had there been a bombardment? Clashes? Resistance? Tariq replied that it had happened in a way unlike anything that had come before it in the history of warfare.

That caught the ears of everyone present. They stopped their whispering, and all other conversations ceased. It invigorated Tariq to see all eyes trained upon him. He knew that this was his opportunity to make such an impression on those assembled that they would never forget him. "It is possible," he said, "for me to give a name to the story I will tell. Something like . . . 'The Snore of the Resistance'."

The attention focused upon him only increased in its intensity, though some smirked or laughed to hear the name he gave his story. And because his friend Tafir had introduced him in such a lofty way, in terms that had given him great pleasure, he felt a need to rise to that level and prove that he merited the sheikh's praise, embellishing his speech with every rhetorical flourish he could muster, even though it was not exactly a heroic tale.

"When the village learned of the approach of the American forces," he began, "they were quite naturally overcome with fear. It meant that the Americans had already vanquished the great armies in the field, mechanised and armed to the teeth, even the Republican Guard. So what resistance could they offer, for they were only simple peasants, poorly armed and with no ammunition? At the same time, however, it was not possible for the men to submit just like that, in front of the women and children, without a fight, without even the slightest resistance. They had their reputation in the region, in the country and in posterity to think of. So they gathered in the village café to take counsel. Abdullah Kafka carried on smoking in his corner, and eyed them with a neutral expression, as though the matter didn't affect him.

Indeed, it didn't affect him much, he who had spent nearly twenty years of his life as a prisoner in Iran. He had seen the forms that death can take and had escaped only by chance. Even so, deep down and for the longest time, he had considered himself dead. So he would smile scornfully whenever one of them put forward a suggestion and almost got the rest to agree with it.

"One said, 'Let's abandon the village to them and hide in the gardens, the fields, the valleys and the thickets that surround it. As soon as they enter, we'll destroy them. We'll surround them on every side, raining bullets.' But there were not enough bullets for even the shortest rain shower, and the American forces were sure to be supported by planes and helicopters.

"Another said, 'Let's set fires everywhere along the road, burning car tyres, piles of wood, old clothes and shoes, everything that can burn, so that the smoke will hide everything and throw them into confusion. Then we'll hunt them down one by one.'

"Yet another said, 'Let's drive all our livestock out into the road: cows, sheep, goats, donkeys and chickens. That will confuse their soldiers, and we'll pick them off from the rooftops.'

"The last suggestion was more temperate: 'Let's pick a delegation from among ourselves to meet them before they enter the village and negotiate with them.' And just as objections had been raised to the various preceding suggestions, an objection was made to this one, in that it would amount to a free surrender and would be a mark of shame upon them for all eternity.

"It went on like that until everyone began to feel the same sense of despair and impotence when it came to arriving at a plan that would satisfy everyone. Then they turned to Abdullah

Kafka, who had been content to watch, listen and smoke with an occasional mocking smile. They asked his opinion. He lit a cigarette from the butt of the previous one, as usual, and said, 'Listen. Everyone dies in the end, whether that death comes from a hail of bullets, a car accident, a kick from a donkey or unseen bacteria, or if time has no more use for him and tramples him down in the street. The important thing is that the end is known. It is extinction, and everything that comes before is just an illusion, vanity, an act in a play, until the whole theatre of existence comes to an end one day, and the curtain falls without even an audience there to applaud it.'

"At this, seeing the faces of the others, I interrupted him. 'Enough, Abdullah! We are familiar with your views and dark sayings. Do you have anything to say about the specific situation we're in or not?'

"'Since, as I say, it is no more than an act in a play,' he said, 'and futility is the reality of this world, free yourselves of agency in this matter. Hamid the Snorer was the first official soldier in the village and is now the oldest. Hand the matter over to him.'

"And who was this Hamid the Snorer?" Sheikh Tafir asked his companion. "I don't remember meeting anyone by this name when I visited your village."

"That's only natural, for he is a man approaching seventy who moves little and sleeps a lot. Because he has been lazy ever since he was small, he did not even complete elementary school, and his father used his connections at that time to help him become a police officer. He was the first of our village sons to join the police, even though he was the calmest and most agreeable of us all. No-one can remember him quarrelling or fighting with anybody, not even as an adolescent. After his retirement from the service, his qualities of speaking only a little and sleeping a lot became even more pronounced. He would sit with you and talk, but he would be asleep and snoring at the same time. He would open his eyes a little, speak a sentence, and then close them and snore as he listened to your reply. Even while eating meals, he would sometimes fall asleep between one bite and the next. He would chew with his eyes closed. He would stop, give a little snore, and then continue chewing."

When Tariq saw surprise and curiosity in the smiles of those present, he began to take pleasure in relating the details, or, indeed, inventing them.

"The villagers have so many stories about him sleeping. In one of them the owner of the café locks up the place, shutting him inside until morning. In another, when he goes to hunt sand grouse in the countryside, he falls asleep in his hide, and when they find him, a grouse has actually laid an egg on his back. Sometimes, when he went to the bathroom, he would be slow to return, and when his wife went to check on him, she would find him asleep on the floor, his trousers round his ankles. She would wipe his bottom, pull his trousers up, and lead him back to bed.

"Everyone loved Hamid, but no-one loved him like Abdullah Kafka did, and no-one spent more time with him. Indeed, Abdullah wished to be like him, abandoning the cares of this world in sleep. Most of their long sessions in the café were spent in silence, which they both treasured, or else they would exchange a few fragmented sentences. Occasionally, Abdullah would speak at length, overflowing with words, pouring out whatever he wished and freely revealing whatever was on his mind. It was as though he was talking aloud to himself as Hamid snored beside him. Perhaps he would ask a question based on some word snatched during his moments of wakefulness, and in exchange, Abdullah would feel that he was speaking to someone and not just talking to himself as he had got used to throughout his life, a habit that became even more ingrained during the bitter years of his captivity.

"Abdullah said to us, 'Hamid the Snorer is the first and oldest military man among you, and you are all united in your firm love for him. Turn things over to him. In that way, you will have entrusted the matter to one in whom you all have faith.'

"Hamid was sitting beside Abdullah at that moment, his head resting on Abdullah's shoulder. So I asked him, 'What do you think, Hamid?' And without opening an eye, Hamid said, 'Of course, of course,' and carried on snoring.

"I turned to the rest of the men, and they indicated their support because they had grown tired of the endless deliberations and were willing to accept any solution they could agree on. So I went back to Hamid with another question: 'And what is it you would have us do?' Hamid stopped snoring and replied, 'It's none of your business. This is a military matter, and you don't understand it.' Then he let out another loud snore. So I said, 'And what do you need from us?' Hamid opened his eyes a little, raised his head, and said, 'Fifty men.' And he went on snoring."

Those present laughed until the grease from their dinner

jiggled in their bellies, increasing all the more their feelings of contentment. Tariq continued with his story.

"And then I asked, 'What else?'

"'Your agreement...' – deep snore – '...to one condition.'

"'What condition?' I asked.

"'Obedience. For obedience is the very soul of the military spirit.'

"Everyone hurried to gather all the weapons they had, such as old hunting rifles, pistols, AK-47s, sticks of T.N.T and hand grenades they used for fishing. They prepared dozens of bottles full of gas and diesel fuel, stopped up with rags that they would set fire to and throw at the Americans. Each one could burn a jeep or a tank, especially if they were thrown from a rooftop. They filled cooking pots with dynamite and nails to make mines that they would plant in the enemy's path. Then, from among our sons, we gathered fifty of the best and strongest young men, and we ordered them to obey the orders of their general, Hamid the Snorer, fully and to the letter even if he commanded them to throw themselves at the enemy in a suicide attack. We made the young men swear it in front of everyone on a copy of the Qur'an in the mosque.

"When we had everything ready, we doused Hamid's face in cold water. To wake him up even more, we gave him seven cups of tea and coffee to drink. Not content with that, we gave the young man selected to be Hamid's aide-de-camp a pot of coffee so he could pour him a cup whenever he noticed that sleep was overcoming him. And because the belly of the supreme commander of the armed resistance forces, Sayyid Hamid the Snorer, was large and hung low, hiding the belt beneath it, we gave him a small pistol to put in the chest pocket of his robe.

"The general gave the first of his orders, which was that they dig trenches along the length of the main road leading through the village. These trenches would be spaced out so that a shout from someone in one trench would reach the trenches before and after him, allowing orders and updates to travel from the front to the rear lines, and from there to the village itself. Each of these positions was garrisoned by five fighters, and, since he was the general, Hamid placed himself in the first trench, on the outskirts of the village, where he expected the invasion to begin. The last trench was in the centre of the village, right in front of the café, so that everyone would be aware of what was happening and what the orders were, and could pull together and cooperate.

"Some objected, arguing that fifty fighters were too small a force, not nearly enough in the face of the most powerful army in the world. Hamid replied forcefully, rejecting any meddling in military matters, and insisting that, in his experience, the decisive factor was rarely strength of numbers. Often it was precisely the opposite, just as when he, with a band of no more than five police officers, had taken entire villages by surprise – and who was to say that the small units deployed were not the main reason for victory? In order to settle the matter and reassure the others without wasting any more time arguing, I put my literary and linguistic training to use, reminding them what was written in the Qur'an, which says, 'How many times has a small band triumphed over a larger force by the permission of God? And God is with those who are patient.' I cited God's prophet,

Ibrahim, who fathered an entire nation. Then I raised my voice to perform some lines from the great Arab poet Al-Mutanabbi: 'Do not disdain the small in a dispute; verily, the gnat can bloody the lion's eye.' I followed that up with some lines by the twelfth-century religious scholar Najm al-Din Amara al-Yemeni:

> Do not despise the trap set by the weak, for perhaps
> the asp may die by the poison of the scorpion.
> Long ago the hoopoe undermined the throne of Bilqis,
> and the rat's burrow ruined all progress towards the goal."

Sheikh Tafir, in order to keep his friend from digressing even further and divulging the full contents of his memory, said, "Well? What happened next?"

"By the time evening fell, everything was ready for the battle. A group of old men remained in the café together with a pack of children who could run to bring news and orders to the rest of the village, spreading the word from neighbour to neighbour, as soon as it arrived from the front line, where their leader, Hamid the Snorer, was positioned.

"Before the sun went down, they heard the thunder of Apache helicopters. Then they saw the choppers themselves, flying close to the ground. This was followed by the rumble of tanks and other enormous machines, which they saw drawing near. They grew larger and larger, little by little. The five men with the general in the forward position didn't know what to do. Their nervous, fearful eyes flitted between the approaching column of vehicles and their leader, who had rested his head against the side of the trench and plunged into a deep sleep. He began to snore, and his snores harmonised with the roar of the enemy machines. His hand was on the small pistol in his breast pocket. The young man with the coffee pot woke him and poured him a large cup, and Hamid ordered him to serve out the rest to the others. Then he went back to sleep. And when a shout reached his men from the next trench, asking for orders, they did not know what to answer except what they were hearing from their general, so they replied with a shout of their own: 'Snore! Snore!'

"And so, the orders were passed along the line, all the way to the last trench outside the café, and from it to the café itself, and the children set off at a run through the streets and alleys of the village, all of them shouting, 'Snore! Snore!' Everyone laid their head on the nearest pillow. Some actually did sleep, exhausted by the tension, anxiety and fear. Others just pretended. When the vanguard of the American soldiers arrived at the first position, they found a fat old man and five youths lying in a trench dug across the road, snoring with their weapons in their hands. The soldiers took the weapons without any reaction from the sleepers, who continued to snore. They examined the weapons and found them to be old and rusty, so they threw them aside and advanced towards the next trench, and then to the one after that, and so on, until their forces were spread out through the village, covering its most prominent roads and vantage points, without needing to fire a single bullet, for everyone they saw in the café, in the shops, in the gardens of the houses and in the houses themselves was fast asleep. And because the soldiers were actually very tired from the distances they had travelled to get there, after the battles, skirmishes and fierce resistance that had surprised them in other villages, and because their clothes and their heavy weapons were weighing down their exhausted limbs and spirits, they felt suddenly relaxed, and they remembered what it was to sleep, just as someone might remember a lover whom he longs to embrace. The soldiers saw an opportunity to rest before moving on to the next village. They lay down where they sat, inside their vehicles or on their roofs, and gave themselves over to rest, to sleep and to snoring, just like the villagers, the whole night through."

General Adam shot an inscrutable look at the American soldiers gathered in the hall. He brought his gaze back to Sheikh Tafir and smiled. Then he turned his eyes back to Tariq, giving a slight nod to indicate that he wished him to continue speaking.

"With the first light of dawn, when all the cocks in the village crowed and the old women and old men woke first for the dawn prayers, followed by the mothers who would soon prepare breakfast, the good-natured ladies of the village approached the foreign troops sleeping in their jeeps, still wearing their boots and heavy helmets, parked there in the gardens and the alleys. The women woke them up with a mother's gentle sympathy, just as they woke their own children. I saw one woman shake the shoulder of a young soldier, holding out a cup of curdled milk, water or tea along with a piece of bread and butter, and say, 'My son, my son! Wake up, my son!' The soldier started, and before he'd even opened his eyes his fists tightened around the rifle in his hands. But as soon as he saw the face of the old lady bending over him and heard her gentle voice, speaking a language he didn't know, his grip relaxed. Some of the soldiers said 'thank you' in English and went on sleeping. Others woke up, sat up and looked around in astonishment. A woman was urging a soldier to take a cup from her hands and drink, and the soldier was politely and gratefully pushing it away. And on it went for two hours, until all the soldiers had woken up, without any of them taking a sip of what the women were offering them. They withdrew in a column, just as they had arrived, and headed towards the next village. Nothing in the village they were leaving merited any attention or was worth stopping for: no oil, no factories, no government installations, no military camps. Nothing with any strategic importance to American national security or the security and peace of the universe."

Sheikh Tafir stroked his beard, not at all sure whether the story his companion told was true, or whether he had invented it to win the approval of the American general and to amuse all the others. He knew that Tariq's village had not seen any clashes with the Americans, but he had not heard any details like that. He did not want to dwell on the matter, considering that the truth of it, or the lack thereof, was not important so long as the story brought them the desired outcome. He looked at the general. "Extraordinary!" he said, to prevent himself from dwelling too long on the details. "Occupying the village without a single bullet being fired, or any blood being spilled, or any buildings damaged, or any trees knocked down. And without any of the birds or animals of the village being panicked. Truly an astonishing event."

Tariq picked up on Tafir's cue. He felt his tongue had become even more fluent and effective as a result of the story he had told. Directing his words to the general as well, he said, "Yes, praise be to God! The village agreed that this was the greatest victory that can be won in a war, one that is secured without any destruction at all. And it was all thanks to the cleverness and prudence of our leader, Sayyid Hamid the Snorer. Their love for him has only increased, and he has remained a symbolic figure for them. They've been calling him 'Leader' ever since that day. Some even consider him to be a true exemplar of the new climate of freedom and democracy, because he leaves them their freedom to speak and act without any interference on his part."

CHAPTER 4

A Breach at the Council of Men

Sheikh Tafir whispered in the ear of General Adam, "Honestly now, dear General, honestly, would not this village of Nakhila, and above all the honourable Sheikh Tariq, deserve all consideration and care from you since it cost you not a single bullet, not a single drop of blood, to pacify?"

"Of course," the general replied.

"Would you permit me then to give him your personal mobile number, and will you advise your officers to cooperate with him?"

"Of course, of course. Absolutely."

With that, Sheikh Tafir felt he had achieved his victory, and he vigorously slapped the knees of the two men sitting with him, crying, "By God's blessing!" Then he called for his young son, Shakhbata, who was playing quietly with another boy at the far end of the hall: "Shakhbata! Tell Rahib to raise the call for the evening prayer."

The boy set off, and not five minutes later they heard a voice calling from the highest point of the house, heard clearly despite the closed doors and windows, echoing throughout the village and shattering the stillness of the night. It was calling them to prayer, and had the guests seen the owner of that voice, the power of which surpassed that of any megaphone, they would not have believed their eyes, for it came from the throat of a dwarf who stood barely a metre tall. As for the people of the village, they considered him to have become – and indeed he had become – one of the distinguishing features of their village and their lives, for not only was he the only dwarf among them, but he was stronger and more vigorous than any of them. His name was Rahib al-Shakhabiti, and when he was born, and his father saw that his head was larger than his body and his limbs were the length of a finger, he stepped back and sat in a far corner – far from him, from his wife, from the midwife, and from the female neighbours who were present – balled up as though he were a child who had committed some crime, as though he were afraid of the form of his newborn. After that, his parents decided not to have any more children. They were getting old, and Rahib was the last of nine sons. If they produced any more, God alone knew what its size and shape would be.

It goes without saying that Rahib soon realised that he was different from everyone else, thanks to the mockery of the children, their refusal to include him in most of their games, and, indeed, through the beatings they handed out at school. So Rahib redoubled his efforts and his energy in all things that could compensate for his feelings of inferiority. He applied himself even harder to playing sports, working the fields and stretching his limbs, in the hopes that he would grow taller. But while his muscles grew stronger and firmer, his height did not change. His hands and feet were like rocks, so much so that the other children became wary of provoking him. He likewise distinguished himself in caring for animals, in farming and in hunting, including tracking down snakes, extracting them from their burrows and pulling out their fangs. Rahib became an artist in torturing animals – strangling them, slitting their throats, skinning them, burning them alive – until the animals themselves would become alarmed at the merest hint of his scent. Whenever he approached, some of them would flee at once, while others would become confused and lie down where they were, frozen by the intensity of their fear. People said they even saw plants and trees bending in the opposite direction out of fear, for when Rahib passed by, he would kick them, snap their stems, scrape off their bark and strip their leaves.

Rahib needed only four hours sleep, and he would spend the rest of his time, both day and night, on the move. People swore there were two of him, so often would they see him about. When he did sleep, however, it was sometimes as though he had died, and it was not easy to wake him before his four hours were up. He just would not wake – even if you danced on his chest and stomach, even if you picked him up by a leg and threw him into the river – until he himself decided to do so. Most people loved him and were wary of him, and some people flattered him, for as well as being party to the secrets of the whole village, he was a master of almost everything he did. Rahib liked to feel needed, and he was not slow to offer his help. People asked many services of him, which he rendered with generous good grace. He was in his element at weddings, singing, dancing and telling jokes, creating an atmosphere of joy and merriment, playing the role of jester. You would also find him at funerals, overseeing the preparation of food for the mourners, for no-one could match the delicious flavours of the dishes that he cooked. He would do things that no-one else could do, such as going down deep wells, where all kinds of spiders, snakes and worms made nests that weakened the walls, or he would slip through small windows to extract forgotten keys, enter clogged sewers to let rainwater drain, climb trees to save a cat he might afterwards kill, cram himself inside the engines of large trucks to plug a leak or repair some damage. In this way, Sheikh Tafir found him to be one of the most useful members of his inner circle, and he showered him with gifts.

Rahib left school early because reading annoyed him. Anything that required staying in one place for a long time, not moving, was unbearable to him since it did not develop either his muscles or his body. He preferred to expend his energy on actions rather than words. As a result, he was able to build himself a house of his own before his brothers or anyone else his age. His most cherished dream was that he would get married, but there was not a single female dwarf in the village, nor in the neighbouring villages, nor in the entire Shakhabit tribe, and all the widows and unmarried women refused him, though they were legion thanks to the former President's many wars. It was as though they did not consider him to be a man, even though he could beat most men in most things. Because of this, no-one objected to his slipping in and out of the rooms set aside for women and associating with them or the children. From the very first day Rahib had come to work for him, Sheikh Tafir had pledged that if a bride could be found who would be content with him, he himself would underwrite all the expenses of the wedding, and, indeed, would provide everything that the bride demanded as a condition for the wedding, even if that should be Rahib's weight in gold.

As soon as Rahib finished the call to prayer, everyone got up. Sheikh Tafir asked his friend Tariq to lead the prayer on the grounds that he was a guest and also the most learned in religious law. They stood behind him, with Tafir and the general in the front row along with three of the general's soldiers who were also Muslim. Tariq led such a prayer as he had never achieved before. His heart had been gladdened by the warm welcome he had received here and all the distant horizons that this visit would open up to him later on. Perhaps the excellence of the dinner – which included half a bull's heart and an entire bull's testicle fried in oil – had also played a part. He shone when it came to selecting his suras from the Qur'an and even more so during the ritualistic recitation, which he performed in a way that enchanted everyone, as though they had been joined by a chorus of angels. From his lips the prayer itself was a sweet spiritual celebration, filling the room with such grace that even the two soldiers who were not Muslims, standing at the door, thought for a moment they might convert, lulled by the dreadful awe of the spectacle and the sweet sound of the recitation, which each and every listener felt pass through their skin to grip their very soul.

In the women's hall, meanwhile, the scene was very different, thanks to the great number of children in the room and the way they flitted about between food, games and their mothers. Chaos reigned, and the women were unable to finish the conversations they started due to all the interruptions from their children. Qisma did not like spending time with women the way she liked the company of men. Nevertheless, she was able to win the affection of Sheikh Tafir's wives, and of his daughters and daughters-in-law, who were about her age. In a short time, she learned a great deal from them about Tafir, about their village and about the Shakhabit more generally. At the same time, she was kept informed of everything that happened in the men's hall, again thanks to the children, whom the mothers sent one after the other to investigate. The children would race through the rooms and passageways, competing with each other to be the first to relate what was happening and what was being said. There was also Rahib, who roamed between the two rooms and the kitchen, and who could hardly be distinguished from the children except by the remarkable size of his head.

After Qisma had finished feeding her child and had put him to sleep in the room set aside for her on the second floor, she managed to persuade two of Tafir's wives, the second and the third, along with a few of his daughters, to join her in an audacious plan, even though the elder wife tried in vain to dissuade them. It would set a dangerous precedent, the results and penalties of which could scarcely be guessed at, for nothing like that had ever occurred throughout the long history of the tribe. It would be a breach of all customs and all certainties, so firmly established as to be almost sacred. Indeed, it seemed to the old lady to be a breach of the rules that bound the universe itself. In her confusion and dread, she stayed rooted to her seat, as though crippled and unable to move – for how could she stop them? – while Qisma and seven other women stood up and arranged their clothes as they waited for their little spies to bring the news that the prayer was over and the men had returned to their seats.

Qisma's entrance into the men's hall was a thunderbolt striking them all. She walked forward and called out in a loud, clear voice, just like the men: "Peace be upon you!" Behind her were her seven accomplices, and behind them and between their legs were a crowd of children, staring in surprise and delight.

All the men in the room stood up in a single movement, as though not governed by their own will, and returned the greeting in one voice, as though it were an anthem. Then, for a moment, complete silence and stillness reigned. It was up to Sheikh Tafir to seize the initiative and take control of the situation, and the only available option was to make the best of it. Employing the self-mastery that carried him through most difficult situations, he called out with exaggerated courtesy, "Welcome, welcome! A thousand greetings to Madame Sheikh Qisma." Then he introduced her to everyone. "This is our honoured and esteemed guest, Madame Sheikh Qisma, the new wife of our great guest, my brother, Sheikh Tariq, and the daughter of the happy martyr – now in paradise, God willing – Sheikh Ibrahim al-Nakhili, may he rest in peace. Come in! Come in, sister!"

Tafir motioned for her to sit beside her husband, while his two wives pushed forward to sit beside him. Tariq hid his feelings with a small, fixed smile even as his insides were bubbling like a boiling pot, the flames of his heart rising all the way to his throat and drying out his mouth.

Before Qisma sat down, Sheikh Tafir introduced the general, saying, "And here is another guest and friend, General Adam, who is a Muslim like us, praise be to God!"

Qisma approached and shook his hand, saying, "We've met."

When he had said goodbye to her some hours earlier, she had had a feeling that she would see him again. She sat beside Tariq, leaving Sheikh Tafir to wrestle with his surprise at her revelation. Then she turned towards the general as everyone sat down after her. General Adam confirmed to Tafir that they were acquainted, and, addressing Qisma respectfully by reference to her son, said, "We are deeply sorry, Madame Sheikh Umm Ibrahim, for what happened today."

Qisma was delighted to be addressed as "Madame Sheikh", feeling it strengthen her own self-confidence. She wondered if it would be possible to adopt the title formally for everyday use.

The general went on to explain in a polite and eloquent tone that "exceptional circumstances oblige us to enforce certain restrictions, much to our regret, and although we do our best to warn and inform everyone who approaches, mistakes still happen, unfortunately."

"Deadly mistakes," Qisma said.

"Unfortunately, yes. Some of them do prove fatal."

"In essence, your invasion and occupation of our country is itself a deadly mistake. It is only natural, therefore, that it should lead to innumerable other mistakes. The strange thing is that you are not ashamed to speak of 'friendly fire' or 'mistakes'.

Then again, it is not unusual for you to refuse to call things by their true name. Killing is killing. It is a crime and more than a mistake, because a mistake can be corrected, but a dead man can never be restored to life. It's like when you call your occupation a liberation, and you call the resistance – those who are merely defending their country – terrorists. You distort everything like that."

In an attempt to forestall a quarrel between his guests, Sheikh Tafir grasped the staff in the middle, directing his words and his glances at both Tariq and Adam to enlist their support in neutralising Qisma's provocations. "Listen, everyone," he said. "The truth is, as Iraqis, we are at a loss as to what to do, for with the Americans have come many Muslim soldiers. Take, for example, the honourable General Adam and his men. Here they are, having prayed with us just now. They join us for the Friday prayer in our mosque. According to our religion, they are our brothers, Muslims, whom it is haram to kill. But if we consider things from the point of view of the nation, they have occupied our homeland, and it is our duty to oppose them. It is a true conundrum, wouldn't you say?"

"Of course, of course," said General Adam. "I understand you perfectly, sheikh."

When Tafir turned towards Tariq to solicit his view, Tariq said, "Yes, sheikh. In my opinion, it is incumbent upon us to see our religion triumph over our worldly concerns, for it is the most important thing, above all else. Indeed, it is above the concept of the homeland itself, which is a worldly, conventional concept, rather than religious and divine."

No sooner had everyone relaxed, fully convinced by this reply, than Qisma confounded them by rejecting it. "First of all," she said, "it is necessary that religion play no part in the building of the state, especially since the Americans themselves claim they want it to be a modern, civic, democratic state, an example to the other nations of the region. What is more, Iraq, in its essence, was never a religious state, because it was home to different religions and sects. And even if we suppose that the entire American army and the other armies allied to them were composed of practising Muslims, our religion says in unambiguous verses, in clear lines from the Qur'an: 'If two sects of believers are fighting, make amends among them. And if one of them oppresses the other, fight against the oppressor until he submits to God's command.' And who but the Americans can we consider the oppressor?"

In that moment, there was not a single man – or woman – who was not thoroughly impressed by what Qisma said and how she said it. Even though she had been ostensibly addressing Sheikh Tafir, her glance kept straying to the general, and it was largely for his benefit that she spoke, though she intended all present to hear. She thought about raising the issue of the gang rape of Abeer al-Janabi, but she held back at the last moment.

Tariq, who had never in his life felt such anguish as had been prompted by what Qisma had said and done that day, now experienced a warm swell of pride. It was as though he said in his heart to Sheikh Tafir and to all the men present, "This is my wife, mine alone. My own property. How grand I now am among you, for there is no man among you who has a woman like her. She truly is a madame sheikh and suitable for a sheikh like me."

For his part, Tafir was filled with admiration, to the point of profound jealousy. He wished she were his wife, or, if not she, another like her who suited his station, a woman so impressive that he and the rest of those present had quite forgotten the shock that came when she and her confederates breached every expectation and convention by entering this council of men. Nevertheless, he had to maintain his equanimity and save the situation again. If he did not, he was absolutely certain that, were she to continue talking in this way, in this clear, serious, persuasive and affecting manner, so beautiful and bewitching in the way she pronounced the words, they would reach the point that if she said, "Kill the Americans," those present would do it. Indeed, even if she did not say it explicitly, and just continued to speak in this way, she would bring about some irredeemable tragedy, as some zealous or headstrong fellow among them would take it upon himself to kill one of the soldiers who were their guests. After that, the American army would wipe him from the face of the earth, together with his family, his village and every last Shakhabit. For that reason, he thought about how best to change the direction of the conversation, shift it away from these topics of occupation, religion and homeland. And because he knew that talking about men and women fascinated most people no end, women in particular, he decided to take refuge there. What is more, it would allow him indirectly to rebuke the women of his house for their impudence.

"Friends," he said, "let us set this topic aside for now, for this is a matter for men, falling on their shoulders alone. It is for them to discuss, reach a decision on and conduct themselves in the most fitting way with regard to that decision."

This pronouncement was to lead to an even greater surprise, one culminating in an incident that no-one present would ever forget. They would tell it to everyone they knew, and the story would be passed down to subsequent generations.

CHAPTER 5

The Contest of Male and Female in the Presence
of the Americans and the Tribe

What Sheikh Tafir had not known when raising the different spheres concerning men and women was Qisma's great sensitivity when it came to this topic. It was like a raw wound inside her, provoking her at the least reference. Even though she did not much like the company of women, neither their subjects of conversation nor their interests, and even though she positively hated their weakness and submissiveness, she was not prepared to listen to him dictate what was or was not an appropriate matter for her sex.

Deep down, she felt a kind of doubt and ambiguity about her gender. Throughout her childhood, and even on occasion after puberty, she had wished that she were a man, and she had acted under the pressure of this feeling. Her estrangement from her father stemmed from her frustration with the way he submitted to fate, being content with patience and endurance, to the point that his friends had called him Ibrahim the Fated because of his perennial refrain: "Everything is fate and decree." Indeed, it went so far that he named her Qisma, meaning fate, due to the intensity of his faith in this matter and its deep correspondence with his personality. And so Qisma had sought a husband who was his very opposite, strong and ambitious, jealous of other men and determined to overpower them, to the point where he took part in an attempt to overthrow the former president, ultimately resulting in his execution. But deep down she had not loved him. Despite her love of strength and her hatred of weakness, she did not care for arrogant men, infatuated with masculinity, virility and strength. For although she venerated strength, she hated it to be used without consideration for what was right, just as she hated it when those in the right surrendered to weakness. She did not know how to unravel the interwoven threads of contradiction within her. She sometimes said she loved justice and hated tyranny, and that she considered all people to be individuals without distinguishing among them on the basis of sex.

For most people in this world, this matter is settled, and they feel a congruity with their sex, being satisfied with it and with the role that is expected of them – happy even, feeling no desire to be the other gender. Some are satisfied, others demand equality, and yet others claim superiority or seek to impose it. Nevertheless, whenever they debate, their debates never end, and they still have more to say. Were the waters of the Tigris and Euphrates to turn into ink there would still not be enough to transcribe it. A person such as Qisma, who had an internal dialogue that formed a balanced, internal counterpart to this external discourse, would perhaps be able to argue the topic for the whole of her life.

As the conversation with Sheikh Tafir unfolded, Qisma spoke at length, clearly and passionately, provocative in her replies. The words left her mouth almost like slaps. Among the points she made was that she rejected this masculine, reactionary discourse of his, and insisted that issues related to homeland and honour concerned everyone, men and women, old and young – indeed, even cows and donkeys! – because the outcomes concerned everyone. It is like the gift of life and like the enigma that is death, neither of which distinguishes between male and female, young and old.

But the sheikh defended his point of view and his reasons for it, arguing that every being has a role entrusted to it in nature and in life. Just as the tree is a tree and has its role, the cow is a cow, and the bull is a bull, each assigned its station and function. The same is true for men and women. There is no shame in adapting as best one can to one's role and function; trying to change that would be a mistake. "A disaster even! It is impossible, for example, that we ask the bull to supply us with milk."

"You are mixing up innate nature and that which is foisted upon us by culture," she told him.

As the sheikh did not precisely follow her point, but was merely pretending to do so in front of his guests and followers, he shifted the discussion to a point that had long annoyed him and which he and his fellow sheikhs had criticised at length, which was that the country's new regime had imposed a rule that required that the percentage of women in parliament should not fall below twenty-five per cent, even if female candidates did not achieve the necessary votes. Thanks to this quota, the sheikh had been prevented from obtaining more than two seats in parliament, one for his son and the other for the husband of his eldest daughter, because although his tribe had enough votes to obtain more seats, he had refused to nominate any of the tribe's women. He said that he was not able to imagine a woman in such a position of influence, "because that had not happened before and would be an affront to our customs and traditions."

"That does not mean that women are incapable," Qisma told him. "Think how many women have led great empires across history, and how many are now the heads of states in our own era."

She gave him numerous examples, but he insisted upon his convictions, repeating that a woman could never, ever be like a man. She countered that women were more than capable of performing all the functions that men perform – indeed, they held the upper hand in that they were able to become pregnant, bear offspring, and raise children, being both a mother and a leader at the same time, while men were not able to do that.

The sheikh tried to overpower Qisma's arguments and claim victory by resorting to scorn. "But we men," he said, "would refuse the duties of pregnancy and childbirth even if nature granted us the ability to carry them out."

Some of Tafir's followers laughed, which further puffed up the sheikh's feathers as he added, "To draw a line under this dispute, I will give you a simple example that provides conclusive proof that women are not like men."

A hush greeted this sweeping statement from Tafir. No sound was heard apart from Qisma's question: "And what might that be?"

"Men can piss while standing up," he replied. "Women can't do that!"

The sheikh's hall shook with everyone's laughter. Even the women and children joined in, agreeing with the men that their sheikh had secured the last word in this matter thanks to his wisdom, intelligence, and the truth of his argument, just as they had expected, and that he had silenced his opponent with a decisive blow. But after the laughter and admiring comments had died down, and all eyes and ears turned towards Qisma, she surprised everyone with what she said next. "Look, O sheikh! Despite the simplistic nature of this proof of yours, and how inappropriate it is to apply to our disagreement, nevertheless I say to you that you are wrong. Indeed, I challenge you on it, here and now, in front of everyone."

The gathering was utterly stunned, stupefied as never before. If they were told that camels could fly, they would have believed it. And if it were said to them that the Americans were going to completely slice up all of Iraq like a birthday cake – the land, the sky, the people, the fields, the animals, the cemeteries, and the toilets – and take it away piece by piece in ships and planes to that place beyond the oceans, just as they had taken Iraq's historical antiquities and its oil; that they would restore it, repair it, and rebuild the schools, hospitals and bridges that they had demolished; that they would cleanse it of all the pollution from their bombs; that they would teach its people democracy according to its true foundations; and that they would teach them about human rights and how to eat a hamburger instead of okra soup with tomatoes, they would have believed that too. Or, at least, they would have believed it more readily than they believed what their ears now heard from Qisma.

The sheikh was all the more certain that he had struck a decisive blow because her challenge was impossible to fulfil. This woman, even if she were crazy, would not have the audacity to do a thing like that in front of such a large audience. And if she did, it would reduce her to a laughing stock, as all she would achieve would be to wet her legs and her clothes. No, the important thing was to save his friend Tariq, a lifelong friend whom he loved, from this distress and ignominy, for the shock visible on his face was mirrored by the shock etched on the faces of everyone else present. The blood had frozen in his veins, and his mouth went dry no matter how much water he drank. His whole body was paralysed down to his very pupils, for whoever looked into them at that moment would have sworn they were the eyes of a dead man.

In a tone entirely different from the one he had adopted during the dispute – a tone that was calm, fatherly and empathetic, a tone that was confident, firm, masterful and triumphant – Sheikh Tafir said, "By God, sister Madame Sheikh Umm Ibrahim, you have honoured us today with your visit, truly. You have lit up the house, the village and our hearts. On this evening of celebration, you, sister, have bestowed a delightful, clever joke, one unlikely to be equalled and never forgotten. I take that as a kindness and an honour, for with such destruction and tragedy around us, we can reach the point where a man knows not how to respond or express himself except through sarcasm and jokes."

But what Sheikh Tafir did not expect, nor Tariq, who had recovered his breath a little, nor the general, nor Rahib, nor any Muhammed, Mahmud or Ahmed present in the hall, nor the children of the neighbours or young Shakhbata or anyone else present, was that Qisma's reply would retain its former sharpness, its confidence – indeed, becoming even sharper and more confident – as she said, "But I am not joking, sheikh. I am speaking in all seriousness."

It was not easy for the sheikh to swallow this challenge in the presence of this audience, which comprised the tribe, their neighbours and the Americans. Even so, he tried to stay calm at first with an ironic reply. "No, no, Umm Ibrahim. For even this son of mine, Shakhbata, would beat you." He pointed to his son, who was watching his father from the far end of the hall and who laughed with delight to hear his name.

"Not a chance," Qisma replied. "For we were speaking about women and men, not about a woman and a child."

"Fine," said the sheikh, continuing in jest. "Even this half-man would beat you." He pointed towards Rahib, who was circulating among those seated and offering cups of tea. Rahib had spent the whole day in the kitchen, and the smell of cooking emanated from him. Laughter rose again to fill the hall. Rahib set the tray of cups on the floor and leaped in the air, clapping exuberantly, going through the motions of the clown dance he knew so well. The laughter rang out even louder. Qisma noticed that the only ones who did not laugh, but were content to echo the others' laughter with a smile, were the American soldiers, who did not understand what was being said. General Adam also limited himself to smiling and watching intently, even though he understood perfectly well. For that reason, Qisma sometimes caught his gaze, as though challenging him too, or as though she were telling him that he was the one she meant, something which kindled the flame of the challenge in her blood all the more.

"Not at all, O sheikh," she said. "Rather, I was challenging the most manly person here. Choose for yourself the person here who best exemplifies your conception of manhood. Indeed, I was challenging you alone! In this way, each of us will defend our words with deeds that prove our point. And one more thing: it is not right to describe this man as half a man just because he is shorter than most, for men are not judged by their size, as though they were bulls, but by their values and their qualities."

Everyone fell silent. The sheikh said nothing. He stroked his beard as he thought, certain that he now had no choice but to see this predicament through to the end. "So be it," he said. "And what if you lose the wager?"

"You may ask whatever you want from me."

Everyone gasped, while the women recoiled in embarrassment at her words and what they imagined them to mean. Tariq's only wish was that the ground would split open and swallow him.

"Very well," said Tafir. "I shall receive just one request. In exchange, if I lose, you will have the right to demand three wishes from me, whatever they may be, and I pledge before everyone present to fulfil them, even if it should cost me my neck. Agreed?"

"Agreed," Qisma replied immediately. She rose to her feet, and everyone followed suit. Everyone except Tariq, who had lost all feeling in his legs and feared that if he stood up, he would fall on his face. He pretended to adjust his headdress and robe as though preparing to get up. Qisma made for the door. Sheikh Tafir went behind, followed by all the rest, with Tariq last of all, repeating prayers and verses, beseeching God for his protection from Satan and begging for a good outcome to what was about to happen.

No-one knew how this pissing contest would take place, and no-one could guess how it would end. But the one thing certain was that it was going ahead, and, just like a boulder rolling down a steep slope, it was no longer possible to stop it. Everyone was swept before it in apparent submission. As soon as they were in the wide courtyard of the house, they formed a semi-circle. The rest of the women, daughters and children – all those who had remained in the hall of the women – climbed up to the roof of the house and looked down on the scene from above, with the exception of the elder wife, who remained behind, seated and trembling, and, like Tariq, prayed to her Lord for a satisfactory resolution. She was almost slapping her cheeks as she imagined the horrors that the insanity of this woman, their guest, might lead to. All the same, she was not able to absent herself now that Rahib and the children, who had been providing her with information, had withdrawn. Using the wall for support, and extinguishing the light so that no-one could see her, she made her way to the window of the kitchen, which looked out onto the courtyard. Having seen the whole assembly stream out from every door of the house, the soldiers and guards at the main gate also made their way over and waited inside the courtyard. Sheikh Tafir stood before the gathering, flanked by Qisma and the general. Tariq rather reluctantly joined them after everyone made way for him to pass through to the front.

A murmur rose up from the crowd as everyone whispered to his neighbour amid a dozen stifled laughs. And because no-one had any idea how to conduct the contest, Rahib took it upon himself to stand at the front and propose that it take place on a spot of earth near a section of the outer wall, which had been planned as a flowerbed and was half-illuminated by light from the house. The two contestants would face the wall, their backs to the light and the audience. Thanks to the dryness of the earth and the smooth concrete wall, it would be easy to see the line of urine and the distance it travelled along the ground – or if it reached the wall, should God grant either of them such success. The winner would be the one whose stream proved the longest.

Everyone was pleased with the idea, and Rahib set off at a run to the agreed spot. Using the handle of a knife that he took from his belt, he drew a straight line in the dirt, parallel to the wall and about two metres away. Then he leaned back against the wall, waiting, whereupon Sheikh Tafir yelled at him, "You will stand behind the competitors, and not in front of them, you bastard!" Everyone broke out into laughter so loud it woke the chickens and the pigeons in the coops scattered around the courtyard, just as it startled the birds sleeping in the treetops, sending them flying into the darkness without knowing where they were going. Rahib kept smiling even after his hopes were dashed of seeing the genitalia of the contestants, and he stood behind them, in the space between the audience and the line he had scored in the ground.

Sheikh Tafir said, "Let Madame Sheikh Qisma go first." Then, with a show of courtesy, he added, "Ladies first!"

"No, we will go together," replied Qisma. "And we will stand on the line side by side, for we are competing to establish equality."

The audience supported her with nods and more murmuring, in a fever pitch of excitement. Sheikh Tafir moved forward, and Qisma could sense his confusion and suppressed distress, which, she was certain, would affect his performance. She advanced with him until they stood on the line that had been marked, one step apart, their cloak-covered backs to the audience, their eyes fixed on the wall.

"Ready?" Rahib called from behind them.

Qisma raised the hem of her cloak by lifting it off her shoulders and draping it from her head in the way women do. The sheikh spread his legs apart and then gave a thumbs-up with one hand to indicate he was ready. Counting slowly to build the tension, Rahib shouted, "One ... two ... three!"

The audience could see the contestants moving their arms, and they imagined the rest of the unseen steps involved in preparing to urinate. The sheikh was the first to shoot off his stream. Though he squeezed hard in the attempt to reach the wall, he did not succeed before the stream weakened and was exhausted, ending in a soft fart that only Qisma heard.

In a low voice, as her hands continued rolling up the edge of her dress under her cloak, Qisma commented, "That alone is enough to proclaim your defeat – indeed, your disgrace – forever!"

"Hide my disgrace," the sheikh replied. "And may the Lord hide yours!"

"Have no fear," she said. Then she asked, "What do you want me to write or draw for you on the wall?"

The sheikh's voice almost faltered, but he regained control and said, "It is enough for you to do it a handsbreadth in front of your feet so that you do not piss on your clothes. Look how far my line goes: it almost touches the wall." Then he raised his voice so the audience could hear him and said, "I've finished, but the madame sheikh hasn't done a thing!"

Calls of congratulations rose from his followers, along with claps and whistles. But Rahib raised his short arms and his voice rose over all of them as he yelled, "No, no! It doesn't matter who starts and finishes first. The timing isn't important. The crucial factor is how far it goes."

Silence fell, and Qisma seized the moment to expel what was stored in her bladder, which was full since she had used the toilet no more than once with her child after their arrival. She pushed it out so powerfully that those in the front row could have sworn that they heard its hiss. The whole assembly was stunned to see the word "woman" being written on the lower half of the wall, albeit in a terrible script, right in front of their eyes. Their voices rose in surprise despite themselves, coming from mouths gaping as far open as their jaws would allow. Then a trill rang out from the gathering of women, followed by vehement applause. The children started clapping, whistling, cheering and jumping about, just as though they had witnessed a goal scored by their team in a football match. After that, the men clapped and Rahib hurried up to the competitors, who had turned their faces towards the audience after having rearranged their clothes. Since there was no need for him to measure the distance because the result was visible to all, it was enough to announce at the top of his loud voice, with boundless enthusiasm, "The madame sheikh has beaten the sheikh!"

Without thinking how the sheikh would react or what punishment might follow, everyone started to shout in a single voice, clapping along to the rhythm: "Madame Sheikh! Madame Sheikh! Madame Sheikh!" The general made a secret sign to one of his soldiers to go and take a photograph of the site of the contest before the evidence dried. After everyone had had their fill of cheering, they withdrew, going back inside the two halls.

CHAPTER 6

Of Dawn Events and the River

Unlike Qisma, who, the moment she put her head on the pillow beside that of her infant, plunged into a deep sleep on account of the pressure of travelling and the exciting events of the day and the evening, Tariq kept tossing and turning in his bed, which they had made up for him in the guest hall. He pictured the things that had occurred and been said that day, and they clashed together chaotically in his head, wave after wave. All of it tormented him. His body was exhausted, but his mind was mercilessly alert, disbelieving everything that had happened and wishing that he might fall asleep and wake the next day to find that it had all been a terrible nightmare.

He thought he had been too hasty in agreeing to marry – indeed, ensnaring himself with – this creature, whom he actually did not know that well. The truth was he had always looked on her like one of his children. But what baffled him most was how she had been able to urinate while standing. Was she actually a woman after all? It can only have been Satan who had impelled him, tempting him with desires, dreams and illusions, to commit this great mistake. So he beseeched God's protection against Satan and rolled onto his right side. He told himself that God was the one who desired it, according to some wise plan of His that no-one but the Most High knew, and he would just have to be content with God's decision and decree.

Tariq rolled back onto his left side, thinking he ought to get rid of her as soon as he could, before she led him into even worse situations, scandals and disasters. Given that he had only married her by an oral agreement up to that point, it was possible for him, according to religious law, to divorce her orally as well, merely by telling her three times, "You are divorced." Thus he would be finished with this ordeal.

But when he rolled again onto his right side, he couldn't help thinking that this woman might produce a change in his life, a transformation, something he had long dreamed of, even more than glory, money and connections. For he had seen yesterday how the men's eyes were drawn to her, nearly snapping her up in the intensity of their admiration, including the general and Sheikh Tafir, and how she had all the confidence in the world in herself and what she said and did, even as doubt assailed everyone else, until she triumphed over them all.

Rolling back onto his left side, he began to worry that this woman would be master over him, and not the other way around as he had been expecting, or as he was used to with his first wife, an obedient, simple and compliant cousin on his father's side. Indeed, she might distance him from his family, his work and his friends, using him to further her own ends and not the other way round. Turning again to his right side, he decided that this woman was the great test of his life, perhaps the trump card that would open for him the doors to everything he wanted and desired. But as he rolled onto his back a voice whispered: "Or she may lead you to ruin."

Exhausted, he may have dozed off, but it was not long before he resumed his tossing and turning, wrestling with his thoughts. This continued until he heard through the window the crowing of the first cockerel at dawn. His heart fluttered with joy at the approach of day, but then he fell asleep again until, some minutes later, he felt a hand gently shake his shoulder and heard his name called in a whisper to wake him up. He opened his eyes and saw the face of Tafir looking down into his own from where he squatted close to Tariq's head.

"God bring you a good morning!" Tafir said. "Get up, my friend. Wash yourself so we can perform the dawn prayer together. Then I want to speak with you about a personal matter before anyone else wakes up."

Tariq got up quickly despite the heaviness in his body. If Tariq had snatched a few short moments of interrupted sleep, Tafir had not even closed his eyes. Lying alongside one of his wives, whom he scarcely noticed, he had turned over even more times than his friend. Tafir had been so distracted by the evening's events that he had not even considered whose turn it was to spend the night with him, though it was his habit to parcel out his attention to them equally, just as religious law required.

Tariq came back from the bathroom, and the two of them performed the fastest dawn prayer of their lives, feeling not a drop of spirituality or submission throughout, and indeed remembering none of it, not even the short suras from the Qur'an that they recited. Afterwards, Tafir gave Tariq one of his traditional fur pelts, a thick heavy one made by hand from the hides of baby lambs. One side was soft wool, and on the other, on top of the leather, was a special kind of cotton, embroidered around the edges with gold thread. The wearer of such a pelt would not feel the cold even if wandering the mountains in winter.

The two of them went out, wearing their fleeces, into the cold of the dawn before the thin mist had lifted. When they passed the checkpoint at the main gate, only one guard was awake, sipping a large cup of tea and rubbing his hands around his rifle. He hurriedly stood and greeted them. Then he hastened to wake his two sleeping colleagues, who quickly did up their belts, put on their shoes, picked up their rifles and followed the two sheikhs, who continued their walk along paths that ran through the fields and gardens that lay between Tafir's house and the river. The guards kept their distance to prevent the sheikhs' conversation from reaching them clearly, and each of them followed a line on either side, one to the right and one to the left of Tariq and Tafir.

Tafir began to talk about the plants they passed by, complaining about the reduced harvest returns since the beginning of the war and telling Tariq how the pollution levels in Iraq had multiplied, affecting the soil, the water, the air, and, worse still, the birthrate. So many women were unable to bear children these days! Farmers were no longer receiving any support from the Ministry of Agriculture and Husbandry as they used to in the days when they were furnished with fertilisers, insecticides, machinery and loans. Tafir said that he had an appointment with a minister in the new government about this matter. But it was not, of course, to speak of these matters that he had woken his friend so early and led him out into the fields, and he soon moved on to inform Tariq of his plan for carrying out the first of Qisma's three requests, which she had announced to him the night before in front of everyone, postponing revelation of the remaining two until their time came, as she put it.

Qisma had asked him to join her and her husband in the search for her father, contributing whatever he was able and all the men and connections at his disposal, until they came across the body or else decided to abandon the search. He told Tariq that he would have done all that anyway, even if she had not asked it of him. "The deceased Ibrahim deserves that from us; he was your lifelong friend and is now the father of your wife." Tafir said that they were used to collecting the corpses of those killed alongside the highway leading to Baghdad and those that were brought by the Americans to be buried; not a day passed that they did not bury one or more unidentified bodies. He would make it known to all the people of his village and the neighbouring villages that they were not to bury any corpse before it could be examined, "now that the main characteristics of the corpse of the betrayed man are known to us – roughly fifty years old, head recently cut off, right foot amputated long ago and perhaps replaced by a prosthetic. Likewise, I will contact our acquaintances in all the hospitals and in the police departments of the towns and villages, giving them this description, for they too receive dozens of unidentified bodies on a daily basis. As for Baghdad, if you need to contact the authorities to facilitate your mission, just let me know, and I will notify my son in the parliament, who will get in touch with them. And thus it may be that our Lord will make our path easy, and we will come across his pure body so it may be buried with his head in peace, and both his soul and yours may rest."

He was silent for a while, staring at the nearby river, wondering how best to broach the sensitive subject that was the main reason for this conversation. At that point, Tariq surprised him by providing a suitable opening, going straight to the heart of the matter when he asked Tafir what he had intended to demand from Qisma had he triumphed over her. Tafir tried to dodge the question, saying that he had not thought of anything at the time, and that he would have come up with some pleasantly witty thing, perhaps, for instance, that she promise to take care of her husband and not fail to obey his commands. But Tariq, who had known his companion well since childhood, recognised from his hesitant tone and lack of eye contact that he was not telling the truth. So he insisted, reminding Tafir that they were brothers, and that nothing in the world would ever come between them, that they knew of each other's dreams and shameful secrets, and that their confidence in each other would remain absolute, no matter what happened.

Tafir confessed that he would have imposed upon her the condition that she marry him in the event of her divorce from Tariq or if she became a widow – God forbid it should come to pass! – or that she seek for him a wife matching her description exactly in terms of age, dress, education, intelligence, courage, culture, personality and everything else, perhaps one of Qisma's friends or acquaintances in Baghdad.

Tariq felt a sense of relief after everything Satan had been whispering to him in the night about conditions far worse than this. He gave his friend a playful slap on the shoulder, as he used to in their youth. "You like her that much, eh, you bastard?"

Reassured by this, Tafir replied, "Yes." He had liked her very much indeed. "And if she were not your wife, I would have said that I loved her. But . . . But, brother, since what happened – her victory in the wager, I mean – I've been thunderstruck. I couldn't sleep all night. I just couldn't understand how! I still don't understand. And that is what I wanted to ask you about."

Tariq revealed that he had not been able to sleep either, and that he was no wiser because he had not yet touched her or explored her body. Some images from old wives' tales had crossed his mind: men in women's clothing, or vice versa, men with two sex organs, or women with two sets, one male, one female, and other fabulous things like that.

When they reached the riverbank, they sat down facing each other on two boulders near the edge of the water. The scene was magical. The river flowed peacefully past. The white light of dawn was tinged with a soft orange glow as the sun approached the horizon. The air was mild. There were delicate drops of dew on the leaves of the plants and the river-washed rocks near the bank. The stillness and silence, broken only by the chirping of the birds, led each man to vow to himself that in future he would go more often to visit the riverbank in his village at dawn, something neither had done for a long time.

Tafir confessed to his friend that his liking for Qisma had been shaken by what had happened, because, although he still thought of her as a splendid, strong, beautiful woman, this image he had of her was now in doubt because he no longer knew whether she was truly a woman. Likewise, he did not hide his significant anxiety that her outrageous, scandalous violations of the social conventions that governed his life might provoke his wives, daughters and daughters-in-law to rebel against tradition, and then to rebel against him and his own authority and dignity in front of his followers, his village and his tribe. He did not know what the result of all that would be. But then he assured Tariq, in an attempt to reassure himself, that he would know how to suppress such rebellions. His women had no refuge apart from him, and the members of his tribe would not abandon him and head off on their own in a country as broken as Iraq. "For we know from history and our own experience: during moments of danger, creatures will take refuge in gatherings of their own kind, or in the shelter of the nearest stone or stable tree. Right now, there is no strong government to speak of, nor any system that guarantees life and livelihood to them, apart from the tribal blocs … This is as it ever has been, my friend, and it will continue as long as this country lacks a government that guarantees the rights and safety of its citizens. Even the Americans are seeking refuge in tribalism, trying to make use of it now they understand the difficulty, the impossibility, even, of establishing control over this country, no matter how extreme their use of force … I believe that I am able to mend this breach quickly and easily, but what about the breach of nature itself? It concerns you more than it does me, and I worry for you. What if you do not find her to be a woman as we understand the term? You see what I am getting at?"

"Yes! Yes, of course. And I am nearly going mad, just like you, because it makes no sense to me at all, and I can only fear what the future will reveal to me about her."

"But then again, Tariq, from another standpoint, a woman her age, with her beauty, her power and her characteristics . . . She is nothing less than a gift from heaven, especially to a man of our age. She will renew you. She will force you to be younger, more vigorous. Her rhythm of life will infect you. It will be just as our people say: 'A new bed, a new life'."

"But I have discovered that I do not know her. I thought she would be like any other woman."

"That is precisely the beautiful and exciting thing about it, that there will always be something new for you to learn. This path of discovery, with enjoyment and renewal, will recall your first emotions in the days of adolescence. Anxieties, desires, delusions, dreams . . . dreams upon dreams."

Feeling the magic of the moment and place, Tariq took a stone and threw it into the river. The atmosphere and that conversation with his friend calmed his soul, though the anxiety within him did not dissipate entirely. "I remember a saying from Nietsche," he said, "that woman is a trap set by nature, and that when a woman has masculine traits, a man must approach her with caution."

Tafir abruptly slapped Tariq's shoulder and said, "Enough of this madman and his ideas! If he had known anything about women, he would not have failed in his relationships with them and died alone, with only his sister for company. It is up to each of us to create his own personal philosophy according to his make-up and his circumstances, and nobody's resembles anyone else's absolutely. Just as no two fingerprints are identical. Coming back to Qisma, if she were a man, she would be the best of men, and there is nothing that could force her to conceal that fact. She is certainly a woman, and, indeed, the most that any woman can be: a blazing fire, hellfire hot, a recalcitrant horse, wild and unbroken. In my opinion, a rider finds more enjoyment in a wild horse that he breaks in his own way, than in a horse he acquires already broken at the hands of someone else. It appears that all who have tried to tame Qisma have failed. Didn't you tell me that even her father gave up and despaired of her ever obeying him? Just imagine, even her father, who had her since birth to mould like clay, did not succeed. It is all the more enticing, my friend, because it means an even greater challenge for you. The greater the challenge, the greater the pleasure in meeting it."

As their conversation flowed back and forth, they felt the light increasing, reflecting off the surface of the water as the top limb of the sun broke free, try as the trees might to block it from sight. In that moment, they heard voices and laughter coming from upstream, though they could not make out the source on account of the nearby trees, some of which hung low and leaned over the water. The voices came closer, as though travelling with the current, until there appeared in the middle of the river one of the wooden boats favoured by farmers in that area. They were surprised to see Qisma standing in the boat, with the first light of the sun anointing her head as she tried to get her child to stand up so she could teach him how to fish. And although they could not see him, they heard Rahib's booming voice and infectious laughter.

When Qisma turned around and recognised them, she greeted them in a voice loud with excitement: "A blessed morning of roses in all their beauty, O sheikhs! A morning of hope and action! I am now a seagull!"

Instinctively, they both stood and waved at her. Then they saw the large head of Rahib rising like a watermelon over the gunwale in the middle of the boat. He was bending over or lying down, working away at a fishing net. "Me too!" he said, laughing. Then the little one turned and said to them joyfully, "I'm a seagull too." He added that he had seen some fish and ducks. Oh, and he had seen a little fish too!

"We will catch you a fish for breakfast," Qisma said.

"We will catch you a fishy fish fish!" Rahib repeated after her as he threw the net into the water. He began to sing:

> Fisherman, fisherman, catch me a girl
> My heart caught in the net, what can I do?
> Together we sit, between shore and palm
> Whispering glances with healing balm

All Tariq was able to say to them as they drifted away on the current, midstream, with no need of oars or motor, was that they must take care and not go too far. But he was secretly annoyed. In his whole life, never had he known a woman of his family go out without permission, and, even worse, at a time like that, in a strange place, with a strange man.

His friend sensed what was troubling him and said soothingly, "There's no need to worry so long as that devil Rahib is with them."

On their way back to the house, following a different path through the fields and gardens, as the two guards kept pace at a distance, Tafir pointed out a low green dome at the edge of the village. "That's the shrine of Abu al-Anwar. Do you want to visit it?"

"No, not now. On a future visit, God willing. But who is this Abu al-Anwar? I haven't seen his tomb before."

"I'll tell you his story another time. For now, I want to be sure that you will strengthen your resolve when it comes to your second wife. The most important thing is to make the most of every opportunity at a time when we are all at each other's throats." He counselled him on the necessity of believing in himself and in his future family, which would bring him both money and glory, for the two went hand in hand. "Our fathers risked their lives," he said, "working to smuggle weapons, tobacco, and so on in order to get another mouthful of bread. But today, the threshing floor stands open, with no-one to guard it, just like this river, open to anyone with an ounce of intelligence and initiative who wants to dip his bowl. For example, we are coming up to elections, and we may sell our votes to the highest bidder. For what are these votes anyway? Nothing at all! We did not know them before; it's just as though we are selling the air. Our true votes are those we cast with our tongues, and they stay with us. What we're selling is something we cannot see, touch or know. They call them our votes, our voices, and they tell me, 'When election day comes and you have the pieces of paper with a certain image on them and the names of so-and-so, tell your tribe to put down "Shakhbata" in exchange for money, glory and offices.' You have to do that too, Tariq. I'll teach you this and other things that will make you see with your own eyes, and touch with your own hands, the fruits of this democracy that they have brought us."

Tafir informed him that in the ranks of his guards there were seven of his nephews he had picked himself, yet it was the government that paid their salaries, in addition to providing two cars and weapons. As for his oldest son, he had forty guards, all chosen from among their relatives, five armoured cars and a whole arsenal of weapons, under a system that was known as "allocations". His son was now thinking of undergoing plastic surgery on his nose and ears, with the government picking up the bill. "Why shouldn't he," Tafir asked, "when his female colleagues in parliament are spending millions on plastic surgery, all paid for by the government? I encouraged him, of course. By the way, most members of government and parliament take a pilgrimage to Mecca nearly every year, for, as you know, whoever takes a pilgrimage to the house of God is purified from his sins and returns just like on the day his mother gave birth to him. My son and I are thinking of doing that at the beginning of next year."

CHAPTER 7

Arriving in Baghdad

Rahib prepared a delicious breakfast, roasting some of his catch over the coals of a fire and frying the rest in oil with sliced onions, tomatoes and spices. The delightful odour wafted as far as the noses of the guards at the main gate, and they started sticking their heads over and looking in under the pretence of checking the lock. Carpets were spread on the grass in the garden in front of the house. Rahib joined the guests for the meal, choosing to sit close to Qisma, so close that they were touching. In their conversation, they passed quickly over the fasts that they had missed during Ramadan, agreeing that most people's failure to abstain stemmed from the injustices they were suffering, their subjugation, and the daily threat of death that hung over their heads. Tariq hinted that foreign occupation forces were aware of this and saw it as a way of distracting the people from their religion, insisting that war had a firm, religious spirit as well, lacking which there would never be a sufficient justification for it.

"We have to think about the actual moment," Sheikh Tafir said, "and try not to use the phrase 'if only' too often. It's good for nothing but ushering in the devil's whispering."

Then he began to review what he had said to Tariq, with the intention that Qisma hear it as well, for she was part of his plan to persuade them to plunge themselves into this new great game and get their share of the meat from the feast. They soon seemed close to being persuaded, with Qisma showing more enthusiasm than Tariq. Tafir proposed they spend another day as his guests, especially as every hour brought news of fresh unidentified corpses, their murderers also unknown, discovered in the fields that bordered the Baghdad highway. They decided, however, to leave immediately after lunch in order to arrive at the capital before nightfall, for the corpses were also accumulating in the police stations, hospitals and morgues. They must make haste with their search for Ibrahim before the authorities got rid of his corpse to make space for another, or it was covered by the rapidly accruing bodies.

Tafir advised them to seek an audience with a son of their village, Sheikh Jalal al-Din, and he gave them the private telephone number of his own son, who was a member of parliament. Rahib surprised them by producing one of his colourful business cards, with his name, address, telephone number and, in place of a profession, the phrase "Jack of All Trades". He pressed it into the hand of Qisma, seated beside him, saying that he too would be glad to help them in any way he could.

The guests said their farewells with a ceremony to rival their reception. Sheikh Tafir insisted on accompanying them with his guards and followers in a convoy of cars halfway down the dirt road, where he got out and embraced his friend again. He remained standing there with his entourage until Tariq's car appeared no larger than a box of matches.

On the road, the thing that most occupied Tariq's mind was

finding an appropriate moment to ask Qisma how she had urinated standing up, and he jumped between different topics, searching for anything that would provide the opportunity. He praised his friend's hospitality towards them; he ran through the advice they had received; he flipped through the stations on the car's radio. All the broadcasts talked about new conflicts between political factions, about fresh murders, and about the sales of weapons with silencers – or other weapons that killed at full volume. They talked about masked men, booby-trapped cars, explosive devices and mosques, houses, cafés and whole streets that had been blown up. They talked about suicide belts. Land mines. Trucks loaded with tons of explosives and bombs placed in cars, motorbikes and bicycles – even on donkeys and in the bodies of the dead so that they would explode in the ambulance. There was news of blood drowning the country in a merciless dance of destruction.

"There's no power or might except with God," muttered Tariq. "Everything is stained with blood. Everyone's killing everyone."

They managed not to come into conflict with the numerous convoys of American military vehicles, keeping the specified distance of one hundred metres. They endured the boredom of waiting at the checkpoints, and the humiliation of passing through them, and as the hours passed it grew harder and harder to distinguish between them and judge the nationality of the soldiers manning them, given the chaos of similarities and differences in their uniforms and the insignias on their shoulders. It was an affront in the greatest sense of the word, to the point where Qisma began to wish she were wearing a suicide belt in order to blow herself up at one of those nauseating, humiliating checkpoints and finally get some rest.

What calmed her in those moments was the way her child would smile at her whenever she stroked his head. He would raise his face towards her and smile, and she would lift him up, press him to her breast and breathe in his scent. He returned the embrace with his arms tight around her neck as the love stole from his small chest into hers. Qisma's eyes filled with tender tears. She was afraid for him, and, in equal measure, determined to do anything she could to keep him safe – all the more so as it seemed to her that a masked man had threatened her that same day. She was not entirely certain about what happened, so she had not told Tariq about it. It had occurred when the two of them were waiting in the line of cars at the last checkpoint. Tariq had been busy flipping through radio stations, while Qisma stared out through the closed window on her side. An official-looking black car had passed alongside them in a lane designated for military vehicles and cars that were not subject to inspection. She saw a masked man sitting in the back seat of the car. He looked straight into her eyes and drew his finger across his throat. Qisma felt her heart judder. Not believing what she had seen, she turned away. Then she looked back and found that the man was still looking at her and did not avert his gaze until the car had pulled away and was lost in the press of vehicles. Her mouth went dry. She did not know how to explain it – to herself or to Tariq. Could it have been some strange apparition conjured by her own imagination, or just some idiot making an idiotic gesture and meaning nothing by it? Or perhaps his sign had been for someone other than her among all the people piled up in the crowd of cars . . . Because the alternative was . . . She didn't want to think about that. She drank more water and held her son to her breast for what remained of the journey.

They reached Qisma's Baghdad home, which overlooked the Tigris as it wound its way though the city centre. Tariq parked the car in the designated area behind the house. They made their way into the house through the front courtyard, which had a small fountain in the middle (no longer working, of course), a miniature replica of the famous statue in Baghdad of Kahramana, heroine of *Ali Baba and the Forty Thieves*. Tariq was astonished at the size and elegant splendour of Qisma's home. The ground floor was dominated by a large room with doors on both sides, which Tariq later learned led to a kitchen, two bathrooms, a study and a guest room. There was also another door, which Tariq never saw opened, and which he did not ask about. On the floor above there was a smaller hall that ran the length of the building, with the stairs at one end and a balcony that looked out over the garden and the river at the other, which was flanked by the balconies of two bedrooms. All the balconies were furnished with two chairs and a low table. Distributed around this upper hall were the doors to four bedrooms, including Qisma's master bedroom, which led to a smaller room for her child.

As soon as they went inside, Qisma busied herself by giving the child a bath, changing his clothes and feeding him before putting him to sleep upstairs. Tariq explored the ground floor, astonished by everything he saw, starting with the furniture – the couches and chairs in particular. He was certain that he had seen them somewhere before, and he kept standing in front of them, pondering their gilt embroidery, sometimes sitting on the edge of a seat as he scoured his memory. It came to him in the end and he jumped up with a shudder. These were the chairs and couches from one of the palaces of the former president. They had appeared many times on television when the president received dignitaries. He deduced this from the way they were arranged: two large chairs at one end of the room; a pedestal between them beneath the Iraqi flag; couches along both sides; and above the flag a large framed photograph of a man who, with his military uniform, moustache and glasses, closely resembled the former president. On both sides of the picture were smaller frames displaying the decorations and medals worn by the man in the picture.

Against the wall behind one of the couches was a broad bookshelf. It was virtually empty save for a few sets of crockery and a row of books. When he got close enough to read the titles on the spines and pull out others to look at their covers, he found they were a mixture of military history, memoirs of politicians and generals, tracts on law and economics, and a few novels. It delighted him to find books in the house, even if it wounded his soul that there was not a single religious book among them, and he decided he would make remedying this a priority. He spotted some packs of Marlboro cigarettes lined up at the end of the row of books beside a silver cup. He looked towards the low tables in the hall and noticed the glass ashtrays, some of which were trimmed with gold. Tariq felt reassured when he saw that they were clean and empty, concluding that they were for guests and not for Qisma, whom he had not seen smoke throughout the journey or on any other occasion. In one corner, he saw the casing of a large artillery shell, which held an imposing bouquet of plastic flowers.

Heading towards the bathroom, Tariq washed the dust off his hands and face. As he sat on the toilet, he contemplated the size and elegance of the bathroom with its marble fixtures, and took note of the numerous expensive-looking bars of soap, bottles of shampoo, and so on. It was even more impressive than what was in Sheikh Tafir's bathroom. After finishing his business, he went through the next door and was appalled by the size of the kitchen and all the modern appliances he found there. He began to explore the cupboards, finding bags, boxes and cans of all sorts of packaged food. It shocked him to see that one of the cabinets was filled with bottles of alcohol and beer. He shut the door quickly, as though he had seen the naked body of a woman.

Poking his head around the kitchen door, he looked to see if the lights were on upstairs. Having checked that Qisma was still up there with her son, he went back into the kitchen and opened the drinks cupboard a second time. It horrified him that Qisma might have drunk from these forbidden bottles, and he tried to tell himself that they must have been for her former husband or some of their guests – even though that too was distasteful to him and his religion. He looked at the bottles without daring to touch them. Then he closed the cupboard door and turned towards the wide window looking out on the high wall that separated Qisma's garden from that of her neighbours. He did not know what to think, and, desperate to distract himself with any task whatsoever, he called out, "Do you want tea or coffee?"

"Tea," came the reply.

The process of making tea calmed his thoughts – and possibly his soul – and while busying himself in the search for what he needed, the sugar, the tea itself, and so on, he heard from the upper bathroom the sound of water splashing in the shower – reflecting that instead of the common word, *doosh*, he preferred *mishah*, as it was called in proper Arabic, a term he learned from his second son, the one interested in language and books as he himself was. And did he imagine that he also heard Qisma singing? He went to stand at the foot of the stairs. Lifting his gaze to the floor above, he saw the door to the child's bedroom pulled to, with the light off, while the lights were on in the room next door. He could not make out the words she was singing.

"Singing?" he wondered aloud to himself in a voice only he heard. Then he added, "But of course she's singing. What else? Do you recite the Qur'an in the shower, you idiot?"

Tariq smiled at this conversation with himself, then went back to making the tea. He interpreted it as a positive sign, for, as the proverb says, "The flourishing soul sings." She would be relaxed now, and the night promised good things. With his imagination running away from him, he singed his fingers on the fire. Luckily there was no-one to see it. He had never imagined that he would end up trading roles with a woman. He was in the kitchen, making tea for her, while she was in the shower, singing. Content nonetheless, he said to himself, "It's O.K. All men do these things at the beginning of relationships. Men win women's affection with gifts, attention and simple sacrifices. Then, later on, they resume their allotted roles. It's alright. The girl is still a bride, and she deserves to be pampered a little by me, at least for a limited time at the beginning."

Having clarified this with himself, he carried the tea into the living room on a tray. Two cups, a teapot and the sugar bowl beside a small plate of biscuits. He sat and waited for her. He did not have to wait long. Her scent reached him first, and, turning towards the stairs, he watched her descend. She was like a princess in his eyes. He rose and stared, utterly dazzled. She had changed into a long green dress, light, diaphanous even, for it clung to the curves of her body. He realised how slender she was, not at all like his first wife nor like most of the women he had known. Short sleeves revealed two tender-skinned arms that shone despite the dim lighting in the room. Her long hair, black and shining, was draped over her shoulders, and he could almost follow the length of each hair as it rippled down her back like water from a fountain.

As she reached the bottom step, he was moving towards her, hands outstretched to take hers with delighted praise. "My God, my God! What beauty God has made! Blessings and prayers upon his Prophet! O earth, preserve these feet that walk upon you!"

She thanked him with a smile and allowed him to take her hand and lead her to a seat beside him on one of the couches. He poured the tea into the two cups and offered her one, saying, "To see you now so elegant, a man would not believe you were the same woman he saw yesterday and earlier today."

"You haven't seen anything yet," she said. "I promise you, you won't have time to be bored when you're with me, but you'll need to double your capacity for patience and endurance."

"If the result is this beauty," he said flirtatiously, "then I am ready to endure even more for your sake than the suffering of camels in the desert."

Influenced by the magic of her appearance and her perfume, which dominated the room, Tariq was encouraged to move even closer until his thigh was touching hers. At the contact, he felt an electric pulse that propelled the blood through his veins. He stretched his arm around her shoulders and whispered, "I had wanted our wedding night to be more beautiful than in *A Thousand and One Nights*, but you know how things are these days, the complications of these strange times in which we are living." With that, he dared to plant a light kiss upon her cheek, aroused by the softness of her skin and its scent.

She pulled away a little and said, "Yes, though I no longer dream of a wedding night like that. I experienced all that before, in the presence of my father. I had everything a bride could hope for or even imagine. I have become more practical and pragmatic now. Results and tangible realities are what interest me – more than dreams and fantasies."

Her shift away made him anxious, and he replied, "Yes. Yes, I understand you. Indeed, I agree with you, for this is a sign of maturity and wisdom." Tariq became more anxious still when she stood up and headed towards the desk. She pulled out a cigarette, lit it and sat back down on a chair opposite him. She crossed one leg over the other and took a long drag.

"You smoke?" he said in horror.

"No, no. Only on certain occasions, or when I need to put in order the thoughts running through my head. Right now, we have to plan our next steps and decide what to do tomorrow."

Tariq stole a glance at the white calf she had revealed when she crossed her legs. It looked like a piece of fresh cheese, and he wanted to eat it up. Then he glanced at her throat and the opening of her robe, where he could see for the first time a suggestion of her breasts. They were not large, but they would fill his hands. How they tempted him. He imagined setting his head on those marble breasts and tasting the honey of her womanhood with his tongue.

They agreed that first they would visit the office of Sayyid Jalal al-Din to see if he was able to help them. After that, they would go to the registry office to change the name of the child, and find out how and when they might obtain passports. Tariq was surprised by this mention of passports and questioned her motive, since she had not spoken of leaving the country.

"Who knows?" she said. "The situation changes every day; it is not remotely stable. Many of the people I know, including these neighbours" – she pointed towards the high wall that Tariq had seen through the kitchen window – "have emigrated. Some of them sold everything they had and left the country with no intention of returning. Most of those in the current government even have dual citizenship in some foreign country. There is no security here, and no-one knows what will happen tomorrow. No clear future for the children, no education, no health care, no laws. Indeed, it's hardly a country at all in the full meaning of the word."

"But ..."

"Don't worry. As I said, we aren't going anywhere, but we will ask about passports and obtain them, if possible, as a precaution. After that, we'll make the rounds, starting with the Ministry of the Interior. Then we'll go to the medical centre, the agency of forensic medicine and the hospitals, to ask about the latest corpses to have reached them."

Tariq's mind remained full of questions, many of them concerning her contest with Tafir. But he put them to one side, resolving to mull them over by himself a little longer. Besides, talk about such matters would be better in bed. He asked her instead about the furniture and where it was from. She replied that her late husband had admired the former president very much, while at the same time harbouring a deep resentment and jealousy of him. He resembled him in everything, and it got to the point where he wanted to take the president's place. So he took part in that doomed coup attempt, which led to his execution. He had seen this furniture on television and in the newspapers. Maybe even in person too, given that he belonged to the unit that guarded the Palace of the Republic. He took a collection of photographs to a craftsman he knew and asked him to make a set exactly like it, no matter what the cost.

At that, Qisma's narrative trailed off for a moment. Then she told Tariq that she planned to remove the photograph and put in its place the picture she had taken of her father with a smile on his face as he carried her son, laughing, on his shoulders. "It's a small picture, but I will take it to a studio to have it enlarged to fill the frame." In that way, she would see the smiles of both her Ibrahims every day.

She told him that she was thinking of making other changes to the house, including the furniture. Tariq asked if it was her property, and she said yes, because her husband had registered all his possessions in her name before embarking on his ill-advised plans. Had he not done so, it would all have been confiscated. When she saw Tariq looking at the medals, she said, "As for those, I don't know. I'm thinking of keeping them until I figure out what to do with them. I've heard of many officers and soldiers who sold their medals and decorations for bravery during the years of the sanctions in order to feed their children, as some of the badges have silver or gold in them." When Tariq pointed to the flag, she said, "I'll change this too, of course."

"Change it for what?"

She thought for a moment and then said, "The flag of the Shakhabit, perhaps." They laughed together, laughed as loud as they could, until they caught hold of themselves so as not to wake the sleeping child. Tariq took this as a good sign. It was the first time he had heard her laugh like that, free, high and alluring. Then she said, "Wait a minute. It occurs to me now that in place of the flag I'll put my father's chequered headscarf. I still have it."

At that, a tear came to Tariq's eye. Deeply moved, he went over and embraced her where she sat, rubbing her back to show his sympathy and compassion. When he went back to his seat, he saw that her eyes were bright with tears too, and the light had gone out of her face. He realised how greatly she felt the pain of her father's death.

After a few moments of silence as they recovered their composure, she said, "Well, we have to go to bed now for we have a long day ahead of us tomorrow. Do you want to sleep with me in my room or in a room of your own?"

Her question surprised Tariq, and he did not know how to reply. And because she was watching him, waiting for his answer, he stumbled over his words and made a few inarticulate sounds. Then, in a way that hinted at what he meant, he said, "Ummm . . . I get scared sleeping on my own."

She laughed, and he laughed with her. Standing up, she said, "Fine! Let's go then. But don't get any ideas. Tonight is just for resting."

"Yes, of course!" he said, relieved that she had understood his meaning and given him something of a promise.

He followed her as she ascended the stairs, watching her tight, round buttocks rolling under her dress as her scent transformed the whole universe into a garden within his soul.

CHAPTER 8

A Dinner of Sheep and Bombs

At ten o'clock the next morning, Tariq called the private number of Sayyid Jalal al-Din al-Iraqi, the title the man had adopted and by which he was known, rather than Jalal Isma'il. Tariq used the landline in the house since he still did not have a mobile. As for Qisma, she scarcely used hers at all and sometimes forgot where she had left it.

Jalal seemed delighted to hear from him and said he would be waiting for them in his office in an hour's time. He described the building in detail to Tariq, but when they got there, Tariq could not see how it matched Jalal's description. The approach was heavily guarded, but at the first checkpoint they found that the full names of the three of them were on a list, which sped up the process of inspection and entry. One of the guards led them to the sayyid's office. Jalal rose to receive them with an effusive salutation. He embraced Tariq, shook hands with Qisma and kissed the toddler's cheek. Abandoning his official chair behind the broad expanse of his desk, he sat with them on the visitors' chairs. Jalal asked what they would like to drink, and then had instant coffee brought to them and a cup of orange juice for the child.

This was the second time Tariq had met Sayyid Jalal. After a brief introduction the previous year in the company of Sheikh

Tafir, Jalal had given Tariq his private number and asked – insisted even – that they meet again. It was then that he informed Tariq that he was the oldest son of the now deceased mayor of the village, Ibrahim, and his wife, Zaynab the Kurd. He had fled over the border to Iran, where he had settled at the age of seventeen. He had never forgotten his village, and he had a great desire to visit it after the passing of these long years, but he would only do so after the country's perilous position had stabilised. His responsibilities now were many and great: he was one of the deputy ministers of national security and chief of security for the Commission on Public Integrity.

Something he did not mention, however, was that he was afraid to confront his past and face his son, Abdullah Kafka. He did not know what Abdullah's reaction would be upon seeing him. He was also afraid of visiting the village cemetery, where Zakiya – his victim and Abdullah's mother – was buried, and so too his father, whom he had loved but who had forsaken him and died with his heart still turned against him. How often had the same nightmare returned to haunt him? A nightmare that left him sweating and panting as he fled their bloody frames, flesh torn and bone bleached, clawing their way from their graves. She carried a pickaxe and he a rifle, and behind them came an army of villagers, both living and dead, those whom he had wronged as a spoiled youth, carrying clubs, knives, pistols and torches, howling and out for blood.

He did not know Qisma, of course, nor her father, for they had been born after he left the country, but he remembered Sheikh

Tahir, father of Tariq, because he had been the intimate friend of his father, and he began asking the two of them about old acquaintances from the previous generations. For the most part they replied that they had died, but when they mentioned the dull-witted shepherd Isma'il, he surprised them with his joy at hearing the man was still alive, tending his sheep and the village's cows just as he had always done, despite his great age. He had not married, they told him, and his honoured mother had continued to care for him until the final moment of her life. Deeply saddened by her death, Isma'il still visited her grave every day after bringing the two herds he tended to graze beside the new cemetery.

Then Jalal told them how, after leaving the village, he had crossed the Kurdistan mountains and settled in Iran. He studied there, married, had children, and joined one of the Iraqi opposition parties based there. Presently, the conversation moved on to the reason for Qisma and Tariq's presence in Baghdad: to search for the body of Qisma's father, since they had buried only his head in the village, alongside eight others. Jalal told them he had heard about that distressing incident, and he offered his condolences to Qisma in the most elegant terms. He said there was no need for them to undertake the search on their own, that he would contact the top officials in the Ministry of the Interior and the Ministry of Health right there and then to give them all the information they would need to make their enquiries. They would report back to Jalal, and he would convey their findings to the two of them. Qisma and Tariq looked at each other with satisfaction, then at Jalal with gratitude, and thanked him.

"There is no need to thank me," he said. "You are my family, and he who cannot help his family is no good to anyone."

He asked if they had any other requests. Encouraged, Qisma informed him that she wanted to change the name of her son, who bore the name of the deposed president, and bestow on him the name of her father.

"That is an even easier request to grant than your first," Jalal said. "What else?"

"If possible, to obtain passports as well."

"It's expensive, but it costs nothing to ask. Do you have passport photographs?"

When they said they did not, Jalal said, "It's not a problem." He picked up the receiver of one of the many telephones on his desk and began speaking into it.

Tariq whispered to Qisma: "He's the very image of his father! Right down to the cut of his moustache and beard."

"I never met his father."

Tariq asked if she had seen his picture in the reception room of his house in the village.

"Once, maybe," she said, "and I no longer remember it. But I see a certain resemblance between him and Abdullah Kafka, the difference being that Abdullah appears like a crumpled version of him."

When Jalal had finished his call, he turned towards Qisma and said, "Done! All is in order, and everything you request will be accomplished within the hour. Now, is there anything else I can do for you?"

They said they were incapable of properly showing their gratitude and that they did not have any other requests at this time.

"In that case," he said, "it is my turn to ask something of you. Namely, that you do me the honour of visiting my home and meeting my family, so that they may get to know my own people, and through them my village, which I have been telling them about for so long."

Overcome by his generosity and eager to respond in kind, Qisma replied, "Only on condition that you and your family do us the honour first, and visit our house here in Baghdad, or in the village, as you prefer."

Jalal agreed and said that he would let them know as soon as he was able to.

At that moment, one of the sayyid's guards entered, accompanied by two men in civilian clothes. One of them carried a case full of documents, the other a camera. He asked them to stand, one after the other, against a space on one of the walls that was the only spot free of paintings, flags, photographs and framed certificates. He took photographs of the three of them and then withdrew to develop them, while the other man recorded their information in official documents and took their fingerprints. Tariq was surprised that Qisma registered her son as Ibrahim Qisma al-Nakhili al-Baghdadi, taking his second name from the mother, and not the father as was the custom. But of course, this was not the moment to stop and debate that. The proceedings were quickly concluded, and in what seemed like no time at all Qisma held in her hand all the documents they had requested, just as they wanted them, including three passports and an official marriage contract.

When Qisma and Tariq left, the sayyid accompanied them to

the door of the building. They all promised to keep in touch, and, when the time came to say goodbye, Qisma was not content to shake hands, but took the sayyid's head in her hands and kissed his forehead in gratitude. It was as though this kiss sealed the contract of an unshakeable relationship founded on mutual trust and goodwill.

"What would you think if I were to visit you alone this evening after dinner?" Jalal said, while they were still standing by the door. "To allow us to continue our conversation far from this official setting, to share memories and perhaps touch on other important topics?"

They welcomed the idea – indeed, they rejoiced in it. Without asking them the address of the house, he told them he would be there around ten o'clock. And when Qisma was about to mention it to him, he said, "I know it," and ordered some of his guards to go ahead of them in a car to make it easier for them to pass through the checkpoints on their way back.

Qisma and Tariq went straight home. They could not have been more delighted and relieved by how easily it had all been accomplished. Without Sayyid Jalal al-Din, they would have had to endure a long search, and it would have taken them months of application forms, queues and bribes to acquire these documents. They discussed how best to thank Jalal that evening in a way that befitted his station and what he had done on their behalf. They began by liberating the entire house from the dust that had accumulated during Qisma's long absence. Tariq set about cutting the grass in the garden and pruning the branches of some of the more unkempt trees.

In the afternoon, they went for lunch at one of the grandest restaurants in Baghdad, one Qisma seemed to know well, rewarding themselves after the day's accomplishments. They also put in an order for the restaurant's signature dish – a small grilled sheep stuffed with rice and raisins – to be delivered to the house at nine or nine thirty so that it would be fresh and warm when their guest arrived. Although he had said he would come "after dinner" and not "for dinner", they still wanted to do something to demonstrate their gratitude. They paid no attention to how much their order came to. Tariq gave them all the money he had in his pocket, which covered just half the bill, and said he would pay the other half upon delivery.

After lunch, Qisma suggested that they drop by the house of the parents of her late husband to greet them, introduce Tariq, let them know the new name of their grandson, and perhaps leave him there to spend the night with them, just as she had done many times before.

Tariq, of course, approved of this idea enthusiastically. When they got there, he was surprised to find that they addressed Qisma by the name Nisma, that the house was not far from hers, and that it was even larger and more luxurious, with furniture and carpets that were in the old Baghdad style and clearly very expensive. The two parents lived there with a daughter who was Qisma's age. Tariq later learned that she was a widow, and that she ran the family's jewellery shop. She had poor eyesight and wore glasses. The three of them were elegant, kind and refined. They rejoiced to see the child, for whom they had set aside a room of his own when he was born. They also approved of changing his name, because his bearing the name of the former president would expose both him and them to constant danger. But they found the addition of the name Qisma strange, as they did the insertion of the title al-Nakhili before that of al-Baghdadi, which was their family name that went back generations. This was another opportunity for Tariq to learn more about Qisma and her way of thinking.

She explained to them that she had decided to do away with her former name of Nisma, which she had adopted for herself unofficially and by which people had known her since her arrival in Baghdad years ago, and would revert to her true name, which her father had given her, and by which he too had been known in the village. Qisma pointed to Tariq, saying that he was responsible for giving her father that name back when they were boys. Tariq laughed, then recounted the names the Sons of the Earth Crack had devised for themselves: Tariq the Befuddled, Ibrahim the Fated – Ibrahim Qisma, that is – and the last of the trio, Abdullah Kafka. The parents and their daughter were amused by the lively way he told the story. Qisma stressed that she would adopt the name with a new meaning, not the old one, which derived from her father's lifelong submission to fate and his repetition of the phrase "Everything is fate and decree". In her case, it symbolised that she was resolved to respond to, be revenged upon and to strike fiercely against anyone who threatened her or her son. To the point of tearing them into two pieces – or more – if necessary!

From the edge in her voice, each of those present felt that this warning was directed at him or her, in one way or another.

She explained she was giving her father's name to her son as an apology for the way she had neglected him, and as a way to honour him and preserve his memory for future generations, including her son and his children and grandchildren. Likewise, she had put her name where the father's usually went in the hope that it would help her son to feel that she was both his mother and his father.

"As for al-Nakhili," she went on, "it comes from our village, and it is also my title and Tariq's in the new documents we obtained today. And al-Baghdadi . . . Well, that's because he was born in Baghdad, and you, his grandparents, carry this title."

Qisma and Tariq left the child in the care of his aunt, who had been the happiest of them all to see him. They returned to Qisma's house, Tariq not commenting on what she had said about little Ibrahim's names, nor about her late husband's family, except to declare, "They are good people." Then the conversation moved on to something they had been talking about since they had left Sayyid Jalal al-Din's office: the important topics that he wanted to discuss with them. They had no idea what those could be, other than news of the people of the village, including who remained from his family, how they lived now, and things like that. Then again, perhaps not, since he already seemed extremely well informed about goings-on, though there was nothing strange about that given that he was an important official in a government security agency.

As soon as they arrived at the house, Qisma took the best glasses from the bookshelf in the main room and brought them to the kitchen, where she washed them in preparation for the sayyid's visit. Once everything in the house was ready, they went to shower and put on their best clothes, Qisma telling Tariq that he should wear a suit and tie instead of a robe and headdress. He objected, saying he preferred traditional dress, which painted him as a religious man, a tribal man – and in any case, he had not brought a suit with him. Qisma suggested that he put on one of her former husband's many expensive suits. Tariq was startled and resisted further, but Qisma went on trying to persuade him, insisting that changing clothes did not mean changing one's identity, and that it was incumbent upon a man to change as the situation demanded and to wear clothes that suited the occasion and the place. If his reluctance was on account of the clothes having belonged to her dead husband, that scruple was even more frivolous, for if he had agreed to take the wife of a dead man, what objection could he have to taking his clothes as well!

Tariq did not want to clash with her or enter into a prolonged discussion on minor matters such as this. He decided to go along with her wishes since it would not harm him in the slightest to do so. Indeed, perhaps she was right, and it would work to their advantage. When she opened her late husband's wardrobe, which covered a whole wall of one of the bedrooms, the number of suits – and their elegance – shocked him, not to mention the number of shirts and ties. Qisma picked out a jacket for him to try, but they found it was too tight on him, for her former husband had been a slender, graceful officer. He tried on several more, but the result was the same.

Qisma slapped Tariq's stomach and said, "You need to shrink this belly a little."

Her words cut him to the quick, but he knew how to turn the matter into a joke. "This belly is part of any sheikh or notable's outfit," he said, "just as it's a sign that a man is happy with his wife and the way she feeds him."

Qisma laughed. "Really! Enough with these feeble excuses! Now go and shower."

"If I'm going to wash my back," he said to her with a wink, "I'll need you in there with me. And when you shower, I'll repay the favour."

She laughed a second time, a pleasing sound that melted his heart, and he tried to catch her in his hands. But she moved away, saying, "Later! Later! You go to the downstairs bathroom, and I'll shower here in the bathroom off the bedroom to save time."

By nine thirty, they were both downstairs reading on one of the couches, dressed in all their finery and drenched in scent. Qisma wore one of her suits – exceedingly elegant with its short skirt and jacket – along with a set of slender gold bracelets and an elaborate necklace that appeared to Tariq to be more intricate and expensive than the one he had seen the previous night. She was wearing the same perfume as the night before, so he knew it must be her favourite. Tariq had put on one of her late husband's expensive colognes after changing his white dishdasha for another that he had brought in the car. He wore a red headdress, held in place by an iqal, and he had trimmed his moustache and beard. Qisma sprayed the entire house with perfume and turned on more lamps. She also hastily replaced the flag in the main room with her father's black and white headdress, just as she had been planning to.

The intercom at the outer gate rang. It was a car from the restaurant. Two youths began carrying covered dishes into the house and arranging them in the kitchen according to Qisma's instructions. There was so much food that it took close to a quarter of an hour to unload it all. Qisma paid them the balance of the bill, adding a tip for the two of them. Before they left, they thanked her and told her that their boss, the owner of the restaurant, sent his best greetings and thanked them for their confidence in him and his food. If they needed anything else – at any time – they just had to call.

At ten o'clock precisely, Sayyid Jalal al-Din arrived, just as he had promised. A few armed guards remained in the car at the gate while he went inside. One guard stood at the front door and another at the back door, which opened onto the garden overlooking the river.

Qisma and Tariq showered their guest with extravagant words of welcome and ushered him in to the main hall, where they hastened to set out tea, coffee and fruit juice on the table so he could choose whatever he wanted. After sitting down, Jalal took a packet of cigarettes from his pocket, offering one to each of them. Tariq politely refused, saying he did not smoke, but Qisma took one, and the sayyid lit it for her himself. Before they embarked on any serious conversation, Qisma told Jalal a little about the history of the house and its location, and explained the picture of her late husband, which looked down on them from the column. The sayyid said his sacrifice would work to her advantage because her husband was considered a martyr in the eyes of the new government, and she should hurry down to apply for a martyr's certificate, with all the entitlements that come with it, including a monthly pension for her and her child, a plot of land, and a—

The sayyid was interrupted by a sudden explosion in the kitchen. Shattered dishes and glasses splintered through the air, adding violence to the shock, and for a moment the whole house shook. Directly after came Qisma's involuntary scream of terror, almost louder than the blast itself. Most of the guards came in at a run and cautiously entered the kitchen. Jalal, Qisma and Tariq followed, the sayyid calm but the other two as frightened as they had ever been. Had they not seen how composed the sayyid was, they would have collapsed from fear, for their legs, hearts and lips were trembling, along with everything else apart from their blood, which had frozen in their veins. They looked through the door and saw that the stuffed sheep had burst open at the belly, its limbs strewn about and the rice-and-raisin-stuffed cavity burnt out. They could just about make out remnants of electric wiring, and one of the guards said, "The sheep was booby-trapped." The sayyid, standing close to the charred, broken remains of the sheep, surrounded by dozens of scattered dishes, destroyed cabinets and broken glasses, told Qisma and Tariq to take photographs of everything with his camera while he investigated the scene.

CHAPTER 9

Founding the Party

As he led his hosts back to the main room, Sayyid Jalal al-Din ordered his guards to clear up the chaos caused by the explosion and restore as much order as possible. He gave Tariq and Qisma each a cup of coffee, and, carrying his own cup, suggested they go out and sit at a table in the corner of the garden. There he calmed them as much as he was able to, though Qisma kept trembling. She got up and went quickly back to the house, forgetting to take leave of her guest. She called the home of her late husband's family and asked after her son. When they told her that he was sleeping, she warned them not to buy any food prepared by a restaurant, though she did not tell them what had happened. Then she returned to the garden.

Sayyid Jalal al-Din told them that the bomb had only strengthened his convictions regarding the matter he had come to discuss with them. They had absolutely no choice, he insisted, but to act, and to involve themselves in shaping their country's future. They could not stay on the sidelines with no role, no view, no position. What was happening touched the life of every person – indeed, everything and every living being – within the borders of the homeland, however much he might try to deny it. He told them he could not be sure who the target of this explosion was – for it could very easily have been him – and that he would personally oversee an investigation. Otherwise, no-one would take any notice of it, for dozens of explosions, accidents and assassinations took place every day in Iraq, to the extent that the government had given up issuing proclamations of feigned condemnation. Likewise, the media grew tired of mentioning them because they no longer represented fresh news. As for the largest explosions, which claimed a hundred lives or more, or the kidnapping or assassination of a well-known personage, the most the media would do was demand that a committee be appointed to investigate. Of course, when such committees were formed – or were said to have been formed – no results were ever announced. Such demands were nothing more than a hollow gesture to mop up anger, and people quickly forgot because some new atrocity would displace the old one. And so it went. Death had become a fact of life, with or without an explosion.

He asked them where the food had come from, and they told him the name of the restaurant. He said he knew it and that he had no doubts about its owner, but perhaps one of the workers or cooks had planted it, or one of the men delivering the food, or maybe someone had gained access to their car without their knowledge. Perhaps . . . maybe . . . "There are many possibilities. As for the true target . . . If it were me, it wouldn't be the first time there's been an attempt to liquidate me; the threat has been present since I began opposing the former regime and doubled when I became part of the current one. My enemies are many. The important thing is that we fortify ourselves against them as far as possible, and never let them deter us from our plans. The two of you must take steps to protect yourselves and your families, and your village after that. It is time for you to take advantage of the new lay of the land."

When Qisma's throat was no longer too dry to speak, she told them what she had seen at the last checkpoint before they reached Baghdad – the masked person who had threatened to cut her throat. She had not found any explanation for it. Tariq was deeply disturbed. After a moment's thought he suggested that it might have some connection to the people who slaughtered her father.

"Anything is possible," said their guest.

The sayyid was leaning against the garden wall, Tariq too, with Qisma at his side. She asked the sayyid what he thought they should do. It was the question the sayyid had been waiting for, and he led them over to sit once more around the table. He began talking in a low voice, bringing his head close to theirs.

"It was always my intention to take you out into the garden to discuss these matters. For no-one can guarantee there won't be cameras or microphones planted in my office – or even in this house of yours. Everyone spies on everyone, and we no longer know all our enemies or their agents because of how many there are. Ever since the change, Iraq has been transformed into a table spread out for everyone to plunder: individuals, organisations, countries; those from within and those from without. The Americans dissolved the army and left the border open. They have installed a power-sharing government, with a new prime minister from a different sect, tribe or party every three months. It's the same with the other institutions. Everyone rushes in turn to take what he can. All the neighbouring countries – and many others that do not even border Iraq – seek to make it their own back garden. Do you understand what I'm saying?"

The sayyid meant to keep talking until his hosts forgot the explosion, or at least confined it to a distant corner of their minds. He could tell they were becoming calmer and listening more closely, early signs that they would be open to anything he suggested. When he felt they were ready, he looked them in the eye, each in turn, and said, "What you have to do is form a party, an organisation or a political bloc so that the thousands of votes from your village and the neighbouring villages are not cast in vain."

"Why doesn't Your Excellency do that," asked Tariq, "you being a son of our village? Why don't you return to take the lead?"

"No. In the first place, I belong to one of the largest parties sharing power now, one that was formed years ago in exile. Second, I belong to a vital security organisation, and I do not want to work in the open, publicly, in full view of the people and the media. I am one of those who pulls the strings behind the curtain. That is my role."

"And how do we do what you propose?"

"Either you or someone you trust must become a member of our party there. Or you form a party of your own that you ally with mine after the elections. We will support you in everything, and if you do not want to form a political party, then at least make it a tribal confederation, with you at its head as sheikh."

Tariq relayed to Jalal his friend Tafir's thoughts on the same topic, and the sayyid confirmed that Tafir was right in everything he had said. You had only to look at the success he had seen. "And in the future, you will be able to cooperate with him and form an alliance on the bedrock of your friendship, perhaps even persuading him to ally with our party."

Tariq turned to Qisma to gauge her reaction. He could see that she was excited; the way she moved her head towards the sayyid's as he was talking made it look as though she was going to kiss him – or eat him up. Qisma interpreted Tariq's turn towards her as a sign of deference, and, seeking any quick solution that would guarantee the safety of her and her son, she said, "Perfect. We're agreed. Let's get to work!"

The sayyid was delighted. He looked at Tariq, who nodded in confirmation. "Yes!" Tariq said, infected by Qisma's enthusiasm. "Yes! Let's put our trust in God."

The sayyid squeezed the shoulder of each and said, "Excellent! Excellent! This is excellent!" Then he took a packet of cigarettes out of his pocket and offered one to Qisma.

She took it and, with the scene of the shattered kitchen still looming large in her mind, said, "I'll bring coffee and tea. Is your Excellency hungry?"

"No, no, thank you. I had dinner before I set out. Coffee is enough. But please take a seat." Jalal summoned one of his guards from the far side of the garden and told him to bring a tray of tea and coffee from inside. Then he lit Qisma's cigarette and his own.

"In my opinion, it should be more of a regional, tribal organisation than a political party, even if it has the form and mechanisms of a party. That way you won't have to spend time setting out the ideology and manifesto of your party. In essence, what your friend Sheikh Tafir has done, and what he has recommended you do, is the best way: easiest, fastest and least costly. I will personally register your demands for protection at the country's expense, which will cover your guards' salaries, plus cars and weapons. But first you must choose them from among your close followers and supporters. It should be no great matter to entice them with the promise of work, since, as you know, most young people are out of work these days, and it is in my power to employ them, or to give them access to dozens – hundreds, actually – of jobs at different institutions, even if they are jobs in name only, with no actual work required."

As they listened to the sayyid's fine words, it was as though they had forgotten the attempt on their lives. They were imagining themselves as dignitaries, with a dignitary's bodyguards, connections and possessions. They would finally make something of themselves. They wanted it. They yearned for it deep down, without knowing exactly what it was they were yearning for. Their ambition opened up a vista of an undefined paradise.

The sayyid stoked their enthusiasm, assuring them, until they could almost touch it with their fingers, that it was all within their reach. He said that everything was laid out before them, that they had advantages not possessed by others. For Tariq was a well-known religious figure in his area. A sheikh himself, he was friends with a powerful sheikh who was the son of a famous sheikh, "and now you have a relationship with me and with my party." In addition, Qisma had roots in the countryside and connections in the capital. She was the widow of a man who was a martyred hero in the eyes of the new government. Her father could also be considered a martyr and a hero, regardless of who killed him. It was possible for her to receive a separate pension and a plot of land for each of them. He also promised her a comfortable salary, even if she didn't need it, to cover daily necessities, for she had left her job as an employee in the central bank a long time before, and it was also possible for the years she had been away from work to count towards her pension. He explained the laws of "political separation", which had been enacted for the benefit of those who lived abroad, so that the years they had spent out of the country were credited to them as years of service, since they had been forced to flee the previous regime. They drew salaries and gained advantages in proportion to their years of absence, and were given a helping hand up the career ladder, so that now they were general managers, government officials, military officers, and so on.

Qisma was stunned by the impudence of it all, the magnitude of the plundering and injustice. Those who had enjoyed security and freedom in other countries had received enormous compensation and advantages, while those who had remained in the country, at the mercy of the dictatorship, the storms of war and the bitter years of sanctions, were given nothing. But she did not persist in this line of thinking because she knew perfectly well that injustice was the master of all situations. She had to work with how things were, not how they should be, to try to bite off as much of this reality as she could chew, without thinking about those less able to sink their teeth into a slice of the pie. She was not to blame for their situation, and it was her right to try save herself and her son, so as not to become just another victim. Qisma tuned back into the conversation and found that Tariq was expressing a preference for playing it two ways at once, starting a political party and a tribal organisation at the same time. This made sense to Qisma, who argued that it would allow them to include those of their acquaintance who were not from the village or from the tribe, for she knew many people in Baghdad and in the other cities and provinces of Iraq, in part thanks to her father's archive of the victims of the former regime. Tariq had connections in Mosul from the days when he studied there, and in other cities and villages. The sayyid was by no means against this idea. "The more the merrier," he said, laughing. "I will facilitate the process of getting you funding for party offices, maybe even some houses, just as is enjoyed by the other political parties, who took over the offices of the old ruling party, which is now outlawed, and the houses of its ministers and officials."

Ideas and plans were flowing thick and fast. It was as though creative inspiration had descended upon all three of them at once. They felt able to speak freely without any sense of suspicion or restraint. Qisma accepted another cigarette from the sayyid, who, after he had lit it for her, moved on to another topic, one closer to his heart than anything that had been said thus far, namely, his desire to see his son, Abdullah Kafka, the fruit of his fornication with the mentally handicapped orphan Zakiya, with whom he had passed his childhood, when she was living – she and her brother Isma'il – under the wings of his family. That incident had turned his entire life upside down and forced him to flee the country of his birth when he was seventeen years old.

"I know you have a friend named Abdullah," he said, "and that he was a prisoner in Iran for nearly twenty years. If you could persuade him to join you in this venture, it would be of the greatest benefit to you both. He would be the magic key to it all."

This struck them as odd, given what they knew of Abdullah's character – withdrawn, depressed, pessimistic, rejecting everything and everyone. How could a person like that be the key to anything when he seemed hardly willing to utter a single word?

"He knows the Iranian language and culture so well, you understand," Jalal went on, "along with their way of thinking. You two are aware, of course, of the extent of the Iranian incursions into our territory, their meddling, and the influence they have wielded over Iraq ever since the fall of the regime. If you could persuade Abdullah to cooperate with you, he would be a smooth bridge to all kinds of support, to your advantage as well as his." He told them he would be able to appoint Abdullah to whatever post he wanted – with an unimaginable salary and allowances – be it in security, the intelligence services, diplomacy, or anything else he wished. "Try, at least. Please do whatever is in your power to persuade him, even by some trick, to meet me so I might ask him myself. I will know how to persuade him."

Jalal's comments surprised them. They looked at each other and then back at him. He told them that, as far as he was concerned, this matter was the most crucial of any they had discussed, though it was all of grave and vital importance. They said they would not be able to make any firm promises, for with Abdullah, though it was possible for things to be easier than expected, the exact opposite was also possible. It might be impossible to persuade him. But they would speak with him when they got back to the village and do their utmost to persuade him.

The sayyid called over one of the guards and whispered something in his ear. The guard left, returning with two boxes and a bag, which he gave to the sayyid before taking up his position once more. The sayyid offered them both a box, saying, "This is a mobile phone, a gift for each of you. They are for you to use just for these private matters – you will have to use your usual devices as before for your day-to-day business." Then he pushed the bag towards Tariq and said, "Here is ten thousand dollars. Consider it a gift, or as compensation for this evening's mishap, so that you can renovate the kitchen and repair the damage. If there is any left over, you will be able to use it to fund the opening stages of the project we have spoken of. And of course, for every major expense thereafter, you will receive full reimbursement."

They thanked him profusely for his generosity. As he made ready to leave, he insisted that it was he who should thank them for their hospitality and their confidence in him, and for their willingness to serve the people of their village and the country. He would order two guards to be placed at the door of the house to ensure their safety – a temporary arrangement until they were able to appoint private protection for themselves, just as they had discussed.

They thanked him again and walked with him to the gate leading out of the garden. There, Tariq embraced him, warmly and gratefully. Qisma shook Jalal's hand, giving it an extra squeeze as her other hand went to the sayyid's shoulder. She offered her most heartfelt words of thanks, promised to stay in touch, and said that he would be pleased – nay, astonished! – by what they would accomplish.

CHAPTER 10

In Which She Uncovers Her Legs

As soon as they had closed the gate, they went straight to the kitchen. They peered inside apprehensively, expecting to find piles of rubble, and were surprised to see that the kitchen had been cleaned and put back in order. The dishes that had been saved had even been washed, while pieces of thick cardboard were placed over the windows where the glass had been shattered.

Tariq felt a great sense of relief. He was already buoyed by the comfort he had received from Sayyid Jalal al-Din's words and gifts. "Ah! How quickly his wisdom is put into action!" he exclaimed, as much to himself as anyone else. Then, directing his words to Qisma, he said, "No doubt it was the sayyid who was the target, and not us. A man like him has many enemies, as he said himself. How brave he is!"

He advanced into the kitchen with Qisma behind him. When they opened the refrigerator, they found that it was full of the small dishes of food that had not been affected by the explosion, and that a great and varied feast awaited them: kibbeh, vine leaves, meat and fish, rice, bread, fruit, and so on.

They estimated that the damage – the doors of the cabinets, the shattered glasses, the plates and other ceramic dishes, some cracks in the walls and the ceiling, the counters and the window-panes – would not cost ten thousand dollars to put right. Indeed, for that sum they could make it better than it had been before. They rubbed their hands together in delight and carried some of the food up to the bedroom, where they put it on the dressing table. Tariq moved quickly over to Qisma and embraced her warmly. He spun her around him in delight, saying, "I can hardly believe everything that has happened to us these past two days. It's almost enough to fill a whole lifetime." Qisma agreed, smiling. Throwing her onto the bed, he stretched out, half beside her and half on top of her, his face close to hers and his speech broken. "It seems as though our marriage has brought down a blessing upon us and all those who belong to us, and that our lives and theirs will change entirely. It's as though the doors of heaven have suddenly opened before us."

"Yes indeed," she said. "Something like this happens only in Iraq. Everything can change in a single day. The poor become rich, and the rich poor. The president becomes a prisoner, and the prisoner a president. The ignorant man is made director, and the director is put out of work. That which lives dies, the dead man is sanctified, and if there were such a thing as the dead coming back to life, that too would happen only in Iraq. That's how it goes."

"It's a country of marvels, home to every blessing and every evil. Just look how civilisation took root here, spreading throughout the world. Then, from one day to the next, it collapsed and disappeared. The man who treads this ground has to expect everything, from the greatest success and conquering the highest summit, to plunging into the deepest abyss . . . Do you know what? I think I should offer a prayer of thanksgiving to God this very instant, for all of this is by God's grace. He alone is the master of miracles."

Tariq planted a quick kiss on his wife's lips and got up from the bed. He asked her about a prayer mat and the direction of Mecca, and Qisma pointed towards one of the corners where there was an empty space between the wardrobe and the wall. Noticing a rolled-up rug resting against the wardrobe, he quickly spread it out and began to pray.

Qisma got up slowly and changed out of her formal clothes, putting on a dress that resembled the one she had worn the night before and that matched its beauty and grace. Then she pulled one of the small bedside tables away from the wall. She made a dining table out of it, placing a chair to one side and bringing over the plates of food they had prepared in the kitchen. Then she sat down on the edge of the bed opposite the empty chair, waiting for Tariq to finish praying. He took a long time, holding his raised, open palms in an extended final supplication. Qisma caught a few of the words he was whispering and felt the depth of his sincerity.

They ate a little and talked a great deal about what had happened, what had been said, and what they would do the next day, which included bringing in people to repair the kitchen. Tariq suggested that young Ibrahim stay with his grandparents for two days so that the noise of the workers with all their hammering would not frighten him. Qisma agreed. They also made a rough plan for all they hoped to achieve over the coming days in Baghdad and when they returned to the village. One possible name for the party they were to form was "Date Palm and Homeland".

That would join the name of their village to the new title of their tribe, giving both a nationalist slant. Enthusiastic about the idea, Tariq suggested they might adopt a saying by the Prophet about the excellence of palm trees and the importance of honouring them, a saying that also contained a reference to the Virgin Maryam: "Honour your auntie, the palm tree, for it was created from the clay left over from your father Adam, and among the trees there is none more precious to God than the tree under which Maryam, daughter of Imran, bore her child."

Among those whom Qisma named as a possible supporter was her neighbour, Amira, whose husband had been slaughtered along with Ibrahim. She was literate, loved books, and had been born in Baghdad. Of all the women in the village, she was the only one who truly loved Qisma. She would also consider hiring Amira's oldest son as one of her bodyguards. She would ask for a public library to be established in the village, to be run by Amira, so that she could earn a salary in addition to what she could expect to receive as a pension in the name of her martyred husband. Surely it would be impossible for her to refuse such inducements? Qisma was convinced she would agree if only for the sake of their close friendship. The rest of the guards would come from Qisma's cousins on both sides of the family. Tariq, meanwhile, thought that his oldest son, Zahir, would be his primary supporter, either taking charge of his personal security or else acting as his representative and delegate in political and tribal matters, among other things. His second son, Mazhur, would serve as his secretary since he was younger and more bookish. Like Qisma, he would pick his bodyguard from among his nephews.

The images and ideas poured forth, one after the other, brewed up in Qisma's head and dispatched from her lips. Tariq the Befuddled was more astonished and impressed by her than ever, by the things she said and how she phrased them. She told him she would call everyone she knew there in Baghdad – her classmates, her friends, her own acquaintances and those of her former husband and his family – to find among them those who had the wherewithal to further their ambitions. Likewise, she would make contact with all the families she had helped across Iraq's distant provinces and cities by means of her father's notebooks, which had granted them the bittersweet peace of knowing what had become of their loved ones. This she saw as a preparatory step towards opening party offices beyond the capital and in their own village. Qisma began drawing up a roster of friends, identifying their characteristics and skills, making judgments about who among them would be the most suited to each task.

All this mental exertion left Qisma in need of a cigarette. She told Tariq she would take the dishes downstairs, and that she would bring back the two telephones and the bag of money, which she had put in one of the drawers of the desk in the main room when they had passed through to see the sayyid to the gate. While she was gone, Tariq took off his robe and sat back on the bed in his long johns and a short-sleeved undershirt to await her return.

When Qisma came back, Tariq noticed at once the cigarette between her fingers, but before he could utter any objection, she said, "Don't say it! I feel the need for this at the moment. And I won't have you getting upset if I smoke again in the coming days."

Tariq chose not to respond to that, and they began to open the boxes after first checking the stack of money in the bag, which Qisma placed in a dark corner of the wardrobe. Each of them took their new mobile from its box and examined it eagerly. As they were doing so, Qisma reminded Tariq that they needed to use them thoughtfully and with care. For perhaps – almost certainly – Sayyid Jalal al-Din had devised some way to spy on them by means of these devices. Tariq agreed, feeling deep admiration for her acuity.

Afterwards, they launched into a discussion of how best to convince Abdullah Kafka, and how it would be necessary for them to pursue a variety of paths in order to do so. First, they would offer incentives, and, if that failed, they would try to frighten him into accepting their proposals. They would attempt to persuade him to marry Tariq's sister Sameeha. They would try to convince him that the government was likely to cut off his pension, or that there was a price on his head, for how often did they hear of the Iranian secret services murdering combatants, generals and leading figures from the former regime who had participated in the war against it? How often did they hear about everyone killing everyone? Religious men killing secularists, and secularists killing religious men. Tribal sheikhs killing politicians, and men from the parties killing sheikhs. The ignorant killing the intelligent, and the intelligent killing the ignorant. Men of one sect killing men of another. Collaborators killing insurgents, and insurgents killing collaborators.

That's what this country has come to, Abdullah, they would say. It is as though a person is wandering through a thick dark forest, and in order to make his way through it, is willing to burn it to the ground. And because everyone wants to become president or be the head of something, he tries to cut off the head of anyone who stands taller than him.

Tariq even thought about putting pressure on Abdullah by rescinding the services of Anwar, the young man who worked Abdullah's fields. Faced with this on top of the prospect of his pension being frozen, Abdullah would surely have to agree, for he would have no way to cover the cost of the cigarettes he smoked. But in the end, they stopped thinking of ways to threaten him, because, after all, their love for him outweighed their ambition. They would focus instead on attempts to persuade him, painting a glorious picture of the advantages he would gain if he joined them in their project. If they failed, they would encourage him to meet with Sayyid Jalal al-Din, or even trick him into meeting him, just as the sayyid himself had said.

It was past two in the morning and, despite the fatigue in their bodies, their minds were still racing on account of the new horizons they sensed were spreading out before them. Nevertheless, they agreed that it was time to sleep. Qisma got up and went into the bathroom while Tariq remained on the bed, thinking. In effect, tonight was his wedding night. On the previous night, exhaustion had been her excuse, and he had not pressed her after giving her a kiss on the back of her neck and embracing her from behind. She had moved away, and he had followed suit, saying, "Goodnight! Sweet dreams!" They had both slept deeply.

The night to come, the night already at hand, would be quite different. It would crown all the events and triumphs of the day with the most important victory of all – so far as Tariq was concerned, at least. That was what he was telling himself when Qisma came out of the bathroom. He sat up, watching her as she moved. She stopped in front of the mirror and looked herself up and down. She rearranged her hair with her fingers. She picked up one of the many bottles of perfume on the dresser and sprayed it on her neck and between her breasts. Tariq got up and gently embraced her from behind. With exaggerated vigour, he sniffed the white skin at the base of her neck, and, intoxicated, whispered in her ear, "My God! It revives the soul."

Then he went into the bathroom. He was at the height of his confidence, his hopes climbing to the sky. But when he came out several minutes later, he found she had turned off all the lights except the small lamp on his nightstand. She was lying on her side of the bed, covered by the soft white sheet.

The atmosphere was poetic, charged with his own expectancy. Tariq walked around the bed to his side. He raised the sheet a little and slid quickly underneath it. Turning to Qisma, he embraced her. She did not move, so he took hold of one of her breasts through her nightgown, but still she did not respond. Tariq pressed himself closer to her from behind. He felt his erect penis against her. She did not pull away, so Tariq began to push her nightgown up towards the top of her legs. At this, Qisma took hold of his hand and lifted it off her. Tariq lay still for a moment. Then he put his hand on her hip again. She pushed it away a second time. At that, Tariq sat up and gave voice to his annoyance.

"What is this? What is this, Qisma?"

"What is this yourself? Don't you see what time it is?"

"Indeed I do. There's no better time in the world."

Qisma did not reply but simply drew the sheet over her head, covering herself entirely. Tariq pulled it back sharply and said, "Later, later ... But for how long? This won't do!"

"Later," she said again.

Once more, she drew the cover over her head, and, once more, with greater force, Tariq pulled it off her.

Then Qisma sat up in the bed and turned angrily towards him. "Listen! Don't give me a headache with what will or won't do, for what won't do is what you're doing right now. How can you think of such things now after the explosion that took place in our house just hours ago? Or after all the plans we've made, when the important thing is that we rest so that we may put them into motion in the morning."

"All the more reason to reward ourselves, after our close call and all we have achieved."

"And what have we achieved? We haven't done anything yet. And what is this reward you speak of, anyway?"

"Listen: you're my wife now, by religious and civil law, and I have a right to you."

"And this right is the most important thing to you? What about my rights?"

"What rights do you mean?"

"The simplest of them is that you respect me, that you respect my wishes and desires."

"And do you know that the woman who goes to sleep when her husband is angry with her is cursed by the angels until morning?"

"No. No, I did not know that. And what about the man who

goes to sleep when his wife is angry with him? After all, it is you who asked to get married with such haste."

"There's no blame in our haste! For the great imam, Abu Hanifa, when his wife died in the morning, got married again the same night. And when he was asked about it, he replied, 'I would have hated to die in the night and meet God as a bachelor.'"

"And what if a woman had done that?"

"Religious law does not permit it, for she must complete the *iddah*, the necessary waiting period after her husband's death."

"As usual, you proscribe everything in favour of the male. And no wonder, for you are the ones who set down these laws!"

"No, they are the laws of our Lord, and they are not to be opposed."

"You are not a bachelor."

"No, but my condition is worse than a bachelor's, for I have two wives but I spend my nights as tormented as if I had none!" He was more furious than ever now, saying, "Listen, my wife – that is, if you are my wife at all–"

"Of course, I am!" Qisma interrupted him loudly. "Why would you say such a thing?"

"It is my right to say it! Indeed, I have been going crazy waiting to say it ever since the scandal of your contest when you stood and pissed like a man!"

At that, Qisma's anger reached its peak, and she nearly sent her foot flying into his belly with as hard a kick as she could muster. But she ground her teeth, bit her lip and swung her feet abruptly down to the floor. She ran from one light switch to the next, turning them all on. The bulbs shone brilliantly, bringing back the light of day. She stood there in front of him and lifted her nightgown to her waist. Then she pushed her underwear down to her knees, spreading her legs to reveal what was between them. With a fury that nearly burned her lips, she said, "Take a good look! Push your eyes right in and look. Are you satisfied now? Can that slow brain of yours relax? Is your bestial heart reassured?"

Then she let her nightdress drop to the floor, covering herself again. Qisma turned off the lights, came back to bed and wrapped herself in the sheet. She was panting, liable to explode at any moment – not unlike the booby-trapped sheep.

Tariq lay where he was, not moving or saying a word. Qisma sat back up, turned towards him, her anger not in the slightest diminished, and said, "Do you want a party in exchange for what you have done? What we have done? And what is it that we have done? Well? Have you forgotten so quickly the main reason we came here? Our fundamental task. Indeed, the reason for our marriage? Have you forgotten? In that case, let me remind you! We have come to search for the rest of my father's body after he was slaughtered with a knife and we buried only his head. My own father, Ibrahim Qisma – do you know this name? Your dearest friend, your lifelong companion, from your days in the cradle when I was not yet born."

Qisma fell silent for a moment before adding in a low voice that burned with pain, "And would that I had never been born at all."

With that, she threw herself on the pillow, pulled the covers over her head, and began to sob, waves of tears coursing down her cheeks.

CHAPTER 11

A Visit to the Refrigerators of the Dead

Tariq got up late because he had fallen asleep late. In his few hours of sleep, he had had disturbing dreams of exploding sheep and naked women screaming in his face. He did not find Qisma in bed beside him when he woke. She was not in the bathroom either, so he assumed she must be downstairs in the kitchen or reception room, or perhaps in the garden. He pulled aside the curtain hanging between him and the balcony over-looking the garden, but there was no sign of her. He stared for a while at the seagulls circling above the river. They looked happy, blissfully ignorant of the flames that were engulfing Iraq. Tariq leaned his head against the glass and contemplated the scene until he felt a degree of peace, his mind clear and entirely empty.

He went into the bathroom and took a shower. Afterwards, he went downstairs, but he did not find Qisma. He looked for her in the reception room, the bathroom and the kitchen. He called her name more than once, but there was no reply. He went into the kitchen in search of food.

Qisma had been reunited with her child in his grandparents' home an hour earlier. She held him close to her. A feeling of longing, a desire to embrace him, had come over her in a way she had never experienced before. She pulled him to her chest, breathed deeply the scent of his neck, his cheeks and his forehead, as though to inhale him right back into her womb. She buried her head into his hair from time to time, as though to take refuge there. She did not release him from her embrace until breakfast was brought to her.

Tariq made his own breakfast. He put a pot of tea, some bread and some slices of cheese on a tray and brought it up to the bedroom, and from there out onto the balcony. He set the tray on the low table and sat on one of the chairs facing the river, contemplating once again the movements of the gulls and the small boats floating by. He looked towards the far bank, thick with minarets, distant columns of smoke rising over the buildings, and watched the cars crossing the bridge that spanned the wide river. Pure air entered his lungs, propelled by a cool breeze from the river. In that moment, he felt the tea had a different flavour. Even the steam was somehow delicious. Even the burning heat of the hot cup against his fingertips was a pleasure. He took a deep breath and said aloud, "Praise God!" Then he saw fishermen and police pulling a body out of the river. He thought about Qisma and where she might be at that moment.

He began to review what had happened the night before: Qisma's terrifying anger, her heart-wrenching sobs. He was willing to admit that he might have moved too fast, and that he had been stupid to doubt her womanhood, for the child could not have been born out of her ears! On the other hand, it was a comfort to be free of his stupid misgivings about this matter, even if he was no closer to knowing how she had managed to win that damned contest! He regretted his bad behaviour, which he had not observed in himself before – his haste, his lack of intelligence, patience and wisdom – and told himself that her allure had blinded him and made him forget his wound and hers caused by the loss of Ibrahim.

She was an intractable woman, and he had no idea how to communicate with her, or where his relationship with her would take him. Never had he known someone whose wife spoke to him like that. In his mind, he said "like that" to avoid the words "insolence" and "impertinence". Would it be correct for him to consider her the greatest challenge of this life? He did not know. But in any case, it would be improper and not at all becoming for a man of his stature to abandon her too soon. Tariq decided to be as patient with her as possible, if only for the sake of his love and respect for her father. At the same time, there was much about her that attracted him, including aspects of her character that might appear shocking to others. From another point of view, their relationship marked him out for distinction, for she possessed something not found in any of his friends' wives. And that was before one considered her intelligence and her ability to do all that a man could do and more. It was possible to work with her as a partner and to rely upon her, whereas most women were content to rely on their husbands.

Tariq kept turning the matter over in his mind as though he were two people debating with one another there on the balcony. With every thrill he experienced at the thought of her youth, intelligence and passion, he felt a gentle longing for his first wife, his good-natured and submissive cousin, who gave him blind obedience.

Tariq did not arrive at any firm decision and contented himself with the thought that it was still too early to decide anything. It was true that this was a time for mourning, not for amorous advances. He resolved to avoid provoking Qisma or coming into conflict with her for the time being. He would see what the coming days and weeks brought. After all, they were embarking on a number of important projects together, which necessarily relegated their marriage to a side issue. Tariq's thoughts moved on to what they had spoken about with Sayyid Jalal al-Din, and their excited conversations thereafter. He imagined that before long he would possess a magnificent house in Baghdad – not unlike Qisma's – as well as followers, bodyguards, power and money. At that point, the balance of power between Qisma and himself – and between himself and many others of his acquaintance – would be very different.

Tariq's thoughts were interrupted by the sound of a telephone ringing inside the room. He hurried to answer it. It was his mobile, the one Sayyid Jalal al-Din had given him the day before, and it was the sayyid who was calling. He greeted Tariq and asked if he was well, taking an interest in him and showing concern as he had done since they had first met. He told Tariq that he should go with Qisma to the medical centre. His sources had let him know about a corpse that matched the description they had given, and the official in charge of the refrigerators of the dead was expecting them.

Tariq thanked him and confirmed that they would speak again after they had seen the body. Using the same telephone, he called the mobile given as a gift to Qisma. He heard it ringing and saw that it had been left there amid her bottles of perfume and make-up on the dressing table. He called her other mobile, which she answered. She gave a happy gasp at his news and said she would be there in a few minutes, so they could go together.

At the medical centre's information desk, a man in his fifties was waiting for them. Like most of the staff there, he was wearing a long white apron and safety goggles. He checked with Qisma and Tariq that they were the ones who had been sent by Sayyid Jalal al-Din, then he led them through long corridors permeated by a humid, medicinal odour. As the corridors stretched on and on, Tariq's pulse grew faint; he was afraid he would pass out. Qisma's heart, meanwhile, was beating faster and faster, twice as fast as the rapid striking of her heels against the floor tiles as she outpaced her two companions. At each turn, she would point a finger, asking, "Which way: right or left?"

By the time the official gestured for them to come to a halt, Qisma and Tariq felt that they must have passed from the first building into another, so long had they had been walking through those featureless, oppressive corridors. The man opened a heavy set of doors for them, revealing a large room lined on both sides with rectangles: the refrigerator doors. He led them to the relevant door and, before opening it, turned towards them to check that they were ready to see the corpse, for many people, in his experience, retreated at the last instant or collapsed on the spot. The man watched as Qisma drew closer, her jaw set with fierce determination, almost reaching her hand out ahead of his to open the door, while Tariq backed away and stared about in alarm.

Qisma helped the man open the door and pull out the mortuary slab. She quickly uncovered the legs and found that the corpse was indeed missing its right foot, and the scars from the amputation were long healed. But Qisma realised at once that it was not her father, because the cut was higher, towards the middle of the calf, while her father's leg had been severed at the ankle. Furthermore, she remembered well how the healed wound had looked. This one was tapered, with the skin folded like wrapping paper around a gift, bulging out at some points, whereas her father's had resembled a sliced cucumber.

The man watched as Qisma examined the corpse, then, after a time, asked if she wanted to see the rest of the body, warning her that the man had been decapitated. She nodded, while Tariq turned his face towards the door.

Qisma saw that the corpse was fat and said, "No, my father was never fat in his entire life."

"It might just be the swelling," the man told her. "Look at the hands and arms."

When he revealed the left arm, Qisma saw a traditional tattoo of a heart pierced by an arrow with the Arabic letter "ayn" in the middle.

"No," she said at once. "This is not my father. I'm certain that there's not a single tattoo on my father's body."

The man expressed his regret and went to cover the corpse again, but Qisma stopped him and asked him to show her the severed neck. He stood frozen in silence for a moment, caught off guard, then, without a word, did as he was asked, watching her as she studied the severed neck without batting an eyelid.

After a while, the man cleared his throat and said, "I'm sorry."

Qisma asked if there were other decapitated corpses in the facility.

"Yes, many," he said. "Among them are those whose necks have been severed by an explosion or through the application of torture, by sharp or dull instruments. But they don't match the description I was given, particularly the part about the right foot amputated long ago."

She was about to say, "It doesn't matter: I want to see them all," but then she noticed Tariq's discomfort. Tariq thanked the man and urged him to get them out of there quickly. He felt faint, as though he were suffocating, and thought he might collapse at any moment.

As soon as they reached the exit, Tariq ran to the edge of the lawn. He grabbed the end of a hose, which he carried over to the outside tap, and turned it on to wash his face and neck in the water. Lifting the hose, he let the water play over his head for a full minute. Then he turned off the tap and sat on a nearby bench, letting threads of water run off his head onto his clothes. He leaned back to let the air dry him, deeply shaken.

Qisma remained with the man from the morgue. She repeated the detailed description of her father's body, and gave him her telephone number, asking him to call her immediately if he saw a corpse in any way similar to what she had described. She then thanked him, pushed into his palm a number of dollar bills, and came to sit beside Tariq without uttering a single word.

Qisma was recalling the raw wound that was the severed neck, focused on the act of the slaughter, the moment of the slaughter, the sting of the slaughter, the edge of the knife as it passed over the skin, the way it plunged in, going back and forth through sinew and flesh, the spurts of blood, warm blood, the gurgling of the pharynx, what might be passing through the mind of the slaughtered man in those last seconds of his life. How many times had she brought these details to mind ever since the head of her father had arrived in a banana crate! How many times had she imagined it! How greatly had she suffered! Then, gradually, her brutal imaginings were transformed into a desire to slaughter someone or something. To have someone slaughter her. She wanted to feel exactly what her father had felt. She wanted the blood to choke her guilt, the pain to obliterate the torture inflicted by her conscience day and night, for she had been disobedient towards him since childhood, she had felt an aversion to him ever since she saw his severed right leg for the first time. It was no fault of his that all that had happened to him. So why had she increased his anguish by looking down on him, disobeying him, refusing to embrace him? She was tormented by her guilt, and she derived a grating pleasure from her suffering because she felt she deserved it: it was a punishment of sorts for the way she had tormented her father's heart his whole life. And now that she was a mother – now that she had come to understand the magnitude of his goodness – she felt the extent of his torment further still.

Qisma touched her fingertips to the skin of her neck. She had started to do that more and more over the last few days. She would trace her fingers across the likely path the knife of slaughter had taken. Sometimes she would do that with the nail of her index finger, and sometimes she would squeeze tighter and tighter with her entire hand as though she longed to choke herself. She would recall the blood and horror of the slaughter whenever she used a knife to cut fruit, vegetables or meat – or, indeed, whenever she saw a knife. When this phenomenon first began to dominate her, she resolved to rid her house of every knife, but soon she found herself feeling, deep down, a desire to be slaughtered, and she began to stare at knives, contemplating their shapes, their sizes, the sharpness of their blades, which she would sometimes test with her fingertips. How in the world could someone crave to be slaughtered? Qisma felt this desire grow steadily stronger until she began to imagine that to be sliced open in this way represented a pleasure that had no equal. A unique experience, the deepest, broadest, strongest and most complete pleasure possible in this life. There, sitting on the bench beside Tariq, she forgot where she was and what she was doing, lost in recalling the jagged bloody wound of the severed neck. She did not know how long she stayed like that before she noticed Tariq beside her, urging her to go home.

They remained silent throughout the journey and even once they had arrived back at the house. Tariq went into the bathroom on the ground floor while Qisma hurried to the bookshelf to get a packet of cigarettes, which she took into the garden. She leaned against the wall, smoking and looking at the river. When Tariq came out of the bathroom, he was content to throw himself on one of the couches in the reception room, watching Qisma through the broad windows, resolving to respect her silence and avoid disturbing her, to let her be the one to initiate conversation.

At the same time, he felt a kind of weakness before her, unable to imagine what was going on in her mind and in her soul at that moment, unable to assess what she might be capable of after all he had heard and seen from her recently. He felt a desire to return to his village, a desire to flee this stressful, asphyxiating powder keg of a situation. He pushed away this momentary impulse, telling himself to maintain his resolve – even if, in truth, he was not as strong as he imagined himself to be. He had not seen as many bodies as others he knew – not ones mutilated by violence, iron and fire, at least. In his youth he would help his father wash the dead and wrap them in shrouds, but they had been whole, unbloodied, at peace. He used to feel that they were just sleeping. And when he took part in prayers for the dead and burials, the corpses were covered by the cloth of the burial shroud. As for the moment when he embraced the severed head of Ibrahim, he did not remember it well, affected as he was by the horror and shock of his friend's death. All he remembered was that his heart was burning, his eyes were streaming with unbidden tears, and his stomach was gripped with sorrow, contracting in pain and then going numb, so that if a needle had been stabbed into him at that moment he would not have felt it. It had, without doubt, been the most momentous and most painful thing that had ever happened to him.

He thought about going out to Qisma and embracing her, pulling her to his chest with a fatherly tenderness. Or just standing beside her in silence, perhaps even taking one of her cigarettes to smoke with her. But he banished the thought and remained stretched out on the couch, staring at the ceiling. He would abide by what he had resolved: to leave her alone without bothering her, no matter how long her silence lasted. After what seemed to him like hours, Qisma came inside again. She went straight upstairs and into the bedroom. Tariq heard her close the door behind her. He strained his ears in order to discover what she was doing up there – listening out for any sobs or cries – but he heard nothing. He remained like that until he passed out where he was, lying on the couch.

Qisma woke him at four in the afternoon. Tariq saw that the coffee table nearby had been transformed to a dining table, overflowing with plates of food. He took a glass of water and drank it down. Qisma refilled it for him. Tariq headed to the bathroom and washed his hands and face. He came back to find her sitting waiting for him, fully dressed, though he noticed a redness around her eyes, despite the eyeliner and mascara she had applied. She must have been crying for a long time. He also thought that she might be angry – whether with him or with someone else he was not sure – for she had a serious air about her, and she seemed tense, which he supposed was the result when someone had been crying.

As they were eating, Qisma told him, more in the manner of someone issuing commands than initiating a discussion, that from that moment they must begin to put their plans into practice. As soon as they had finished their food, they would set off for a print shop that she knew, which she had used when she was studying in Baghdad. An old man whom everyone called "Uncle Papers" worked there. He did not mind the name. Indeed, he liked it, for he had spent his life in the business. He had worked at a printing press in his youth, and from there had opened his own shop specialising in printing, copying and design. One of his sons was a partner in the business. They would discuss with him all the printed materials they would need for their party – membership cards, publicity pamphlets, and so on.

While they were speaking, Qisma took a small notebook from her bag to record observations and ideas, and Tariq could see that she had already committed to paper a great deal of what they had discussed. Since he had already decided to go along with her and follow this path until he saw where it led, he did not raise any objections to her suggestions and itineraries. When he got up to change his dishdasha, she got up too and helped him while holding forth on all the things they must put in motion or seek to achieve by the end of the day.

As they were driving towards Uncle Papers' shop, Tariq understood that a bone of contention had arisen between them, one he had not for a moment anticipated. Which of the two of them would be the party's president, leader or secretary general?

CHAPTER 12

The Laureate of Liberation Square

This question of who should be the figurehead of the party kept them both occupied over the next few days, though they were reluctant to address it directly. As they sat down for breakfast one morning, Qisma's thoughts were with Tafir. Although she had beaten him in their contest, it was clear that he was a capable and shrewd leader, whose example they could do worse than follow.

"Tell me, what is the secret of your friend Sheikh Tafir, who has managed the affairs of his own tribe so well, to his advantage and for the benefit of his kin?"

"As you have seen, he is more than just a friend. He is like a brother to me, and that is what our fathers urged us to be, insisting that we should preserve our sense of brotherhood as much as they had. His father did not have the same quick wits that his son and the rest of the elders in their family enjoy, so he used to seek my father's advice in most things. They also conducted a secret trade in arms. Among the members of their tribe, there were those who stood with the former regime and those who supported the resistance, and yet others who were on the side of the Kurdish fighters in the mountains of Kurdistan. Many tribal chiefs have followed this course, placing one foot here and the other foot there, so that the one would stand firm if the earth should shake under the other. And this is what my friend Tafir does even now – allowing certain members of this tribe to ally themselves with the Americans and with the exiles the Americans brought back to rule the country, and others to align with the factions that oppose the occupation. In this way, his influence is such that he can begin to play one side against the other. And he has increased his control and domination over the tribe, unifying it still further under his command. All this is helped by the collapse of the state, for if it is unable to provide protection, then who else can they turn to? He has also strengthened the tribe's sense of identity by bestowing upon it its own slogan and flag, indeed, even an anthem that resembles the national anthems of actual countries."

"Really?"

"Of course! Didn't you see the yellow banner fluttering beside the Iraqi one at the gates of his compound?"

"Yes. Yes, of course."

"You remember? Pure yellow, with a great mass of drawings surrounding the words "The House of Shakhabit". A sword, a flower, a cup of coffee, a stone bench, a hat, the head of a male duck – I forget what else. It's said that each of them relates to a story about a former sheikh of the tribe."

"And the anthem?"

Tariq laughed so heartily that a bird hopping about on the lawn took fright and flew away. "The anthem – now there's a story. In fact I learned it by heart along with the rest of the tribe, just because it's so unusual. Check this out, *habibi*." He hummed the opening bars of the tune, in part to distract from the first flirtatious words he had said to Qisma since her outburst a few nights before. Then he began to tell her its story.

"When Sheikh Tafir decided that his clan must have an anthem of its own, the suggestions poured in: a large number of traditional wedding songs, circumcision songs, harvest songs. But he didn't like them. He wanted the song to have its own words, unique to the tribe. Some people recommended old poems they had memorised, but he wanted the words to the anthem to be composed by someone within the tribe. At this point, the name of the most notable poet the tribe had produced in the past two decades came up – none other than the brother of our friend Rahib, would you believe? His picture, alongside articles and several of his poems, had been published in the newspapers. He had even been on television. It seemed obvious, but there were objections. For one thing, he wrote only in formal Arabic and he wrote prose poetry in the modern style. He was also known to speak ill of both the family and the tribe. Even of poetry itself! No-one from the tribe could make head nor tail of his poems.

"It was said that he had been a bit strange from childhood, forever on his own, refusing to join the other children in their games, with the exception, on occasion, of his brothers. As soon as he learned to read and write, he went crazy for reading, and no-one ever saw him without a book, reading on the roof of his house, in the fields beyond, or on the banks of the river. He did not join the family or the tribe in any of their traditional practices or customs, neither in joy nor in mourning. He did not like to work in the fields, nor with the livestock, and he did not like hunting – the very opposite, of course, of Rahib. He did not like anything except reading, and his sole positive characteristic, in the eyes of his family and the people, was his excellence at school, which naturally stood him in good stead. When he began his university studies in Baghdad, that was where he found himself – and lost himself at the same time. What I mean is that he liked the city and everything it had to offer almost too much, to the point of getting lost in its bookstores, cafés, bars, nightclubs and literary circles. He came home to the village only during the summer holidays, when the student residences closed their doors. He became involved with a group of young people like him who spent their time loitering in cafés and on street corners, rebelling against society, swapping jokes and banter late into the night. They praised what was negative in life and positive in poetry. But when I tried to read what they published, I couldn't understand a word of it, and I certainly didn't see anything positive in their poetry! Honestly, it was all scribbles within scribbles, a real *shakhbata*, you might say.

"They called themselves the Prose Poetry Explosion. What is this country coming to! Everything in it ends up exploding, even the poetry. They published a poetic manifesto. It is said that this young Shakhabiti man dreamed it up, and his fellow poets co-signed it. It calls for going beyond the prose poem, which didn't make much sense to anyone even then. Among the nonsensical drivel I remember from his manifesto were sentences like: 'It is necessary to explode the text of the prose poem and liberate it from the strictures which define it. In addition, we need to liberate it from any shackles of earnestness, for life, when you get down to it, cannot be taken seriously.'

"His name was Bara al-Shakhabiti, but he published the manifesto as Breton al-Shakhabiti, taking the name from the French poet André Breton, who wrote the *Surrealist Manifesto*. Since then, he has continued to publish under that name and has become quite well known."

"Oh, yes!" cried Qisma. "Yes, I know him."

"How?"

"He came to our institute to put on a poetry night and present one of his collections. He was truly strange. He looked like some kind of hippy with his long, dishevelled hair, long coat, long beard, and these thick-framed glasses covering half his face. I recall a certain resemblance to your friend Abdullah Kafka. More in attitude than appearance. I think that if they met they would understand each other – much better than people tend to understand them. Some of the younger students liked him, because he embodied the avant-garde in rebelling against everything that is traditional and fixed in both life and poetry. They applauded him enthusiastically, even though I didn't understand anything of what he said. Yet this strange charisma of his made the whole affair rather enjoyable. Memorable too."

"Yes, yes. It is said that the son of the deposed president embraced him, him and his group, and helped them to be published, both in newspapers and by poetry presses – perhaps because they avoided writing about what was happening in the country and the oppression of our freedom at that time. He encouraged them to write poems that were obscure, mysterious and experimental. They went along with it, believing that refusing to write about real life was an expression of true freedom. They ended up influencing the popular poets who wrote in the common dialect as well as the traditional poets who clung to classical rhyme and metre. Rather than striking a blow against the regime as is surely the role of poets, they ended up helping to sustain it."

"Wait," said Qisma. "Just a minute. I remember that at the end of that poetry evening of his he imposed a strange condition. He wouldn't sign any books except in exchange for a hug and a kiss on both cheeks. This applied both to the male students and the female students. And the strange thing was that most of the audience were satisfied with that, and they stood in line to kiss and embrace him."

"Even the women?"

"Yes. Indeed, most of the people who purchased his collection were women."

"Indeed. O Shakhabiti, you bastard! And you?"

"Me, no. Just the thought of it made me shudder! I remember thinking how the title of his book was *Toot, Toot*, referring to the sound of a car horn, and asking myself why I should pay good money and submit to his smelly embrace for the sake of a written toot, when I could hear it in the original form from my car whenever I wanted. Leaving aside the fact that the streets are filled with that sound night and day!"

"Yes! Yes, I remember that poem. It's the one that made him famous. In fact, he may have been reading it the only time I saw him on television, on one of the culture programmes on a channel run by the president's son. All the newspapers published it. As far as I was concerned it was complete and utter nonsense. All I remember from it is:

> Toot, toot
> The car of iron said to me, "Toot"
> I, a flesh and bone car, replied, "Toot"
> The car of iron tooted back
> I, a toot; it, too, a toot
> The shop, the street, the house a toot.

"He listed many things he called a toot, and then he finished the poem with:

> Life's a toot, love's a toot
> being and existence and death a toot
> everything's a toot
> and no-one knows the essence of a toot
> or the meaning of a toot ... toot ... toot.

"But on the radio and in the newspapers people were inventing all these interpretations for this toot. Some said it meant 'who gives a fuck' – if you'll forgive the expression. And some said, in a whisper, that it was another word for 'arse'." Tariq spoke the word in a quick low voice. "Some said it represents a lost truth, or it's like the letter 'x', which symbolises the unknown in mathematical equations. Some people considered it a philosophical or political or musical symbol. There were countless more interpretations, each more ridiculous than the last."

"During the event," Qisma said, "he told us how the inspiration for this poem came to him. He said he had been drunk one night, staggering in the middle of the street, when a car nearly ran him over. It had braked sharply and come to a stop just short of him, and the driver began angrily hitting the horn: toot, toot! And he responded with his own 'toot, toot' without getting out of the way. The traffic began to pile up, all of them honking their horns with a 'toot, toot'. He replied to them all, as though they were holding some kind of a conversation: 'Toot, toot.' Then some passersby and a couple of drunks joined in, and it turned into a big celebration, with everyone laughing in delight, even back at a time when people would scowl at everything."

"How extraordinary," Tariq said, though he did not laugh or even smile. "And now, my dear, let's return to the anthem of the Shakhabit tribe. Sheikh Tafir became convinced that this poet was the one and only person fit to write it. But the problem was that no-one knew of an address where they could contact him, for after the fall of the former regime, which, as I say, had to a certain extent adopted him, he roamed about alone, homeless, on the streets, and people came across him sleeping in a different place every night. You would have thought the occupation might have been an opportunity for him, for he studied English language and literature at the university, and he surpassed all his peers."

"Yes, I remember he read some poems he had written in English. The language was dazzling, but the poems were strange and hard to understand, just like his Arabic poems. I mean, and I don't know exactly how to put this, that these poems were–"

"Tooty poems," Tariq finished for her, and they both burst

out laughing, startling the birds again. Tariq swelled with pride. Humour could be a vital tool in his campaign to win Qisma's heart and mind, for women and children love men who can make them laugh.

"Now, back to the story, *habibi*," he said at last, when her laughter had died down. "After graduating from university, the tooty Shakhabiti poet refused to work as an English teacher, saying that to spend his life teaching the Roman alphabet to children who couldn't even master Arabic was beneath him. If it were possible for him to work as a professor teaching other academics the recondite nuances and grand ideas of English language and literature, then all well and good. Otherwise, work was not for him. But in the end the president's son appointed him editor of the cultural supplement for one of his newspapers, and he continued in that role until the regime collapsed at the hands of the Americans, along with all its newspapers and television stations – and its poets, too, of course. And since every regime has its poets and drummers, the new rulers had their poets and drummers too, and among them were those who had skilfully transitioned from praising the former regime to praising the current one. It is said that the militia of the new rulers detained our poet along with many other followers of the former regime, and that after torture and quick, arbitrary trials they executed many of them with a bullet through the mouth. When it came to Breton's turn, he challenged them to produce any texts in which he had praised the former regime. On the contrary, he argued, he had always written in opposition to it – he just did so using symbolic language. And he began showing them, explaining some of the poems to them, to show that they were actually written to denounce the former president. He kept going until they grew bored with him, semi-persuaded by what he said. They fed him one last meal of torture, breaking two of his teeth and cracking a lens in his glasses, and threw him back onto the street.

"After that, the Americans picked him up and threw him in Abu Ghraib prison with a diverse range of criminals and suspects: militants, thieves, politicians, extremists, the homeless, former soldiers and the like. But they eventually realised that he was just an innocent poet, and that his command of English out-stripped theirs, to the extent that he would occasionally explain in great detail the origin of a particular word. He would recite for them the Shakespearean sonnets he had memorised, and poems by T. S. Eliot, Walt Whitman, Charles Bukowski and others. They offered him a job as an interpreter, with a good salary. He agreed on the condition that they arrange for his glasses and his teeth to be repaired, since, as an interpreter, he feared losing his precision when it came to pronunciation. But he only stayed in the job for a few months, and whenever he received his salary, he would immediately invite his vagabond friends to squander his money in a bout of inebriation, during which he would disappear entirely, leaving the Americans with no idea where to find him. In the end, they got rid of him, and he returned to wandering the streets, which, so far as I know, he still does to this day.

"No-one knew where to find him, but Sheikh Tafir was deter-mined that he should write the anthem, so he sent Rahib to the capital to search and search until he was found. As you can imag-ine, Rahib took to his task like he takes to any task he is given, and within days he had located him. The sheikh himself travelled to Baghdad to speak with him, accompanied by Rahib and a bottle of whisky. He came across him at sunset, finding the poet sprawled on the ground under the Freedom Monument, his arms folded under his head as a pillow. A great reek of alcohol emanated from him, and he was clutching an empty bottle to his chest. Near his head was a tattered piece of cardboard that read, 'POEMS FOR SALE'. The sheikh kicked the cardboard sign away and prodded the poet's head with his shoe until, with some difficulty, he opened his eyes. The poet looked up and murmured, 'Who are you?'

"The sheikh said to him, 'I am your master, the sheikh of your tribe.'

"The other man stared at him for a moment, then he leaned his head back again and closed his eyes. The sheikh gave him another kick and said, 'Wake up! You're a disgrace! You could have been a source of pride, but instead you've sullied the reputation of the tribe. The time has come for you to return to the bosom of your people and make amends for the wrongs you have done us.'

"'What do you want from me?'

"'I want you to write an anthem for our tribe.'

"The poet laughed. 'And how do you expect me to do that?' he asked. 'If a poem could be called an anthem, then it can't have come from my pen. And this tribe of yours means nothing to me.'

"The sheikh used his shoe to grind the outstretched hand of the poet into the ground until he let out a wail and said, 'If you want, I'll sell you a poem I've already written.'

"'No! We don't want any of your tooty nonsense! We want a new poem, something of our own, something that will be understood by all sons of the tribe and all the Iraqi people. Indeed, by all peoples of the world.'

"'Impossible, impossible!' repeated the poet, as he burst out laughing a second time. 'You're asking the wrong poet. I don't concern myself with such trifles.'

"'Oh but you will – in spite of yourself and all your followers!' The sheikh ground the poet's palm down harder, at the same time gesturing for Rahib, who displayed no emotion at Tafir's mistreatment of his brother, to wave the bottle in front of his eyes. At this, the poet ceased his lamentations to gaze at the bottle with naked desire. The sheikh continued to torture him, pausing between each stomp to repeat, 'Well? Well? Well?'

"'Fine, fine. Give me the bottle, and when you return tomorrow you will have your anthem. And bring another bottle.'

"The sheikh pressed his foot down harder, gesturing for Rahib to bring the bottle right up to the poet's face. 'No, now! Immediately, without delay. If you don't, I'll crack your head open on the spot.'

"'Alright, alright. Just give me my hand back. We're right under the Freedom Monument, after all.'

"The sheikh lifted his foot from the man's hand, and indicated to his secretary, who had made the journey with him, that he should write down whatever the poet might recite, this notorious poet who was sitting propped up against the base of the monument, reaching for the bottle, trying to open it, and begging for help from his brother to do so. He took a slug of alcohol and laughed as it went to his head. Then he began to speak lines of poetry, pausing between each one to take another swig and laugh:

Life is truly a scribble, a quibble and a dribble
We are the first people, the most noble of people, and ours is the
    seat of honour
The fount of civilisation and art, and of the first word, a scribble
We are the Shakhabit and whoever stands opposed, we blot out
Life is truly a scribble, a quibble and a dribble

"He had finished half the bottle and was well on his way to intoxication. Laughing, he repeated over and over again, 'Life is truly a scribble, a quibble and a dribble,' without adding any new lines.

"The sheikh asked his secretary, 'Is that enough?'

"'Yes, it's enough. This is excellent!'

"'Listen, Bara,' the sheikh said to the poet. 'We are your family. This is your brother, and I am your lord. Our homes and our hearts are forever open to you, for you are our flesh and blood. And therefore we hope that you will choose to return to us. If you want, I'll even give you work as an interpreter and marry you to one of the daughters of the tribe.'

"It appeared that the poet had not heard him, for he merely raised the bottle towards his mouth and slurred, 'To your health!' Then he collapsed into uncontrollable laughter, repeating again and again, 'Life is truly a scribble, a quibble and a dribble.'

"The sheikh thought for a while, looking down at him. Then he bent over and put the piece of cardboard he had kicked back in its place. He took a stack of dinars out of his pocket and threw them down in front of the poet. Then he turned away, followed by Rahib and his secretary."

Tariq's story gave Qisma an idea. Should their party not have an anthem and a banner too? They began to discuss the matter, light-hearted at first, but more in earnest the deeper into it they delved. When it came to the party's banner, they lit upon the idea of three palm trees on a white background, two of the same height with a third, taller one in the middle. Tariq proposed to Qisma that they add the image of a foot, alluding to the foot her father had lost in the war, but she preferred to leave it out so that they would not be forced to explain it to all and sundry.

As for the anthem, it made perfect sense that they search out the poet Bara al-Shakhabiti. They agreed that he could do a great deal to help them if he could be so persuaded, and in exchange they would furnish him with whatever he wanted – a salary, fine wines, and a newspaper to edit. They had decided that they too would publish a newspaper – for every party, organisation and community seemed to have one now. Hundreds of new publications had been launched since the fall of the former regime, which, for decades, had allowed just four or five newspapers to be printed. It was important for their party to have a journal, even if only a few hundred copies were printed each month. It would carry on its masthead the name of the party and their symbol with its three palm trees. Its first page would display their photographs and whatever news they had, while they would leave the rest to the Shakhabiti poet to fill as he saw fit. They agreed that if they could persuade Bara to cooperate he would be a great asset, for he had experience and connections in the spheres of journalism and culture, and was equally adept at writing in Arabic and English. Perhaps they could even publish their paper in both languages to win over the Americans.

Qisma suggested using Rahib's influence to persuade him to work with them, and even floated the idea of enticing Rahib himself to work with them, for she had gained a great deal of respect for him in the short time they had spent together. But Tariq feared that his friend Sheikh Tafir would be most displeased if he heard they were trying to poach one of his most important men, one he had come to depend on. Qisma persisted with the idea, convinced that his services would be of inestimable value to their cause. Did he not have access to Sheikh Tafir's secrets, and would he not know the best way to convince him on any future matter? Tariq admired the intelligence and perspicacity of her idea, but maintained that it would be playing with fire, so they put the idea aside for consideration at a later date.

For now they would go to Liberation Square, to the Freedom Monument, to seek out the poet Breton al-Shakhabiti and reach an agreement with him. And if they were unable to persuade him, perhaps he could point them to someone he knew who had the qualities they needed.

CHAPTER 13

The Trunk Boat

For the next two weeks, they worked tirelessly to put their plans in motion. Tariq continued to give ground whenever conflict threatened to arise between them, becoming deferential and passive if a discussion became heated, as it did when the matter of the party leadership finally came to a head. After a preamble about the equality between men and women, Qisma told him that the great advantage of her being the leader was that her contacts spanned both the countryside and more urban regions – the capital in particular. What was more, her being a woman would attract attention, and help the party to stand out from the hundreds of parties and movements led by men. Qisma did not neglect to highlight, naturally, her relationships with many notable figures, whether in the army (friends and acquaintances of her former husband) or the merchant classes (friends and acquaintances of her husband's family) – not to mention the people she had met during her studies. On top of that, she reminded him, she was the daughter of a man considered by many to be a martyr, and she had used her father's notebooks to help scores of families across the country. She was also the widow of a second martyr, one who had given his life in an attempt to overthrow the former president.

Tariq set out the reasons for his own primacy. The first was that he was a man in a man's world. The tribe, for example, would not accept the leadership of a woman, and he would not be able to draw people to the party if they saw him as a mere follower of his wife rather than a leader of men. Indeed, he would be unable to convince even his sons if they considered him to be subordinate to his second wife, who by the natural order of things should show deference to their mother.

The conversation took them down various meandering paths and cul-de-sacs until Qisma found a solution – one that suddenly burst into her head in a moment of pure inspiration. Why not make her son, Ibrahim Qisma al-Nakhili al-Baghdadi, the leader of the party, with the two of them as his deputies? Tariq the Befuddled was surprised – nay, astonished – by what she proposed, for the child had scarcely reached the age of three. But Qisma quickly convinced him that his leadership would of course be symbolic, and that this symbol was a way to honour her father, for the child bore his name. Their relationship, their marriage and their partnership were nothing more than the fruit of their love for her father, while her son's name also contained references to the tribe and village (al-Nakhili) and the city (al-Baghdadi). But the key advantage to installing him as leader was that he would necessarily be an absent leader, which would lend him an aura of reverence, just as with religious, mystical or even divine leaders and authorities.

"For we will be able to paint him just as we wish, and speak his name with awe. It is customary for people to tie their hopes, their dreams and their aspirations all the more to one who is absent, for reality never measures up and can never satisfy them. We may even reach the point of sanctification and blind obedience. That will prevent our future enemies from getting to him in an attempt to harm or kill him. We'll record just his name in the official papers of the party, and we won't publish any photographs of him, leaving the people to imagine how he looks, each according to his or her own taste. If our policies and our message earn us enemies, they will not know who to strike at. We too will be protected by this ruse because we will just be followers, acting in his name, and anyone who tries to kill us will think that he will only be bringing more troubles upon himself if he does not do away with the head of the party. In the same way, we will be able to change our policies at any point, just by saying that His Excellency or His Honour, our Leader, objected to our former position, obliging us to adopt a new one."

Tariq liked the idea very much. After all, throughout his life, he had excelled at speaking on behalf of absent religious, tribal and historical authorities. He began adding further arguments to support hers, reminding her that for the official papers they needed to register, it would be possible to use her father's identity card since her father's death had not yet been officially recorded, just as was the case with thousands of dead Iraqis. Indeed, if it was necessary in the future for any reason, they could produce a photograph of Ibrahim and refer to him as the party's spiritual founding father, or words to that affect.

Tariq was moved to embrace Qisma, kissing her cheek in approval of this ingenious idea of hers. But he insisted that he be named the first deputy to the leader, with her being the second, as she would take precedence when the party was inaugurated in the name of her son or her father. She agreed without hesitation, for in her mind's eye she could already see what a glorious future she was making for her son.

Later that day, when they visited Uncle Papers' studio to sign off on the designs, he persuaded them to have an additional image under the three palm trees because dozens of parties and organisations had used them in various forms in their logos, not surprisingly given that Iraq had once been known as the land of thirty million palm trees. When Tariq again suggested a foot, Uncle Papers slapped his desk in his enthusiasm for the idea. The foot would be unique, and no-one who saw it would forget it. No-one had included a foot in their logo before. It could symbolise standing firm. It could represent movement, progress, initiative. Theirs would be the first flag to carry something human, for didn't all flags boast plants, animals, birds, swords, shields, and so on, which suggested that they were not fundamentally in the service of human beings?

As for Bara – the poet Breton al-Shakhabiti, that is to say – they did not find him on either of their two trips to Liberation Square. The homeless people they spoke to said that that was how he was, he would appear without warning, then disappear just as suddenly. The tips they were given about his whereabouts and his habits were contradictory, and they had no option other than to call Sheikh Tafir so that he might help them locate the poet. Tafir promised to lend them the best tool for the task, his own right arm indeed, the brother of Bara himself, the clever dwarf Rahib al-Shakhabiti.

It was also during this time that Tariq and Qisma employed a couple to look after the child and see to all the housework. One of Qisma's friends, the widow of one of the officers who had participated with her husband in the failed coup, vouched for their trustworthiness and diligence. They had worked in her house, but she no longer had need of them because her children had grown up. With nothing standing in her way, she had married another man who did not need or want to bring servants into his household.

Sabriya and Sabir were in their mid-forties, and it was a testament to the strength of their commitment to one another that Sabir had adopted this name – instead of his official name of Sadiq – to match his wife's, whom he had loved since they were young children, playing together in one of Baghdad's suburbs. It was because she never left him, even after he was arrested and tortured, his tongue cut out because he had cursed the former president. Sabir and his wife were prohibited from taking any government job, so he worked as a porter in the market and as a waiter in cafés until the War of Occupation began. He wrote his name, Sabir, "the patient one", on a piece of paper for everyone who met him for the first time and for everyone who knew him from before and still called him Sadiq, for his wife had confirmed for him, once again, that she was his sole support and safeguard in this world, no matter what happened. As if his muteness were not enough, he was made lame when the old house they had been renting collapsed upon him and their two daughters during an American bombardment immediately after the war against Iraq was declared. The house was next to a government building, but they had not known it belonged to the state intelligence agency. Their two children were killed and Sabir's shinbone was shattered. Sabriya received only light wounds because she was in the kitchen at the moment the bombs struck, protected by the strong stone staircase. In the wake of that tragedy, impoverished and heart-broken, they began working in houses together, desperate not to be parted for a single moment. Lean, good-hearted and simple-minded, their dry wrinkled faces hinted at their buried grief, while their eyes inspired instant confidence in whoever saw them.

Qisma gave them one of the rooms on the ground floor next to the kitchen, and they carried out their tasks with great industry and very little noise. If Sabir tried to speak, only a few unintelligible sounds came out of his mouth, so they were accustomed to communicating with gestures. They scarcely left one another's side, even going to the bathroom together at times. As soon as they knew what was expected of them, it was as good as done. Tariq loved them and Qisma loved them too. Their services cost Qisma only a quarter of the salary that she received as a consultant in the Central Bank, a position that Sayyid al-Jalal had obtained for her, just as he had promised. This was on top of her former husband's pension now that she had registered him at the Agency of Martyrs' Affairs. Tariq, likewise, received a number of contracts and licences, including one from a communications company to open a branch for them in the village. There was another from the Ministry of Health to build a clinic, one from the Ministry of Education to restore a school, and one from the Ministry of Transport to repair the roads in and around the village. He also received a certificate from the Ministry of Trade for importing and exporting, which he immediately sold to a Baghdad businessman at a handsome profit.

As for their fundamental mission, searching for Ibrahim's body, they received two more telephone calls, one from the same official in charge of the refrigerators of the dead in the medical centre and the other from a different facility. In both cases it turned out that the body in question was not Ibrahim's, but Qisma nevertheless examined each corpse closely, gazing for a long time at the edges of their severed necks, just as she had the first time.

During one of Tariq's early morning sessions on the balcony, as he gazed at the seagulls and fishermen after having performed the dawn prayer as was now his habit, he watched the fishermen pull from the river a body with only one leg and no head. He had taken to using Qisma's late husband's military binoculars, which he had found in a drawer, and now he adjusted them to their maximum magnification to confirm what he thought he had seen. He ran down the stairs, jumped over the garden wall, rushed down the slope and reached them as they were piling three bodies on the sandy shore. He greeted them and told them that he had lost a brother who was also missing a leg. They were happy to let him inspect the bodies as much as he pleased until an ambulance or a police car came to take them away. When Tariq saw them close up, their clothes were proof enough that none of the bodies was Ibrahim's. Tariq looked at the corpse with a single leg and no head, and saw that the leg had been amputated at the thigh, that the hair on the chest was thick and black, and that this was the body of a young man in his twenties, not a man Ibrahim's age. He turned away from the corpses, his stomach starting to heave, and told the fishermen in greater detail about the body he was looking for, pointing to Qisma's house so they would know where to find him if they ever came across a body that matched the description. Unaffected, they promised to do so, as they went on separating the strands of the fishing nets. They could do without these corpses interfering with their attempts to earn their daily bread by catching fish.

On one of the few times that Qisma went to the offices of the Central Bank to which she was attached as a consultant, she established that there really wasn't any work for her to do there. She spent the morning browsing through a stack of papers – the resumés of people who had applied for work. From among them she chose the C.V. of a young woman in her twenties who had finished her studies at the same institute where Qisma had studied but had not yet found a job, a situation faced by thousands of the country's graduates. The fact that she wore a hijab in her photograph indicated that she was from a poor family – as did the particular kind of hijab. Qisma called her, interviewed her, then appointed the young woman as her secretary. She converted another room on the ground floor for use as an office for the administration of the party, furnishing it with three desks, chairs, computers, telephones and filing cabinets.

The new secretary worked diligently, recording the telephone numbers and addresses of potential supporters, and acquiring the necessary papers for registering the party. It was not hard for Tariq and Qisma to amass some five hundred names, along with the serial numbers of their identity cards, starting with Sabir and Sabriya, the secretary herself, Qisma's late husband's parents and sister and their neighbours and acquaintances, the owners and employees of the restaurants they frequented, Qisma's old friends and acquaintances, with their families, neighbours and acquaintances, and the acquaintances' acquaintances, as well as Uncle Papers, his son, his acquaintances from the market and the surrounding cafés, and some of the customers who passed through. They even took the names of some of the homeless men they had met when asking around for the Shakhabiti poet. People seemed happy enough to give them their details, since it did not require them to pay anything or make any great effort. It cost them nothing beyond the time it took to take their I.D. card out of their pocket and pop it back in a moment later. Then they would forget all about it.

The process was accelerated when one of Qisma's friends proposed enlisting the help of her husband, a police officer who manned one of the checkpoints guarding the Martyrs' Bridge. This officer, along with his colleagues manning other checkpoints, gathered more than two thousand names in the course of a single day. The actual registering of the party was easily accomplished, the wheels of officialdom greased by a call from Sayyid Jalal al-Din, whom they visited immediately after it was completed to update him on all they had achieved. He congratulated them on their zeal and energy, reaffirming his willingness to support their every endeavour. He also raised once more the matter of Abdullah Kafka, emphasising that persuading Abdullah was paramount as far as he was concerned, and that if they were able to bring him to Baghdad for a meeting, that would be the best way to thank him for everything he had done for them and would continue to do for them in the future. They promised him they had things in hand, for they would be returning to the village in two days' time, as soon as they finished putting a last few affairs in order.

Tariq and Qisma asked Jalal to pay them the honour of coming in person to the village for the large celebration they were planning to mark the inauguration of the party. Anyone Jalal wanted to invite would of course be most welcome – ministers, officials, celebrities or journalists. But Jalal declined on the grounds that he belonged to another political party, and that it was vital for his intelligence work that he not be known by the public and did not appear in the newspapers or on television. His presence in the village would be of no real use to them, but he promised to send two or three ministers and members of parliament who often appeared in the media. That sort of event appealed to them, and since they did not have any real work to do, of any practical value, it was with such appearances that they made their living. They liked being wined and dined, wearing ties, and waving for the cameras. Each one would be sure to bring his personal media team.

Rahib al-Shakhabiti arrived with the first light of dawn. Tariq, up on his balcony, saw him before anyone else. As usual, he was watching the seagulls and the fishermen when he suddenly noticed a tiny boat, no larger than a suitcase. "It's the smallest boat in the world!" Tariq said to himself in amazement as it approached the shore, and when the figure sitting alone inside it stood up, Tariq saw that he was very short. The person jumped out of the boat and secured it just like one would tie up a cow, using a rope with a stake on one end. He planted the stake in the ground and pounded it in.

Tariq picked up the binoculars, which were sitting on the table in front of him, put them to his eyes and adjusted the focus. As though he were only a metre away, he could see Rahib al-Shakhabiti, who was wearing the very same clothes as when he had last seen him. Having secured the boat, Rahib took a bag from inside and headed towards the house, ascending the slope with a wave of his hand. Delighted, Tariq stood up at once, waved back and hurried down. They met at the garden wall. Tariq spent no time wondering how Rahib had managed to arrive before him, despite having to cover more ground. It was because Rahib was truly *rahib* – terrifying – by name and by nature.

They shook hands across the wall. Then Tariq picked him up and hugged him, holding him against his chest like a child and welcoming him with surprised delight.

"My uncle, Sheikh Tafir, sent me," said Rahib. "I bring his warmest greetings."

Tariq, still holding him, replied, "A million thanks! Both to you and to your dear uncle."

"He told me to put myself under your orders," added Rahib, only a few centimetres from Tariq, his chest and belly pressed against Tariq's chest. "And obey your every command." He paused, and when he found that Tariq was still thanking him with sincere words of welcome and seemed to have forgotten to put him down, he pointed at Tariq's arms around him and said, "And here I am in your arms!"

Tariq realised what was happening, and they laughed aloud in unison. Then he set Rahib down on the grass. They were still laughing when Sabir and Sabriya came running out to greet them, rubbing the sleep out of their eyes.

CHAPTER 14

Cleaning up the Homeless Poet

By the time Qisma awoke, the poet Breton al-Shakhabiti was already present in her home, lying on one of the magnificent couches in his dirty rags and smoking her cigarettes. Rahib had insisted on carrying out his mission even before eating the breakfast that Sabir and Sabriya had prepared for him. He told Tariq that he knew his brother's haunts – the bars where they had drunk together many times and the places where Bara would bed down for the night. He also knew some of Bara's circle of poets and intellectuals as well as a few of his homeless friends.

Tariq went with him, taking the car into the city centre and following Rahib's instructions as to which road to follow, which alley to go down, and which square was a good place to park. Rahib did the talking when they were stopped at checkpoints. He told the police on duty that he was looking for his poor lost brother because their mother's last wish was to see him before she died. This led a number of kind-hearted officers to convey their sympathies and wave them through, often pointing out the shortest routes to get to where they were going. When Tariq asked the truth about this bereavement, Rahib just said, "Little white lies."

They found Bara sleeping outside an old tavern, wrapped in a dirty blanket, sprawled across some cardboard, using his arms as a pillow. On his head was a moth-eaten woolly hat. Without even trying to wake him, they picked him up and spread him across the back seat of the car. Then they drove him back to the house and carried him inside just as he was and draped him over a couch. In his brief moments of wakefulness during the trip, Bara realised that he was in the company of his brother Rahib, but he did not embrace him until they had laid him on the couch, whereupon he clung to Rahib, pulling Rahib's small chest against his own with genuine tenderness and longing. This went on until Rahib was nearly choked by the intensity of the embrace and the foulness of his brother's odour, for the poet had wrapped his arms around Rahib's head and pulled his face into his beard. Rahib began coughing and finally escaped his brother's arms by offering him a cigarette. The poet released him instantly, and Rahib drew a cigarette from a packet that was lying on the table. He lit it for his brother, and then went straight to the bathroom. While he was gone, the poet took one cigarette after another from the pack, lighting each one from the butt of the last, as Tariq watched him in disgust, murmuring, "Forgive my sins, dear God Almighty! Indeed, our religion warns us of these crimes. Glory to God Most High! These are the consequences of disobedience against the Lord."

It was at that moment that Qisma woke up. Hearing voices below, she crept out to stand on the stairs, observing the scene below her in the salon and listening to the conversation between Bara and Tariq.

"You're a sheikh, right? That's clear from your beard and the way you talk. But are you a religious sheikh or a tribal sheikh?"

"Both."

"Ha! Me too! I have a beard, and I'm the sheikh of poetry and the sheikh of vagabonds." He let out a loud laugh and sucked greedily on the cigarette. "But you are bound by old traditions and ancient texts, whereas I chase after new ideas and produce new texts. Do you want to hear the last English poem I read, or one of my poems in Arabic?"

Qisma felt a certain affection for the vagabond poet, so self-assured, so direct, so unique in his speech, so liberal: a free spirit casting only a fleeting shadow. Indeed, even his filthy rags struck her as a symbol of rebellion, of his rejection of the societal norms that she herself sometimes wished she could escape. She found that he looked older than he had when she had first laid eyes on him at the institute; he was also more handsome and certainly dirtier – never in her life had she smelled such a terrible odour. She smiled at his conversation with Tariq, who stood over him, stroking his beard as he regarded him with pity, loathing and confusion.

Breton sat up, saying, "Poetry deserves respect when it is being read." Then he began reciting his poem with a focused seriousness. He enunciated each word, syllable by syllable, savouring every moment, fingers dancing along in time with the words and their varied intonations as though his digits were producing the sound, not his tongue.

"It's called 'Clarity over Perfect Absence'."

Oh, for the infamy of the surety
Language is a rift
The one is an embrace of what's ruined
And the other a treatise on the rude
On the prescription of praise is reaching the goal
Even in the middle, a demagogue on your belly
The rejection of presence, the missing number
Compromise being a watchword for non-existence
A man wakes to his total absence
The rabbits thirst for all their fearful sojourn
This is the path of flight, even if you justify it
There's no logic to existence; so what would you say to its lack?
Provoking speech about the end, a true lie
And this exemplary babble, deafness

When Tariq found that Bara had fallen silent, he clapped his hands in sarcastic applause. "Finished? What is all this gobbledygook? This strong talk with no head and no . . ."

"No arse? Say it! Say it! I don't know why people avoid uttering a word like that. It's no different from other words like finger, nose, foot, arm, sheikh and all the rest." He laughed again, even louder this time.

"Listen. That's enough of this nonsense. Take off that filthy cap of yours. Why are you wearing it when the weather is nice and you have a thick head of hair?"

"Because I live in a mad, upside-down world, and I want to be able to tell my head from my arse!" the poet said, hardly able to breathe he was laughing so hard now.

Tariq was extremely irritated by him, by his nonsensical poems, by his smell and by his laughter. Exasperated, he said, "You really are a strange, upside-down creature. You shit from your mouth and talk out of your arse."

Bara burst out laughing so hard he fell off the couch onto the floor. At the same time, Qisma's laughter rang out from where she stood on the stairs, bouncing off the walls of the house. She came down to join them, and a moment later everyone in the house – Rahib, Sabir, Sabriya and the secretary – had gathered to find out what all the noise was. They surrounded Bara, who was writhing on the floor, gripping his stomach and kicking the air, and none of them could help laughing themselves at the peculiarity of Bara's laughter.

Then, once Bara had calmed down a little, he said, still lying on his back, "I knew you were an empty reed."

"What's that?" Tariq asked. "What do you mean? A reed is an old pen. So why am I an empty reed?"

"Lift me up," said Bara, raising his arms.

Rahib and Sabir quickly pulled him up onto the couch again, then Rahib grabbed his brother's woolly hat and threw it in the bin in the kitchen before returning to the salon.

"Have a seat," said Bara, as he pulled out another cigarette, making no mention of the loss of his hat. "Please, take a seat."

Everyone sat down on the nearest seat. After taking a long drag of his cigarette, Bara said, "I call people who swear by tradition, people who cling to old books with an old point of view, the empty reeds. The kind who always call a pen a 'reed', or the heart 'the quick', or death 'the grave', a lion 'the king of the jungle', or dirt 'soil'. Things like that. And you, my friend, are a perfect example of these reedy types. It goes without saying that the only poetry you know and like is that which sticks to classical metres and has been extinct for centuries, talking about camels, swords and sandals. But do you know, O Sheikh Reed, that your inability to understand my poetry is precisely what my poem wanted to convey? For poetry is not meant to be understood to the extent you expect to understand it. It's not an article or a Friday sermon, O sheikh. Poetry is one of the mysteries and miracles of existence, like love or like life itself. We may think we understand it, each in our own way, yet it still remains a mystery. Poetry is an attempt to express what cannot be expressed, to describe what cannot be seen. An attempt to shift what is motionless and let movement pervade it. It is 'a seed', as André Breton puts it. A seed that will grow and flower into something. Maybe a seed of doubt or certainty, of despair or hope, of laughter or tears, of ignorance or knowledge. It is a cleansing of the–"

"I think if you got up and took a shower," Tariq said, interrupting him, "it would be better than all this nonsense."

"Yes," said Qisma. "Take him to the bathroom, Rahib. Sabir, you help him. Cut his hair or his beard or both, and give him a good wash. I'll get him some clean clothes."

Bara tried to resist. He was not a child, he was not ill, and he was quite capable of washing himself once he'd had a rest. Rahib laughed and said, "And what would you be resting from? You haven't done a thing since our mother squeezed you out!"

They carried him off by force, Sabir holding him under the armpits and Rahib by the knees. Bara kicked like a petulant child and cried, "Leave me alone! Leave me alone, you empty reeds!"

They took him into the bathroom and closed the door. The clamour inside could be heard as clearly as if there were no door at all, and soon Bara's cries of protest gave way to raucous laughter. Among the merry sounds, Sabriya recognised the laughter of Sabir, and to everyone's surprise she ran over to press her ear against the door. They watched her smile with an inexpressible joy, then squat down, leaning against the wall and bringing her ear close to the keyhole in order to hear better. She was as happy as a child, and her smile broadened whenever she heard a fresh bout of laughter. When she noticed that Tariq, Qisma and the secretary were staring at her in amazement, she leaned her head back against the wall, the tears pouring from her eyes. Qisma ran over and knelt beside her, placing her hand on her head. Fighting back tears, Sabriya said, "This is the first time I've heard Sabir laugh since they cut out his tongue."

Qisma pressed Sabriya's head to her breast and caressed her shoulder. Sabriya was still crying, but another crescendo of laughter made her turn aside and press her ear to the door again. She wiped away the tears that had washed her face and her soul. She smiled and laughed softly, trembling from the intensity of her joy.

After a while, they all withdrew, the secretary to her office, and Tariq and Qisma to their bedroom, where Qisma began looking among the shirts and suits of her late husband for something she could offer Bara. Meanwhile, Tariq was telling her about their search for him, and his doubts about working with an intransigent vagabond like Bara.

When Qisma came down with some clothes, she found Sabriya still had her ear pressed against the door, and when she saw Qisma approaching, she beckoned for her to come closer. Qisma, amused, did so, listening to the racket – splashing water, singing, curses and yet more laughter. The sounds of three men returning to childhood, yelling spontaneously as they played and quarrelled, cut off from the outside world and forgetting everything beyond the confines of the bathroom and that exact moment in time.

Qisma patted Sabriya's shoulder and pushed the clothes into her hands. Then she went back up to the bedroom and told Tariq that she was thinking of keeping Rahib with them a while longer. He would provide fresh impetus for everything they were planning, as well as keeping his brother in line. But Tariq did not approve the plan any more than he had when she had first raised it, for what she was suggesting was tantamount to exploiting – betraying, even – his great friend. Rahib was the most important of his men and his followers. He was Tafir's right arm! Besides, he did not think that Rahib himself would agree to leave his village and his home to work for her. Qisma said she knew exactly how to persuade them both. She would promise to find Rahib a wife, and when it came to Sheikh Tafir, he had already agreed before their contest to grant her three requests, so he had little choice in the matter.

After they had both showered, dressed and gone downstairs, they found everyone waiting for them in the salon where breakfast had been prepared. The change in the poet's appearance struck them dumb. It was as though he were a different person.

Rahib and Sabir had cut his hair and had shaved off his beard and moustache. Qisma noticed that the clothes of her late husband fitted him rather well, though he was a touch more slender, so the white shirt bunched up around his belly.

They told him that with his clean-shaven, slender face and round glasses, he looked younger and more attractive. In a far calmer and more polite manner than before, he told them that he was grateful for their kindness, and that they should hurry up and take a seat and have some breakfast because he was starving. As they all gathered round the two tables, crowded with eggs, cheese, butter, warm bread and cups of tea, it struck them all as a moment of harmony and joy, almost as though they were a family. Qisma asked Bara if he wanted a tie, but he refused, saying he did not like them, and that he could not bear to dress like one of those starched-shirt empty reeds. He apologised to Tariq for his lapses of courtesy earlier, then said that he had now changed and was no longer a bearded sheikh like Tariq. Then, jokingly, as he stroked his smooth chin, he added, "Now you represent tradition, and I represent modernity."

"Yes," commented Tariq, "this tooting modernity of yours."

Everyone laughed, and Tariq went on, "I wish you would alter your precious modernity, so it would become something practical and useful, where tradition and innovation are in harmony with one another, connected through dialogue rather than left in isolation."

Everyone approved of this sentiment, and Tariq was impressed with himself for the way he had put his cultured language to use. But when Bara asked him what he meant, Tariq decided to take a different approach, by throwing in a joke. He said, "I mean that you should make it accessible, so one can make sense of it. You should give it a head and a . . . and a . . . tail."

"Say it!" Bara laughed as he shouted the words. "Say it! A head and an arse!"

Everyone joined in the laughter that followed this, and once it had died down, Tariq asked him about poetry. "Do you know about rhyme, metre, rhythm, and so on?"

"Of course. Of course, I know them very well. I experimented with them at the beginning of my poetry career, but it was only natural that I should move beyond all that. Otherwise I wouldn't have been able to create anything new."

"Excellent. The first thing we'll ask of you is that you return to them one last time to write us a short poem that we can use as an anthem for the Palm and Homeland Party. We want a simple poem with traditional metre and rhyme. Even a few empty-reed words, because people are still moved by that kind of old-fashioned language."

Bara laughed at the sheikh's adoption of his term. He knew this was a kind, tolerant and affectionate man, and he felt himself warming towards him. So he asked about the identity of this party, and Tariq explained, with Qisma's help, and Qisma asked the secretary to bring him the sketches for their logo. Bara liked what he saw. He liked the palm trees, and he liked the foot even more, and was moved by the story of Ibrahim when Qisma explained its meaning. His approval delighted both Tariq and Qisma, and they were more delighted still when he said he would write them a poem, on condition that they not reveal his name as the author of the anthem, since he was known to nurture a deep aversion to this kind of poetry. When they pointed out that he had written an anthem for his tribe, the Shakhabit, Bara was taken aback and denied it, even when Rahib and Tariq started to sing it.

Bara laughed and said, "Impossible! It's impossible that I could have written something like that." He did concede, however, that from time to time, for a laugh, when he stayed up late to drink and talk with his poet friends, they would compose dirges like this to mock the popular, empty-reed style of poetry.

It was then that Tariq and Qisma made Bara an offer he could not refuse. He would be named the party's communications director, and would edit a monthly journal in exchange for a salary, room and board. He would present their news and the news of the party on the journal's opening pages, but it was up to him to fill the rest of the journal with whatever he wished, on the understanding that the publication would be in both Arabic and English. Bara immediately agreed. How could he not, given that their offer fulfilled his dream of being a literary editor? For all the poet's self-confidence and bombast, he had never been able to rise beyond being a proofreader or, at the very most, sub-editor of a cultural journal. He made only two requests of them: that he need only put his name to material if he wished to, and that they provide him with a computer, an internet connection, cigarettes and alcohol. Qisma quickly agreed before Tariq could raise any moral or religious objections, then said that his office was ready for him. He would share with Sister Wafa – the secretary – who would help him with the journal's design and with research and other similar tasks. "As for the cigarettes and all the rest, Brother Sabir will bring you everything you need. He will also fix up a bedroom for you. All this is temporary, until we can establish an office for party business. But now, your first and most urgent task – to be done today, actually – is what Sheikh Tariq requested: an anthem for the party."

Everything seemed to be going as well as could be, and after they had finished breakfast – which lasted nearly two hours – Rahib announced that he was leaving, having fulfilled his mission to perfection. Qisma took him aside and, in a low voice, told him that she wanted him to work with them too, to be responsible for all manner of things, but with an emphasis on supervising his brother Bara. He told her he was not able to do that, his uncle, the sheikh, would never permit it, but that he would be there whenever they needed him. She assured him that she would take responsibility for persuading the sheikh, and then promised that if Rahib agreed to work for her she would find him a wife. At that, Rahib fell silent, with a smile on his lips. After a thoughtful pause, he said that he agreed, in principle, if she meant what she said, though he had no great love for the city and hoped they would grant him leave to return to his village whenever he wished. With the matter now settled, he told her that he would be leaving as planned, but that he would return when his uncle Sheikh Tafir gave his blessing.

Before he left he gave his brother a long embrace, his nostrils filled with the scent of soap this time rather than the stench of alcohol. Tariq asked about his boat, and Rahib said, "I sent it on ahead of me. I'll hire a car to take me home." When Tariq expressed surprise, Rahib explained that this was not the first time he had come to Baghdad in this way, and that a taxi driver he knew was always willing to drive his small boat back to the village for the price of an item of luggage – for that, in fact, was what it was. "It was my mother's wedding chest, which my grandparents gave her when she got married. It's made of the finest wood, and I adapted it into a boat for myself." Travelling by boat was faster, since he was able to avoid the numerous checkpoints and queues. Not to mention safer. If any part of the river flowed north, he would have returned in the same way. He loved the river, and most of his trips from the village to the capital were made in this way.

They all saw him off at the gate and then went back inside, each settling down to their task.

CHAPTER 15

The Secret of Her Victory, and the Graveyard Meeting

Although Tariq was unable to persuade Qisma to abandon her plan to poach Rahib from Sheikh Tafir, he was at liberty to refuse to call his friend to make the request, so she called herself. The sheikh fell silent at first, such was the force of the surprise. Then he explained that it was simply impossible, putting forward various justifications – most of them entirely reasonable – related to his reliance on Rahib. Qisma reminded him of two things: he himself had encouraged Tariq to establish some kind of political bloc, and – more significantly – he had to grant her three wishes according to the rules of the competition. This would be the second of them. There was nothing Tafir could do but grudgingly agree, though he implored her to grant Rahib leave if he should have need of him, and to send the dwarf back as soon as their affairs were moving forward and their need for him had diminished. Then he congratulated them on all they had accomplished so far and made great promises regarding future ties between their parties. He went on to tell her about his continuing search for Ibrahim's body, though there was little to report, as among all the corpses they had come across since her visit they had not found a single one that matched the description. Tafir ended the conversation with a plea that they proceed with caution, since entering the political arena was like playing with fire in a tinder-box, and he himself had been exposed to two recent assassination attempts.

Sitting on the balcony at sunrise two days later, Tariq saw the trunk boat anchor by the riverbank once again. When he was sure that the figure jumping out of it like a little duck and waving to him was Rahib, he hurried down, just like last time, to welcome him at the garden wall. A small bed for Rahib had been installed in the room set aside for his brother Bara, as well as a third desk in the office Bara shared with Wafa. Even if he were not likely to use it, it would be there if he wanted it. They put him in charge of managing the practical affairs of the party and the house as a kind of major-domo.

Once Tariq and Qisma had satisfied themselves that they had put all the necessary arrangements in place, they left to go back to the village. Before the occupation, the trip used to take around four hours, but now it was closer to ten on account of the various hazards and checkpoints they would face, and the fact that the American army columns took priority on the roads. The long drive served as an opportunity to review what they had accomplished in Baghdad and remind themselves of what they had to do in the village. At the top of the list was the task that Sayyid Jalal al-Din had insisted was his priority, namely, persuading Abdullah Kafka to meet with him. As the journey dragged on, Tariq tried from time to time to draw the conversation back to their relationship. Qisma had informed him that while they were in the village she would stay in her house, the house of her father, and that she would not move into his house to live with his first wife. She said it was only right that someone who married more than one woman should arrange a separate house for each of them. Tariq agreed with her entirely, but he wanted to know if he would be allowed to spend the night with her. Would she grant him that intimacy, or would he spend each night with his first wife? Either Tariq was not able to express the idea clearly, or else Qisma was stubbornly pretending not to understand him, for all she said was that he should stay for as long as he wanted in his own home, in the company of his first wife and their children, since he had been with Qisma in Baghdad for some weeks now. Besides, she needed some rest and some time to think and put things in order at her father's home and in his fields.

When they passed near the checkpoint guarding the dirt road that led to Sheikh Tafir's village, Tariq thought again about the contest, seeking, as he often did, an explanation for how she could have beaten his friend. Of course, Tariq was careful and oblique in his approach, afraid of arousing her anger lest she get out of the car and expose herself to him here, in full view of the long line of passing cars and military convoys. He had no doubt that she was capable of doing that if provoked. He managed to express in the mildest terms possible his surprise at what she had done that day, and his confusion, which had weighed on him ever since. He confessed that despite all that had happened since they arrived in Baghdad, he had not stopped thinking about it and trying to find an explanation. Qisma understood what he was getting at but merely smiled. It was a smile that had a mix of haughtiness, cunning and satisfaction – with the result that it was exceedingly beautiful. Beguiled by what he read as flirtation,

Tariq recited lines of classical poetry he had memorised about smiles. He had not known she had this bewitching smile because he had never really seen her smile. Certainly not a feminine, bewitching smile like this.

By four o'clock in the afternoon they were more than halfway to the village. They turned off the highway at a rest stop with a restaurant, a car repair shop and a shack that sold fruit and vegetables. Tariq parked the car among the others in front of the restaurant. He told Qisma to stay in the car to deter thieves, for cars in those days were often stolen so they could be used as car bombs. Tariq went to the restroom at the restaurant, and then he bought sandwiches, Pepsi, some extra bottles of water and a cup of tea before going back to the car. Then Qisma got out with the child, and they headed for the restroom. On her way back to the car, she bought a packet of cigarettes from a boy sitting near the door to the restaurant.

Once Qisma had sat her son down on the back seat and buckled him in beside her, offering him half a cheese sandwich, she opened her handbag on her lap and said to Tariq, "Look."

Tariq turned round to see what she was holding. It was a small pink funnel made of plastic or silicone. "What is it?" he asked.

"This is what I used to beat your friend in the competition," she said. "Are you satisfied now?"

Tariq's eyes bulged in astonishment. "Ah, yes. But what is it?"

"Haven't you seen one of these before?"

"Never. It looks like the kind of funnel we use to fill lanterns with kerosene. But it's smaller, and its spout is different."

"It's called a Shewee. It's made of silicone, and women use it when they don't want to sit down in the filthy public toilets of restaurants, cafés, clinics, government offices, and so on. It attaches to the skin like this, allowing women to do their business standing up. So, for the contest, I put it on, raised the spout up, and squeezed a little here, on this opening. I would have been able to shoot it even further if the wall hadn't been right in front of us. It helped that my bladder was full to the point of bursting, though!"

As she explained, Tariq kept repeating, "Oh my, oh my. Women! How sly and shrewd! As it says in the Qur'an, 'Verily, your cunning is great.' God is great and he speaks the truth."

Qisma went on, delighting in her secret now it was revealed. "These things are available in certain pharmacies and in markets. You can also buy them online. One of my friends got it for me as a gift when she visited London." Then Qisma held up a curious plastic tube in her other hand. "And this is the case. I carry it with me whenever I leave the house."

By the time she put the funnel back into the case and the case back into her bag, Tariq's surprise had died down. He started the car and pulled out onto the highway, reassured at last that his wife was indeed a natural woman. He told her that what she had done in the contest was unjust, that it had been a trick, and that the end did not justify the means.

"It's not a matter of the end justifying the means," she said, "but rather of defeat stemming from ignorance. All of you claim to have such a great knowledge of women, and you boast about it among yourselves, but in reality you are ignorant of our nature. The simplest woman is able to deceive you whenever she wants, make you believe whatever she wants you to believe, and afterwards you imagine that the seed she planted was something you knew all along thanks to your experience of women. Believe me, no-one understands a woman except a women. And women don't understand women. Some women don't even understand themselves completely, me included."

"Perhaps," said Tariq in a more delicate tone. "And that is why God created five senses for us to communicate with them. Because words alone fail to convey precise understanding. So in addition to hearing, we have sight, smell, touch and the tongue's ability to taste."

"Even so," she said, "I believe that even if you had ten senses you'd never understand us."

The closer they got to the village, the more Tariq felt his spirit relax. He was like a child returning home from his first day at school to the embrace of his mother, who knows and comforts him. The boy tries to cut the distance by running full pelt, leaving behind the world with its crowds, systems, clamour and responsibilities. Tariq had had enough of cities. Village life was simpler and more suited to his temperament. Indeed, he felt his breathing change. In the city his chest constricted, but in the village it relaxed and he could breathe freely and deeply. It was just the opposite for Qisma, who needed noise and complications because they made her focus less on her interior self. The village, on the other hand, forced her into prolonged periods of introspection, which yielded nothing but a sense of futility and feelings of guilt, isolation and uncertainty.

They drove in silence for a while, as Tariq was unable to think up a response to Qisma's withering assessment of the empathic capabilities of men, and Qisma was satisfied that she had delivered the last word on the matter. But as they came closer to their village, the dust now settled on their dispute, they began to discuss the tasks they had planned for the following morning. They would meet with those they had chosen for their bodyguards, helpers and assistants, and get to work persuading them to join the party. And in the evening, they would visit Abdullah Kafka in an attempt to persuade him to join them, or at least meet with Sayyid Jalal and marry Tariq's sister Sameeha. Then, after that, they would meet separately with Sameeha.

By sunset, they were drawing near to their village, having passed through several smaller villages on the way. The clean air revived Tariq as he looked out of the window at the herdsmen coming back from the fields with their sheep and cows. Their dogs rushed around their flocks, and small boys imitated the way the older herdsmen carried their staves on their shoulders or rode their donkeys. Clueless but assured chickens wandered through the villages and blocked the road, heedless of the few cars they encountered. And when the outskirts of their village, Nakhila, the cradle of their birth, came into sight ahead of them, Tariq let out a deep, long sigh, and cried out, "Ahhhh! My God, how I've missed it!" Then, after filling his lungs with air that tasted truly sweet, despite the smoke wafting from some nearby bread ovens, he said, "I want your father to be the first person we see. Let's pass by his grave and recite the opening sura of the Qur'an. We'll kiss the headstone and tell him that we have returned from our journey to seek his remains, that we are together because we love him. Indeed, we love him more than any other person in our lives, and it's for that reason that we go to him first, even after a long and tiring journey."

Not hearing any reply, he looked in the mirror and saw tears streaming from his wife's eyes as the car approached the hill topped by the new cemetery built outside the village, where her father's head lay. Tariq's eyes filled as well. He turned onto the side road that led to the cemetery, driving with care so that the sleeping child in the back would not be woken by any jolts from the ruts in the dirt road. The car slowly climbed the hill, and, just as slowly, the sun sank in the sky. It touched the top of the mountain that stood behind the river on the opposite bank. How large and magical it was! A round disc, a necklace on the breast of the sky. Clear and bright, a radiant harmonious blend of red, yellow, orange and gold.

When he at last tore his eyes away from it, Tariq noticed the shadow of a man sitting by Ibrahim's grave. Tariq turned towards Qisma to be sure that she saw him too. "Who could that be?" she asked him, wiping her tears away.

"I'm certain," he said, "nearly as certain as I am about the existence of God, that it is Abdullah, and no-one else."

Fresh tears filled Qisma's eyes, though she quickly wiped them away. It was indeed Abdullah Kafka sitting on the ground, pressed against the headstone. One of his hands was resting on top of it, the other held a cigarette. He was looking down the length of the grave, and in front of him was a bottle of water. He went on smoking, not even turning to glance at the car that had come to a stop behind him. The first to get out was Tariq, moving with the greatest haste. He ran to Abdullah and embraced him where he sat. He embraced him hard, with a flood of affection. He kissed Abdullah's forehead, his cheeks and his beard, repeatedly squeezing him against his chest. Abdullah squeezed him back, and they cried together in each other's arms. When Qisma got out of the car and saw the two men clinging to each other, she could not hold herself back but hurried over to embrace both of them together, her tears falling, despite herself, upon their heads.

They remained like this for several minutes, silent apart from the stifled cries and shudders that escaped them, accompanying the tears that flowed from each of them in turn, provoked by the sobs of the others. But at last their tears were exhausted and their souls grew calm. They disentangled themselves from their embrace and Qisma kissed their foreheads, like a girl reverently kissing the brow of her father. Then she kissed the top of the gravestone. She stroked it with her hand and then went to sit down at what she thought must be the foot of the grave. Meanwhile, Tariq sat beside Abdullah, their knees touching, and said, "What are you doing here at a time like this?"

Abdullah picked up the cigarette that he had thrown on the ground, took a long drag, and said, "What else would I be doing at any time at all?" He fell silent, then added, "I don't have anything to do, or anything I want to do in this life. For that reason, time is no longer important to me, just as I no longer make a distinction between my interactions with the living and the dead. Indeed, I sometimes feel the dead are closer to me than the living because they are the ones who are alive. Or else because they truly embody nonexistence, while the living are just counterfeit beings who settle temporarily on the edge of nonexistence. If life for you is a series of successive gains, for me it is a series of losses until the final loss of all."

They let him go on as they sat with their heads bowed, running their hands over the pebbles that covered the grave in front of them. They noticed that the surface of the grave had been sprinkled with water, and some of the pebbles were still wet. Abdullah informed them that he visited the two graves once or twice each week. The older one in the morning, and this newer one in the evening. Indeed, he sometimes visited them in the middle of the night. It was not clear from his words if the night visits were to both graves or just to the old grave, namely that of his mother Zakiya, or if they were confined to times when the moon was shining, because they had killed her at night not long after she had given birth to him. They had sat her down, blindfolded, in the trench that would be her grave and permitted her to embrace him one last time. She had named him Qamar, after the moon. Then they put a bullet in her head to wash away the shame. Their shame, for the one who had violated her was the son of the same mayor who then killed her. The son who had raped her was Jalal, the man who now called himself Sayyid Jalal al-Din.

He told them that he missed Ibrahim, and whenever he needed to talk he came here, for, living or dead, Ibrahim was the one who understood him best. It was not exactly by means of language that he understood him, but he was good at listening silently and feeling everything Abdullah wanted to communicate. Spiritual intuition sometimes goes beyond words.

Then Abdullah said, "Where is the little one?" Abdullah had never called the child by his name because he bore the name of the deposed president.

"He's sleeping in the car," said Qisma. "And from now on you can call him by his new name, his true, official name: Ibrahim. Ibrahim Qisma."

Abdullah let out a deep sigh, like someone who has been relieved of a heavy weight on his shoulders. "Ahh!" he said. "Excellent. I want to see him now."

He got up and went towards the car, looking through the window at the child sleeping on the back seat. Abdullah pressed his hand against the glass, whispering in a rattle that he alone could hear. "Ibrahim . . . Ibrahiiim."

CHAPTER 16

The First Wife's Heart

Tariq took Qisma to her house. He helped her unload her luggage while she attended to the child. Then he sat in the salon. It was not because he hoped she would yield to him that night, for they had already spoken about the matter. In any case, both of them were tired from the long journey as well as emotionally drained by the meeting at the cemetery with Abdullah.

Once Ibrahim had been put to bed, Qisma joined her husband in the salon and they began talking about what they could do with this stubborn, depressed Kafka of theirs. After they had told him about the results of their quest, their failure to find Ibrahim's body, he had said, "A countryman's body, lost in a lost country, on a lost planet, amid a terrible universe swimming in meaninglessness."

After lighting another cigarette, he had added, "I wonder if this is not better for poor Ibrahim after all. Or that it might be assumed that it doesn't matter to him. For he was born, he lived and he died without any choice in the matter. An unknown victim in his life, an unknown victim in his death. I too was like him in my birth and life, and it would not surprise me or matter to me if my end were like his. Or if my end did not matter to me at all."

When they enthusiastically told him about the party they

were forming, he responded with predictable sarcasm. "Dogs fight over their prey," he said. "Two roosters unite to peck a third. Everyone pecks everyone else for a mouthful of shit. Nothing but chickens confined to a cage."

Qisma replied sharply, reminding him of the conversation that had taken place between them when she had asked him to accompany her in the search for her father's body. He had said: "Even shit has its uses! Don't go on talking about shit or your shitty outlook, if you please. Let's think practically. Here we are, still alive, and this is the complicated and unfortunate situation. We have to deal with it somehow until we die. Deal with it and make something better for us and for our children coming after us, just as every living being has the instinct to defend himself. That is his right. Indeed, his duty."

"I don't have children," he said, "and I don't care about anyone coming after me. Likewise, I don't consider myself among the living. For many years I've considered myself dead. Nothing in this futile world tempts me, for it's nothing but wombs putting out what graves then swallow. I'm a stranger to it, and it's a stranger to me. I need nothing more than what I have, my food and my cigarettes, which bring me closer to my end and keep me company through the melancholy and boredom of my long wait for death."

They told him of the intention to cut the pensions of former prisoners, possibly even to expel them or kill them, as had happened to many of their fellow countrymen who had been liquidated by foreign hands.

"If they had wanted to kill me," he said, "they could have done so easily when I was their prisoner for twenty years. As for this shitty pension, it doesn't matter to me, for the little that I get from my field is enough to fulfil my simple needs, and I give all the rest to Anwar and his poor family."

They told him that powerful enticements awaited him in Baghdad, and that Sayyid Jalal al-Din had promised to obtain for Abdullah an exalted position and more money than he could imagine. At that, Abdullah spun round in anger, spitting on the ground in fury. "I could shit upon him and his money and his promises. Upon all his ilk. Shit upon these murderers, these criminals, these rapists, these greedy, ugly, filthy, savage men! They are the ones who have destroyed the country and its people, collaborating with the occupation so they can grind down the simple folk, squeeze them dry and drink their blood. Keep away from them! I do not want to hear them mentioned before me, especially this shit sayyid of yours, son of that other shit. Leave me in peace! Leave me alone! Forget me! Consider me dead, and don't even bother to search for my body or my memory."

"However much a man tries to get away," Qisma said, "people just won't leave him alone."

Abdullah snorted like a furious bull, gripped by a rage they had never seen in him before. Tariq wrapped his arm around his shoulder, trying to calm him down. He gave Qisma a significant look that she understood to mean they must let things be for the time being. In an attempt to change the subject, Tariq said to his friend, "Fine, fine. It's O.K. Calm down now, brother. Just calm down. Tomorrow we have a beautiful surprise for you. Something totally unconnected with all this."

Qisma stood in front of him and added with a smile, "And

I'm certain that you won't utter the word 'shit' in the face of that surprise."

Darkness had begun to creep up around them, and Tariq asked Abdullah if he wanted them to give him a lift home. Abdullah shook his head, but Tariq guided him by the arm towards the car, saying, "Come on! At least to the outskirts of the village, or halfway. Come on!"

Back in the salon of her house, Qisma offered Tariq a glass of water, and Tariq asked her what she thought they should do the next day to persuade Abdullah to marry his sister. And how would they broach the matter with Sameeha herself?

"Go to your family now," Qisma told him. "They're waiting for you, missing you. Let's rest before making any decisions. I'll think it through and let you know. And you do the same, if any ideas come to you. Come back tomorrow evening. In the meantime, we can keep in touch with our mobiles."

He stood up, and she got up too and saw him to the door. Before opening it, he turned and cautiously embraced her. Standing stiffly in his arms she let him do it, then gave his shoulder a pat. He brushed her cheek with a quick kiss, then left, saying, "I wish you a pleasant and happy night!" Before she had a chance to shut the door behind him, he stuck his head back in, smiling and stroking his beard, to say, "And if you have any romantic dreams, I hope I feature!"

"Go!" she said, smiling at him. "Sleep well!"

Tariq was welcomed back to his family home with a great outpouring of love and emotion. As they took turns to embrace him, he realised that he had felt their absence more keenly than he had thought, particularly that of his youngest child, a daughter named Zaynab – ten years old – whom he cherished above all, and his wife, who was reserved and somewhat cold in her greeting. He felt that he could hear the depths of her heart fluttering like a sparrow's wings as it evades a cat. But this was not the time to address that. First he would ask Zaynab to inform her brothers Zahir and Mazhur of his arrival. Their official names were Zahir Ibrahim and Mazhur Abdullah, in honour of his father, Zahir, and his uncle, Mazhur, as well as his friends Ibrahim and Abdullah, though people generally called them by their first name alone.

"Let them come, along with their wives and children!" Tariq said, pressing a chocolate bar into Zaynab's hand, and she set off excitedly for the two neighbouring houses where they lived.

Once the whole family was gathered, he began to tell them about his trip to Baghdad, about his friend Sheikh Tafir, and about the new political party that would shower gold upon them all and guarantee their futures and those of their children. He cautioned them against behaviour that would hurt his reputation or the reputation of the party. He spoke at length about the operation to give his wife the sense that he had been busy with all these practical matters from dawn to dusk every day from the moment of his departure until the hour of his return, that he had not been on a honeymoon – not even a honey-half-moon – as she might have imagined.

Nevertheless, when they retired to bed, she remained silent. Her face was calm, but there was a sadness about her, and when he embraced and kissed her, she did not react in any way, offering neither resistance nor an encouraging response. Instead, she just gave herself over to him. She was cold towards him, colder even than on those nights when they went to sleep after a fight. He knew he had wounded her soul, her heart, her feelings and her dignity when he had taken a second wife after a long life together, years that she had devoted entirely to him and to his house and to his children, obeying him in everything. And how had he repaid her? By taking for a wife a young woman the same age as their first-born son! Tariq pulled her to his chest and used his usual gentle, intimate, whispering tone to tell her that he had missed her dearly, swearing to God that he loved her, that she was the love of his life and the mother of his children, that he had married Qisma for many reasons, not out of love, but rather out of responsibility and duty, in order to protect her and protect her child, and to keep faith with his lifelong friend Ibrahim. She, more than anyone, knew how much he had loved him. Likewise, he swore to her – truthfully, though not for want of trying – that he had not been intimate with Qisma. They had been too busy inspecting the bodies of the slaughtered and laying the administrative groundwork for their party. He went on to say that he had no interest in being intimate with Qisma, and although this was a lie, he said it in a tone that conveyed truthfulness, a tone he had learned from his father by working with him on tribal affairs and hearing him preach the Friday sermon. For his father had perfected the art of sounding serious and honest and convinced by what he was saying, even if deep down he wasn't, for in order to persuade others you must be seen to be convinced yourself. It is a skill that all politicians need to master, and anyone else who seeks to make a living out of manipulating people for their own gain. And it was thanks to this tone that during his long, whispered embrace he felt his wife's body soften a little, even if he could not see her face, which she kept buried in his chest. He became more daring with his hands, which caressed her naked back and shoulders.

He felt a degree of distress, however, and his conscience pricked him. His heart was hurting at the hurt in hers. But he was not the first man, nor would he be the last, to take a second wife, or more, and pass through moments like this. He would endure them and, in the end, he would put them to use. That was also his father's way. He had not been one to let his conscience get in the way of his ambitions. And yet Tariq knew he needed this wife of his more than anyone else in his life. She was the one who understood him best and who had loved him since they were young. Because her face was still hidden from him, he turned off the light and laid her on her back. He lay on top of her, embracing her and placing her arms around his back so that she would embrace him. And she did. She was soft and desirable, more than at any other time he could remember. Her surrender to him like this, without any reaction, brought him a refined, unique pleasure. He felt the return of his strength, his manliness – and his sense of authority, which Qisma had undermined.

After exhausting his desires, he lay beside her, pressed against her body, feeling a deep relaxation. A purity, a release from the mound of worries piling up in his brain, dense and chaotic. He kissed her cheek and pulled her close to him, saying with all sincerity, "Thank you, Umm Zahir, for your understanding, the forbearance of your intellect and the goodness of your heart. May God reward you with all good things. You are a great and remarkable woman, and you will always be the great woman in whom I seek refuge – I and the children."

She patted his hand, which was on her breast, with hers, and, satisfied, he felt an overwhelming desire for a deep sleep, a delicious sleep that would take over his entire being. Even so, the last thought to pass through his head was that he had broken something inside this good person, broken it forever, broken it beyond repair. He recalled the prophet's description of women as glass vials in his injunction to "Be gentle with the vials!" Tariq had broken his vial, and what had been broken could never be restored to what it had been. The only thing to do was to continue living with it and to tread as lightly as he could. He did not remember whether he kissed her a second time, or she said anything to him. All he remembered of that night was that he slept the profound sleep of the truly exhausted, something he had not done for a long time.

He woke at eleven in the morning, which was late for him. He felt no regret at having missed the dawn prayer, and offered thanks and praise to God with all his heart as he stretched out his body, entirely naked, fully relaxed, and alone in the warm bed. His mind seemed especially clear; he felt capable of anything. He was ready to undertake whatever he wanted, vigorously and generously – even joyfully and with elation. He felt he had recovered full power over himself and the affairs of his life.

When he went to the bathroom, Tariq took his mobile with him and called Qisma from there. He greeted her in a low voice.

"Good morning, Madame Sheikh, my lovely, you most beautiful of women and sheikhs. Did you dream of me, as I did of you, throughout the night in a thousand dreams and visions? Each one was beautiful and left me as befuddled as my name suggests!"

He learned that she too had slept well, and that she was about to go out to visit her neighbour Amira, having finished breakfast with her son. He asked her if she had had any thoughts regarding Abdullah and Sameeha, and she suggested that he send one or more boys to follow Abdullah's movements from afar: "So that we know where to find him at any given time. I believe it will be best if we bring Sameeha to him suddenly, without any warning, and then leave them alone together. If we try to convince him again, we won't get anywhere, with him being so withdrawn, contrary and stubborn. In matters like this – indeed, in most matters – the woman is best placed to persuade a man, for if she is convinced of something, she'll know how to attain it, and how to make the man consider it his own idea. Indeed, the majority of events that men have set in motion in this world have, in truth, been driven by women. They are the ones pulling the strings from behind the curtain . . ."

Tariq was so satisfied with life that morning he would have agreed to anything, but in this case he was truly convinced. He liked her idea very much. But how should they approach Sameeha and persuade her to cooperate with their plan?

"We'll do the same thing with her," she said. "We won't tell her anything except 'Get yourself ready, we have a surprise for you.' Then we'll take her with us in the car to where Abdullah is sitting alone, and we'll drop her off and leave. We won't talk to them till later on, when they've spent some time alone together."

Tariq rejoiced at her idea, praising her with delighted enthusiasm. "You're a marvel! Haven't I told you that, above all others, you are the madame sheikh of this world?" Then, before ending the call, he took a risk and said, "I kiss you! I kiss you all over!"

He nearly told her, "I love you", but he composed himself and held off from saying that word until another, more powerful moment. For it was a powerful word. A desire to sing swept over him, but he was afraid someone would hear him. All the same, he was not able to check the feeling. There was a song bubbling up in his chest, thrusting itself upon him, and he secretly hummed it, singing voicelessly while the echo rose high inside him. His lips followed along under the water, and his body moved in a dance. It was an old wedding song. A song taught to him by the first girl he had known, when he had taken her off alone to the threshing floor among the sheep. She was Fahda, the Bedouin girl, whom he would never forget because she had given off a ewe's woolly scent, and this smell came back whenever he remembered her and her breasts, big as two rabbits.

Tariq put on the best clothes he had, a shining white robe and an ironed headdress, held in place by a firm iqal. He combed his beard and moustache and sprinkled more of his favourite cologne over his head, neck and beard. He wished he could put kohl around his eyes as well, as the Prophet Muhammad used to do, he who liked scent and kohl.

Tariq went to the salon where he found breakfast ready and waiting for him, along with his daughter Zaynab and his wife, who was perfumed and elegant in a country dress with branching patterns and a necklace that he knew she liked. He smelled her perfume when she came close, holding the hot teapot in order to pour him some tea.

"Good morning, my sweet princesses!" he told them. Tariq kissed his beloved daughter and pulled her to his chest. Then he began eating his breakfast voraciously. His daughter joined him despite her mother's protests – she had already had her breakfast. "Let it be!" Tariq said. "Let her eat a second time with me. And you too!"

He asked his wife to prepare as many pots of tea and coffee as possible and make ready to receive guests in the diwan. Tariq also asked her to tell their sons to summon to the diwan everyone he had mentioned the day before – cousins as well as other relatives and friends –so that he might distribute the tasks among them. He had decided who should oversee the projects for which he had received contracts and permits. The other tasks related to the formation of the party. Who should be his driver and who should form his bodyguard? He would not put any of his sons in the bodyguard that would accompany him in Baghdad lest they realise how marginal a figure he was there or discern the nature of his relationship with Qisma, for if things did not develop as he wished it would diminish his stature in their eyes, and, if they did, it would stir up jealousy within them on behalf of their mother. In the end, he chose the seven members of his bodyguard from among his nephews and cousins. He entrusted to his eldest son, Zahir, the role of filling in for him and conducting all party and tribal business in his absence, while control over the affairs of the mosque, the family and his fields were given to his second son, Mazhur. Thus, all that he had been planning was at last set in motion, and he revelled in his complete mastery of the situation and his audience as he spoke with commanding fluency and confidence. This went on till noon in the presence of nearly one hundred men – and not one of them bore the name Abdullah Kafka.

Abdullah had followed his usual routine that morning. Breakfast in the café, consisting mostly of cigarette smoke and tea, as he sat beside Hamid the Snorer. Both were silent and equally heedless of who entered and left the establishment, and of the passage of time, for neither wore a watch. A little before noon, Abdullah woke Hamid, who had fallen asleep on his shoulder. He accompanied him to his house on the outskirts of the village, and then headed off in the direction of his field on the bank of the river. There he sat with his labourer, young Anwar, at the edge of one of the irrigation canals, satisfied that all was as it should be – as it was every day because Anwar loved his work in the field and loved Abdullah. Abdullah offered him a cigarette, just as he always did, and Anwar refused apologetically, just as he always did.

Abdullah's mind was calm because he had not dwelt on yesterday's conversation with Tariq and Qisma, even though the sins of his fornicating father, Jalal, were the only reason he had been born. Not that Tariq and Qisma were aware of this. No-one on earth besides Abdullah and his rapist father knew who his true mother and father were. As for the delightful surprise they had said they had for him, he had forgotten all about it the moment the words left their lips. As far as he was concerned, nothing could surprise him, be it pleasant or painful, so the long silences that passed between him and Anwar were broken only by reflections and thoughts that had come to him since they had last spoken. Anwar, for his part, was used to that. He regarded Abdullah as a kind of father or uncle, for beyond his having given Anwar the means to feed himself and his family, and beyond his general kindness, forbearance and generosity, Abdullah had suffered from the war and his imprisonment in Iran, just like Anwar's father and uncle, who had been broken by it.

"Listen to me, Anwar," Abdullah said, "and I beg you not to forget this. When I die and you visit my grave, scatter bread-crumbs over it so that the birds will visit me. Sprinkle water over it too. It's not so that I'll have company in the loneliness of the grave, because I was born alone and I will die alone. But because the birds are alive, and we can at least lessen their hardship in life until they die. As for the water, it is so that the seeds, locked up and suffering in the dirt, revive a little. In the end they will die and find rest, but it is better than being tormented under-ground when they still have some life in them. The only goal is to ease hardship and pain for all those living for as long as they are alive. Nothing apart from that. There is no need for hardship and pain in life. A living being suffers enough hardship and pain just from the fact that he exists without having desired it or having ever known why. The pain of knowing from the time of his birth that he will die, and that he was not born for anything except death."

After a moment's thought, Anwar confirmed with a nod that he would do so. Abdullah lit a cigarette and said, "As for you, I advise you not to believe that if you are good you will be spared other people's evil, for being good means only that you spare other people your evil, not the opposite. The good animals – chickens, cows and sheep, for example – are not spared being slaughtered and eaten by humans. Quite the opposite, in fact: they become the preferred food with which humans fill their bellies."

After that, they ate together, sharing Anwar's lunch, which his mother prepared for him every day. After they had washed the traces of oil from their hands and their mouths, Abdullah departed for the riverbank, where there was a boulder he liked to sit on, and where he often stayed until sunset.

CHAPTER 17

Lovers Meeting after Long Years

Tariq's car approached the isolated spot by the riverbank where the river turned and where he knew he would find Abdullah, for this had been a favourite haunt of theirs since childhood. Besides, the boy to whom he had given a few dinars to serve as a spy had confirmed Abdullah's presence. Tariq parked at the end of the dirt path, where a slope led gently down to the river – light brown sand giving way after fifty metres to a belt of pebbles that gradually increased in size the closer one got to the water. A few larger boulders were scattered about on this bed of rocks, one of which Abdullah had chosen as the perfect setting for his reflections. At high tide the water would lap against it. At other times it would recede, leaving the rock high and dry. As it was a sandy, rocky area, people seldom disturbed him there. They would go instead to more accessible stretches of shoreline, surrounded by willows and lotus trees.

Abdullah's face was turned towards the river and the western bank, dense with trees and thick undergrowth, and beyond it the mountain, behind which the sun was accustomed to taking its rest. As dusk was approaching, it was hard to make out his figure sitting on the rock in the fading light. From a distance he appeared to be nothing more than an extension of the boulder. His shadow too was one with the boulder's shadow, all the more obscure when set against the calm water glistening with reflected sunlight. Only Tariq and Qisma knew it was him. In a low voice they said to their companion Sameeha, "Do you see that man sitting on the boulder? He is waiting for you. He will reveal the happy surprise. Go to him."

Sameeha was more confused than ever. Throughout the journey she had been unable to guess at the surprise they had prepared for her or persuade them to give her any clues. They had just said over and over again that it was a wonderful surprise that could change her life.

"Go on! Go up to him slowly, and surprise him from behind."

She took two steps down the sandy slope, then looked back at them and saw that they were smiling. Qisma signalled for her to keep going. So she did, slowly at first, feeling her feet sink into the cold sand, which seeped inside her soft shoes, its touch somehow kind and sympathetic, soothing her racing heart. Every few metres she would turn back towards them and see them gesturing for her to continue, which she did, until she had covered more than half the distance.

At that point Qisma said to Tariq, "I think we should call out now to Abdullah and alert him. Otherwise, she may come running back if she gets closer and recognises him."

"You're right," Tariq said. He put his hands around his mouth to amplify his voice and shouted, "Halllooo! Kafka! Hey, Kafka!"

Abdullah turned. Sameeha stumbled and fell at the shock of hearing his name, rolling over on the sand. Tariq was about to run down to help her up when Qisma reached out to grab his robe. "No, stop!" she hissed. "She's not hurt. It's soft sand, nothing more. And it's in a woman's nature to want the man to be the one who comes to her, rather than the other way round."

Abdullah stood up and hurried over to the unknown woman he had seen fall in the sand. "Take care of my sister! I'm entrusting her to you!" Tariq called down from above. Then he and Qisma returned to the car. As soon as the engine had started up, Qisma yelled through the window to them, "Set the wedding date soon! We want to celebrate with you. Get married, get married! Life is short!"

Tariq supplied the line with which to finish her message to them: "Truly, a soul does not know what it will gain on the morrow, nor does a soul know in which land it will perish."

In a loud voice, Qisma repeated the Qur'anic verse, then the car pulled away. Tariq tooted on the car horn the rhythm of a well-known wedding song until they were far down the narrow dirt track that led between the fields, leaving a cloud of dust behind them.

Back down the slope, Abdullah was squatting in front of Sameeha, a little lower than her because of the incline. He pulled her shoe out of the sand, shook it off and pressed it into her hand. "Are you alright?" he said, looking into her eyes for the first time. Before she had a chance to answer he lost his balance and found himself sitting on the sand, bowled over by the enormity of the shock. His entire being trembled, and it was as though his heart had stopped and his mouth had suddenly dried up. In his whole life, he had never felt such confusion and paralysis, not even in the moment of his capture, or when he was a witness to death on the battlefield or at a torturer's hands. They remained staring into each other's eyes for several long, solemn minutes, scarcely blinking as the tears fell unbidden. Their glances conveyed a tempestuous flood of words stored up for a quarter of a century.

They had no idea how long they remained like that, statues frozen on the sand, their eyes fountains of words and tears. The living dead. The only living dead in the country. Finally, Sameeha blinked. The universe seemed to move once again, and Sameeha murmured with difficulty, "I'm fine. I just twisted my ankle a little."

Abdullah blinked, and he croaked out her name as though it were his final word: "Sameeha." He broke into a sob.

"Abdullah," she said, as she shook with tears.

He stretched out his hand to her injured foot and shifted its position on the sand. He looked into her face again and found her wiping it with her hand. Then he looked behind her but did not see anything, not even the dust thrown up by Tariq's car, which was long gone. Referring to Qisma and Tariq, he said, "What is that crazy girl doing? And that foolish dog, that son of a bitch?"

Sameeha laughed. "Now you're insulting me – he is my brother after all."

Abdullah smiled and began to apologise. "Not at all," she said. "He truly is foolish. I've lost count of the stupid things he's done. But deep down, he is good. A child even. And that playful, befuddled child's spirit still lurks within him."

"Yes," he said. "Yes, I know him well."

Abdullah helped her get up, and when he saw that she was finding it difficult to walk, he took hold of her arm and draped it across his shoulder so he could support her, wrapping his other arm around her slender waist. It was the first time he had ever touched a woman's body. He had swallowed forty-seven years of life, during which he had imagined a million times what it would be like to touch a female body, but he realised that he had got it all wrong. He was unable to describe what he felt in that moment with his body pressed against hers as his fingers trembled on her waist, like the fingers of a drunkard playing a tabla drum.

When he had sat her down upon his favourite rock, with her feet dangling into the water, he squatted down to wash them. His soul trembled as he gently felt the soft skin of her feet – like two pieces of cheese. He wanted to eat them, and the desire to cry came over him again. But tears of a different kind that he did not know how to describe.

He found that she was as slender as she had been in her youth, maybe more so, and as beautiful as she had ever been – again, perhaps even more so. The few wrinkles on her face and at the corners of her eyes made her all the more attractive. He saw her face above him like the moon. Like the sun. Like the sky. She was the gentle, compassionate sky that had sheltered his soul throughout his life.

"How are you, Abdullah?" she asked him tenderly.

"I don't know," he replied, looking down at her feet in the clear water. "As you can see, I've suffered greatly."

"Me also. For you and because of you."

"You didn't have to do that, not at the cost of your own happiness."

"It wasn't my choice. You were my life's dream, ever since I knew what it was to dream."

"And in my entire life, not a single thing has happened because I wanted it to, not since my birth."

"And now?"

"I don't know. All I know is that I do not want anything from this world. I am not of this world, Sameeha. Some unknown person – or a vile twist of fate – cast me into it by mistake. I've been paying the price of that mistake my whole life."

They fell silent, and he continued washing her feet tenderly. Sameeha took off the necklace she was wearing. The pendant was a small white stone in the shape of a heart, in which Abdullah had bored a hole and upon which he had etched their initials, one on each side. He had given it to her when they confessed their love for one another more than twenty years before.

"Look," she said.

Abdullah looked up at her and was so astonished that he nearly fell backwards into the water. He stood up and stretched his hand to the stone pendant hanging from her fingers on its fine white thread. Taking hold of it, he kissed it, still not believing his eyes. Then he closed his fist tightly around it and let out a deep sigh. "Ahhh! How can this be, Sameeha?"

"All religions have sacred stones. My religion is love, and this is my sacred stone."

He wanted to squeeze her to his chest with all his might. After a short silence as he mastered the trembling of his lips he said, "In my captivity, I had a Christian friend I loved very much. They tortured him to death. He knew all about religion, and many times he repeated the Messiah's saying, 'If you believe in a stone, it shall make you whole'. But this stone has been making you sick for years."

"On the contrary, it was the only thing that reminded me I had ever been alive, for the person who has never loved has never really lived. And I have loved."

"And your daughter?"

"She paid the price of my love. And in exchange, I've given my life to care for her."

"How is she now?"

"She's like me in every way, both in appearance and spirit. She has never married, though all the girls her age in the village have. She's the same age as Qisma, and Qisma's father used to buy the same presents for both girls. Qisma has married twice and had a child, while my daughter still sleeps in my bed, just as she has done ever since she was a nursing infant."

"Why?"

"Because she is stubborn like me. She refuses to get married except to a man who truly loves her, and, at the same time, she is afraid to love after she realised what love did to me."

Abdullah raised his hands to his head as though to start ripping out his hair. He began turning around on the spot as though he had been stung by some in the creature in the water. He seemed to be slapping himself. Then his hands closed into fists and he began striking them against his thighs as he continued spinning. He took a cigarette out of his pack and lit it. He sucked in the smoke with a full deep breath and kept on spinning. "God! God!" he was saying. "God!"

Sameeha climbed off the rock and reached for his shoulder. She stopped his spinning and said, "You're not to blame for any of it, Abdullah. It's just that we insisted on being ourselves in a world that does not allow that. Nevertheless, we did it. We chose to be true to ourselves no matter what the cost."

Abdullah remained standing, drawing down into his lungs as much smoke as he could.

"There are many crimes that the law does not hold to account," Sameeha went on. "But time is its own judge, jury and executioner. Mistreating a guest, abusing an orphan or breaking a lover's heart. My father committed this last crime, and he paid the price in the final year of his life. A strange, wasting illness struck him, and he disintegrated before our eyes, his still-living body rotting away until there was nothing left."

"Yes, I know. And his crime against me was greater still."

He thought about telling her the secret, but the sun was about to set, and there was not enough time to tell her everything he would have liked to. Each of them was reluctant to open the door to release the storm of words that still raged inside their hearts after all these years. They were unsure of where it would lead. So they were content to let it flow from them gradually, little by little.

The sun had disappeared behind the mountain. Darkness began to overpower the light. They heard the croaking of the frogs and the chirping of the grasshoppers. The sound of the river flowing past and the rustling of the trees became clearer. It was time to go back to the village. They chose a narrow path that ran between the fields to avoid being seen. The path ran alongside one of the fields belonging to Sameeha's family. It was the very field where they had declared their love when their hands met during the cotton harvest. A fleeting touch, initiated by Sameeha, one that Abdullah had never stopped replaying in his mind. He wished then that she would recall that youthful daring of hers and take his hand for the rest of the way. It was inconceivable that he make the first move. He was not skilled in normal human interactions. He had no experience of taking the initiative in this way, and he could not guess at her reaction.

Because each of them was used to conducting an internal dialogue with the other in their absence, they continued in that way. They walked together, slowly, silently, each addressing the other in their heads. Sameeha limped a little because of her twisted ankle. Abdullah hunched over a little because of what so much smoking had done to his lungs and as a result of his ribs being broken when he was tortured as a prisoner. If anyone saw them, they would know, despite the darkness, that they were old. But that's not what they felt inside. It was as though their bodies had each shed twenty years because their souls were living a moment stored up ever since the time of their young love.

Abdullah told Sameeha that her image was what had enabled him to endure the torture, and that thinking about her and remembering her had fed his soul and kept it alive. Beyond her, neither his life nor this world held any meaning for him.

Sameeha told Abdullah that her love for him was what had made her content with herself, even though she had no hope or dreams for her future. She told him how she had run away from her cousin, whom they had forced her to marry, and how her father had beat her and sent her back to her new husband wrapped up in a blanket. She told him how she had found a strange pleasure in that torture, which was how she had endured his torments.

She ran away again, and her father beat her again. This went on until she gave birth. A week after her baby daughter was born, she left her behind and fled. Her husband returned the child to her and divorced her because he was no longer able to endure the shame.

They did not know if they actually said these things to each other, or if these details were just part of their internal dialogue. Abdullah was not even certain that Sameeha was truly there with him, for how often over the years had he come alone to his rock by the river to think about her and talk to her in his head.

They were drawing close to the outskirts of the village, the lights from the windows like tiny holes in a dark tent. They stopped to swat at the mosquitoes swarming around them, and Sameeha wondered aloud what they should say to Tariq and Qisma when they asked them about their time together.

Confused, Abdullah said, "I don't know. For my part, I don't have to tell them anything, and if they insist, I can easily ignore them in silence or else curse them. What do you think?"

"I don't know either. I understand their intention in pushing us together. I'm grateful to them. For if they hadn't, perhaps we would have remained afraid, and we would have avoided meeting each other until it really was too late. But . . ."

"But they also have to understand that we're not like them. Our lives have run their course. It is not just death that is the end of life, and there are numerous endings that go before it. I have considered myself dead for a long time. My body is exhausted. Inside and out, I give off the odour of smoke. No money, no family, no children and no hope. It would be a wanton injustice against you: you fast for your entire life, and then you break your fast with an onion."

She smiled and said, "To break my fast with an onion is better than fasting until the point of death. It does not matter to me that you are an exhausted old man, or that you are poor in material wealth and rich only in sadness and regret. What do I have to offer? I have no hope of bearing children now. And I do not mind your smoking and its smell. I would be happy for you to teach me how to smoke so that I could share that with you. Why should I care what people say? I've never paid them any attention, not even when I was young, so why should I start at this time in my life? I have been content my whole life just to have a pebble from you, so how could I not be content with you, yourself, whatever condition you are in?"

Abdullah did not know what to say. At her words, his love for her welled up to the point of overflowing. He bent over, all the way down to her injured ankle that he had wanted to kiss when he was washing it in the river. Now he did. Then he sat on the dirt path, placing his head between his hands. Sameeha sat in front of him. She took his head and drew it to her breast. He cried inaudibly, like an orphaned child.

Sameeha pulled him closer still, rested her cheek on the top of his head and, in a compassionate voice, said in his ear, "It's our right – and our souls' right – to spend the rest of our lives together, to reduce the pain of life for each other and take away the loneliness. Even if we just sit together in silence. Better that we spend it like that than finish it alone."

Abdullah took her hand from where it lay on his head and

kissed it. Then he kissed the stone necklace hanging near his lips.

Sameeha felt him growing calm. She lifted his head so he was facing her, wiped the tears from his cheeks and beard with the side of her hand and said, "The only obstacle is that it is impossible for me to get married before my daughter does."

"If you tell them that, they will hatch a plot to get her hitched in no time, those two old bastards."

"Let it happen. It is not unusual for love to be born from a trick. Love is a great mystery. The important thing to me is that she want it, that she be happy and completely certain. I will never force her to marry, nor will I permit anyone else to force her. My daughter will not leave my bosom except for one she loves, one who loves her – or at least someone she is content to share her life with."

They got up, and when they had reached the end of their shared path, before they set off separately for their own homes, Sameeha stopped again and stood facing Abdullah. She took his hands in hers and said with a smile, "I'll keep fasting, and I'll never break my fast – not even with the smell of onions – until my daughter breakfasts first on whatever she's hungry for."

They felt a rush of love as they held hands. Then, both still smiling, they parted.

CHAPTER 18

The Great Celebration

At last it was the day of the great celebration, a historic moment,
for the village had never witnessed a party like it since it
was founded – just five huts on the riverbank – and it might not
witness anything like it again in the future. After days of preparation, Qisma and Tariq's guests of honour arrived to witness the
inauguration of the village's first political party: three ministers
– without ministries – sent by Sayyid Jalal al-Din from Baghdad,
a busload of journalists, Sheikh Tafir and his entourage, General
Adam and his bodyguard, the American officer responsible for
the district and his bodyguard, the sheikhs of the surrounding
villages and the imams of their mosques, and prominent friends
from among the Kurds, the Turkomans, the Yazidis, the Shabakis,
the Christians and the Sabians.

The Americans and the local police organised a security detail,
which was joined by forty individuals appointed by Tariq as a
bodyguard for him and for Qisma, overseen by his son Zahir. A
cordon was set up around the village and its outskirts to prevent
suicide bombers and other enemies of the newborn democracy
slipping in.

No-one in the village cooked dinner that night, for the feast
which Tariq had ordered to be prepared under the supervision of

Rahib surpassed, in quantity and variety, what the village would cook in the space of a week. Ten fat cows were slaughtered, half a ton of rice was cooked, and thousands of round pittas were baked as the ovens worked from noon until sunset.

The streets and alleys of the village were decorated with hundreds of posters bearing the party's slogans and policies and large photographs of Sheikh Tariq and Madame Sheikh Qisma. Dressed that night in all their finery, they resembled a prince and princess who had stepped out from one of the old stories. The first issue of the party's journal was distributed for free to the people crowding the village square. It set out the ideas and principles of the party, as well as its promises, which were no different from those of any party in any time or place. Uncle Papers had worked late into the night to have it printed in time, and Rahib had brought it down with him in a hired car, along with his brother Bara, Sabir and Sabriya, and Wafa, whose mother had given her permission to travel. In addition, they brought with them a professional photographer.

Upon arrival in the village, they were assigned tasks by Qisma. Wafa was to gather as many business cards as possible from the guests and the journalists. Bara would work his charm on the most important personalities present and interview the guests so he could fill the next issue of the journal with their platitudes. As for Sabriya, her role was to stand beside Qisma with the child Ibrahim in her arms, while Sabir was at hand in case the two of them needed anything. A troupe of singing and dancing gypsies had been hired to close the event. That had been Qisma's idea, and Tariq had been unable to persuade her to drop it.

At the height of the celebrations, Tariq planned for Hamid the Snorer to be honoured by General Adam for saving the village from a bloody occupation. The medal was an old brass one that Tariq had kept in a drawer in his bedroom since winning it in a sack race at school. It had been burnished by the passage of time, like a rare antiquity, since Tariq's frequent handling of it had made it all the more shiny and had worn away the inscription and the design. Its ribbon was in the colours of the Iraqi flag, so it already had the appearance of a military decoration.

Hamid the Snorer had arrived that morning in his uniform, as Tariq had requested. He had put it on without question, though his belly defied his attempts to button it fully. In a few quick movements, Tariq took the medal out from his pocket and gave it to General Adam, who was sitting beside him. In full view of the crowd and the photographers, General Adam hung the medal around Hamid's neck and stepped back to lead the applause. Then Hamid left the podium and made his way through the crowds in search of Abdullah Kafka, so he could sit with him and fall asleep on his shoulder. He was pleased to be honoured, and fondled the medallion proudly, though he had no idea what it was to reward him for. He would have preferred to receive it when he was younger, but he said to himself, "Oh, well. Better late than never!" Failing to find Abdullah anywhere, he stretched out on the grass on the fringes of the festivities and went to sleep among children playing and dogs sniffing around for scraps and bones from the feast.

Abdullah Kafka was the only one of the village's inhabitants not to attend the celebrations, content just to comment, "What is

227

the meaning of all this vanity?" After listening to Tariq's speech, and taking down the comments of the three dignitaries, Bara slipped off to look for him, for he had heard his name often while staying at Qisma's house in Baghdad. More than anything, he was curious to know why he was called Abdullah Kafka. What could the connection be? After wandering for a time down the village's deserted back streets, he found a boy who could lead him to Abdullah's house. He followed the boy, carrying a bag more filled with beer and Lebanese arak than with party papers. They arrived at the gate to the courtyard and saw a cigarette smouldering in the dark. "That's him," said the boy. Bara thanked him, pressing a few dinars into his hand, and the boy scampered off. Bara made his way into the dark courtyard, heading for the glowing tip of the cigarette. He found Abdullah sitting on the ground with his back against the wall of the outdoor toilet, which was set apart from the house. He was staring into the darkness in the direction of the fields and the river, which could not be seen at this hour from where he was sitting. Bara greeted him and sat beside him, saying, "I'm the poet Bara – or Breton the Shakhabiti. I'm responsible for the journal of the party of the two sheikhs, Tariq and Qisma."

"The two sheikhs?" asked Abdullah, incredulously.

"Beyond the requirements of my work, thanks to which I'm able to eat – or rather, drink," continued Bara, patting the bag, "my most important motive in coming here from Baghdad was to see you."

Abdullah felt an immediate liking for Bara, despite his connection with Tariq and Qisma's contemptible enterprise. He offered him a cigarette and lit it.

Bara took out a can of beer and offered it to Abdullah. "My curiosity was piqued when I heard the name Kafka. Are you the one who chose it?"

"No," said Abdullah. "It is a joke coined by your sheikh when we were young. And once I'd learned about Kafka, I came to like it."

"But Kafka is a pessimist, not a nihilist," Bara said, for he had heard Qisma complaining to Tariq that it would be impossible to come to any agreement with a man who believed in nothing and no-one as Abdullah did.

"Classifications don't interest me. I myself don't know what I am or what meaning my existence has in this world."

"Maybe if I had been your friend, I would have named you Abdullah Schopenhauer."

"Yes, I like Schopenhauer. I feel we would have understood one another, had we met."

"You live alone?"

"Yes. They found me as a baby half a century ago, right here where we're sitting, next to the toilet. And here I am, still beside it. We are born and we die, and in between there is nothing but shit, for all we pretend to forget that."

"Do you like poetry? I could recite some of my poems for you."

"I do not like anything at all apart from smoking. Though actually, I did love one creature in this world."

"A woman?"

"Yes, but a woman like no other."

"Love, yes. It's the great mystery of all. Besides poetry. And life."

229

"Yes, a mystery. We do not understand its secret. We do not know exactly what it means. But it provides us, or rather it seems to provide us, with the gift of a reason for living. In our ignorance of love's secret, love becomes the meaning behind an even greater unknown, which is life itself."

"Yes, and the strongest proof that love is blind is that we love Iraq despite it having tortured us ever since we were born."

"Leave aside Iraq for now. We are talking about love. Perhaps we cling to love because it provides us with an illusion, a delicious sense of perceiving the secret of our existence, despite the fact that it causes us pain too. But we are not able to deny our inclination towards love, our need to love and be loved, to share with someone the loneliness and melancholy arising from ignorance of our ultimate fate."

"Yes, we were born to love, my friend, and for my part I love poetry."

"We were born for pain. We are beings who take pleasure in love because it torments us. Perhaps if love were a soft, easy thing, it would not have assumed the value it has for us. We are beings who seek the pain that we fear. We create it and bring it into existence. We torment ourselves and become artists of torture. We invent instruments to torture each other's bodies. We even torment our souls with love. Indeed, the world is built on war and love."

"Yes. Humans are remarkable creatures, tied to pain, as you say. And the strange thing is that, in the future, they will open shops that will charge enormous sums to torture and kill you in the way that you long for. And when they come into competition with each other, they will begin to advertise the methods and means of torture and death that they can offer us."

"Yes, humans are the only creature that carries evil in its heart and practises it consciously."

In that way, they continued to exchange cigarettes, drinks and conversation, each reply beginning with the word "yes", confirming that each understood the other's point of view.

"Yes, it tears my soul that for the most part our tragedies and misfortunes are down to our fellow men. Why is this? The earth is big enough for all. There is food enough for everyone. There are places enough for everyone to shit." They laughed. "Your health, my friend."

"Yes, and that is why the dream of the simple, the poor and the oppressed throughout history has been justice. But unfortunately we have lost all hope of achieving that. The dream has become an equal distribution of injustice instead."

"Yes. And we dream of peace too, which is the original, first condition, and costs us nothing – all we need to do is leave each other alone. Peace, the one thing that doesn't require us to do a thing, has become the scarcest commodity."

"Yes, I do not know why they do not just grant us this temporary existence of ours, which doesn't cost anyone anything. Not even the air we breathe. We will leave them all this air in a few years' time when we depart forever."

"Yes, death is waiting for us at the door. It might push it open and come in upon us at any moment. Indeed, it is even found in this air that we breathe. Life is nothing more than a small margin running around the edge of the page of non-existence. Our lives are only a temporary reprieve from non-existence, whence we have come and where we shall return."

"Yes, life and death are neighbours, with only a delicate line between them. In any given moment, you have no idea whether you will be pushed, or whether you will take a step and then fall, ending up on the other side."

They kept exchanging that "yes" until the cigarettes and drinks ran out. Then they passed out where they sat, intoxicated, repeating that "yes" and other inaudible words that mixed with the saliva dribbling from the corners of their mouths onto their clothes. The echoing harmonies of the singing gypsies continued to rise up from the middle of the village until the first light of dawn.

In the days following the magnificent celebration, the star of the two sheikhs, Tariq and Qisma, continued to rise, for most of the newspapers covered the party's inauguration, splashing images of its placards and posters across their pages. No-one in the village dared touch any of the party's promotional material, leaving the task of taking it down to the wind and the passing animals that tore at it with their teeth. Most of the girls of the village began to imitate the way Qisma looked in her photograph. They pushed back their hijabs, which used to cover their heads entirely, to reveal half their hair, so their hijabs amounted to little more than handkerchiefs, draped over their heads for decoration. This innovation annoyed the village elders and religious men, but they kept silent out of fear, and muttered their complaints only in the ears of those they trusted.

Sheikh Tafir had given Tariq two pieces of advice the night he spent with him in the village. After praising everything he had done and congratulating him on his resounding success, he said, "You have to prepare an armed force on the margins of the party, just as all the other parties have. Otherwise, your life, the lives of your family – and, indeed, all your interests – will be in danger. I myself have been exposed to two assassination attempts. But this militia of mine has its other uses. For example, if a project I have accepted a contract for does not come to fruition or is delayed, I can instruct my men to blow up the construction site, leaving no trace. If it happens before the deadline for completing the project, no-one will take account of what has and has not been accomplished. Everyone does it – the sabotage is merely chalked up to terrorism. And this is not the only deception you can profit from. Listen, brother, you must find some intangible symbol, something abstract, superstitious or even sacred for your people to put their faith in – even if you have to invent it. For is it not the case that people are always more willing to put their trust in superstition than in logic or science? The proof lies in the fact that they are prepared to kill for the sake of superstition but not for the sake of science."

Tafir then told him how he had worked hard to burnish the reputation and legend of a small, forgotten tomb on the outskirts of his village. No-one knew exactly whose tomb it was, or how or when it had been built, but a poor woman claimed to have seen a light emanating from it. She persuaded the women to seek a blessing there, and the women persuaded their husbands and their children, and so on.

"So I set about building a dome over it, and we called it Abu al-Anwar, 'the Father of Lights'. The people spontaneously began to weave stories around the miracles of the resting place of this saint, to the point where it is now one of the most sacred sites in the country. It is necessary to plant the burning fire of faith within the hearts of men, so that afterwards you can use it to move and inspire them. There will come a time, my friend, when you need to harness this too, if you are to succeed as I have. And remember, whenever you want to discourage people from discussing something or thinking about it too deeply, just add the word 'sacred'. It could be a stone, a person, a tree or a cow. Or even a rotting watermelon. Just call it 'the sacred rotting watermelon'." Tafir laughed loudly, clapping Tariq on the back.

"This is dangerous talk, my friend. I am surprised to hear it coming out of your mouth – you being a religious man."

"If you think it through carefully, you will see that it works to the advantage of religion too. It is in these tense times of ours that religion finds its true calling."

The successes that Tariq enjoyed in terms of rank, authority, reputation, contracts and money had made him forget that all of it was down to the patronage of Sayyid Jalal al-Din, in exchange for bringing him Abdullah Kafka. Suspecting as much, Qisma reminded him of their promise and told him what she had learned from Sameeha about her meeting with Abdullah: that they had decided not to marry for the time being and that Sameeha's daughter was the reason. Qisma had herself tried to persuade the girl to marry, reminding her of their childhood friendship and the dreams they had shared as teenagers. She offered her the choice of any of the young men of the village that she liked. She even offered marriage to Rahib, citing – and exaggerating – his many qualities: his intelligence, his industriousness, his courage, his strength, his sense of responsibility, his ambition, his good humour, and so on. She pointed out that it would be an opportunity for Sameeha to move to the capital instead of spending her life there in the village, where nothing ever happened. Qisma promised to undertake all the arrangements.

"But the girl is as stubborn as your sister, Tariq. One way or another we need to honour our promise to Sayyid Jalal al-Din. Rahib, too. I promised him I would find him a wife. If we're able to persuade the girl, we can kill two birds with one stone."

Tariq scratched his beard, at a loss for how to reply or what to do. He settled for a general platitude. "Be patient awhile, Qisma. Sometimes time itself takes responsibility for resolving our dilemmas."

But Qisma had run out of patience. She paced around him, wringing her hands. "We don't have time to wait for miracles. We have to do something."

Abdullah, meanwhile, having recovered from the hangover that had greeted him the morning after his meeting of minds with Bara, was having lunch with Anwar, whom he surprised by uncharacteristically speaking about love. Since his talk with Sameeha, he had been reliving every detail of what had occurred between them, every word and every touch. His longing for her was like a storm inside him. It had deprived him of sleep and kept him in chain-smoking isolation, so he could enjoy recalling her every move and gesture in peace. He yearned to see her now more than at any time in the past, but he did not know how he should behave or what he had to do in order to see her, or what he would do or say when he did. He wished to see her with every atom of his being, and although he did not dare to believe that she might feel the same, he felt that his life had changed. There had developed in him a single certainty, a single desire, after years of having no desire for anything at all. He was entirely certain that he loved her and wanted to see her. His talk of love was instinctive, spontaneous, inevitable, for there was nothing in his heart or his mind apart from it.

"Love is a mystery, Anwar," he said, "just like life and . . ." Abdullah broke off here just as he was about to say "like poetry", for that was the expression of the poet who had stayed up drinking with him two nights earlier without Abdullah ever having seen his face. When he woke up, there was no sign of him. Abdullah would have doubted he had ever been there at all were it not for the pounding in his head. After a moment's thought, he changed tack and asked Anwar, "Have you ever been in love?"

The young man lowered his head, confused by the question. Abdullah realised then how strange it must seem coming from him, for it was not his custom to show any interest in the personal lives of others. The question had escaped him involuntarily, but he did not regret it when he saw its effect on the young man. Anwar trembled, his face turned red, and he appeared to be struggling to speak. Abdullah repeated his question in a soothing tone, to which Anwar replied, "Yes, but . . ."

Abdullah put his hand on the young man's shoulder. "But what?"

"I do not know if she loves me or not."

"Tell me."

"I've loved her for two years and she doesn't know. She's a little older than me and from a family that is richer than mine, so I don't expect she thinks of me at all. And if she did think of me, I don't think she would want me."

"How do you know that you love her?"

"Because my entire body trembled when I saw her for the first time, and whenever I've seen her since. I think of her every moment of every day. I've begun dreaming of a life with her, so that now I have two lives, one of them real, in which I live and in which people see me, and the other private and internal, which no-one apart from me sees or knows anything about, and in which I see no-one but her."

Abdullah felt a great affection and kinship for the boy because what he was expressing resembled that which Abdullah had experienced his whole life, an existence split between reality and daydreams. He asked Anwar to explain the feeling in greater detail.

"It's good and it's not good," Anwar said. "On the one hand, there is nothing to limit us in the lives we live in our dreams. We can construct them just as we wish. We can flee to them whenever our real lives close in on us, and it reduces life's hardships. Indeed, it sometimes makes us forget them, which helps us to go on enduring. But because it's not real, it can't be touched or held onto and our lives can blossom in our dreams without producing any fruit. When our dreams seem out of reach, the burden of our real life increases, because that which we do not love remains real, and that which we love is still imaginary. And sometimes we are afraid to realise our dream, afraid that it will upset the balance between our two lives, between the dream and the reality . . . I don't know how to describe it."

Abdullah patted his shoulder and stroked his head with affection and encouragement. He resolved to listen to this good young man more and to help him resolve his internal difficulties. "You've described it very well. I think I understand you."

CHAPTER 19

The Stone Heart Speaks of Love

After Abdullah left Anwar, he headed in the direction of Hyena Valley, on the distant edge of the fields, to the slope where he would often go as a boy to sit alone and contemplate the village below him as he waited for sunset. The entire way, he was thinking about Anwar and how he might help him. He did not want what had happened to him to happen to this young man. Shame and his family's poverty were preventing him from being joined to the woman he loved. With each step Abdullah took, his resolve to do something to help him grew stronger. At times, he felt that Anwar was a young mirror of himself, and that he needed to change the course of his life to keep him from ending up like him.

When Abdullah reached the top of the slope, he sat down and started to play absentmindedly with the pebbles on the ground around him. He remembered that it was there that he had found the white stone that had taken on the shape of a heart after he had filed the edges a little. Then he had bored a hole and etched with a hot tool his initial on one side and Sameeha's on the other. The most beautiful gift she had ever received, she had told him, just days before. Abdullah proceeded to search the top of the hill and its slope for another white pebble resembling a heart that he could file, bore through and engrave. He would tell Anwar, "Take this to her. This pebble will convey all the words you wish to say but don't know how, the words that you are too afraid or too embarrassed to say yourself."

For half an hour, Abdullah circled around, examining and discarding pebbles. Anyone who caught sight of him from afar would assume he was looking for mushrooms or truffles or something he had lost. At last he came across two delicate stones capable of being whittled into the shape of a heart, just as he wanted, and he hurried home.

When he reached his house, he fetched the tools he would use to carve, etch, file and burn, and set up a workshop in the salon, working with a patient and careful joy until, as night fell, he had finished fashioning one of the two stones into the shape he wanted. It looked beautiful to him, exactly like the one he had given Sameeha. After he had etched Anwar's initial into one side of the stone, he realised that he had not asked the boy for the name of his beloved. He put down the stone and his etching tool, deciding to leave everything in place until the morning, and spent the rest of the night thinking of Sameeha until he finally passed out in the sitting room, holding between his fingers one last cigarette that sleep had not granted him time to light.

Qisma smoked even more cigarettes than Abdullah that night. She broke out in a sweat as she paced between the sitting room, the kitchen and her bedroom, all alone in the house now that her son had fallen asleep, anxious, gripped by an obscure desire and energy to do something. Or for something to be done to her. Perhaps if Tariq had been with her in those moments, she would have granted him her body there and then, for no other reason than to exhaust her body so she could sleep. She was thinking of many things and scenes all at once, blending them together in a random way. In the sitting room, she remembered her father, and she sat for a while in what had been his favourite place. In the kitchen, she fingered the knives, thinking of the masked man who had threatened her. She touched her neck, and for a moment she wanted that man to burst into the house there and then, and for him to slit her throat, or she his. She peered through the kitchen window into the darkness outside, seeing nothing in the shadows except a faint light emanating from somewhere in the house of her neighbour, Amira. Suddenly, it occurred to her that she could marry Amira's son to Sameeha's daughter. The release of having found a solution to one of the matters weighing upon her filled her with renewed energy. She smoked with frenzied pleasure as she turned the idea over in her mind, becoming more and more convinced by it. Had it not been so late, she would have gone straight to her neighbour to persuade her of the idea, offering to take care of all the arrangements.

As soon as Abdullah awoke in the morning, he hurried out to the field without having anything for breakfast except for a cup of water and a few cigarettes. When he came upon Anwar, already hard at work, he asked him without any greeting at all, "What is the first letter of the name of your beloved?"

"S."

"Perfect." Abdullah turned to leave, but after a few steps he came back to ask: "What is her name?"

"Salma."

"Perfect."

He turned to head home, but after a few steps he returned with more questions, for doubt and curiosity had filled his head. Her name was Salma, and she was older than him? And from a rich family? Which Salma did he mean?

"Which Salma? Whose daughter?"

"The daughter of the Sameeha who is the sister of Sheikh Tariq, son of Zahir."

Abdullah fell silent for a moment, then he smiled with pleasure. It was the first smile Anwar had ever seen on his face. Then he said, "Perfect. More perfect than perfect. I'll be back soon." He set off for his house, and this time he managed to leave the field without returning to ask another question. He was moving quickly, running, almost flying like a butterfly, dodging plants and slipping down dirt paths, leaping over puddles and muddy irrigation canals.

Abdullah was excited, and his excitement had stoked up his appetite. He went straight to the kitchen as soon as he got home. He put the teapot on the stove, then spread butter and sugar over half a pitta and poured what was left of the previous night's dinner onto a plate. He carried everything to the salon, where the tools were where he had left them and the white stone was waiting for him on its tile, lacking only the letter "S" on one side. He scratched it into it as he ate his breakfast. Then he began looking for some thick white thread like Sameeha wore round her neck to pass through the hole so it would become a necklace ready to be given and worn. He could not find any white thread in the house, so he unpicked some from his blanket. Now he needed a box or special bag to present the necklace in. Because such things were rare in his house, he dug out the relics of his childhood and found among them a small cloth bag containing bracelets made of soft beads and a small wooden box with Damascene engravings in which his adoptive mother Maryam had stored his baby teeth. He put them in the cloth bag with the bracelets, blew the dust off the wooden box, wiped it with the edge of his sleeve, and put the stone necklace inside.

Abdullah went out again, moving just as rapidly as before, singing to himself as he went. When he came to his field, he showed Anwar the box and told him, "Look. Send this to her with some child you trust."

Baffled, Anwar took it. He turned it over in his hands. "Open it," Abdullah said.

Anwar took out the white stone heart and touched it gently with his finger, as though it were a real heart. He traced the two etched initials with his fingertip, and Abdullah explained their meaning.

"It's truly beautiful," said Anwar. "But what message should I send with this gift?"

"Not a word! She'll know that this stone heart says in silence what you are unable to say with words."

Anwar embraced Abdullah. "Thank you, uncle."

"There's no need to use such terms of respect with me. Call me Abdullah or Kafka."

Anwar wrapped the thread around the necklace and put it back into the small box, closing its lid. They remained there in silence for a moment, staring at each other and smiling.

"Now go," Abdullah told him, "and don't come back until you are sure it has reached her."

"Now?"

"Yes. Don't let an opportunity for love pass you by. Don't repeat the mistakes I made!"

"And the field?"

"The field is permanent, but love is fleeting. Go! There isn't any field in the world more important, more beautiful or more fertile than the field of love. It demands more tending, but from it you'll reap the richest harvest."

Anwar went over to the shed to change his clothes while Abdullah sat down by the irrigation canal and lit a cigarette, one that tasted better than any he had smoked before. As Anwar was leaving, he brought Abdullah a pot of tea, saying, "It's still warm. I prepared it just a little while ago."

Abdullah thanked him and said, "Now go. Warm up your spirits, young hero, and go!"

Anwar set off quickly, running, almost flying like a butterfly, dodging plants and slipping down dirt paths between the trees, leaping over puddles and muddy canals, his mood matching Abdullah's that morning.

The widow Amira's reply to her neighbour Qisma was positive – enthusiastic, even. She was excited by the prospect of being related by marriage to this sheikh family. It would be an honour. But she warned Qisma that it would not be easy to arrange. First it would be necessary to discuss the matter with the two young people. She did not know whether her son was ready for marriage yet, or whether he was already in love with another girl, for she had noticed recently the increased care he was taking with his clothes and his hair, and the way he was listening to music. They agreed that Amira would broach the subject with her son and try to persuade him, and that Qisma would approach Sameeha.

When Anwar's little sister, the infant messenger, entered the courtyard of the house, she saw Salma scrubbing a dress in a washtub, squatting in a way that revealed the soft skin of her legs. Anwar was watching from afar, hidden behind a fig tree. His heart was beating violently. The girl gave Salma the box, saying, "This is for you. It's from Anwar. My brother Anwar, son of Sabry."

She came back at a run, just as Anwar had instructed her, while, breathless with tension, he waited to see Salma's reaction. He saw her open the box and take out the necklace. Her mouth fell open as she turned it over in her fingers. Then she closed her fist around it and pressed her fist to her chest as she sank back onto the ground. At that, Anwar came out from behind the fig tree. He took his sister in his arms and ran off home with her. From time to time he kissed her and thanked her, urging her to keep quiet about what had happened, saying it was a secret between the two of them and she must not mention it to anyone.

When he had dropped his sister off at their home, Anwar returned to the field to look for Abdullah, who was still sitting there, smoking, having drunk the entire pot of tea. Anwar gave Abdullah a detailed account of all that had happened. "You're sure she pressed the necklace to her chest?" Abdullah said.

"Yes."

"Then rest easy. That delicate stone heart has the power to soften human hearts." He added with a wink, "Ask the man of experience, not the sage." Then he got up, patted Anwar on the shoulder and left.

As for Salma, as soon as she had caught her breath after the surprise, she got up and went inside, looking for her mother. She found her in the kitchen, and without a word led her by the arm into their bedroom. Having closed the door and sat her mother down beside her on the edge of the bed, Salma silently offered her the box.

Sameeha gasped the instant she opened it, reaching unconsciously for the almost identical necklace at her breast, as though to make sure that the one in the box wasn't hers. She lifted it out from beneath her dress and took it off, placing the new one beside it to compare them. They were exactly alike, with the exception that the new one was a little more delicate and a brighter white. She knew without doubt that the same person had made them both – the love of her life, Abdullah.

With difficulty, her throat tight and parched, she whispered, "Who is this from?"

"From Anwar, son of Sabry. He sent his little sister to give it to me."

Her mother's first thought was that this must be a plan of Abdullah's devising, conceived out of love for her, confirmation that he wanted her as much as she wanted him, for why else would he want her daughter to be married if not to allow them to marry too? She wept tears of joy when she saw the tears glittering in her daughter's eyes. They embraced.

"What did she say?"

"Nothing. Just that this was for me from her brother. Then she ran away."

"How long have you had a relationship with the boy?"

"I've never had a relationship with him. I don't know anything about him beyond what everyone knows – that he is a good, unfortunate young man, who works to provide for his mother and his siblings."

"And polite, a good Muslim, bashful, and with a heart as white as this one," her mother added, pointing to the new necklace, which was still in her hand. She separated the strands of the white thread and hung it around her daughter's neck. Then she turned her round to examine her with pleasure. "How beautiful it looks on you!" She wiped the last of the tears from her daughter's cheeks, then from her own, and smiled at her. Her daughter returned the smile, and they embraced again.

"At last I have a necklace like yours. How I have dreamed of one my whole life! Maybe even since I was an infant nursing at your breast."

"I hope the matter does not stop with a necklace, but rather that your fate will include the one who gave it to you."

"Do you think that will happen?"

"The only opinion that matters is yours. I will support whatever decision you make."

"What should I do?"

"Meet with him, talk with him, get to know him – and then decide."

"How?"

"I'll take you to him this evening myself. We'll go together to Abdullah's field where he works."

At five o'clock that afternoon they went down from the village in the direction of the fields. They had both put on the same perfume, and they wore similar dresses that they had bought at the last Eid, turquoise blue and decorated with small flowers. Both also wore a green shawl and their stone necklace. Just as their preparations had been festive, so too was their journey to meet their two men; with trembling hearts, intertwined hands, they were more like two friends or sisters confiding in one another than mother and daughter. It was not necessary for the mother to say to her daughter, "Open your heart to him," for the daughter's heart had opened the moment she had set eyes on the stone necklace just like the one she had dreamed about her whole life and had sensed the chance to live a true love story like her mother's, which she had talked about for so long. "Some women choose a man for the depth of his pockets," she had said, "and others choose a man for the size of his heart. You and I are the second kind."

Before they reached Abdullah's field, the mother said, "Men are more embarrassed and obedient than women at first, so conduct the encounter however you want. Ask him anything you want to know. Most often, it's the woman who decides that a relationship should burst to life out of nothing."

They approached the shed in the middle of the field. They saw a man with his back to them sitting on the edge of one of the irrigation canals. Even before he turned towards them, they knew that it was Abdullah. Cigarette smoke rose in a cloud above his head. He got to his feet with lightning agility and covered the distance between them with surprising speed. The daughter resembled her mother so closely she was like a copy stamped from the original. She was the very image of her mother in her youth. She greeted him politely, "Good evening, uncle," and he wanted to seize her in his arms and press her to his chest. He wanted to address her, "O my daughter," for he felt as though she truly were his daughter, this daughter of his soul's beloved, who resembled her mother so closely that there was no trace of her biological father in her features.

"Where is Anwar?" the mother asked.

"In the shed, making tea."

"Go in to him," she said to her daughter.

The daughter moved forward with slow confident steps, buoyed by the faith in herself that her mother had instilled in her.

The mother remained standing behind her, urging her on with her glances until she went inside. Then they sat down, she and Abdullah, where he had been sitting before, and she asked him, "Oh my! How did you think up this plan, my love?"

"It wasn't my plan, but rather the plan of destiny, or 'fate and decree', as Ibrahim used to say."

"I mean, how did you convince him?"

"I didn't convince him of anything. He has been in love with her for two years."

"Really?"

"Yes. All I did was to help him dig the irrigation canal to channel this torrent of fate. My love for you led me to ask him if he had ever been in love, just as it gave me the idea for a new stone necklace."

She stared into his eyes until the tears glimmered in her own. "I love you so much, Abdullah."

"And I do not just love you, Sameeha – you give meaning to my existence."

She wrapped her arm around his neck, drew him close and kissed his cheek. Then she said, "You have to trim that beard – better shave the whole thing off."

"I'll do whatever you ask of me." He took her hand, kissed it, and went on speaking. "For a long time, I have not been able to distinguish between dreams and reality. Right now I can't believe that this is not a dream." He brought his arm close to her and said, "Pinch me. Pinch me so I know this is real."

A mischievous impulse gripped her. She swooped down upon his arm with her mouth and bit it until he cried out. They laughed. When her daughter's face appeared at the small window of the shed to find out what was happening, Sameeha smiled to indicate that all was well, then gestured to her to get back to what she was doing. Sameeha and Abdullah continued to talk for almost an hour, all the while expecting a pot of tea to emerge from the shed. Among the things Sameeha told Abdullah was how "parents think they define their children's future, while the truth is that we give our children their beginnings and they fashion our endings. That's our situation now, you and I: two old people sitting and waiting for our future to be decided by the choices of these two youngsters."

Abdullah smiled. "So let's chivvy them along then. We don't have as much time left for our love as they do." He turned to the shed and called out, "Where's the tea, my boy?"

Anwar came hurrying out, carrying a pot of tea in one hand and two cups in the other. Embarrassed, he offered them to Abdullah and stammered, "I'm sorry, uncle! Sorry! I forgot."

"I know. But listen: how many times have I reminded you not to call me 'uncle'? Don't worry, I'll forgive you – but only when you marry her!" Abdullah fell silent for a moment and then added, "My daughter, that is. When you marry my daughter."

"The matter is in her hands."

"Then get back in there! And do everything in your power to persuade her. Beseech her, if you must. Kiss her feet, even. There's no shame in that. Indeed, it's an honour for a man to kiss the feet of his woman. Napoleon himself did that."

When Sameeha and Salma returned home, hand in hand once more, the mother said to her daughter, "Well, tell me."

"I love him, Mother."

CHAPTER 20

Tension and Release

The four of them continued to meet in Abdullah's field every evening. Sometimes the younger couple would talk in the shed while the older two sat by the irrigation canal; other times, the opposite happened. They created for themselves a private world, a small, happy world, cut off from the chaos, violence and tragedies that dominated their country. They said it was their right after all they had suffered.

Abdullah proposed that the two young people live with them in his house after the wedding, if they wanted, but Anwar and Salma had already decided that they would live with his widowed mother and his younger siblings, who they would help to raise and look after. Salma loved Anwar's devotion to his family, just as she loved the idea of living with a new family that would become her own, fulfilling an only child's dream of being surrounded at last by laughter and mischief.

It was clear that their love could not remain confined to their private world forever. Abdullah proposed that he raise the prospect of the two weddings with Tariq, while Salma said that she would have to talk with Qisma, who had recently been urging her to get married, suggesting the names of some young men from the village and beyond, including the son of the widow Amira, and offering to handle all the arrangements. Perhaps it would be better to speak to Qisma first, if Tariq was likely to object, since it was whispered in the village that her word was now his law. They drank endless cups of tea as they discussed the matter, so much that the teapot turned completely black from being set so many times in the coals. They agreed at last that they would do both. First, Salma would inform Qisma, her uncle's wife and her childhood friend; after that, Abdullah would talk with his own lifelong friend.

Not one of them imagined that Sheikh Tariq would start dancing on the other end of the line when Qisma called to give him the news, and that he would rush over to her house to embrace her. He lifted her in the air and spun her around the salon. After putting her down, he danced around again, forgetting for a moment that he was in the house of his friend, the slaughtered Ibrahim, for whose body they were still searching. And if Qisma's explanation for this explosion of joy was that he had found the key to fulfilling Sayyid Jalal al-Din's request to meet Abdullah, and he would at last be freed from the expense of his sister and niece's upkeep, the real reason could be found in Tariq's youth, in the guilt he felt at persuading his father to refuse the match the first time round, resulting in so much torment for them both.

Nevertheless, pragmatism soon resurfaced at the forefront of Tariq's mind. When Abdullah spoke with him about the matter, asking for the hands of both mother and daughter, he agreed and expressed his happiness – indeed, his joy – and promised to take care of all the necessary expenses, but on one condition: that Abdullah meet Sayyid Jalal al-Din first.

Abdullah's reaction surprised the family members present,

who thought of him as a calm person. He stiffened like someone stung by a scorpion. "Fuck you and fuck this sheikh of yours!" he screamed in rage.

Then he made to leave, as Tariq yelled back, "Why are you always as stubborn as a goat, brother?"

Abdullah turned round in the doorway and replied just as loudly, "And why are you always as fickle and acrobatic as a monkey, brother?"

Silence fell. Anxiety, fear, anger and apprehension filled the room, and the two friends did not speak again for two whole days. Qisma tried to think of a solution, while Sameeha resolved to see Abdullah in secret to find out what had angered him so. She was eaten up by anxiety, faced with the collapse of this great joy for her and her daughter. Her heart hurt more for her daughter, who had never suffered a disappointment like this before. Tired of waiting for a second sleepless night to drag by, she got up a little before dawn to head to Abdullah's house in the dark. He surprised her by opening the door at her first knock, a cigarette in hand. She could tell that he had not slept either, and as soon as he closed the door behind her, she threw herself into his arms. He held her in a long powerful embrace until they had both calmed down a little.

"What's going on, Abdullah?" she asked him. "And who is this man that Tariq has made it a condition that you meet?"

Abdullah took a turn around the room, scratching his head in thought. He kicked the cushions on the floor as he went, and from time to time struck the wall with his fist. Then he stopped in the middle of the salon and said, "You need to hear a secret that no-one in the world knows apart from me and that shit they call Sayyid Jalal. It's your right to know the truth so that your decision to marry me is an informed one."

Abdullah fell silent and lit another cigarette. Sameeha stood in front of him, waiting and looking into his eyes, until he said, "I'm a bastard, and the man who seduced my mother is this Sayyid Jalal al-Shit, the son of the old mayor, who is long dead and buried. My mother was Zakiya, sister of our dull-witted herdsman. They grew up as orphans in the mayor's care after their parents drowned when they were young. They were a year or two younger than the mayor's first-born son, Jalal, and when Zakiya reached the age of seventeen he raped her. As soon as the pregnancy began to show, Hajja Zaynab, the wife of the mayor, found out what had happened. She informed the mayor, and he sought the counsel of your father. Your father was complicit in everything that unfolded. They confined my mother to a storeroom under the house until she bore me and named me Qamar. Then they killed her, claiming that they had married her off to a distant relative or a wandering Bedouin. They expelled Jalal from the village, and he crossed into Iran, where he joined the opposition, allowing him to return and obtain a position of power after the fall of the regime. As for me, they left me to be found by a poor and barren couple who became my parents: my mother, Maryam, and my father, Salih. Hajja Zaynab told me all of this when I came back from captivity. She died the next day."

Abdullah was crying as he told the story. He sobbed and wiped away the tears, saying, "That's the short version of the story. Tariq knows nothing of this, nor anyone else."

Abdullah broke down in bitter tears, his whole body shaking. Sameeha too was crying and trembling. They remained like that for a moment, standing apart and crying with their heads bowed. It was as though they were looking down at the body of a loved one lying between them. Then, without warning, Sameeha leaped towards Abdullah and embraced him. She began raining kisses upon him, on his eyes, his beard, his nose, his mouth – wherever her mouth landed. His face, his chest, his shoulders and his hands were all smeared with tears.

"So much pain for one soul to carry, my love. I understand you better now, and I love you all the more. I will never abandon you. I will be mother, doctor and wife to you. We will get married in spite of them. Indeed, we will get married here and now, right away. No-one, no matter who he is, will separate us after today, even if they force us to flee the village and the country – or even the world, all the way to hell. From now on, when it's just the two of us, I will not call you by any name other than the one your mother chose for you: Qamar."

Qisma had managed to persuade Tariq of a new plan: that they agree to the two marriages and give them a week to prepare everything necessary for their wedding. In the meantime, Qisma and Tariq would return to Baghdad, meet Sayyid Jalal al-Din and let him know how Abdullah had reacted, putting the matter once more in his hands. Perhaps they would be able to persuade Jalal to come to the village and attend the wedding himself, the thought never crossing their minds that Abdullah might go so far as to attack Sayyid Jalal, turning the wedding into a funeral that would draw the wrath of the government and invite retribution on the whole village.

Tariq thanked her for providing a solution yet again. He wrapped his arm around her waist, drew her towards him, and rubbed his body suggestively against hers. She peeled his arm off her, and moved away, saying, "Leave all that for now, and go to Abdullah yourself. Ease his mind. Let him know you are happy to bless the weddings without any conditions, and whatever you do, don't mention the name Sayyid Jalal al-Din. Give him some money in case he needs it, and I'll give some to Sameeha and her daughter. Pick a night for the wedding – sometime next week. Then you and I will set off for Baghdad early tomorrow morning. I don't want a lifelong friendship like yours to be severed for any reason whatsoever. You, Abdullah and my father were the Sons of the Earth Crack."

They took ten members of their bodyguard with them, travelling in two cars, one driving ahead of them and one bringing up the rear. Naturally, none of Tariq's sons were among them. He left behind his oldest son Zahir in the village, not only so that he could serve as his deputy but also to keep him far away from the ever-present danger of kidnapping and murder in the capital – and to keep him from seeing how his father interacted with Qisma when he was away from the village. Qisma had noticed her stepson's antipathy towards her during the party's inauguration. His sour glances, the sullen tone of his replies to her and his habit of avoiding her and focusing only on his father, showing obedience towards him while ignoring Qisma's minor requests, made it all too clear.

As they drove, Qisma asked Tariq how his meeting with Abdullah had gone. He informed her that, true to form, Abdullah had not changed his mind and did not appear likely to do so after the wedding, despite his genuine and rather touching joy at the prospect of marrying Sameeha. He had also gathered that Abdullah had no intention of fathering any children once he was wed. In the course of their conversation he had repeated what Tariq referred to as his pessimistic mutterings, such as "We are nothing more than fertiliser for the earth. Some of us sprout to produce yet more fertiliser, believing that we prolong our existence, when actually we are just keeping the soil fertilised. Of course, the earth couldn't care less about us, whether we exist or not. Indeed, we damage it more than we benefit it. To tell the truth, the one thing that we prolong is death, for if we all passed out of existence, death too would be extinct."

When Tariq had tried to converse with him using the language of religion, which he knew so well, Abdullah had asked, "What do you want, Tariq? This world or the next?"

"Both. This world and the next. Everything. Why not?"

"But you use religion for worldly goals and purposes."

"What is your objection? Isn't religion here to serve and benefit mankind? It's a means to ensure the happiness of mankind, not an end in itself. It's the path leading to happiness in this world and the next."

"For my part, I am with the great al-Shafi'i, who pointed to the verse, 'By time itself, mankind is uttely lost,' and said, 'If God had sent down only this verse, it would have been enough for people.'"

"Why this insistence on loss alone, ignoring things like prosperity, success and victory? All living creatures seek their daily bread, and they compete to get more of it. All except you.

Look around you at what people do. They strive and exploit and compete with one other to secure an advantage. Don't you realise that the entire country has turned into a jungle?"

"Even if the country has turned into a jungle, that doesn't mean that you should turn into an animal."

After Tariq had relayed to Qisma the rest of his conversation with Abdullah, he concluded by saying, "I honestly don't know. Sometimes I feel that his view is correct, that he's right. And sometimes I feel that my view is the one that's right."

The military checkpoints that punctuated the highway were less of a nuisance now. They would skip the lines of cars waiting for the humiliating inspection. The guards in the first car drove straight to the front, flashed their party badges, and told the soldiers in a haughty and intimidating tone that they were leading a convoy of important dignitaries. Those manning the checkpoint would invariably wave them straight through. Sometimes the soldiers and police officers would salute as Tariq and Qisma's car drove past.

"Leave all that for now," Qisma told Tariq. "Abdullah knows what suits him, just as we know what suits us. And one thing I think suits us is putting the advice of your friend, Sheikh Tafir, into practice. That we too should look for a spiritual symbol to consecrate. In our village, there is nothing religious or spiritual except the mosque."

"What should we do then? Should we carve out images for the people from stone, or else from dates, for them to worship and then eat, just as the idolaters did before the blessing of Islam came and they turned to God?"

"No, of course not. And please don't make fun of me. Maybe if we give it some serious thought, we'll find a solution."

Qisma fell silent for a while, then she said, "Perhaps we could do exactly what he did with that anonymous grave."

"And who's to say that the stories that the people of Tafir's village tell each other about that grave aren't true! That some people really saw light emanating from it, and some were healed by virtue of its blessings. That grave may really belong to a godly saint. Perhaps it belongs to some foreign sufi who died while passing through."

"Regardless of the truth of the matter, it's just a grave, and we have two cemeteries in our village. They contain hundreds of graves. We can choose one and create a legend around it." Qisma fell silent. She swallowed, then took a risk and said, "It could be, for instance, the grave of my father's head."

"God forbid!" Tariq cried in dismay, shuddering. "God forgive us! Impossible! Have you gone mad, woman? How can you dare think such a thing? Seek God's forgiveness for what you have thought and said, woman, and never speak of such a thing again."

When Qisma found that he was truly angry, she hastened to soothe him. "Alright, alright. May God forgive me! It was just a thought. Forget it. I never said it. Let's consider the other issue now: the necessity of founding a military force, a militia, even if it's just a small one, just as Tafir has and all the other parties, tribes, and so on."

"Ugh! It's playing with fire, Qisma. I think it best that we content ourselves with the political party and what we are doing now through peaceful means. Let's not get tangled up in this arms race that's sweeping the country. We have our personal bodyguard. Isn't that enough?"

"Yes, it's fine if you want to remain small and weak – on the margins. The truly powerful won't invite us into their game and let us have a share. If you're not a wolf yourself, the wolves will eat you, and we're in the jungle now, just as you told Abdullah."

Hearing this, Tariq remembered what Qisma had said on their previous journey about her desire to eat Iraq, and it struck him suddenly how far down that road they had already travelled. "No, I'm not convinced," he said. "And I would caution you that anyone who wants to eat Iraq will end up being eaten, while Iraq will remain undigested. Look back through history. It's full of the demise of people who tried that. I don't want to get further entangled in all this, for he who lives by the sword dies by it too. I fear that having started out with the intention of searching for your father's body, we'll end up like him: severed heads, cut off by who knows who, and bodies that will never be found."

Qisma's own anger was aroused by the mention of her father. "You're a coward, Tariq," she said sharply.

Tariq realised what had provoked her anger. He sought to mollify her by lightening the mood. "Yes, maybe I'm a coward, and maybe not, but I prefer not to call it cowardice, as you do, and instead to describe it as wisdom. Every creature develops its own way of protecting itself, and I've developed my intelligence. It's worked well for me, and the proof is that I'm still alive, and that I'm the most successful of my generation among the village's sons. The proof also lies in you, now that you're mine, my priceless treasure," said Tariq, winking at her.

Along the way, they passed by car crashes, a burning checkpoint that had been blown up by a suicide bomber, and ambulances carrying fresh corpses from the day's bloodletting. Each time, Qisma would insist on getting out in case her enquiries led her to a corpse without a head. The third time she came back seething with anger after seeing five corpses, including a woman whose breasts had been blown off, and the man who had carried out the attack. She got into the car beside Tariq and slammed the door violently, heedless of her child sleeping in the back seat.

After they had driven for a while in silence, she reached the climax of her wrath and exploded, shouting, "Humans. What savages!" Then she spat out the window with the utmost disgust and said, "I'll get my revenge. I'll fuck his mother."

She fell silent again and heaved a deep sigh. Then she burst out laughing at what she had said. Tariq relaxed and laughed along with her.

"What crime has his poor mother committed?" he said. "If you're going to fuck anyone, let it be me!"

CHAPTER 21

Love and a Kidnapping

They arrived at noon. Sabriya and Sabir prepared lunch, while the members of their team reported on their progress since the inauguration. Bara had received the first issue of the journal from the printers, his brother Rahib had finished building a covered passageway that ran from an opening he made in the kitchen to the unoccupied house of their absent neighbours who had emigrated, and Wafa had organised all the records after the many names, addresses and phone numbers of those who had attended the inauguration had been added. Because Qisma and Tariq were hungry, they decided that they would continue the meeting over lunch, and Sabir had to find an extra table and ten chairs for the members of their bodyguard.

The first thing they did after sitting down to eat was look over the journal, which pleased them very much. On the front page were large photographs of Tariq and Qisma at the inauguration with headlines in large type describing them as the two sheikhs; inside there were many more photographs from the celebration and quotations from those who had cared to comment. Everyone agreed that the most beautiful photograph was that of Hamid the Snorer in his military uniform at the moment he was awarded the medal by General Adam. Part of Tariq wished that

Bara had put it on the first page, though at the same time, he did not want his own photograph to be any smaller than it was. The next section of the journal had been filled with such material as Bara had seen fit: cultural and literary essays, translations, his poetic texts, poems by his friends, and an article about contemporary poetry in Australia. Tariq and Qisma were surprised to find that most of this content was attributed to Rahib. When they asked him why, it turned out he knew nothing about it. Everyone laughed, and Bara said, "Didn't I say I would do this? Look here: the cooking section is under the name of Sabriya, and the article criticising the Ministry of Culture for neglecting monuments and statues is under the name of Sabir."

The laughter increased whenever he showed them something new, for no-one had taken the time to read through the journal yet, although bundles of copies were stacked in all corners of the house. Bara went on: "Here's a piece by Wafa that proposes the refitting of school libraries and the greater promotion of literacy in the curriculum. A piece by Abdullah Kafka about the dangers of philosophy's marginalisation in the world. And then there are some authors' names I just made up." Turning to the bodyguards' table, he said, "Don't you worry, you'll have pieces under your names in upcoming issues." Pointing at each of them in turn, since he did not yet know their names, he said, "Your article, for example, will be about suicide bombers targeting markets in working-class areas. Yours will be about the liquidation of scholars, cultural elites, university professors and judges. Yours will be on the nuances of kidnapping. You will write about financial and administrative corruption in all the offices of state, and you will write about the crooked weapons deals that the authorities are making, resulting in those faulty bomb detection devices."

Everyone laughed and praised the ingenuity behind his efforts. Tariq asked him for something he had long been dreaming of: space in future editions that he could fill with religious material and ideas about social issues, and even with literary essays about books he had read in his youth and still kept stored away in boxes in his house in the village.

Rahib said that the distributor, after a long negotiation, had agreed to accept just a quarter of the cover price as its share, which was a good deal since the other distributors would not accept less than fifty or sixty per cent.

Wafa confirmed that the response to the journal had been positive. Indeed, the Americans and some government ministries had offered to buy advertising space and a hundred copies of the current issue if they agreed not to criticise them in future editions.

"Oh," said Qisma. "That's excellent. That might be a way to cover the costs of the journal and even turn a profit from it. In the future, perhaps we'll be able to start a radio station or a satellite television channel, like those who have real money behind them have done."

After lunch they set off, with Rahib leading the way, through the passageway he had constructed joining Qisma's home to the house next door. This was something Qisma had told him to do, ignoring Tariq's objections. She said that the house belonged to an important officer in the intelligence services of the former regime, who had fled abroad with his family the moment the regime fell. Since it was common for new officials to take possession of the houses of those they had replaced, and since most of the new parties had taken over the offices of the now defunct ruling party, she could see no reason for them not to do the same.

As soon as they emerged in the neighbouring house, Rahib began to explain how he had divided it up, with the first floor given over to sleeping quarters and the ground floor designated as office space. Pointing to signs he had hung on the doors of the rooms that said things like SECURITY FORCE and SECRETARY, he said, "This is the guards' office, and here is Wafa's. 'Media Director' is Bara's office, and 'Internal Affairs' is Sabir and Sabriya's office." He concluded by pointing to the door of the largest room, upon which he had hung a sign saying HIS EXCELLENCY, THE DIRECTOR GENERAL. "And this is my office."

Everyone laughed, and no-one raised any objection. "You absolutely deserve that," Qisma said, patting his shoulder.

Then he pointed to the door of a small room under the stairs. "We'll talk about that one later on. As for the upper floor, there's a kitchen and some bedrooms: one for me, one for Bara, another for Sabir and Sabriya, and four for the guards."

"Sabir and Sabriya will continue to sleep in our house," said Qisma, "so they can be close to the child at all times."

What Rahib did not report, naturally, was something that only he had picked up on, for few details escaped him, and that was that a romantic attachment had formed between his brother Bara and the secretary, Wafa. Rahib had noticed it when they first started working together in the same office, struck by their constant affectionate chatter and willing cooperation. Every time he walked past the door he wondered if he would surprise them in the act of kissing among the filing cabinets. Even though he was someone who desired every woman he saw, including the madame sheikh, he was truly delighted that his brother was showing a liking for a woman, for that would keep him sober and clean. It was possible it would lead him to mend his ways altogether; he might even marry her and return to the village.

On the drive to Nakhila Village and back, they had sat side by side in the car, talking the whole way, though they were careful to stick to topics connected with work. Likewise, on the night of the inauguration, Wafa was the only person Bara told that he was going to look for Abdullah Kafka, which was how Rahib learned where he was and was able to collect him at dawn. For most of the trip back, he slept on Wafa's shoulder.

When the others learned of this burgeoning relationship, they did not find anything strange about it, for one of the characteristics of love is that it can resemble a magnetic force, in that opposites attract and similar characters can repel. This scruffy, rake-thin poet found in this chubby, mild-tempered, traditionally-minded city girl something he had not found in any of the other women he had met since moving to the capital, whether they were his classmates at university or the rebellious poets he had befriended. He found Wafa to be more accepting, more understanding and more compassionate. There was something motherly about her that he found himself responding to. When he asked her why she was so tolerant of his drinking and his occasional coarse expressions even though she wore the hijab, and why she did not badger him to give up alcohol, as most people he knew did, other than those who shared his addiction, she told him that she had grown up surrounded by bottles of wine, books, poets and dreamers, because her father had belonged to a secular movement on the far left. But he had not tried to dissuade her from taking up religion, praying and wearing the hijab when she had decided to follow that path. On the contrary, when she had accompanied him to one of their gatherings wearing the hijab, and some of his friends had mocked her for it, critical of him for accepting it in his own home, her father had abandoned the group, whose comradeship had shaped his life from his youth. He had responded angrily, saying, "I thought our first principle was tolerance, that we refused to impose our beliefs on others. It seems that we are no better than the racists, the sectarians, the nationalists and the religious bigots."

That was the last he saw of them. From that day onwards, Wafa watched her father drink more and more, and gradually wither away, deaf to his doctors' pleas that he give up drinking, which was ruining his liver. It was not just the alcohol that was killing him, but a broken heart, for his friends had expelled him from their movement and barred him from writing in their journal. They even managed to get him fired from his humble job as a pensions administrator, and not one of them ever visited or called him. He felt his life had been spent in vain, and he confined himself to the house, giving free rein to his beard and drowning himself in drink and despair until at last he died.

"There's nothing more painful for a child," Wafa told Bara, "than to see her father a broken man. But he was a good father. He never made a distinction between me and my brothers in the way he treated us. He never prevented me from reading any book, from talking about any subject, or from making my own decisions. Honestly, he had more truth and sincerity in one finger than could be found in the hearts of all his former friends combined."

Bara told her how his classmates who wore the hijab and his religious friends would always show him more respect and kindness when he was drunk than his companions who would spend all night drinking with him, and far more than the people who used to kick him as he slept under the freedom monument. When he opened his eyes he would see that they were wearing ties, but when he opened his eyes and found a plate of food near his head, he would see a man in religious dress looking down at him. Even in the cultured university environment, he experienced prejudice against him because he was a rural child of the provinces. Everyone had treated him superciliously, including the occupying Americans when he had worked for them. He stood with her, therefore, in her rejection of hypocrisy and narcissism, and her love of sincerity, no matter how different they were from one another.

They shared many long discussions like this, some of them in the presence of Rahib, who did not take part in them and paid less attention to what they were saying than to their tones of voice and the emotional charge behind their words. From those conversations of theirs, Rahib learned for the first time that his brother had travelled outside the country, to Paris, of all places. When Wafa had asked him why he did not think about emigrating like so many other poets and intellectuals, he replied, "Yes, I did once make a trip, taking up an invitation to a poetry festival in Paris.

I could have torn up my passport and stayed there, but I had no love for that city. It was bigger and grander than it needed to be, and I felt myself crushed within it, lost. I'm a poet, and the self is the most important thing to me. Cities like Paris wipe out the 'I'; they crush it. The buildings, for example, are made from massive blocks of stone, impossible for a person to lift by himself. Here, on the other hand, houses are made from bricks fired in bread ovens. They are old, lowly, full of spirits, so that I, to my great happiness, feel that I am able to move them, or tear them down and rebuild them the next day. I felt not so much a vagabond there as a beggar. Here, I feel that I embody the souls of poets and vagabonds, from back before *A Thousand and One Nights* and on through today. The existence of people like me is necessary to preserve a spirit of individual rebellion while all around us they try to transform society into a flock of identical sheep. Baghdad needs me; Paris doesn't. It can't tell my presence from my absence."

That night, Tariq was kidnapped. It was a simple, surgical operation, like the thousands of other kidnappings that had taken place since the fall of the regime and the beginning of the occupation. Some victims were returned home safely after their families agreed to pay an exorbitant ransom, selling all they possessed. The corpses of others who were not so fortunate were thrown into rubbish heaps, into rivers, into gardens, along the sides of roads heading out of the city, onto pavements or into public spaces. And some were never seen or heard from again.

When Qisma woke up, she did not find him beside her in bed or on the balcony where he was accustomed to sit in the morning.

Nor in the bathroom, the garden or the kitchen. He was not to be found anywhere in the two houses connected by the tunnel-like passageway. She called his mobile, and it rang in the place he had left it, on the dressing table in the bedroom. She put the two houses on a state of high alert when it became clear that no-one had seen him since dinner the previous evening. Various wild possibilities were competing in Qisma's mind when a communication from the kidnappers confirmed what had happened. Calling from an unknown number, they warned her not to make any fuss, assuring her that they would release him as soon as they came to an understanding with him on several matters.

When Qisma asked, "Who are you?", they told her, "We are the correctors. We rectify wrongdoing." Then they hung up.

Tariq only realised that the person speaking to him was real and not a nightmare, as he had thought at first, when he found himself pressed between two powerful bodies in the back seat of a car, blindfolded and gagged with wide pieces of tape. His arms were tied behind his back. He had been sleeping when the pieces of tape had been placed over his eyes and mouth with remarkable speed – a matter of mere seconds – and then they had lifted him lightly and silently, still between wakefulness and sleep. He thought that he was dreaming, under the power of Satan's whispers, so he took the measures he had practised since childhood, turning his face towards his left shoulder and spitting three times, if only symbolically, and saying, "I seek refuge in God from Satan, the accursed." Then he would roll over to sleep on his right side, as the prophets slept.

The strips of tape were ripped from his eyes and mouth, and he cried out from the intense pain. He felt as though his eyebrows, moustache and beard had been torn away, if not the skin of his face. He found himself shut up in a small, dark, empty room, with three masked people in front of him. The one in the middle spoke first. "Listen, sheikh. We're willing to cut a deal with you. Your life in exchange for his."

That was the only time they honoured him with the title "sheikh", for he categorically refused their demand when they explained whose life it was they wished to take: "Your friend, Sheikh Tafir."

"Impossible," Tariq had said. "I would never do such a thing."

"It could be as simple as slipping him poison that wouldn't kill him until a few days later, by which time you would be far away from him," the man said, but Tariq stared implacably back at him and shook his head.

Eventually they tired of their attempts to persuade him, which was when the torture began, accompanied as is traditional by threats against his life and the lives of his family. With the first blow, Tariq felt something he had never felt before, an entire inversion of his feelings, his thoughts, his being and his life. For this was the first blow he had received in his entire life. He had been born and had flourished as the pampered son of a respected, venerable village sheikh, until the time had come for him to be named sheikh in his father's place. Moreover, despite the violence, oppression, wars, sanctions and chaos that had surrounded him for years and affected everyone he knew, none of it had touched him. He had not served in the army, he had never been in a fight, whether with harsh words or with fists. He was grateful for that situation, proud of it, proud of his ability to escape violence and to succeed without resorting to it. With the first blow, he felt everything crashing down in an instant, a negation of everything he had built and believed in. As they continued to curse him, to hit him, to kick him, to beat him with belts and cartridges, to spit upon him, to use a stick to poke his chest, his neck, his back and his backside, a feeling of impotence, isolation, terror and submission permeated Tariq. He was truly being tortured, though they were not torturing him as true torturers might. They told him they would set him free in exchange for taking a hostage from his family. But if he did not agree to their demands, the hostage's life would be forfeit. They also threatened that if he did not do as they said, they would kidnap members of his family, one after another, until he did.

When they called Qisma two days later, she could hear that the person talking to her was translating the words of someone nearby – someone speaking Farsi. They told her, "If you want your husband back, supply another hostage from among his close relatives, along with fifty thousand dollars. We will call you tomorrow to agree the details of the exchange."

Qisma was torn. What should she do? She paced around her bedroom like a caged cat. She thought about calling General Adam, Sheikh Tafir, or Sayyid Jalal al-Din. Or telling Tariq's family and Abdullah Kafka in the village in order to get their help with handling the situation. She thought that every call from her landline and even the mobile Jalal had given her might be monitored, that her house itself might be bugged. She called for Rahib and whispered to him, pretending not to notice that he took advantage of being so close to her to press yet closer, focusing instead on making him understand what she wanted from him, which was that he slip away, careful that no-one should see him, and buy a mobile for her from the market, even if it were stolen. Rahib was back within half an hour and attempted to press against her as closely as he had before. She pushed him away. "Go down and sit in the salon."

She closed the door of her room and called Sayyid Jalal al-Din. In a low, confused voice, she said, "It's Qisma. I need you urgently. As soon as possible and with absolute secrecy. I have to see you."

"Two o'clock tonight," he told her. "Wear men's clothing and go out the front gate of your neighbour's house. There will be a taxi waiting for you."

As soon as the call was over, Qisma wondered how he knew that she had taken possession of the house next door. But she did not dwell on this question for long, reminding herself that he was responsible for one of the most important security apparatuses in the country.

Qisma tried on Tariq's robes, but they were too big for her. She tried on some of her late husband's clothes and found that, although they fitted her body, the sleeves were too long and she did not have time to shorten them. As she tried to find something that would fit her, she spent a long time looking at herself in the mirror after putting on one of his military uniforms, which she had not planned on doing. Nevertheless, she liked very much the way it looked on her. She saw herself as a strong, beautiful and capable leader. Her desires became someone's command.

She put a beret on her head, which gave her an additional sense of power, especially when she noticed the Eagle of the Republic glinting on her forehead. She picked up the officer's baton, placed it under her arm and began to swagger about in front of the mirror. Then she held out the baton and began issuing orders to the pillows, the sheets, the dressing table and the chairs in a voice audible only to herself. She stabbed a pillow violently, upbraiding it, until she almost poked right through it.

Next Qisma put on her father's peasant robe and found that it fit her perfectly. She also tried on his only suit, the one he had bought for his wedding and had worn when he attended hers. It was as though it had been tailored for her. In it, she felt calm, filled with compassion and confidence. It covered her legs and chest better than the robe. Just in case she was kidnapped too.

CHAPTER 22

The Rescue Plan

Sayyid Jalal met Qisma in the dark garden of a magnificent house in the Karada district. Talking in the garden, he explained, was more secure, given that walls have ears. "Hidden microphones, that is," he went on with a smile, "and maybe even eyes in the form of cameras."

Jalal wore a white dishdasha, and in her father's suit Qisma appeared the more masculine of the two. Whispering so that the guards standing a few steps away could not hear him, and with his face nearly touching hers, Jalal told her, "You look even more beautiful and alluring in a man's suit."

"The dishdasha suits you too," she replied, "because it is a reminder of your origins."

They remained standing as she gave him the details of her predicament. Then he invited her to sit at one of the side tables in the darkest corner of the garden. "It's not easy to identify the kidnappers in a country where everyone kidnaps each other. We don't know their identity or their motives. We cannot guess how they will react if we try to play a game with them. We have no choice, therefore, but to comply with their demands."

"How?"

"It's less complicated than many of the cases of kidnapping

and murder I hear about every day. You do your part, and I'll do mine. I'll take care of the money, and you take care of providing someone from his family."

"But what will become of them?"

"We don't know what they're thinking or what they really want. Our only course of action is to comply with their demands. We'll take things one step at a time."

"It won't be a problem to find someone to exchange for him, for there are many who love him. All his sons would volunteer in an instant. Indeed, I would too, if I did not have a small child."

"Do you love him that much?" he asked, and there was something scornful, almost malevolent, in his tone.

"It's not how you might imagine. He was my father's lifelong friend, and they loved each other deeply. If my father were here, he would do that for Tariq's sake, and, had my father been kidnapped, I'm certain that Tariq would have done the same for him. I love their love for each other, as well as for their companion Abdullah Kafka. I do not want to see this magnificent friendship destroyed, even if the price of preserving it is that I offer myself instead. If it were not for the child, I mean."

"Wait a minute. Didn't you say you heard one of them speaking in Farsi?"

"Yes. The one talking to me was just translating his words. I'm sure of that – some words are very similar in the two languages."

"Excellent. In that case, I think I have an idea." He fell silent, lost in thought for a moment, then continued: "Persuade Abdullah Kafka to be the replacement hostage that they are asking for. I understand that he learned Farsi in his years of captivity, but they won't know that. With the help of the security agencies, we can plant a tiny chip under his skin, and hide a small microphone somewhere on his body. When they take him away, we will know where he is by means of the chip, and what they are saying by means of the microphone. Then we can send in a strike force to eliminate them and rescue him."

Before Qisma left, Jalal advised her to change her bodyguards, for what kind of guards were they if they could not say how the person they were guarding had been lifted from his own bedroom? Qisma wondered what to do. She had assumed they were trustworthy, having been selected from among the sons of the village, and that they knew how to use weapons, like all Iraqis. But it was clear to her that using weapons was one thing, and that being professionally trained to perform a military task with weapons was another. It would be good to appoint two professionals to take charge of their bodyguard and train them.

When Qisma returned home in the same taxi, she went straight to the neighbouring house and found one of the guards awake in the salon, watching television with his rifle beside him. She ordered him to go up to Rahib's room and wake him, but before he could move she stopped him, saying, "No, wait here. I'll go up to him myself."

When she went into his room, she thought at first that the bed was unmade and empty, for the covers were bunched up towards the middle. But when she drew them back, there was Rahib's short body, curled up in a foetal position, hugging his pillow. He jumped up and stood on the bed, right where he was. He made as if to hop down onto the floor, but she stopped him by pressing on his shoulder, cautioning him to silence with a finger against her lips. Rahib relaxed. It pleased him that he was standing as tall as she was, or only a little shorter. His face was almost level with her chest, and from his store of dreams and fantasies, it briefly occurred to him that her presence might be related to some secret, intimate affair. He had never forgotten that she was the only one who had defended him and described him as a man in front of everyone at Sheikh Tafir's house. What is more, she had not objected when he had pressed his body against hers that morning.

Rahib kept rubbing his eyes to make sure he was not dreaming, and when his eyes had got used to being open, he was surprised to find she was wearing a man's suit. He took a step back. When Qisma noticed his confusion, she picked up a cup of water from the table near the bed. She poured some of it into her hand and splashed Rahib's face with it. Passing him the cup, she said, "Drink this and sit down. I have something important I want you to do."

Rahib sat beside her on the edge of the bed. Qisma asked if he was fully awake. Rahib nodded, and Qisma said in a low voice, "I want you to go to our village and meet with Abdullah Kafka alone. Inform him of Sheikh Tariq's kidnapping, and tell him that the kidnappers have demanded a ransom of fifty thousand dollars and that someone close to Tariq be offered as a hostage in exchange for him. It seems that some of the kidnappers are Iranian. I heard them speaking Farsi. When I secretly informed the police, they suggested that it would be an advantage if the hostage that goes in exchange speaks Farsi. They plan to smuggle in a small microphone so they can listen in on the kidnappers and plan a rescue mission."

Rahib rubbed his eyes again. It all sounded like something from a film, and he was so excited by the prospect that he forgot about the thrill of being alone with a woman at night in his bedroom. "In order to finish waking up, I need a big cup of hot tea," he said.

They went to the kitchen. Rahib quickly made tea, and Qisma repeated the request to him in detail, emphasising the need for caution and absolute secrecy. She told him that he should take one of the cars and that she would assign three guards. He reassured her that he would carry out the task as quickly as he could and to the best of his considerable abilities. He would set off in two hours and be back with her before noon, Abdullah in tow. They would remain in contact in case of emergency.

Qisma warned him not to use his mobile or call hers. He should find another one and call her on the one that he had stolen for her that day.

"Excuse me, Madame Sheikh," Rahib said, "I didn't steal it. I bought it from a thief."

"It comes to the same thing. Someone stole it. Whatever, don't call unless it's absolutely necessary."

She went downstairs, still holding her cup of tea, which she had not drunk. She gave it to the guard at the bottom of the stairs and told him, "From now on, it's forbidden for guards to watch television when they are on duty. They should drink tea and coffee instead."

At the first light of dawn, Rahib's car entered the courtyard of Abdullah Kafka's house. Abdullah was standing outside, deciding where to go first – to his field or to the village café. Rahib got out of the car by himself and approached Abdullah, extending his powerful hand as he greeted him. "Good morning, Uncle Abdullah!"

"I'm not your uncle. I'm not anyone's uncle."

"Fine, Sheikh Abdullah."

"I'm not a sheikh either. Who are you?"

"I'm Rahib, director of the office of Sheikhs Tariq and Qisma, and brother of the poet Breton al-Shakhabiti."

"Really?" Abdullah said, taking Rahib's hand. "How is he? How is everyone in Baghdad?"

"Not good. Madame Sheikh Qisma has sent me to ask your help in an urgent matter."

"By all means speak."

"Do you have any tea in the house? I want to make sure that no-one can overhear us."

They went inside. Rahib noticed how slow Abdullah was in locating everything he needed to make the tea, and said, "Oh, step aside. I can do it faster myself."

Rahib took three cups out to the guards, who had remained in the car, then he came back inside and closed the door behind him. He sat with Abdullah in the middle of the salon with the pot of tea between them. He even accepted a cigarette from Abdullah and smoked with him as he related the events of the last few days. Abdullah was dismayed by the news, full of concern for Tariq. He also had to repress his anger towards his friend for having got himself into this mess, and he couldn't help wondering whether it might be a ploy on the part of Tariq and Qisma to get him to do what so far they had failed to persuade him to do, namely, to go to Baghdad to meet their sayyid, the rapist Jalal.

"And what's to say that everything you've told me is correct?" he said to Rahib.

"Because it is I who have told you."

"And who are you?"

"I am Rahib al-Shakhabiti."

"Listen. I don't know you, and I don't know this Shakhabit of yours. I've never seen you before in my life."

"Really? Didn't you see me at the inauguration of the party?"

"No. I didn't go."

"Ha! That's right. You stayed up late with my brother Bara. Fine. Don't you know these guards? They're from your village. Ask them about me, and they will confirm for you that I am the director general of the sheikhs' office."

"I only know a limited number of people from the village, including – unfortunately – those two idiotic sheikhs of yours."

Rahib thought a little. Then he took out two mobiles from his pocket and used one of them to call Qisma's stolen handset. He said that he was with Uncle Abdullah, but he did not believe what he had told him. Qisma ordered him to give the mobile to Abdullah so that she could talk to him herself. She then confirmed that everything Rahib had said was true.

He voiced his suspicion about it being a plan on their part to get him to meet that shit sayyid of theirs. In her anger, Qisma screamed at him, saying that it was not a laughing matter, that his friend was in real danger. The idea that he should be the substitute came from the police, and if he was going to abandon his friend in his hour of need, then he should say so openly, and Rahib would go and tell Tariq's son so that he could be the replacement. She started to cry.

Abdullah was quiet for a long time. He believed her, saying to himself that this iron-hearted woman would not cry unless the situation was truly dire. "O.K., O.K," he said. "Calm down. I'll come."

Through her sobs, Qisma asked him not to tell anyone what was going on, not Tariq's family, not even Sameeha. Having resolved to undertake the task, Abdullah went to his bedroom and filled his pockets with every packet of cigarettes he had. Then he asked Rahib to tell the driver to take them down the dirt road that ran parallel to the fields. Once there, he told them to wait, that he would be back in a few minutes.

Abdullah hurried to his field and said to Anwar, "I'm off on a trip, and I don't know how long I'll be. I need you to find out how much you can get for the field and the house, in case I want to sell them."

Anwar was surprised by what he heard, and his heart began to beat as rapidly as it did during his meetings with Salma. "Why, Uncle?" he said. "Is it on account of your marriage?"

Abdullah had not prepared a plausible reason, so it was fortunate that Anwar himself had supplied him with an answer even as he asked the question. "Yes," Abdullah said. "Yes. Now, please, do as I ask."

Anwar embraced him. Then they parted. Anwar watched Abdullah receding into the distance, feeling a greater love for him than ever, even as he wondered what could be behind his strange behaviour.

When Sabriya informed Qisma of the arrival of Rahib and a man she did not know, she hurried down from her room without stopping to look in the mirror or even arrange her hair, as she would normally do. She did not recognise Abdullah at first. He looked years younger, having shaved off his beard, trimmed his moustache and cut short his hair.

"Thank you," she said to Rahib and the bodyguards. "Thank you, Rahib. Go, now, and get some rest."

Qisma signalled for Sabriya to prepare a pot of tea, and when she and Abdullah were alone, she threw herself against his chest, crying. What an intense moment it was! Abdullah felt a true sense of fatherliness towards her. She, in turn, wanted to find her father's embrace in his arms. He gave her what she wanted, embracing her tenderly and patting her back to calm her down.

"Why have you done this to yourself? To all of us?" he asked.

Qisma led him by the arm and sat him beside her on the couch. She wiped away her tears and said, "I'll tell you something I've never shared with anyone else. I haven't done this to myself and to those around me, as you say. I'm the victim of the actions of others. When, as a child, I saw my father's amputated foot when he came back from the war in Kuwait, my life changed completely. I began to fear being beaten by anyone at anything. Having less than anyone else. Mattering less. My sole desire was to compete and win. Even now I hate anything that reminds me of my inadequacies, and that makes me defend what I have, and want to add to it. It made me sad, deep down, that my father accepted his loss, and my relationship with him was affected by that. I particularly hate injustice. The injustices we heap on ourselves most of all."

"What happened to your father was not his fault."

"I know. And it's not my fault that this feeling has torn at my soul since I was a child."

"O.K. Perhaps this isn't the time for a talk like this. Let's put it off for now. Tell me what's happened and what we have to do."

Qisma filled him in, leaving out her interview with Sayyid Jalal al-Din and repeating the lie that it was the police who had suggested Abdullah's involvement, saying that they would come that evening to meet Abdullah and arrange with him the details of hiding the microphone and the chip on his person. The kidnappers had called her just an hour before to tell her that the exchange would take place in the early evening, as the mosques raised the call to evening prayer. The rendezvous would be under a nearby bridge. "You are to stand there with the money in a red backpack so they can identify you."

"What about the money? It's a large sum, and there's so little time."

"The police promised to take care of it."

"Who do you think they are? And what do they want?"

"I don't know. And that's why the police asked me if I knew anyone who spoke Farsi. When I mentioned you to them, they agreed you were our best hope, for beyond the fact that you understand Farsi, you are a mature man with experience of confinement, torture and suffering. I'm sorry to say that. The police want to get to know the kidnappers – what they want and what they are planning – through you and though Tariq. They promise to keep a close eye on you to keep you safe and set you free as soon as they can. They'll explain the details to you."

Abdullah took a packet of cigarettes out of his pocket and lit a fresh one from the butt of the last. Qisma took one from his pack and began smoking with him. When she saw that he was lost in thought, she said in a different tone, "You are more handsome without a beard and only a thin moustache. You look younger. What made you shave it?"

He did not reply. With a smile, she said, "Sameeha?"

Abdullah was visibly embarrassed. "She mentioned something about trimming them."

"How delighted I am, from the bottom of my heart, by your decision to get married. At the same time I'm so sorry that this has happened while you two were preparing your wedding."

At that moment, Bara al-Shakhabiti walked into the salon from the kitchen, having come through the passageway from the neighbouring house. He spread his arms wide to embrace Abdullah. "Welcome! Welcome, my dear friend Kafka!"

After the embrace, he added, "I apologise for not having left you any cans of beer after that incredible night, or even a cigarette. Not to worry, my friend! Your coming here is an opportunity for me to compensate you for that, and we can continue our deep conversation. I'll take you with me on a tour of the secret and private Baghdad bars known only to—"

"Not now, Bara," Qisma said, interrupting him. "Later."

Two men came at five o'clock that afternoon. They said they were members of the security forces. After passing through to the house next door, they met alone with Abdullah in the office of the director general, Rahib, while he sat in the main room, trying without success to hear what they were saying. They gave Tariq the red backpack containing the money that he would take with him, and from another bag they produced various electronic devices. After they had explained to him what they intended to do and had persuaded him to let them do it, they planted a microchip the size of a newborn's fingernail under his skin on the inside of his knee. Then they covered the small wound with a delicate, skin-coloured plaster that was hardly visible. They said he could remove the plaster as soon as the wound was healed, and that the chip they had planted under his skin would let them know at any given moment where he was.

As for the second process, though they explained it to him politely and scientifically, he could not hide his embarrassment and, indeed, his reluctance. They had taken out a small microphone, roughly the size of an ant. If the kidnappers stripped off his clothes and beat him, the best place to hide it was under his penis, where it met his testicles. It would be completely hidden between the two, even if they stripped him naked, by virtue of the penis resting on top of it, for of course, there would not be any likelihood of his penis standing up to let them see it. They smiled, making a joke of it to dispel his embarrassment. He told them to think of another place, but they said it was standard practice. This was their trade; they had been trained by foreign experts.

Abdullah was silent for a while, then he said, "Fine. Tell me how it's done, and I'll put it on myself."

They explained it to him, using a finger as a model to stand in for the penis. Taking out a tube of transparent glue, they snipped a small piece off one of the skin-coloured plasters. "It's simple. You stick the microphone here with this glue, which is a powerful adhesive, then you cover the microphone, apart from the tip, with this piece of plaster."

CHAPTER 23

Abdullah, the Hostage

Now that the fishermen had tied up their boats and gone home, and every last wanderer had left, the banks of the great river were empty as darkness fell. With only Qisma there to see him off, Abdullah slipped through the gate at the end of the garden. He made his way down towards the water, following the slope of the hill towards the bridge, which was lit up like a beacon, while the houses on both sides of the river were for the most part dark, since electricity was one of the most precious commodities in the country. Ever since the bombardment at the beginning of the war, people had got used to relying on small generators. Abdullah followed the light from the lamps on the bridge, then stood under it in the dark, just as they had ordered him to. He smoked as he looked around him. He heard the lapping of the water below, the sound of cars as they went across the bridge overhead, the noise of a stifled city, and the receding sirens of ambulances and police cars, all amplified by the still night air.

Abdullah looked around him for a rock he could sit on as he used to on the riverbank near his village. He wished he were back there now, free from this anxiety and uncertainty. He did not find a rock, so he squatted down by the side of the water, expecting a group of armed men to swoop down on him at any moment.

He was not so much afraid as annoyed. He felt no desire to give up a single second more of his life than he already had to captivity, with its insults and indignities, subject to the whims of people he did not know, having done nothing to deserve it. A sense of inertia gripped him at the thought of going through all that a second time. Quite simply, he couldn't be bothered. He would resort to the tactic he had adopted from the time the Iranians had taken him prisoner until they had sent him on his way: to think of himself as dead, without hope. In this way the insults and the blows that he received, the hunger, the cold, the heat and the sickness, would mean nothing to him – they were inflicted on his body, not his soul. "For the body is not the self so much as it was a borrowed robe, a heavy burden that we are forced to carry throughout our lives."

When Abdullah had finished thinking about the denial of the body, he turned to the soul. Who could tell what mattered to it? What did it want, and what did it wish for, shackled as it was to a body that would end up cold and dead? He found within it just one final wish, which was that he might embrace Sameeha, there and then, beside the water, cooled by the evening breeze. That he might fold her into his chest for a long moment, breathe her in deeply, and whisper to her, expressing his sorrow for the pain he had caused her without intending to. In short, he wanted to say a final farewell, and not leave her to the torments of hoping, waiting and guessing as had been her fate during the years of his captivity.

He became so absorbed in his reflections – and his smoking – that he nearly forgot where he was and why. Startled, he jumped to his feet when the loudspeakers surprised him by broadcasting the call for the evening prayer from every corner of the city.

The same happened with Qisma. She felt as though her heart was being torn out of her chest, and nearly fell to the ground. She leaned on the fence surrounding the garden, gripping it tightly as she strained her eyes to see what was happening under the bridge, but the broken shadows cast by its bulky frame made it impossible to distinguish any figures or movement. She did not see the boat that approached Abdullah from the other direction. Because it had a small, modern motor, it made hardly any noise. Abdullah did not notice it until it had anchored directly in front of him. Two men jumped out, their faces masked. They grabbed Abdullah's arms, ripping the backpack off his back. One of them handed it to two others who had remained on board, who began lifting a body that had been lying in the bottom of the boat. Despite the darkness and the confusion, Abdullah knew that it was Tariq: it was his robe, his beard, his build. His hands were bound, and wide pieces of tape had been stuck across his eyes and mouth. Abdullah found himself gasping his name. Tariq, who had been hunched over, submitting to the men in the boat, straightened up and let out a muffled sound from under the tape, as his eyes, sealed in darkness, welled up with tears. The men set him on land and ripped the tape from his mouth.

"Abdullah, my dear brother!" he cried.

Tariq spun round on the spot, searching for him with sight-less eyes, and the men released Abdullah, who pulled Tariq to his chest and embraced him in a way that confirmed to everyone that they knew each other. In a harsh tone, one of them said in Tariq's ear, "We shall see if he really is your dear brother. From now on, his life is in your hands."

Tariq, his head buried in Abdullah's chest, was sobbing like a child, saying, "I'm sorry! I'm so sorry!"

Abdullah held him closer, patting his back to calm him. Then the men separated them, bound Abdullah's hands, led him into the boat and gently lowered him into a sitting position. One of the men got in with him, while the other remained with Tariq, leading him two steps forward and positioning him so he was facing the house. He pulled the tape off Tariq's eyes and pointed. "Go in that direction, straight up. That's it." Then he grabbed Tariq's ear and pinched it, twisting it violently between his fingers. "Remember: do what you were told as quickly as you can. If you don't, we'll be back to take the rest of your family, one after another." He slapped Tariq on the back of the neck and quickly got into the boat with the others. They set off downriver with the current.

Tariq turned round to catch a last glimpse of Abdullah, who looked back at him. They could make out each other's outline, but their features were lost in the darkness. They kept looking at each other until the boat was out of sight, the soft hum of its motor long out of earshot. Tariq allowed all the tears that had been bottled up behind his eyes and in his chest to pour out. Because his wrists were still bound, he dried his tears and wiped his nose as best he could on his shoulders. He took a deep breath, looked around, then made his way along the riverbank, slowly and with difficulty, until he was almost directly below the house. He saw Qisma, who cried out at the top of her voice, calling his name, and beside her Rahib, who tried to keep Qisma from vaulting the fence, telling her to remain where she was, that he would go to Tariq. But she ignored him and climbed over the fence. Rahib jumped over and went down the slope at a run until he reached Tariq, embracing his legs. Tariq sank to his knees, remaining there until Qisma arrived, out of breath. Rahib moved back as Qisma knelt down and pulled Tariq to her chest, crying and saying again and again, "Praise God for your safety! A thousand times over, praise God for your safety!"

Standing behind Tariq, Rahib attempted to untie his hands, but he found them bound with strong plastic and could not do it. He set off up the hill to the house and came back with a large pair of scissors he had taken from the kitchen. He found the two of them getting carefully to their feet. Qisma had wrapped her arm around Tariq's waist to support him. Without a word, Rahib fell in behind them. They stopped, and Rahib quickly cut the ties. Tariq put his arm across Qisma's shoulders. He was still weeping silently, his head bowed.

Tariq relaxed a little in the salon. He drank a cup of water and sipped the tea and bowl of soup that Sabriya had prepared for him. Qisma confirmed that he was unhurt. Although he had lost weight and looked a little haggard, nothing was broken or injured – aside from his dignity and his pride. Qisma ordered the others to return to what they were doing, fixing the guards with a fierce glare.

Qisma went up to the bedroom with Tariq, closed the door, and said to him, "Go into the bathroom and take a long shower. Afterwards, I'll bring you some food."

Tariq obeyed in silence. As Qisma helped him peel off his dirty clothes, she saw many dark spots on his body, blue and red, but she did not find any cuts or dried blood. She did not ask him, as she had intended, whether he needed help in the shower, but was content to accompany him to the door of the bathroom, bring him clean clothes and then shut him inside.

When Tariq came out, clean, calmer and more relaxed, Qisma was waiting for him, the low table in front of her piled high with plates of food. He sat on the chair across from her and set about them voraciously until he had eaten his fill. Afterwards, they sat on the bed, and Qisma asked him what had happened. Who were the kidnappers? What did they want? Tariq told her that he had not seen their faces because they were masked the entire time. They had demanded that he kill his friend Sheikh Tafir, and told him that if he refused they would carry off members of his family one by one and kill them gradually until he did what they wanted. "If only they had killed me!" Tariq said. "I couldn't bear it if they hurt poor Abdullah. I couldn't bear to lose him as I've lost your father. I couldn't stand it if anything happened to any of my friends or family. But of course, I won't kill Tafir. I can't bear even the thought of it."

He was crying as he spoke, and Qisma pulled him in to her breast. "I won't do it," he repeated as he sobbed. "And I don't know what to do."

Neither of them noticed that Qisma's son, who, ever since Tariq's disappearance, had been sleeping in their room in a large crib in the corner, had woken up and was watching through the rails as Tariq cried and embraced his mother. The child climbed out and came over to where they were sitting. He stood there in silence. His mother noticed him and withdrew her arms from Tariq, whose eyes were blurred by fresh tears. Then the child opened his arms towards Tariq, who lifted him up and embraced him. The boy squeezed Tariq's neck, his little hands moving as though to pat Tariq on the shoulders or stroke the back of his neck. Tariq felt a violent sense of tenderness and love towards him and held him tighter to his chest even as his tears flowed with renewed force. Now Qisma's eyes filled too, and she began stroking her child's back with tenderness and pride as Tariq repeated, "Ibrahim, Ibrahim, O Ibrahim." In his heart and his mind was the soul of Ibrahim, his friend, the father of Qisma and grandfather of this child – not the child himself.

Later, once Qisma had reassured Tariq about what she had done and what she had planned with Sayyid Jalal al-Din to ensure that nothing bad happened to Abdullah – with God's blessing – the two of them fell asleep, exhausted, with the child between them.

As for Abdullah, he was surprised to find that once the boat had travelled a reasonable distance from the bridge, his captors began to treat him politely. One of them said, "We're sorry about this, professor. Rest assured that we will not inflict the slightest harm upon you, for you are not at fault. You have nothing to do with any of this. Everything we're doing, we're doing for the general good and the future of the country. Here, have some water. We'll remove your bonds as soon as we arrive. Forgive us, professor."

That was the first time anyone had addressed Abdullah as

"*ustaadh*", a common term of respect. He felt somehow reassured by it, even though he suspected that it was nothing more than an attempt to keep him quiet and compliant until they reached their destination. After all, they had not yet untied his hands, though they asked his permission before they blindfolded and gagged him, and they had not used violence or cursed him. They treated him gently, in fact, even after they took the blindfold off.

He found himself in a normal, clean bedroom with a bed, its own bathroom, a table and a small refrigerator containing some food and bottled drinks. Abdullah noticed at once, however, that there was no window. Before they closed the door on him, they told him to relax, and pointed out a button on the wall near the light switches, saying he should ring the bell if he needed them. Still masked, they withdrew from the room. As the last of them closed the door behind him, he said, "Sleep well, professor."

Abdullah had not been a "professor" or anything like it in his whole life. He had dropped out of school early in order to keep his friend Ibrahim, Qisma's father, company when his father had forced him to abandon his studies. As far as he was concerned, the title applied only to those who taught in schools and universities, though he remembered that people had begun to use it to address officials of the former regime, starting with the president's two sons who had failed in their studies, though they were granted spurious doctorates in any subject they wanted.

As he reflected on this, stretching out on the bed and staring up at the ceiling, Abdullah tried to get a sense of what was happening to him and what might happen next. The only definite conclusion he was able to reach was that the matter related more to Tariq and Qisma than it did to him. He was nothing more than a means of applying pressure on them, as he had gathered from the kidnappers' last few remarks to Tariq. Abdullah got up and headed to the bathroom. On the way, he noticed a small shelf above the refrigerator with a few books and an alarm clock. In the bathroom, he saw that there was a small ventilation grille built into the ceiling, and was reassured that he would be able to smoke as much as he wanted during his captivity.

When he sat down on the toilet, he was reminded of the small microphone under his penis, and he did his best not to make any sound while doing his business, placing his fingertip over the microphone. He was ashamed to imagine the security forces laughing as they listened to his farts, even though he told himself, "They don't deserve to hear anything else . . ."

When he came out again, he stood for a while in front of the bookshelf, examining the titles. He found scholarly history books, in addition to a copy of the Qur'an, the *Epic of Gilgamesh*, *A Thousand and One Nights*, *The History of Torture*, and a few foreign novels translated into Arabic in cheap trade editions, including *The Stranger* by Camus, *Nausea* by Sartre, *Hell* by Barbusse and *Notes from the Underground* by Dostoyevsky. He was surprised to find two novels by Kafka: *The Metmorphosis* and *The Trial*. He flicked through a few of the books then put them back on the shelf, resolving to read all of them if his sojourn should prove long enough. With the exception of *The History of Torture*. He had undergone enough torture himself, so there was no need to read a book about it. In any case, he doubted it would prove exhaustive, since torture had been around for as long as mankind had existed. Man was the only creature that indulged in it, not being content just to kill. He would begin with the two novels by Kafka. He had read them as a teenager, at the height of Tariq's passion for literature. He wondered how he would find them now; nothing but vague impressions remained from his first readings of them.

He kept walking in circles around the room, pausing every now and then by the door to see what he could hear through it, for the most part sentences related to tea making, and words such as "car", "telephone", "the boss", "we're out of salt", "money", and "where did you put the cigarettes?" He did not hear any words in Farsi, as he had been led to expect.

Half the night passed without him being able to sleep a wink, despite his fatigue. He got up and thought about ringing the bell on any pretext whatsoever, such as to ask for tea or cigarettes, and then trying to coax the person who answered into exchanging news with him. But he quickly gave up on that idea. It would be best to avoid contact with them. He returned to the bed, stretched himself out, and continued staring at the ceiling and smoking. A long time passed, but at last he began to feel his eyelids growing heavy. He gave in and closed them.

The second day, from dawn till dusk, played on Qisma's nerves to the extent that she would have collapsed on more than one occasion were it not for the quick actions of those present – usually Sabriya – to calm her. She had received no news of Abdullah, perhaps because the telephone lines were down intermittently throughout the day, and was worried about him. In the only call she had been able to place to the office of Sayyid Jalal al-Din, she was told that he was out at an important meeting. The electricity cut out, there were sounds of explosions outside, and the news they received through the radio carried reports on the trial of the deposed president, and car bombs, assassinations and kidnappings. Qisma paced through the two houses like someone stung by a scorpion. She smoked voraciously and yelled in the face of anyone who made the mistake of addressing her. She went up and down the stairs repeatedly. She went out into the garden and then circled the salon.

Suddenly Qisma heard the sound of high-pitched trilling break out in the kitchen, accompanied by lisping yells and the cry of "Long live justice!" It could only be Sabriya and Sabir. It was accompanied by a chorus of celebratory shrieks and trills from outside, punctuated by the sound of bullets being fired from automatic weapons. Qisma rushed to the kitchen and burst through the door to find Sabriya and Sabir jumping and dancing in a circle, a small radio in Sabir's hand. Panting under the force of her violent joy, Sabriya told her that the Iraqi Special Tribunal had passed a sentence of death by hanging upon the deposed president. Qisma froze where she was for a moment. Then she swelled with rage. She ripped the small radio out of Sabir's hand and hurled it against the floor with all her strength, smashing it to pieces. "What kind of justice is this?" she screamed in their faces. "Such an ordinary death? Sentenced to hang? A gallows! A rope! A tie! Just like that, so easy? What about the rights of the millions whose lives he destroyed for decades?" When she realised that the rest of the household had gathered behind her at the door to the kitchen, she pushed past them on her way into the salon, glaring at them as she kept on yelling, "What kind of justice is this?" And because her anxiety for Abdullah was unabated, she remembered the word he favoured, and put it to use as she reached the peak of her rage. "What kind of shit is this? What shitty justice! How can he die just once and in such an ordinary way, he who killed thousands in such vile ways?" They should have forced him first to listen to the details of the torments of his victims and their relatives, one by one, night and day, until the years of his trial matched the years of his rule. Then put him naked in a cage, like a mangy dog, right in the middle of Liberation Square, line the people up in rows with live cameras broadcasting live to the nation and let them ease their burning thirst for revenge by spitting upon him, striking his face, ripping out his hair, biting him, branding him, taking pliers to his fingernails. Sabir would go up and cut out his tongue. Then Sabriya would approach and kill his daughters in front of his eyes. Someone else would cut off his ear. Another would piss upon him, and yet another would shit on his face. Then someone would rape him. "I'd chop off his foot the way he did my father's. I'd cut his throat. I'll cut his throat the way he slaughtered my father and the whole country. I'll cut his throat!" She kept saying it until she was out of breath, then she collapsed on the couch behind her. At that moment, she heard her child crying in fright from upstairs on account of the shouting and the commotion of those celebrating outside.

Abdullah had also heard the news. One of the guards who brought him food had told him when Abdullah asked about the clamour and gunfire outside. He spent the rest of the day reading Kafka's novel *The Trial*, and thinking about the trial of the deposed president, without being conscious of holding any particular opinion about it. He was not able to determine whether he was happy about the judgment or not, whether it meant anything to him or not, whether it affected him or not. In the end, sleep beckoned just after midnight, and, giving in, he closed his eyes, the book sitting open over his face.

But before sleep could claim him, something, a sound perhaps, pulled him out of it and he opened his eyes. Jumping up, he ran to the door and put his ear to it. A commotion suddenly broke out, the sound of things breaking and orders being shouted: "Stop! Throw down your weapons!"

"Hands up!"

"Don't move!"

"Where are the others?"

"Search all the rooms, the kitchen, the bathroom!"

"Where is the hostage?"

Abdullah quickly moved away from the door and sat on the far edge of the bed out of the way of any bullets that might come through it.

He heard someone shouting very close by: "Open the door! Let's go. Open it!"

Abdullah stood up, confused, thinking he was the one being addressed. But the door was opened by one of the kidnappers, still masked, with two police officers behind him, one of them holding a pistol to his head. Then, with breathtaking speed, the other officer began tying the masked man's hands behind his back and dragged him out. The first officer approached Abdullah and asked if he was alright. He assured Abdullah that everything was fine, repeating, "We are the police," even though that was apparent from his uniform. But the confirmation was necessary, given that many gangs and armed militias dressed in police or army uniforms in the course of their operations.

The police car that carried Abdullah away had tinted windows. From his seat in the back, he could not see through them. Meanwhile, the shriek of the siren on the roof cut into his head, just as it cut the traffic on the road ahead. On impulse he had taken with him the two novels by Kafka when he left his cell. Perhaps he would read them later, with Sameeha, for instance.

The siren stopped after a few minutes, but the car itself did not stop for another quarter of an hour. When they opened the door to let him out, he did not find himself at a police station, as he had expected, but rather in an underground garage. The officers respectfully asked him to accompany them, leading him up a short staircase and down a passage into the living room of a magnificent house, then into a spacious office that clearly belonged to an important person, given the badges, medals, degree certificates, flowers, expensive leather chairs and large coffee table with two comfortable couches on either side of it. They asked him to sit, offered him a cup of coffee, then went out, saying, before they closed the door, "The sayyid will come himself in a little while to congratulate you on your escape."

As soon as he took his first sip of coffee, a powerful desire to smoke came over him. He wished he had asked the police officers before they went out whether it was permitted. He looked around for some indication that would make it clear one way or another, and noticed a large black marble ashtray on the low table in front of him. But he did not see any cigarette butts in it or any trace of ash. It was exceedingly shiny, more so than any plate designed for eating he had ever seen. He took out a cigarette, but then hesitated, running his finger around the ashtray, trying to make up his mind about whether to light it or not.

At that moment, a slender, elegant man wearing a suit and tie came into the room. All his hair was white: head, beard, moustache – even his eyebrows. He approached Abdullah, his cologne preceding him, and extended his hand. "Praise God for your safety!' he said, adding, "Do feel free to smoke, of course." Then, after shaking Abdullah's hand warmly, he said, "If you wish, I'll even smoke with you, though it's not my general practice." Abdullah noticed when they shook hands that the man's hand was exceedingly delicate and soft, and that he wore several large rings set with expensive stones.

Abdullah quickly produced his packet of cigarettes from his pocket and held one out to him. "Just a moment," said the man, and brought out from one of the drawers of a cabinet next to the table a beautiful wooden case. He opened it in front of Abdullah; it was full of expensive Cuban cigars. Abdullah took one, and the owner of the box took another. He left the box in front of Abdullah, saying, "They are for you. Consider them a gift from me."

He lit Abdullah's cigar, then turned round and settled in the high black chair behind the desk. He lit his own cigar and said, "A thousand thanks to God for your safety! We have arrested the criminals and have delivered them to prison so they can be brought to justice."

Abdullah murmured inaudible words of thanks, after which the man said, "I know you well, Abdullah. Do you know me?"

"No."

"I am your father."

CHAPTER 24

The Hardest Meeting

For a moment Abdullah was speechless, his mouth agape, as he scrutinised the face of the white-haired man claiming to be his father. He actually did resemble this man closely, and he knew that he could only be Jalal, who had been trying for so long to arrange a meeting with him through Tariq and Qisma. Abdullah shot up like a rocket, powered by an unanticipated energy and strength, and crossed to the man in a single leap, taking holding of him by the lapels of his suit jacket. Abdullah threw him onto the desk, scattering all the telephones, papers and pens that had been there. One hand was on the man's neck while the other pulled furiously at his tie. His anger was such that, had he struck the wall, his fist would have gone straight through. His whole body shook, and his face burned like a pile of coals. Through gritted teeth, he screamed, "I'll kill you, you filthy pig," closing his fingers around the neck of his father, who offered no resistance.

Abdullah would have choked the man to death if the police officers had not rushed into the office to set him free. They pulled Abdullah back by his arms and kept hold of him while Jalal got up off the desk, coughing and gasping. He loosened his tie and leaned on the desk, facing Abdullah, who appeared more strangled than he did. Struggling to find a way to express the fire raging inside him, Abdullah gasped between ragged breaths: "You filthy pig . . . you animal . . . you criminal son of a criminal . . . you son of a bitch . . . you shit . . . you shit . . . you shit of humanity."

Having got his breath back, the old man drank from a bottle of water he took from a small refrigerator beside his desk. He gave a second bottle to Abdullah and said, "Let him go. Let him go!"

The police officers hesitated, but little by little they released their grip on Abdullah's arms. Abdullah took the bottle of water and hurled it at Jalal's head. It served to wet him rather than hurt him, but the two police officers renewed their hold on Abdullah's arms. Wiping the water from his face and the front of his clothes, their master repeated his order: "Let him go! Let him go!" Once again, the officers gradually loosened their hold until Abdullah pulled his arms away. The sayyid told them, "Go out and shut the door. Don't come back in without my permission, no matter what happens." The officers withdrew, closing the door behind them. Jalal took a step nearer Abdullah. "Kill me if you want," he said.

Abdullah lifted his open hand high in the air as though to deliver a slap that would take Jalal's head right off his body. But with great difficulty he mastered himself, closing his shaking hand and digging his fingernails into his palm so hard they almost drew blood. His arm remained poised in the air for a moment, fist clenched, as he trembled, biting down on his bottom lip. He lowered his fist slowly onto the top of Jalal's head, took hold of a clump of his hair and spat in his face with the full force of his hatred and disgust. Then he yanked Jalal's hair back until he fell against the edge of his desk. Abdullah went to leave, but the door was locked. Turning to Jalal, he said, "You're not worth staining my hand in your filthy blood."

Abdullah had never killed anyone in his life, not even during the Iraq–Iran war, nor had he ever beaten or struck anyone. He looked around him, searching for something to smoke, as Jalal said again, "Go ahead and kill me if you want. I would understand. You are ignorant of the truth of what happened, just like I was at the time, and ignorance is a blindness that drives innocent men to ruin."

Abdullah saw his cigar lying on the floor under the coffee table. But because it had been given to him by Jalal he could not bear to bring it to his lips again. He walked over to his father and said, "No ignorance could justify the crime that you committed, you pig. You can wrap yourself in the fleece of a humble lamb, but you're still a devil and a wolf underneath. You appear in the guise of godliness and piety. You've rubbed a callus into the middle of your forehead as if to prove you spend your life prostrated in prayer. But the truth is that you've never prayed except to kiss the shoes of those sayyids who are your masters, just as dirty as yourself. Do you want more signs of your deception and betrayal? Here, take this!"

Abdullah grabbed hold of Jalal's hair again and stubbed out his cigar on his brow, grinding it in, leaving a black spot. He threw the cigar into Jalal's face and let go of his hair. Then he sat back down on the couch and took out one of his own cigarettes. He smoked greedily, his entire being trembling. Fortunately for Jalal, the cigar had already gone out, so it just left a smudge of ash on his forehead.

Jalal brought another bottle of water, set it in front of Abdullah, and sat down on the couch facing him. "You are calling me to account for a sin I committed in a matter of moments," he said, "when I was young and ignorant, a pampered teenager. I've been paying the price of that mistake my entire life. Do you still want to make me pay? With my life, perhaps?"

"It was a deadly mistake, one that destroyed the lives of many, not least my own mother."

"And would killing me correct that mistake?"

"That's what your father did, a pig like yourself. He killed my mother and abandoned me as a baby next to a toilet. All to cover up your mistake."

"I didn't know what happened after I was thrown out of the house and forced to leave the country. Even if I had, what could I have done?"

"How could you have known, given that the whole thing was a secret known only to your mother?"

"I am grateful to my mother, for she entrusted this secret to one of her childhood friends in Kurdistan. The same woman who gave me refuge for a few days before my flight to Iran."

"What did you do in Iran, while I was being tortured in their prisons for nineteen years?"

"My life was not as easy as you imagine. I suffered greatly. I behaved like any living creature seeking to preserve its life against the odds. Telling you everything I went through would take days. Simply crossing the border was a terrifying experience. A spoiled brat who had never left his village being smuggled across the border between two hostile countries by people I did not know. Long days and nights of travelling among rough mountain tribes. Many years later I joined one of the groups of Iraqi exiles based in Iran that opposed the former president's regime. Then I found myself fighting alongside them."

"So you were fighting against your country, on the same front as me but on the other side? Don't you see how vile and despicable you are?"

"I was fighting a dictator who had thrown my country into chaos. I fought to save it."

"That dictator lived a life of luxury in his palaces, while you were killing the innocent soldiers he drove to the front by force. How are you any different from those you are fighting now? They kill police officers and soldiers while claiming to be fighting to save the country from your thieving occupation."

"Listen, if we enter the labyrinth of these discussions, we'll never get anywhere. The situation in Iraq is more complicated than we can imagine, and all of us have contributed to the nightmare. What I'm interested in now is the personal, not the political. You and me."

"What do you want from me?"

"I don't want anything from you. I want to give you whatever you want from me."

"Why?"

Jalal was silent for a moment, wrestling with the difficulty of what he was trying to say. But there was no other way. "Because you–"

"Enough!" Abdullah cut him off immediately. "Don't say it. I'm not your son, and it would bring me no honour if I were.

I've never hated anyone before, and now I'm full of hatred, resentment and festering rage, all directed at you. How can you expect me to embrace as my father the one person in this world that I hate?"

"Denial doesn't change the facts."

"But choices do. I would choose hell and Satan before I chose you."

"I'm not talking about myself. I don't want anything from you for myself. I just wish you could get to know my sons, your brothers."

"I don't have any brothers except the two who shared my childhood: Tariq and Ibrahim Abu Qisma."

"Do you know the name of my eldest daughter, the one people refer to in my nickname?"

Abdullah lit a cigarette from the butt of the previous one, going straight from one to the other. Jalal continued to work away at him in a gentle, earnest tone.

"Her name is Zakiya."

The mention of that name made Abdullah choke on his cigarette, but Jalal went on. "For that reason, everyone calls me Abu Zakiya, the father of Zakiya. Is that not proof enough that I haven't stopped thinking about her and regretting the mistake I committed when I was young and ignorant? Even though I've been paying for it my whole life? My second child is a son named Isma'il. My first grandchild, Zakiya's daughter, is called Zaynab, and I was the one who named the grandson who was born three months ago ..." Jalal fell silent for a long moment. Each of them stared into the eyes of the other, waiting for the other to speak, until Jalal, who seemed to be the one choking now, said, "Qamar."

Abdullah found himself standing involuntarily, turning a full circle. He could not say why he went over to Jalal and grabbed him by the neck a second time, digging his fingers into his flesh before releasing him and pushing him away. He went back to where he had been sitting and Jalal resumed his monologue.

"You want to kill me for an ancient mistake, and I want you to see and embrace a new baby who carries your name and your blood. You want to salt the wound, while I want to treat it, so far as I am able. Nevertheless, I acknowledge that you are in a better position than I am even though you are alone and poor, while I have power, wealth and children. You are better than me because you are more pure. There isn't anyone who hates you or wishes you dead. You have dear friends, not enemies. You put your head on the pillow and fall asleep at peace, with an easy conscience, whereas I sleep only with the help of sedatives, surrounded by guards. Don't think that I'm doing all this out of affection or compassion. The truth is, I'm the one who deserves to be pitied."

"Stop! Stop this cunning talk of yours, this poisonous speech, for it won't dilute the hatred in my soul for you. You're a fraud, a liar, a cheat. A thief, a rapist and a murderer. You have no conscience, and all the money and power you possess are stolen property, stained with the blood of innocents. Everything you use to feed and clothe your family comes at the cost of the people's rights."

"I realise that. I am content to pay the price in this world and the next to spare my children all its hardships, so that they may live far away, removed from what I do, studying and living in peace, however they wish and however befits their dignity, in the shadow of a wall that protects them and wards off all the blows of the sea – a wall that is me. And what I offer you is to be that wall for you too, a wall you can lean against that will protect you. And I've done that. I've protected you without your knowing it. I've protected you, for example, from having your pension cut off. I've even protected you from assassination, which has been the fate of many who participated in the war against Iran."

"Liar! If the Iranians had wanted to kill me, they would have done it when I was their prisoner. As for those you call my brothers and my nieces and nephews, have you told them they have a brother, a brother produced by your rape of a sick orphan girl? Have you told your wife, at least?"

"Of course I haven't done that. As I told you, I decided to be the wall that protects them from the salt wind and the waves. It would be to no-one's benefit to tell them that."

"Don't you see how deceitful you are? How disgusting? How skilfully you twist everything to vindicate yourself?"

"It's logical, rational, realistic thinking – not emotional, confused thinking like yours. All the same, as I've said from the start, I'm prepared to do whatever you ask of me, and if you want me to tell them about it, to tell the people in the village, to tell people everywhere, I will do that in your presence. But will that do you any good? Will it benefit anyone else? I'm not talking financial benefit here but spiritual benefit. If you want people to know about it, if that's what's best for you and what you truly want, I'm prepared to make that happen, and the same goes for anything else you may ask of me."

Abdullah cleared his throat. Pointing a steady finger at Jalal, he said, "Listen carefully. What I want from you is the following: that after today you never show your face to me again. That you never think of me again but forget me entirely. I also want you to keep away from the people I know and love. I'm certain that you are the one who got Tariq and Qisma involved in what they're now wrapped up in. And that you're behind this disgusting pretend abduction."

"You're wrong about that too. As long as your views are coloured by your resentment and your blind hatred for me, you'll never see things as they really are. What good would it do me? Why would I waste my time, my energy and my money on them? Verify it with the kidnappers if you want. They are just another gang like the hundreds and thousands of gangs in this country who will do anything as long as the price is right, no matter who asks them or the motive behind it."

"You arranged to bring me here. To fill my ears with your lies and your poison."

"There's no truth to that! None! And besides, Qisma and Tariq came to me. They asked me for my help, and I advised them on what I saw to be in their interest and the interest of our village. Or would you rather it remained on the margins, that our people should make sacrifice after sacrifice, decade after decade, and receive nothing in return? I did what I could to help them – you can ask them about that yourself. As for this foolish suspicion of yours, you know that I could have you tied up and brought to me whenever I wanted, without the need for a pretend abduction, as you call it."

"I don't believe you. And I don't want anything from you. I don't want to see you or hear from you again. And if there's a final word I want to say to you, it's this: stop toying with people's blood, their money, their dignity, their safety and their fate. Now, tell those dogs of guards to open the door so I can go."

"They'll take you wherever you wish."

"I don't want them to. I'll go back to the house by myself."

"Which house?"

It was then that Abdullah realised there was more than one house, both in Baghdad and in the village, that he could go home to, and he felt that he was in a happier position than he could possibly have imagined, better than that of the fraud and rapist sitting in front of him. Just as Jalal himself had admitted, Abdullah was truly more fortunate than he. Abdullah felt a certain contentment, deciding that the house he had to go to first was that of Qisma and Tariq, to reassure them of his safety and be reassured about Tariq.

"The house that you kidnapped me from," he said. "The house of my true family."

"Do you know the way? It's still dark outside, and the city is full of danger and checkpoints."

It was not fear of danger that made Abdullah agree to be driven to Qisma's home, but rather his ignorance of her address. As soon as the guards opened the door, Abdullah left the room without a backward glance at Jalal, without shaking his hand or uttering a single word of farewell, leaving his father's hand hanging in the air.

CHAPTER 25

An Evening on the Roof

It was nearly dawn when they brought Abdullah to the house next to Qisma's. The guards let him in, recognising him from the village where his smoking and philosophising were legendary, and gathered round to shake his hand. But Abdullah's priority was to go to the bathroom, where the first thing he did was carefully – though not without discomfort – take off the microphone with water and soap, and flush it down the toilet. He removed the plaster on the back of his knee, opened the wound with his fingers, and squeezed out the electronic chip, slick and bloody, from under his skin. Abdullah cleaned the wound and covered it with a fresh plaster. Then he showered and left the bathroom to find Bara waiting for him at the door.

"Why are you up so late?" Abdullah asked.

"Because Madame Sheikh wants me to publish the new edition in two days' time. Come, friend Kafka, come! Follow me to the roof. I had prepared a magnificent feast for myself, but now I can hold it in your honour."

When they went up, Abdullah found that the feast was just a large bucket of beer bottles on ice, two plates of appetisers – one with chopped cucumber and yoghurt, the other a mixture of salted nuts and dried fruit – and a half-dozen packs of cigarettes.

The table had been placed to give them the best possible view of the river, which reflected back the myriad lights of the city, including the lights of the bridge that Abdullah had been stand-ing beneath not so long before, on his way to an uncertain fate. How quickly things change at times! And how slowly at others.

The two men settled down across the table from one other, revived by the breeze from the river and united by the simple pleasure of sitting up on a roof before dawn, a pleasure that all Iraqis recognise and long for.

"I reread Kafka after meeting you, my friend. You entered my heart and my mind as soon as I met you. We poets have a keen sense of intuition – like women and gazelles – and we sense the sincerity and the essence of the person before us. We can predict earthquakes, love, disasters. You are like me: good, gentle and alone, even when you are in the midst of a group. We feel a high degree of estrangement. Our lives are difficult, therefore, even if we don't have to contend with the difficulties others face, and all we do is run and run and keep running until we disappear over the horizon."

Bara was enjoying this abstract conversation, which concerned his inner life more than it did his work and the daily pressures applied by Madame Sheikh. He enjoyed the sound of his own voice and the fact that there was someone willing to sit with him and listen to him. And it relaxed Abdullah because Bara did not ask how he was doing, where he had come from, or what had happened, allowing him to put his misadventure out of his mind and enjoy the last hour before sunrise in peace.

Bara clinked his glass against Abdullah's. "To your health, my dear friend Kafka! To your health. I'll give you some of his works, if you don't have them. I keep them in my office downstairs. I advised Wafa to read *Metamorphosis* too, so she can understand how the way we work in this new era is transforming us into misshapen creatures because it strips us of our essential selves. In my opinion, man ought not to do any work he doesn't love. He should leave all other kinds of work to machines and animals, and live for knowledge, culture, the arts, and refinement of his language to make it more poetic. I don't know what your relationship to poetry is, but there is poetry in everything, even if we don't realise it. As far as I'm concerned, I have only ever loved three things in this world: poetry, freedom and women. Lately, I've been feeling a true love for Wafa. And you? Tell me about the woman you've fallen in love with."

"It's the only thing that has any meaning in life, even though, like you, I can name three things I love in life: smoking, detachment and Sameeha. I say Sameeha, and not "women", because to say otherwise would not be true. By the way, let me remind you of a piece about love that I like from a poem you read to me that night:

> Love
> It's the other
> You imagine it will keep you company
> In the loneliness of the station
> Waiting for bus number zero
> Or that bus that will carry
> A poster for the movie of death."

"Ah, you're an amazing friend! I love anyone who loves my poems. Do you know something? As far as I'm concerned, even the concept of homeland is alien, and I, as a poet, have no love of borders, flags and patriotism. I believe in humanity, not in homelands and nations. I believe in people, regardless of their nationality, their sex, their shape. I find it shameful and embarrassing that people still say that one person is fat and one is skinny, that this one is tall and that one short, that this one is beautiful and that one ugly. I dream of the day when people stop talking about the sizes of noses, eyes, breasts and bottoms – and ethnicities, nationalities and the other inhuman ways of differentiating people."

As the alcohol began to go to Bara's head – for he had already drunk several bottles of beer before Abdullah arrived – his enthusiasm waxed, and with it the speed of his thoughts, and he began jumping between topics in a scattergun way without any preamble to smooth the transitions. Abdullah realised what was happening and liked it, because it was the condition of a mind that was internally free.

"There's a vanity in everything we do," Bara said again, pointing out some nearby flowerpots containing dry, withered plants. "We covered this land of living soil and diverse plants with cities of tarmac and concrete. Then we began selling handfuls of soil in bags and boxes in our clean shops. We buy the soil and small plastic flowerpots to put on our balconies and rooftops. We fill the pots with soil and seeds from bags, and then we wait for a couple of plants or flowers to appear, as some kind of apology to the land, whose living soil and many kinds of grasses we have buried. This simple process is one we can apply to many other things in our lives. I was trying to write an article along these lines, trying to fill the journal with something other than trivial photographs of the two sheikhs, news of their successes, and their fantastical proclamations – something other than the columns of stupid, worn-out analysis of what's going on in the world that most journals stuff their pages with. There's a vanity in everything we do, brother. Newspapers in the east are filled with news and analysis of affairs in the west, and newspapers in the west are filled with the same about the east. Why don't we busy ourselves with our own affairs, clean our own house and put it in order, instead of keeping ourselves busy by plundering our neighbour's house? That way, every neighbourhood of the world could live in peace."

They paid no heed to the sirens of ambulances and police cars, nor to the rattle of bullets or the distant explosions they would hear from time to time, which spoiled the serene nocturnal soundscape. Everyone had become used to that sort of thing, to the point where it seemed like a natural part of their lives.

At one point, however, responding to gunfire that sounded particularly close at hand, Bara shook his head and remarked, "They're at it again, the fools."

"And for what?" replied Abdullah. "The murdered man goes to his rest, while the murderer will never know peace."

They went on drinking and talking.

Suddenly, they noticed Rahib sitting close by, perched like a monkey on the low perimeter wall of the roof, a cup of tea in his hand.

"I like how he adopts his height as part of his identity," Bara said.

"At the end of the day," replied Abdullah, "what are any of us except disabled beings in a defective universe?"

"A profound thought, my friend." Bara gave a drunken laugh and clinked his glass against Abdullah's. "A very deep and profound thought."

Then he beckoned Rahib over and clinked his glass against his brother's teacup, saying, "Why don't you sing a song for us, Rahib? A happy song so we can dance, or a sad song to make us weep." Turning back to Abdullah, he said, "My brother Rahib: he has a truly *rahib* –that is, awful – voice. Rahib, are you in love?"

"Not exactly. At the moment, I love all women. Later on, I'll be content to love the one who loves only me."

"That's why you aren't moved by the concept of homeland. Homeland is a woman; wherever a man's woman is, that's where his homeland is. So, for a bachelor, his mother represents the homeland. For a married man, it's his wife, and for a father, his daughter. I think it's from this, from love for a woman, that love for homeland comes. It's not a love for borders, flags, soil and shit like that, as some claim. I'm not a nationalist, as I've told you already. I couldn't possibly be. But from another point of view, I feel a certain responsibility towards this country, and I sometimes think it's necessary to do something to save it first. After it regains its strength, it will be possible for me to go back to criticising it and renouncing the concept of nationalism, but for now, each one of us has to save whatever he can save around him first. For if each one of us saves himself and a few of those around him in this world, it will be possible for us to save humanity in its entirety."

"Of all countries in the world," said Rahib, "this is the one that has suffered the most throughout history from military aggression and occupation. It has been occupied more than twenty times – by the Mongols, the Persians, the Ottomans, the British, and so on and so forth. Now it's the Americans. I don't know what to attribute this desire to possess it to, this hostility towards it above all others."

"Let me tell you," said Bara. "It's like when young men start to resent their father as they gain a sense of their own power and become gripped by an obscure desire to supersede him, to neutralise him, to be free of him and to kill him. This is what happens even between us poets, between one generation and another. Iraq is the father of civilisation. Therefore, whenever any nation feels a desire to flex its muscles, when it feels the blood pumping in its balls, it thinks about castrating its father."

Rahib leaned back and laughed so hard that it seemed he might fall off the wall. "I don't agree with you," he said. "I've felt the blood pumping in my balls ever since I was in the cradle, and I've never thought about killing my father."

All three laughed, and Rahib went on: "In my opinion, the time has come for you to stop wasting time thinking about your balls, and actually put them to the use that God intended."

"How's that?"

"It's simple: just as every human testicle throughout history has done since the time of the first two that belonged to father Adam." Rahib had switched to drinking beer after finishing his tea. "You carry your balls, brother," Rahib said, "to the woman you love. And you tell her you want to marry her. You don't tell her that you want her to put your unemployed balls to work! Then you arrange things with her, you come to an agreement about everything, and then you go and sit in front of your father and ask him to go with you to the woman's family and ask for her hand in marriage. That's what people call it, asking for a woman's hand, though in truth it's something else that they're after."

They laughed loudly, clinked glasses, and chorused, "To your balls' health!"

"Yes, my beautiful brother Rahib. How I've missed you, you little bastard. You were the only one when we were children who could persuade me to leave my books and play with you. Only with you would I laugh and play. Why don't you establish a party dedicated to the nation's testicles? Its logo could be illustrated with two testicles and two swords."

After their laughter had died down, Rahib said, "No. I'm thinking about founding a party for short people when the time is right."

"Ah, beautiful! In that case, I should start to think about establishing a party for poets – but only poets who don't think about their balls."

Two guards came up to the roof and joined them, each taking a beer from the bucket.

"That's life, brother. People never say what they really mean. They say, 'We request the hand of your daughter for our son,' and not, 'We request your daughter's vagina for our son's balls.' For the truth of the matter is that he doesn't care – and never will –

about that hand except when it cooks for him and plays with his balls. That's the name of the game, brother, and whoever doesn't play by the rules loses out. And the winners? Politicians who say one thing and mean something else entirely. For example, if they say, 'We fight for the best interests of the people,' they mean their own interests. But if the people say, 'We want our rights, we want justice, and we want the law to be applied,' and so on, they're saying what they mean, and that's why they never get it."

They were still admiring Rahib's insight when a third guard came up to tell them they needed to come down before daybreak, to avoid drawing attention to their presence in the house. On the stairs, Bara suggested they continue their conversation in the kitchen, for he had discovered in the madame sheikh's kitchen a cupboard containing every kind of alcoholic drink, from which he would swipe a bottle from time to time. Abdullah, however, insisted that he was tired and needed to sleep. Rahib proposed that Abdullah sleep in his room, so as not to disturb the two sheikhs in the other building, and Abdullah said, "Yes. Not to avoid disturbing the sheikhs, but rather that they don't disturb me."

As it happened, Abdullah woke after only two hours' sleep to find someone embracing him. Before he had even opened his eyes, he knew it was Tariq, and he hugged him right back, hearing Tariq's heartfelt whisper in his ear. "I'm sorry, Abdullah. I'm sorry, brother, for what I've put you through."

"It's O.K. Don't worry. I'm fine. Nothing bad happened to me."

"Praise God! Praise God forever for your safety! May evil strike me before it falls on you. It did fall on me, brother. And I've decided, therefore, to change my entire life. I will go back to the village once and for all. I will go back to God once and for all. I'll leave all this behind me. Indeed, I'll take my leave of this whole world. In all truth, the more you are able to dispense with others, the more you preserve your dignity and maintain your freedom. I will make a true repentance before God, and I will spend the rest of my life following the path of the Sufi mystics, renouncing all the finery of this world, all its false temptations."

Abdullah did not open his eyes or comment, letting his friend rest upon his chest, embracing him, patting his back lightly and taking in Tariq's soft confession. "We'll go to our village. You will marry Sameeha, and I will detach myself from everything in order to devote myself to God. Do you remember how our village was when we were young? No walls around our houses, doors open even at night, strangers passing through as welcome as a guest in any home. We had fewer possessions and less money; as a result, there was no need to lie and nothing to steal. Do you recall how we would swim in the river, tend our cattle, study, play, laugh and dream? You and me and Ibrahim. Ah! How the world has changed! And none of it for the better, brother. "

"We have reached the point where the best we can hope for is to be buried when we die. Believe me, I wish that when my time comes, I might be able to do it for myself so as not to rely on anyone else."

"When I was in their hands," Tariq replied, "I prayed all the more to make up for the dawn prayers that I've missed in recent weeks. And going forward, I will continue to compensate for any missed prayers, days of fasting and Qur'an readings. They humiliated me, brother. They could have killed me and harmed you or anyone in our families. I was afraid to die in the state I was in. Afraid to face God as the man I have been. And for what? For the sake of meaningless, worldly things. This world has passed away from my eyes, and just as our Lord – the great, the all-knowing and wise – has said, it is not worth a gnat's wing to me. This world is not worth a gnat's wing to me, Abdullah."

"It's been like that with me too," said Abdullah, matching his friend's subdued tone. "Ever since I opened my eyes to it."

"Yes, I know. And now I see that you were right, and I can find no fault in you except that you are content to stand and wait for your end, instead of travelling down the road that takes us back to God."

"God knows where I am, while I do not know where he is, so it is he who will take me to him if he wants. My wishes mean nothing compared to his."

"Yes, but it's necessary to signal your intention, for our Lord says, 'I am present in my servant's thought of me; I am with him when he remembers me. If he remembers me in his soul, I remember him in mine. If he mentions me in a gathering, I mention him in a gathering greater than his. If he approaches me by a hand, I approach him by a cubit. If he approaches me by a cubit, I approach him by a fathom. If he comes walking to me, I go rushing to him.' And now I will go to him at a run."

"You know what? The thing that interests me most is whether there is anything after death. Not paradise, not the fire or things like that, but rather any single thing at all that might inspire this verse from the Qur'an: 'Truly you were heedless of this, so we have torn the veil from your eyes, and today your vision is sharp.' So that I might see and know the truth, the real truth. And I might know the answer to this one question: why all the pain? Who benefits? Where does it go, all this pain that mankind and animals have suffered for the entire expanse of time?"

"Yes, yes! There must be some reality. As far as I'm concerned, that reality is God. And now I have found within me the resolve to anchor this reality in my heart and mind and soul for all the years that I have left, so that there will be no doubt within me that I will touch that reality when it's my time." After a pause, Tariq said, "Now get up so we can make ourselves ready for the trip back to our village."

Tariq lifted himself off the breast of Abdullah, who opened his eyes and sat up, leaning back against the headboard.

"I know you are emotional and easily excited," Abdullah said, "which makes you temperamental, changing your behaviour and your outlook in a spontaneous and guileless – maybe even childish – way at times. Tariq the Befuddled: we called you that for a reason."

"No! This time my resolve is strong, and I have settled the matter within my soul. There's no going back on it."

"What about your other obligations and responsibilities? Your children and their mother, I mean, and Qisma?"

"All my children are grown up, and they have everything they need, with the exception of Zaynab, the youngest. She's her mother's favourite, just as she is mine. Without abandoning her entirely, I'll turn her over to the care of her mother. She won't present any problem – my wife, I mean – for she has always been the one who understands me best and supports me no matter what I decide. She is a good, obedient and patient wife. We have known and understood each other well since we were small. The difficulty is with Qisma. To tell the truth, I don't know what I can do with her, and I don't think she will support my decision. At the same time, for the sake of her father – our brother, the good Ibrahim, nobler than any man I have known – I cannot abandon her and her son. She's a difficult woman, Abdullah: she's rebellious, she refuses to wear the hijab, she smokes and drinks, she interacts freely with men, and she doesn't hesitate to do anything that comes into her head. The Lord will hold me accountable for her sins. He will hold me accountable for not holding her accountable, for not checking her or correcting her. And even if I deceive myself and others in this matter, how will I deceive the Lord, he who knows all things?"

"You are always saying, 'Verily, God gives us time though he overlooks nothing.' Do the same and be patient with her."

"I don't know how I will persuade her, or what I will do with her. But I'll think about it. You too: try to think about it with me, I beg you."

CHAPTER 26

Reorganisation

Qisma was seething with anger. She began walking round the bed, wringing her hands. She was certain she would not be able to persuade Tariq to turn away from his decision this time, but she was not one to give up without a fight.

Qisma called for Sabriya to take away her child, who was sitting on Tariq's lap, then she closed the doors that led to the hall and to the balcony. She brought her face close to Tariq's with a suppressed shout. "For the love of God, what are you saying? Our project is not a passing whim. It's not a game. This is a serious business tied to our lives, the lives of our children, and many others besides. You can't get into it then get out again so easily. After all, you are the one who pursued it so eagerly after your friend Sheikh Tafir persuaded you to take him as your model. He's been exposed to two assassination attempts, and here they are, trying a third time through you. But he hasn't retreated or surrendered. On the contrary! As you see, he has strengthened his hand against all eventualities through money, weapons, the tribe and even religion. Difficulties should increase our resolve, not the opposite."

"Say what you will about me. Call me a coward, as you have before. I am firm in this decision of mine because it emanates from the bottom of my soul and the conviction of my spirit. I am not Tafir, and I don't want to be like him. Precisely because this is not a game, as you say, and it's tied to our lives, and the lives of our families and others besides. So I will gladly abandon it in order to preserve us and them."

"Security comes from learning from experience and our mistakes, through greater vigilance, and – when the time is right – through attack as a means of defence."

"There's nothing left to say on this topic. This is not my field. I'm no good at it, and it's not good for me. I've made my decision, and it's final. You need to look to yourself now and decide what you want to do."

"I won't back down. I won't retreat from any battle, even if I have to fight alone. You don't know me well, but I know myself perfectly. I won't back down."

Tariq thought about asking her for a divorce, but he was embarrassed to tell her what was in his soul, that it was hard for him to accept as a wife a woman who was alone in Baghdad, surrounded by all manner of male associates and colleagues. Though he would never say it, he hoped that she might be the one to request a divorce. He had been trying to convince her of the seriousness of his decision in order to make her realise that for all practical purposes his return to the village would amount to a separation, since Tariq was abandoning the world and all its pleasures, and seeking refuge in a life of renunciation, Sufism, devotion and worship.

Another factor in his reluctance to make explicit his wishes was his love for and loyalty to her father Ibrahim. And then there was the fact that he loved her son, and the child loved him, as he had shown in their embrace the day before, which Tariq felt had not just been the pressing of one chest to another, but rather the move of one heart towards another and one soul towards another, the very depths of one person towards the unspoken depths of another.

He wished, after informing her of the kidnappers' request, that he had had the courage to ask her what she would have done in his place, or if the police had not succeeded in their plan to rescue Abdullah. But he had not done so because he feared she would say that she would have given them what they wanted. Deep down, he was almost certain that she would have.

Qisma, recognising the impossibility of persuading him on her own, considered falling back on Tariq's friend Tafir and asking for his help, or perhaps seeking the help of Sayyid Jalal al-Din. In the end, she decided to start with the sayyid because he was closer and more important, powerful and in the know. She called him on the mobile and thanked him for saving Abdullah. She said she wanted to sound him out regarding an important matter and to thank him personally. After she had hung up, Tariq watched as she hurried to change her clothes, and knew that she was going to Jalal. He told her he intended to go back to the village with Abdullah that same day. She asked him to wait until she returned from her interview with Sayyid Jalal al-Din.

She met the sayyid in his office, and after she had thanked him for helping to secure not only Tariq's safety but Abdullah's too, she asked for an explanation of the kidnappers' actions and motives. Jalal told her what he had told Abdullah, without making any mention of his son. He did not let on that he had met Abdullah, and he had no intention of doing so. Likewise, Abdullah, for his part, had not told anyone about that interview, and had no plans to speak of it with anyone but Sameeha, since she was the only one who knew his secret.

The sayyid told her that the kidnappers were just a gang for hire, that he had interrogated them himself and confirmed that they did not know the party that had paid them. He told her that Sheikh Tafir had many enemies and jealous rivals, for he was the sheikh of a large tribe with hundreds of thousands of votes in the elections. Tafir was a canny operator and had many balls in the air; a number of parties were trying to entice or force him to form an alliance with them, or else were doing what they could to prevent him from allying himself with the opposition. In certain cases, they had been able to persuade (or bribe) his son – the member of parliament – to support them in one cause or another, only for Tafir to refuse. So the attempts on his life were no surprise – and it was possible that his own son was behind them.

"Is he really so influential?"

"Yes, and he has relationships with all sides: the Americans, the resistance, the government, the tribes, religious men, merchants, diplomats, and so on. He befriends everyone, and at the same time he cheats everyone, mixing eggs and rocks together in the game. Ever since the regime change, people like him have multiplied. But the players are many, and the field is small. Everyone is doing what he can to neutralise his rivals or else bring them into their coalition."

"I'm able to persuade him to give me what I want," Qisma said.

The sayyid was surprised – impressed even – though Qisma gave nothing away when he pressed her for details. She did not tell him that Tafir still owed her a third request, so the sayyid concluded that her influence stemmed from Tafir's friendship with her husband. When he mentioned this connection, Qisma reported Tariq's decision to withdraw to the village and isolate himself from the world. She asked Jalal's advice, then expressed her hope that he would be able to persuade her husband to think again. Jalal said it was unfortunate, because he wanted the best for the people of his village, but at the same time he doubted he would be able to persuade Tariq to continue down the path they had chosen if he was not driven by a true and burning conviction from within. He saw no reason, however, why Qisma should not take matters into her own hands, continuing to involve Tariq nominally in order to retain the votes of the people of the village and Tariq's acquaintances. For it would be a disaster to abandon everything that had been put into place, and he was always ready to support and help her. His party belonged to one of the biggest factions in the government at that moment; she would be able to form an alliance with them in the future, and also in time persuade others to join – Sheikh Tafir, for instance. He told her, with an air of total conviction, that what her party still lacked was external support, for not one of Iraq's political parties was without foreign backing. He reminded her that her being a woman would guarantee her a seat in parliament on account of the quota. In order to entice her further, he added, "And who knows how the game of alliances and coalitions will go? Perhaps you will be the first female prime minister of Iraq."

Qisma smiled without comment, and Jalal knew he had appealed to her dreams. With renewed confidence, she resolved to forge ahead with the party, even if she had to do it by herself. She did not raise any objections when Sayyid Jalal al-Din escorted her to the door and embraced her before opening it. Even though his embrace seemed fatherly at first, she realised from his tone of voice and the discreet words whispered in her ear that its basis was lust. As she left the room, repeating her thanks for his help and advice, and promising to stay in touch and maintain their spirit of cooperation, she told herself that she would learn to exploit his interest and desire, taking from him what she wanted without granting him anything in return.

Jalal accompanied her, his hand still on her shoulder, from his office to the main entrance of the building, in the course of which he urged her to caution Tariq and Abdullah against going to the village, at least for the next two days, for conditions were not safe. He had reliable intelligence about an intensification of bombings, assassinations and kidnappings, both in Baghdad and along the highway.

Having agreed to postpone their journey, Tariq and Abdullah did not leave the house during the extra two days they remained in the capital. Tariq had begun to put his resolution into practice. He stepped up his routine of prayers and religious readings, and the child barely left his side, imitating everything he did. Tariq began teaching the boy how to pray, starting with the shorter suras of the Qur'an. At times he even recited to the boy various poems and excerpts he had memorised from Sufi books, which helped Tariq himself to understand them better. They were becoming deeply attached to one another, and Tariq took a profound delight in this unpolluted companionship, something so similar to the companionship of the angels that Tariq had begun to refer to the boy as "this angel". Then he started to call him "*my angel*". He even went so far as to suggest to Qisma that he take the boy with him to the village and take charge of his day-to-day care and education. Qisma gave some thought to his proposal and decided it was the best solution for her and the child. Not in respect to his care and education, which were areas in which Sabriya and Sabir excelled, and which school would provide when the time was right, but rather for the purpose of keeping him safe. If the gang had been able to kidnap Tariq when he was asleep beside her in bed, it would not be hard for them to kidnap her son. She knew that the strategies for her advancement that she had discussed with Jalal were likely to win her as many enemies as allies.

Her acquiescence brought true joy to Tariq's heart. He felt that the boy would compensate somewhat for the lost companionship of his lifelong friend Ibrahim. This child was the soul of his soul. He placed wild hopes upon his little shoulders, imagining that he might be his disciple and successor if Tariq advanced through the various ranks of the Sufi order.

As for Abdullah, he spent the entire first day sleeping in Rahib's bed. Rahib was his usual industrious self, everywhere at once, keeping an eye on every aspect of the daily programme of the two houses. But he found the time and the opportunity to meet privately with Madame Sheikh Qisma in his office when she came there to add to his agenda, and used it to remind her again of the reason for his presence there, namely, her promise that she would find him a wife. With a marriage between Bara and Wafa firmly on the cards, his own lonely situation was beginning to weigh upon him more and more. Rahib told Qisma that he wished his own wedding might be held at the same time. He would take any woman, even a widow or a divorcée. Qisma made no attempt to hide her anger at his plea, taking him to task as she paced the floor of his office. "I can't stand people and societies that look upon widows and divorcées as second-class women," she shouted. "As though they were used goods. Anyone who keeps such an outdated idea in their head deserves to lose it."

Rahib almost retorted, "And what about those who still consider chopping off heads an appropriate punishment for outdated ideas?" But he swallowed the thought to avoid escalating the situation. He suspected that her anger disguised a more mundane message: now was not the right time. He told her that the demands of their work would never let up. Indeed, they would only increase with time, and in order for him to remain with her it was necessary for her first to fulfil her promise. Qisma left the room, muttering, "Later, later . . ."

The moment her footsteps had faded into silence, Rahib hammered his desk with his fist, then slammed the door and began kicking the chairs and filing cabinets in his rage. "The whore, the whore!" he repeated in a low voice, though it felt to him like a shout – or even a bellow. "I won't let her cheat me. I'm Rahib! No-one cheats me and escapes retribution!"

But when he had calmed down a little, he said to himself: "I'll be patient with her for a while, but only a very little while. Then I'll bring up the topic again, and this time I won't give her any excuse to brush off my request. Depending on how she replies, I'll know what I need to do." Rahib also resolved to change his behaviour so that Qisma could not be unaware of his displeasure. He would no longer hurry to fulfil her requests, he would dawdle and be slack in his duties, he would be absent without leave more often. With that in mind, Rahib suggested to his brother Bara that they go to their village with Wafa and her mother, if she wanted, so that Wafa could get to know their family, and they her. They could go to the mausoleum of the Father of Lights and seek the blessing, or maybe make an offering to him. Bara agreed in general but baulked at the idea of visiting the grave, for he had never heard of the Father of Lights, and he did not believe in superstitions, as he put it. Indeed, he did not believe in the holiness of any being or anything that either had a body or could exist in one. For according to him, holiness, if it existed at all, belonged to the spiritual and not the physical, to what was absent, not present, to the principle that was impossible to incarnate, and not to incarnation or what claimed to represent it – even symbolically.

Rahib did not understand a word of this, but he was content to remain ignorant. The important thing was that Bara had agreed to visit their village, which he was missing. There, perhaps, he would raise with his original sheikh, Tafir, his concern that Qisma might renege on her promise to him. "I'll make up my mind when we get there," he told himself.

Bara headed to Wafa's office to make plans with her for the

visit and the engagement. The moment he left the office, Rahib came across Abdullah carrying a cup of tea in the direction of the passage that led to Qisma's house. Rahib greeted him warmly and asked where he was going.

"To the garden, to sit and watch the river," said Abdullah.

"Come with me first," said Rahib, taking him by the arm, "and let me introduce you to Wafa."

Abdullah shook Wafa's hand, then sat on a nearby chair, smoking a cigarette and drinking his tea, while Bara spoke freely with Wafa about arrangements for the trip to his village. It appeared that everything had been agreed, prepared in advance by Rahib, and there was nothing left to discuss.

Wafa felt embarrassed to be talking in the presence of Abdullah about private matters that did not concern him. She tried to include him in the conversation somehow, asking if he had taken a tour of the city during his visit.

"No," he said. "Except for the trip at night they gave me for free when I was blindfolded."

Wafa felt even more embarrassed and said, "It's better that you don't, for the city's appearance is sad and horrifying now, so desecrated by the militants, the occupation and the gangs. Its streets are piled high with rubbish, and the poor, the orphans, the homeless, the lost and the crazy fill every square, street and alley."

"Yes, Wafa's right," said Bara. "Baghdad was never like this. Even just wandering about used to be beautiful."

After a short silence, Wafa said, "It breaks my heart to see the homeless children. I wish I could adopt them all, feed them, give them places to play and study instead of them being ground into the dirt like this. How often I've heard stories of them being exploited, forced to fight and kill, or being kidnapped so that their organs might be sold."

Bara felt the sincerity of her sadness. He had not realised she was so affected by the plight of these children. "What would you say about us doing something for them? There are still many good people like us who want to do something positive for this country, some civic act, peaceful and humane. We could start an awareness campaign, collect donations of things needed by the homeless shelters, educational centres, and so on."

Wafa's face lit up. "Yes! Yes! Or we could found an organisation or an unofficial movement that would spread hope among the people and encourage them to do something positive in the midst of all this destruction."

Bara looked at Abdullah, waiting for a response from him. When none was forthcoming, he prompted him, saying, "Even you, my good friend Kafka, you could help too, up there in your village. We have to do something – we, the good, silent majority. Others are forming militias, fictitious companies and gangs to carve out their share of the plunder. They fight among themselves to steal what they can get their hands on. Why shouldn't we do something to save what can be saved? This country is full of charitable energy, full of young people, idealists, dreaming of a better country. Yes, we'll plan for that, and we'll do it. We'll do everything in our power, and we'll spur on our acquaintances to do something too – in Baghdad, in the other cities and provinces, all through Iraq."

Abdullah got up without a word and made to leave, but Bara grabbed him by the arm. "Do not be surprised, my dear friend Kafka, if you find us swooping down upon you suddenly with a group of friends to establish something in your village too."

Abdullah could not deny that their words had touched something in his soul, despite all his dark pessimistic thoughts. As he left, he told them, "You are welcome any time. I'll be glad to help you as much as I can."

CHAPTER 27

The Salt of the Earth

By mid-morning the next day everything was ready for the trips to the two villages. No-one remained in the two houses apart from Qisma, Sabriya, Sabir and Rahib, whom Qisma had promised to bring to his village on her way to her own in a few days' time. Qisma also kept one of her bodyguards, the son of her neighbour Amira from the village, because she trusted him, both because she chose him herself and because he had lost his father the same time she had lost hers. She dismissed the others, acting on the advice of Sayyid Jalal al-Din, whom she had asked to select and train a professional squad, as he had offered.

Tariq, Abdullah, the child Ibrahim and the nine members of the bodyguard would travel in three vehicles. They would take Bara and Wafa with them and drop them off at the checkpoint on the main highway where the road branched off to the Shakhabiti village, where another car would meet them and take them the rest of the way.

Qisma asked Abdullah to get in touch with her a day before the wedding night so that she could attend. The next few days would be an opportunity for her to reassess and reorganise her affairs. She would call Sheikh Tafir to inform him of the new developments, including the fact that she was acting leader of the party now. It would be important to underline what Tariq had gone through because of him, and make sure he understood Tariq's noble position towards Tafir. Anything that might make him feel indebted towards them was worth a try. She would also remind him, at the appropriate moment, of the third request he still owed her. And she would seek his agreement, in principle, to their cooperating in various spheres.

Qisma also considered meeting with General Adam, the American officer, maybe even trying to invite him, in some private way, to her house. She let him know of her readiness to work closely with the Americans so that he would open for her a communication channel with their embassy. Sayyid Jalal al-Din's advice regarding the necessity of cooperating with the agents of a foreign country was fresh in her mind. Naturally, she would not tell Sayyid Jalal al-Din, who was connected to Iran, nor anyone else, what she was planning. In this regard, the absence of Bara, who opposed the occupation, came at a convenient time. Qisma would also ask General Adam for advice on training and supplying her bodyguard, sound him out carefully about forming a militia, and try to ascertain the extent of the Americans' influence on the elections and their impact on the results through propaganda and analysis – or even through fraud.

When she asked Tariq to send word about the date of Abdullah's wedding – given that Abdullah might neglect to do so, since he did not own a mobile – Tariq let her know that he would personally see to it as soon as possible. He wanted to be free to withdraw from the world, but first there were several matters he needed to arrange, chief among them the weddings of his sister and her daughter. For that reason, he was pushing for them to go ahead without delay, despite Abdullah's attempts to put his wedding off further out of respect for his dear departed companion in silence and cigarette smoke, Hamid the Snorer. The moment they had arrived in the village, before they parted to go their separate ways, Abdullah and Tariq heard the announcement of his death over the mosque loudspeakers. They went straight to Hamid's house on the outskirts of the village.

"The first thing to be done is to confirm he's really dead," said Tariq. "Perhaps he's just sleeping."

He said the same thing to Hamid's wife as soon as they arrived, but she, who knew all the ways Hamid would sleep, confirmed it was so. She told them he had taken an unusually long time in the bathroom, and when she went to check on him, she found him on the floor, naked from the waist down. She had dragged him out on her own, despite his great weight, and laid him out in the salon. She had tried to wake him by calling his name, by washing his face with cold water, and by putting perfume, lemons and onions under his nose, but all to no avail.

When they entered the main room of the house, they found him lying there. It was as though he were sleeping, aside from the fact that he was not snoring. Tariq was surprised to find that his old school medal, the one that Hamid had been presented with at the inauguration, was resting on his chest. Hamid's wife said he had not taken it off since they had hung it round his neck. He would even sleep and shower with it on. Tariq remained silent for a while, turning the medal over in his fingers. Then he said, "In that case, let it be buried with him."

As for Abdullah, after confirming that his companion was dead, he embraced him where he lay, saying, "Sleep in peace, my friend, sleep now forever. No-one will disrupt your sleep after today." Then he kissed him on the forehead and left in sorrow, smoking and thinking about death, without giving any thought to participating in the funeral rites of washing, shrouding, praying and burying. The presence of the members of Tariq's bodyguard and the guards Qisma had dismissed – and later Tariq's son Zahir and his escort – ensured these tasks were quickly accomplished.

Most of the men present were friends and relatives of Zahir. He was the one who had selected them for his father's bodyguard. So when he learned immediately after the burial that they were being dismissed, the news had the force of a small explosive device. Perhaps if he had known about it before the burial, the body of Hamid the Snorer would have remained above ground for a long time. No-one, including his father, expected that he would be enraged to that degree, barely able to contain himself. He uttered words against Qisma that verged on disrespect for his father. "Of course, she sees herself as above us. So sweet and precious – a stuck-up city girl. We're just stupid villagers to her. She wants her team to come from Baghdad, city slickers like her. Not like us, the salt of the earth."

Although Tariq was worn out by the journey and the burial, he found the strength to reproach him. "Silence! Get a grip on yourself and mind your tongue. I'll have more to say to you when we are home."

As soon as they reached the house, he led him into his room.

His wife, Umm Zahir, followed them in. They closed the door, and the long, stormy discussion that followed exhausted them all. The son set things in motion by confessing his dissatisfaction with much that Tariq had done. Hoping to win his mother's affection and get her on his side, he said, "Honestly, you should never have married her. Besides the fact that she's young enough to be your daughter, she's arrogant and she looks down on the people of the village. She doesn't dress, act or talk like us. Everyone whispers about it. Personally, I haven't liked her since we were little. My mother has never fallen short in any way, and she does not deserve to be treated like–"

Tariq could not remain calm in the face of this provocation. A red mist came over him, and he launched himself at his son. He would have struck him had his wife not come between them, pushing Zahir away and shouting, "Be silent! So disrespectful! So shameless!"

"No! She's the shameless one!" replied the son.

This time Tariq was so indignant that his wife could not keep his hand from his son's cheek, and he slapped him hard. "Shut your mouth, you imbecile! How dare you speak to me like this? You fool! Who are you to tell me that? What do you know, you donkey, about what I should or shouldn't do? The only thing left is for a bird to fly out of my butt and teach me to fly. I'll crush this stupid head of yours!"

Tariq managed to strike Zahir's head another time despite his wife's attempts to keep them apart by standing between them. She held onto Tariq, trying to calm him down, until she was able to make him sit on the edge of the bed. Zahir sat in the corner on a chair, while his mother remained standing, her heart aching for both of them.

Tariq took a deep breath. Then he spat in the direction of his son and said, "What has come over you, my boy? Your manners towards me have never fallen short. You've never raised your voice against me in your life. What has come over you? Well? Have you gone crazy?"

Zahir hung his head, and his tone became conciliatory. "I'm sorry, Father. I'm sorry. It's because of the people's talk, grief for my mother, and fear for you."

"Shut up about people and their talk! And what happens between your mother and me is none of your business. We are your parents – not the other way round. Obedience is all you owe us, or else you can get out of our faces and go to the devil!"

Umm Zahir made a sign to her son, indicating that he should approach his father and seek his pardon. He got up, kissed his father's head and hand, and then sat on the floor at his feet. "I'm sorry, Father," he said again. "Forgive me. I thought you would understand me, just as you always understand everyone."

This show of contrition had the desired effect on Tariq, and his wife helped further by bringing him a cup of water from the table. He drank it, sighed, and said, "It's alright, it's alright." He paused, then continued, "What I've been wanting to tell you all this time is that I've come back for good. I've decided to leave everything behind, to abandon it all. What I want is a complete disengagement from worldly affairs in order to devote myself to study and worship until the end of my days."

His words came as such a surprise that they forgot everything that had happened and been said moments before. It put their minds at ease to an extent, though they found it strange. "What about the party, the tribe, and the contracts for the projects, Father?" Zahir asked. "What you have accomplished has given the people hope. It's all they speak of."

"I'm abandoning it all entirely, as of now. None of it will benefit me in the least on the day of reckoning before our Lord."

"I understand completely, Father, and I agree. All this is tiring for you, and it's time for you to rest. From now on you mustn't worry about any of it. Set yourself apart for your worship and leave everything to me. I can manage it all in your absence. I've agreed on some new contracts with the American officer in this area, and I've started work on the projects already in hand. I've also filled the ranks of our party with dozens of young men from our village and those close by, and played host to a number of notable people among the tribes. I have done you proud, Father. Ask Mother about what I've done! Ask anyone!"

"I have no doubts about your abilities, my boy, but I do not approve of this road for you. It's a rocky, thorny path, full of dangers. I think it better to relinquish it entirely."

"No! I beg you, Father. I know I can do it, and I want the chance to prove it. You've lived your life as a sheikh and a sayyid, one of the most distinguished men in the village. My grandfather was just the same. I want to be like you both, to keep the prestige and the sheikh's rank within our family. I'm a young man in the prime of life. I am more than capable, and I want our family to keep its standing, pride and wealth forever, for all our sakes: me, my brothers, our children and our grandchildren after us."

"I advise you not to do this, Zahir. After all I've seen and learned, I fear for you. And for your brothers and your children."

"No, Father! Don't be afraid on my account. I'm your son, and I'm worthy of the name. Everyone will attest to that. Please grant me this opportunity. Let me have it! Please. I'll keep you informed of everything, and I'll come to you whenever I need advice."

"As you wish. But leave me out of it. I'm no longer interested. Now I'm exhausted, and I want to go to bed. Before I do, I have one last request for you. As quickly as you can, have a bedroom made in the storeroom that's connected to the mosque, through the door behind the pulpit. The key is hanging on a nail above the door. There, you'll find prayer mats, books, cleaning supplies, dyes and poison for the rats and cockroaches. Clean it out, and put in it two single beds, a small refrigerator, shelves and a kettle. Like a hotel room. That's where I'll live out my isolation. When that is done, go to your uncle Abdullah's house and to the house of Sabry – may he rest in peace – to seek out Sabry's eldest son, Anwar. Ask them if there are any rooms in their houses they want to make fit for a newly married couple and do whatever they want. Furnish them as lavishly as can be and tell them it's a gift from your father on the occasion of their weddings."

At seven o'clock that evening, General Adam arrived at Qisma's house in Baghdad. He had called to let her know that he would not be able to accept her invitation to dinner on account of his busy schedule, but he would visit and drink tea with her for an hour or two. Qisma was dressed as finely as she could, wearing her favourite perfume, when she received him and the two soldiers who formed his escort.

One of the soldiers stood by the main door to the salon, the other outside the door leading to the garden. Qisma and Adam sat across from each other at a table Sabriya had set with plates of desserts and two pots, one of tea and one of coffee. Each of them was struck by how attractive the other was, how elegant and refined. And as the conversation began to flow, each of them picked out the best words and phrases they knew of the other's language.

"You're a brave woman," said Adam. "Brave, clever . . . and beautiful," he said, pausing before risking the final adjective, which was accompanied by a smile and a steady gaze into her eyes. He went on to say that he liked people who were willing to act in the service of their country, and that he would do everything in his power to help her. When it came to military and security matters, he would handle her requests himself. As for political matters, he promised he would set up an appointment for her at the embassy in order to introduce her to everyone there.

When she asked him his view on Sheikh Tafir, he said, "We know almost all there is to know about him. His kind is common in Iraq, unfortunately."

"You have detailed information about everything," she said. "But you don't use it unless it brings advantage to you. You are not acting for the sake of others, or for the sake of a fixed principle, but in your own interests, even though that contradicts all principles."

"That's true, unfortunately," he replied.

When pressed in this way, Adam kept his answers short, using blunt, functional terms. It was as though he was discussing something that he found offensive or distasteful. But when the talk became more personal, his tone changed, and he was more expansive. He told her he had embraced Islam nine years earlier after falling in love with a young Pakistani woman. She had made his conversion a condition for their marriage. Then, when she was pregnant, she had died in a car accident. It had devastated him. He was hoping to marry again and was looking for a Muslim woman, preferably Iraqi, since his experience in Iraq had changed him so much. It was the deepest and most important experience of his life, and he wanted his future wife to be a partner who understood that and who would be part of that experience and that change. "I embraced Islam for the sake of love," he said, "and now I want love for the sake of Islam."

Before Tariq had retired to his bed to sleep that afternoon, Zahir had kissed his head and then the head of his mother. He left in a state of exultation. He almost skipped as he went on his way. "This is where it all begins," he said to himself. Inside, he felt like a young pharaoh who had just been crowned king – or made a god. He wished he had the magic staff of Moses to realise instantly all the dreams that were swirling around in his head; he had been given a green light and would certainly act on it.

The fifteen members of his bodyguard were waiting for him in the courtyard. They were his friends, people close to him. Some were his relatives or relatives of his wife. Their rifles were slung on their shoulders, and they were drinking tea. With them were the nine who had returned from Baghdad with his father. He hugged each of them in turn, patting them on the shoulder. Then he repeated the words he had said to himself: "This is where it all begins. We'll gather today for dinner at my house. Tell the others to attend as well."

He ordered three of them to gather the village's carpenters and the owners of the furniture shops and bring them to the mosque. He awarded the job to the carpenter who promised to transform the storeroom according to Tariq's wishes by midnight. He left two of his friends there to help, in addition to the carpenter's own assistants. Then he set off for the house of Abdullah, who was taken aback and resisted at first, insisting that he did not need anything from anyone. But Zahir begged him to go along with it, calling him "Uncle" and telling him, "This is my father's wish, his orders to me, and his wedding gift to you and my aunt. My father will be angry with us all if you refuse him."

Abdullah showed them the room. "But please begin tomorrow, for now I want to sleep."

The carpenters and furniture dealers inspected the room. They quickly took its measurements then headed off to Sabry's house, where the response was a trill of joy from his mother. She kissed Zahir on the forehead, expressing her gratitude. Then she directed them to the largest room in the house, her own bedroom, in which she had married Anwar's father. After Abu Anwar had been imprisoned and given up for dead, she had married his brother, Anwar's uncle, there too.

However great Anwar's mother's joy, Zahir's was greater still. He didn't sleep that night. After dinner he gave a speech to his guests, during which it became clear to him that he resembled his father and his grandfather in his powers of oratory, then he stayed up with ten of his closest companions until the break of dawn. He distributed roles and tasks among them. "You are responsible for the finances and contracts; you for military affairs and organising protection; you for communications and public relations; you for social matters in the village; you for advertising and publicity. And make sure the people know to honour me with the title 'professor sheikh' or 'sheikh professor'."

In his address the following evening, he announced that he would be splitting off from the party "in order to correct its course, and for the benefit of the village and the region. As people say, 'Nothing scratches your itch like your own fingernails.' City-dwellers never listen to us or work for our benefit, but instead they exploit us for their own advantage." As an example, he pointed to Qisma dismissing members of her bodyguard, replacing them with men from the capital, commenting, "They're limp trash from the city, while we are the salt of the earth. And that's what the name of our movement will be: The Salt of the Earth."

He was pleased with this name because it reminded him of the name by which his father and his two friends, Abdullah and Ibrahim, had been known throughout their lives: the Sons of the Earth Crack. With great enthusiasm, he shouted it aloud as he pounded his chest with his fist. Everyone present did the same, crying in one voice, "Long live The Salt of the Earth!"

CHAPTER 28

The Great Night of Love

In the middle of that night, Qisma dreamed – or else hallucinated – that she was being raped. Someone – or perhaps there was more than one of them – stole into her bedroom in the dark. With great force and remarkable speed, she was blindfolded and gagged. Her wrists were tied to the bedposts. She was stripped naked. And then it was done to her with a tearing violence she did not know how many times. Likewise, she could not guess who the perpetrator might be – or the perpetrators. That was what increased the intensity of her confusion in the aftermath.

Through the long nightmarish hours that she thought she had spent in bonds, debased and defiled, her blindfolded eyes did not shed a tear. Nor did they after she was untied by Sabriya, who came up in the morning when she noticed that Qisma was late to rise. Sabriya, in fact, did nothing more than pull the covers off Qisma's head and ask what was wrong. Qisma poured it all out as she rose from her bed. She cursed, spat and paced like a madwoman. She kicked or punched everything she saw in front of her: table, wardrobes, walls. She was naked as she did it, as though Sabriya did not exist. She did not close the door of the bathroom behind her when she went in to bathe.

Through the long nightmarish hours when she believed she

was tied up, she had tried to work out the identity of the perpetrator. Was it the masked man who had threatened to slit her throat? Was it Rahib? Was it Sayyid Jalal al-Din or one of his men? Or all three together? Was it General Adam or one of his men? Sheikh Tafir or one of his? Was it Tariq or one of his people? Or perhaps Zahir, Tariq's son, or one of his friends. The son of her neighbour Amira? One or all of the kidnappers? Each of these possibilities seemed as plausible as any other, so she decided to exact vengeance upon them all – without mercy. She would not hesitate to cut off their heads or their dicks. She would make them tear each other apart. All of them were implicated in the crime in some way. That was the conclusion she arrived at as she remembered the young woman, Abeer al-Janabi. She stayed a long time in the shower, scrubbing her skin raw. She wanted to remove it entirely, not just clean it.

"One tyrant raped me before," she said as she stood beneath the jet of water. "I know who he is. I know his face and his name. And I swear I will find his grave after they bury him. I will dig him up and tear apart his corpse with my nails and my teeth. I will grind his bones. I will burn him and then piss on the ashes. But now, many tyrants have raped me. I do not know who they are, neither their faces nor their names. I am like Iraq. That is what has happened to it. I am like my father, for that is what happened to him."

Qisma's desire to slaughter or be slaughtered like her father grew until it had taken hold of her entirely. Over the nights that followed the nightmares were unrelenting, and her waking hours were filled by alternating bouts of hysteria, nervous tension and madness, sometimes so intense that she fainted. She veered between agitation and calm, disbelief and faith, movement and stillness, grief and a wild urge for revenge. Before her eyes swam a blend of incongruous images from her childhood and everything that she had experienced throughout her life. Faces, voices, hands, spirits. A stark desire to destroy was followed by a stark desire to be destroyed, or be riddled by bullets, be mangled in a car accident, for the roof to collapse upon her, for the sky to collapse upon her, for the earth to be torn open beneath her as though by a landmine or earthquake. Sabir and Sabriya alone knew of her distress. They alone understood her, and they cared for her through all her shifting states as though she were one of their lost children.

Several days went by before she went to the village to attend Abdullah's wedding. She did not know how many, but it was long enough for her to have formed detailed plans for obtaining millions of dollars from the central bank, either by theft or by fraud, plans to form a powerful militia, and plans to join forces with the most vicious gangs of kidnappers and murderers. She would work with anyone against everyone.

Qisma had entrusted Wafa with all matters pertaining to the party, including the publishing and distribution of the journal, as Bara had decided to remain in the village with his mother for several more days, while Tariq had now begun his seclusion in the mosque storeroom, which he loved from the first moment he entered it after it had been refurbished. The small bed was for Qisma's son and the large bed for him. Tariq transferred all his religious books to the new bookshelves, and he asked his wife to send him only vegetarian meals, prepared, so far as possible, from what was grown in the garden or in their own field. He spent his every waking moment reading or in prayer and contemplation, or conversing with the child Ibrahim in classical Arabic and helping him to memorise the Qur'an. Even their play consisted of rehearsing the movements used in ritual purification and in prayer. He felt his spirit gradually becoming lighter, cleaner and more energetic. His voice sounded more beautiful when reciting the Qur'an. His prayers felt true and pure, and he felt they were uniting him with the Lord. He began to forget the outside world and did not even join the others in the Friday prayer in the main hall of the mosque, just beyond the door to his chamber. Instead, he performed the prayer alone, speaking in time with the others, for he could hear the imam through the loudspeaker. Tariq did not join them even when he knew – by means of that same loudspeaker – that the one giving the sermon and leading the prayer was his second son, Mazhur.

Tariq's youngest daughter, Zaynab, the dearest to his heart, acted as messenger between him and his wife, bringing him food and clean clothes, and bringing the child Ibrahim. He would sometimes keep her there for long hours. She joined them for meals and for their rituals of reading, prayer and religious games. The innocence of their young spirits refreshed and delighted his own, such that he felt his own soul becoming more childlike, innocent and pure. He was joined in his isolation by angelic spirits, or actual angels, whom he sensed but could not see. At times he thought that one of them had brought him a cup of water or had opened a specific page for him to read. And when his little one brought him news that the weddings of his sister Sameeha and her daughter would take place the following night, Tariq did not want to go. He did not want to leave his chamber of secrets and spirits. But he considered it to be the one last task that would discharge his debt and obligation to the outside world.

The weddings were held in the spacious courtyard of Abdullah's house. Zahir and his friends oversaw all the details. After dinner, dozens of chairs were lined up, in front of which sat the four newlyweds. A brief opening recitation from the Qur'an was followed by words of congratulation. Then they played music through speakers until the gypsy band they had hired began to play. Accompanied by his daughter Zaynab, Tariq arrived when the dinner was over because he no longer wanted to eat meat.

Tariq went up to the newlyweds and congratulated them. He shook Anwar's hand and kissed the heads of Sameeha and her daughter. They were beautiful, resembling each other in every last detail down to their wedding dresses and the two stone necklaces that hung amid the traditional chains of gold. There was nothing to distinguish them except that each was sitting beside her husband, and the two men looked nothing alike.

Tariq gave Abdullah a long, warm embrace. Abdullah had shaved off his beard, trimmed his moustache, cut his hair and dyed it black. He looked like a young man, as Tariq was quick to point out. "You've regained your youth, my friend!" He praised Abdullah's decision for the weddings to be held there, in the courtyard of his house, which had always appeared abandoned even if it was inhabited. That was where the earth crack was; that was where the three had often gathered and played; that was where he had embraced Abdullah with a similarly heartfelt embrace after his return from captivity. "How happy I am for you, Abdullah," he said. "Are you happy?"

"I do not know exactly, but the feeling that has come over me now is unlike anything I've ever felt before. Maybe it is the happiness I've never before tasted. I don't know."

"If it's a relaxing sensation or a feeling of contentment, call it happiness."

"Relaxing on the inside, but not on the outside. In all honesty, I feel embarrassed and constrained. Oppressed, even, with all these eyes looking at me."

"Don't worry! Consider it a temporary tax. It's only a few hours, and then all the people will disperse. Congratulations, my dear friend!" To his sister he said, "Congratulations, my dear! Forgive me all the wrongs I've done you, and all my shortcomings. I wish you peace and happiness! Take good care of Abdullah, for life has not treated him well, as you know."

Sameeha kissed his hand and said, "I'll place him in my eye itself. Thank you, dear brother."

Tariq's newfound serenity caught everyone off guard. They were used to him being lively, excitable, jocular and astonished – befuddled, even – by everything. Now he looked as though he was getting on in years. He had let his beard, tinged by white, grow long. Even his back was hunched a little as he took his seat in the middle of the front row, across from the newlyweds. His son Zahir led him there by the arm, and after he had sat him down, Zahir kissed his head before continuing to direct the ebb and flow of the party. Zaynab sat beside her father, smiling at the many people who came to shake his hand and congratulate him. For the first time in his life he felt that the presence of people was bothering him, just as Abdullah used to say, and he decided that he would leave shortly, as soon as the gypsy troupe struck up their first tune.

Suddenly, Qisma's son Ibrahim appeared from the shadows, running towards him and throwing himself upon his lap. Tariq's heart soared. He felt that the child entered straight into his heart as he pressed him to his chest. Then Qisma appeared, looking just as stunning as she had during the party's inauguration. Her expensive French perfume cut through the mixture of perfumes and scents in Abdullah's courtyard. She shook Tariq's hand and exchanged the usual greetings. Then she sat down with Ibrahim between them. Tariq felt he was protected by the spirits of his two children, sitting on either side of him, by his two angels, as he often thought of them.

When Zahir saw Qisma sitting near his father, he began searching the crowd for his mother. He found her in the back row with Amira, and he led her by the arm and sat her in the front, next to her daughter Zaynab. Tariq was careful not to speak to either of his wives – or even look at them – so as not to stir up any ill feeling or jealousy. The situation had become uncomfortable for him, and he was as keen as anyone for the gypsies to begin singing so that he could depart for his cell as he longed to do. But when the singing began, he decided to stay for a few more minutes when he saw the dull-witted herdsman Isma'il get up to dance, leaning on his cane. He had grown very old. He was not exactly dancing but rather making awkward movements that suggested his intention to dance and celebrate the marriages.

The space separating Tariq from the newlyweds was filled by gypsy women dancing, along with Anwar's sisters and other women from the village whom Tariq did not know. Then Qisma got up. Her dancing both appalled and entranced him, for among the women she was by far the most vivacious and beautiful. She stood out from the rest because of her clothes and the way she shook her breasts, her shoulders, her back, her hips, her feet and her belly, as the bouncing of her hair threw back her shawl. Everyone watching her imagined she was the happiest person there, for no-one knew the extent of her inner torment, that she was like a slaughtered bird, dancing from pain.

When Tariq noticed that she was becoming ever more absorbed in her movements as though she were dancing alone, without the eyes of the village upon her, he kissed the heads of his two children and slipped off into the shadows. He moved quickly in the direction of the mosque. As soon as he entered his cell, he took a deep breath and resolved to put the whole affair out of his mind, to forget what he had seen and reclaim his spiritual serenity.

Tariq put out the light and began to pray, seeking refuge in his Lord. He sank into contemplation in the dark and recited the long suras from the Qur'an that he had memorised. He was not aware of the time passing as he practised his rituals, and the lateness did not matter to him so long as he was able to feel – or at least imagine he was feeling – the purification of his soul on its journey to his creator as he brought it to the edge of manifestation with a transparency and lightness, untethered by the corporeal. It was as though he was at one with the intangible shadows while inside he radiated with light. Tariq thought that the deepest depths of darkness might be light, and the deepest depths of light might be darkness. As he approached the conclusion of his final prayer, without knowing how many he had performed before it, a light appeared in the darkness. A faint light that came from behind him. With it he caught the scent of a beautiful perfume that he recognised. Concluding his prayers, he turned his face to his right shoulder to greet the angel standing there, and turned his face to his left shoulder to greet the angel standing there. Then he noticed what he thought was a third angel, standing in the light of the open door. He was startled that it appeared to him in a captivating feminine form. He did not know the gender of angels, but the soft light bleeding from the lamp above the pulpit in the hall of the mosque, just across from the door to his cell, was illuminating the figure standing in the doorway, and there was no doubt that the body under the white, diaphanous robe was female. Tariq murmured a prayer for God to save him from the devil. Under the light robe, the angel was naked, and he could clearly see the slender legs and the round thighs, the mound between them, the curved hips below a slender waist and the perfectly round breasts. He was transfixed, sitting back on his feet, unable to tear his dumbfounded gaze away from the vision before him. In a low voice, he added a third greeting to follow the two he had bestowed on the angels on his shoulders: "Peace be upon you, and God's compassion and his blessing."

The reply came in an even lower voice, scarcely audible, such that he doubted that he had heard anything at all: "And upon you peace, and God's compassion and his blessing." For an instant, all the visions and trials of the mystics flashed through his mind: angels in white clothes, demons in the guise of angels in order to tempt the faithful or test how long they could hold out in the face of temptation. Tariq's heart pounded, but not from fear so much as awe, because he was not certain whether this thing he saw was real or only an illusion.

Qisma closed the door behind her with total calm. It was approximately two in the morning. The party had ended, and the guests had dispersed. She had left her son with her neighbour Amira, taken a shower and put on more perfume. She had dressed herself in a sheer white nightgown and nothing else. Then she had wrapped a black abaya cloak over it and gone to the mosque. She had cast off the abaya outside Tariq's chamber, opening the door cautiously, softly, without Tariq noticing. She had decided to satisfy his longings for her. She would reward him on account of everything he had done for her and endured for her sake, on account of what had befallen him because of her, and on account of his goodness and his love for her, and for her father before her. At the same time, her decision stemmed from her desire to wound herself, to bring pain down upon this body of hers for which she felt no love. Which she hated. Her body was the means by which her spirit had been hurt. So let her smash it. Others had raped it violently – so she thought and believed and felt and suspected – without any right whatsoever, so let her offer it to a man who had a greater right to it. If other bodies had raped hers by force, the time had come for her body to rape another's. There was a deep satisfaction in what she had resolved to do.

There was a desire for more pain. A desire and a craving for hurt, to harm herself. A recalcitrance. A smashing. A disintegration. A destruction. A revolution. Braving what she was fleeing. Plunging into the heart of her doubt, her pain and her weakness.

Qisma advanced in the darkness and brushed her buttocks lightly against Tariq's knees before sinking into his lap. In so doing, she felt she was satisfying an ancient desire, remembering that moment when her relationship to her father – and her entire life after that – changed as she watched Zahir sitting on his father's lap and felt jealous of him, wishing she was in his place. Instead she had had to suffer the sight of her father, home from the war in Kuwait with only one foot, his disgusting stump stretched out in front of him.

Moving sensuously in Tariq's lap, Qisma took his hands in hers and slid them down over her hips so he could feel her curves. She spread her legs as she pressed against his penis, which was stirring and becoming erect. Continuing to rub against him, she let her head fall back onto his shoulder so that her neck was in front of his face, touching his lips, and whispered in his ear, "Don't worry! You're not committing any sin. You're exercising your right, so enjoy it."

Tariq submitted to her. He knew now that it was Qisma, even if a trace of the uncertainty that had overpowered him still remained. She leaned back against his chest and let her hot breath play over his ear and neck as she moaned softly. She guided his hands across her body, from her waist to her ribcage, then higher still. She cupped his palms around her breasts, encouraging him to squeeze and stroke them. Breathing faster, he trembled with pleasure. When she took his index fingers and touched them to her nipples, he gasped as he felt them harden under his fingertips, just as his penis had hardened beneath her. She took off her dress and threw it aside, then reached under his long dishdasha robe and pulled down his underwear. Flesh made intimate contact with flesh, a touch that made Tariq's torso – his entire being – shiver. Reaching back, she encircled his waist and drew him towards her, bending over in front of him on her elbows and knees. She writhed and purred like a cat being stroked, and there was nothing he could do but act instinctively, involuntarily, now that desire had been kindled to its highest point within him. He bent over her, coming to her, penetrating her with panting thrusts and ferocious lust.

Tariq entered her at the same moment that Abdullah entered Sameeha and Anwar entered Salma. Three husbands tasted in the same moment the sweetest thing life had granted them. A unique moment, unlike anything that had come before or anything that would come after it. A moment in which they clung to true love, forgetting their past, their future, their worries, their dreams, their friends, their village and the entire world. In that moment, they even forgot their names and who they were. A pure moment, the climax of pleasure, complete in itself. A moment that allowed them to acknowledge that they had lived, and that life was a great gift that was worth unwrapping, despite all the pain it contained.

Tariq had never felt a pleasure like that in his life, not even with his first wife when they were both the age that Qisma was now. Qisma, likewise, had never experienced such a strange pleasure, especially not one she had chosen herself, with full consciousness and rapture, without any ulterior goal. Her previous marriage to the murdered officer had been motivated by money, prestige and escape from her village. As for Abdullah and Anwar, whose first such union it was, they had never expected, not even in their most fertile imaginings, that it would be so transporting and captivating.

Afterwards, as she lay beside him, her hair spread across his chest, Sameeha talked to Abdullah about all they had to look forward to. She promised him she would fill the house with life. She would raise two cows, a donkey, ducks, chickens and pigeons. She would make half the courtyard into a garden. She would fill it with the crawling, mewling grandchildren borne by her daughter, Salma, who, at that moment, exactly like her mother, was pressed against her bridegroom, naked but for the stone necklace around her neck. She was promising to take care of her husband, as well as his mother and his younger siblings.

After Qisma had granted Tariq all the bodily positions that she knew, or had heard about, or had imagined, after she had given him everything he longed for, she held him to her breast for several long minutes. Both of them were naked, and he returned her embrace, saying, "It's as though this were the first gift of Sufism, one of their escapades or their sweet shudders. But the strange thing is that a song is coming over me now, rather than any Sufi text."

"Sing it then," she said. "From the little I know of dervishes and mystics I can tell it will be beautiful."

It was a song he used to sing long ago, but it had never affected him the way it did in that moment, for it exactly expressed what had happened and what he was feeling. Some of its lines were from a poem by the classical Arab poet Maskin al-Darami, and he sang them in the style of Sabah Fakhri, a contemporary Syrian singer he loved. He felt each syllable rise up from his throat as though it were something he could chew and taste, and he was aware of an increased richness to his tone, thanks to the hours he had devoted to reciting the Qur'an in recent days.

> Tell the lass with the black veil what you did with a holy hermit
> He had gathered up his robe to pray when you stood before him
>   at the door to the mosque
> You stripped him of his religion and his certainty; you left him
>   confused, not seeing the way
> Give him back his prayers and his fasting; do not slay him to the
>   religion of Muhammad

Qisma stared up into the darkness, listening with pleasure. To her the moment was like a metaphor from the past or some other world: beautiful, but something that held no meaning for her. When he fell silent, she turned around, kissed him and stood up.

Qisma put on her robe and went towards the door. Light entered again. She picked up her abaya from the carpet just outside his chamber. Before she wrapped herself in it, closed the door and left, she said, "Now we'll each continue on the path we've chosen. You have complete freedom to divorce me if you choose. It means nothing to me. So do whatever you want. Farewell."

He remained where he was, his mind floating freely, doubting the truth of what had happened. Then he sang the same love song again, in a low voice, to himself, as he stared up into the dark.

Qisma stole through the hall and the shadowy courtyard of the mosque. She went out the main gate and closed it softly behind her. Night had cast its dark blanket over the village. She walked back towards her house with a freedom, a calm inner peace that she had not felt for a long time. But as she turned the corner of her street, three masked men fell upon her. They gagged her with a strip of cloth. They bound her wrists and picked her up in powerful arms. They put her into a car and sat her in the middle of the back seat, one of them on either side. Then they set off in the direction of the fields without covering her eyes.

CHAPTER 29

Tears of the Seagulls and the Laughter of the Grave

Qisma made no effort to resist. Not only was her body exhausted after the trip, the dancing, the sleepless night and the lovemaking, but she was still overcome by the spirit of peace that she had felt as she left the mosque. In that moment she was tasting the philosophy of submission that she had rejected her entire life, which had led her to reject her father. She was trying for herself the acceptance of fate that her father had practised throughout his life, up to the moment he was slaughtered like an animal, submitting to what he called *qisma* and *naseeb* – fate and decree. She did not even look to see if she knew the three kidnappers. She was content to look out the window as the car made its way along the dirt roads through the landscapes of her childhood. Despite the darkness, which was gradually making way for the light of dawn, she knew where she was, and whose fields were whose. When she looked at the clock on the dashboard, it said five thirty. She knew they were taking her towards the river, and she was pleased that she recognised the fields, falling back on memories from her childhood and her youth that she thought the city had wiped away.

She remembered the times she had accompanied her father and mother through these fields, recalling the songs they would sing to her as they took turns carrying her on their shoulders. She would happily wrap her small arms around the head of whoever was carrying her, embracing it like a doll, looking down from a height that, at the time, seemed impossibly high to her. "I'm taller than you! I'm higher! I'm flying!" she would tell them. Her father would lift up his arms, holding her wrists to stretch out her arms like wings. She felt she was a bird circling in the sky, with the world spread out beneath her.

Heading for the same river at the same time, but in a different village, Rahib was treading a solitary path, awake before anyone else. He longed for the river and for the pastures of his childhood, the dirt tracks he knew like the lines of his palm. He had invented names for most of the trees and stones, and he was talking to them, freely revealing his innermost thoughts. Upon reaching the river, he was surprised to find his brother Bara there, stretched out on the pebbles and sipping beer. It was rare for Bara to wake early, and when questioned, Bara explained that he had been unable to sleep. He was afraid that his muse had abandoned him completely, seeing as he had not written a poem of note since the Americans had occupied the country. The poems he had written recently had failed to satisfy him. He did not know if the Americans were to blame for his inability to write, or if his facility for poetry had simply dried up, a fate that befalls so many poets whose inspiration passes with their youth. He had come to the place where he had written his first poems in the hope that being there would stir something within him. Rahib would normally have mocked these concerns of his, but he resisted the urge in case his brother revealed another cause for anxiety. After a brief silence, Bara did just that. He was passing from one stage of his life to another, he said. He would be married soon, and he did not know whether it would suit his free and wandering spirit. Or if Wafa, that sweet young woman, had really understood what she was saying when she promised to respect his freedom and his choices. Either way, there was no doubt that obligations were closing in on him, now that he had decided to share his life with another person. He feared that his obligation to Wafa would lead him inexorably into a series of fresh obligations to other people, for an obligation to an individual leads to an obligation to a group, and then to a society, and ultimately to the nation as a whole.

Rahib did not understand all the words his brother used, but he understood what he was getting at. He grasped the gist of the problem and tried to calm Bara down by urging him to embrace this new chapter in his life. A life passed through different stages, and if it were confined to just one, stretching out endlessly, with the same colour, taste and rhythm, it would become boring and meaningless, no matter how free you imagined yourself to be. Then he reminded him what would happen if Sheikh Tafir learned he was consuming alcohol in the village and said Bara needed to be more cautious and secretive when he drank, before ordering him with a laugh to pass him the bottle.

Rahib immediately drained it, taking great pleasure in the flavour of the beer and the sensation of the bubbles on his tongue and teeth. The two of them drank all the remaining beer, and threw the empty bottles into the river. Then Rahib suggested they go to the grave of the blessed saint, the Father of Lights, to lick the salt in the jars and vessels set there, and to take strips of the green banners to hang around their necks or tie around their arms, under their clothes, like everyone else who came to seek a blessing. Perhaps that would lighten Bara's spirits somewhat.

Bara smiled. "But you know I don't believe in those tall tales."

"It doesn't matter. It can't hurt. And honestly, most people around here talk about positive changes and problems cleared up after a visit to the grave."

"Where did the grave come from? How did it appear? There was no mention of it when I was living in the village."

"No-one knows exactly. It's almost as though it was a gift from heaven. A woman saw a flash of light one night and it led her to a small grave. She sat down and confided in it, complaining about an illness she was suffering. Before she knew it, she had recovered. She complained about a problem, and the solution presented itself. After that she began tending the grave, building up the mound of earth above it. She told the other village women about it and brought them to visit. Soon the stories about its miracles were on everyone's lips. That led Sheikh Tafir to start looking after it himself, cultivating the area around it. He built a small dome and ordered me to bring running water there and to build two toilets. He installed benches for visitors. Before long, a visit to the grave became part of the ritual celebration of births, marriages, deaths, holidays and other occasions. Now people from neighbouring villages and even distant regions have started coming to seek a blessing and request the return of lost loved ones, the safety of those away at war, success for a student, a cure for sterility or a disease, and things like that. They also offer vows, and the sheikh oversees their fulfilment."

"Where is it?"

"Just over there on the outskirts of the village."

Standing up made them realise how drunk they were.

"I'm feeling better now," said Bara. "Lighter."

Rahib laughed. "Me too! No doubt it's the Father of Lights blessing us even before we've reached him!"

They both laughed, and Bara fell in with his brother's short strides as they left the river at the same moment that the kidnappers reached its shore near Qisma's village.

They took Qisma out of the car and ordered her to kneel. They started to cover her eyes, but she shook her head. She was facing the water, receiving its cool breeze, her eyes fixed on the gulls circling in the white pre-dawn light.

The men spoke for the first time since seizing her. One was wearing black gloves, and his heavy hands pressed down on her shoulders. Another man held a pistol with a silencer in one hand and an army knife in the other.

"Which do you want?" he said. "A bullet in the head or your throat cut with the knife?"

She answered by turning her face towards the knife. The kidnappers looked at each other, surprised and even a little frightened.

"Are you sure?" the man with his hands on her shoulders asked.

She nodded and resumed staring at the river, stretching out

her neck to make the task easier, as though she were waiting for a kiss, not a knife. The man who had given her the choice returned the pistol to its holster and twisted her hair around his free hand. He began to saw at her trembling neck with the knife. It did not offer any resistance, and Qisma did not react save for a murmur stifled by the cloth that gagged her mouth and a shudder of her shoulders as the edge of the blade reached bone. Blood spurted out, spraying the pebbles by the shore. Her body sagged forward, and her gaping neck streamed and bubbled with blood. Severing the spinal cord with one last powerful movement, he raised her severed head aloft and took a step back. Her body fell onto the rocks, the edge of her neck touching the edge of the water as though she were drinking. The frogs nearby scattered, alarmed by the red stain spreading in the water, while distant fish approached. Qisma's dead body twitched and shivered in the final throes of death before it went still. Still forever. Her black abaya had fallen away to reveal her sheer white dress, through which her desirable young body could be seen. The men expressed their regret at not having taken their pleasure with it before they killed her. One of them wished they had removed the gag to talk to her before her death, but they had been afraid she would scream. Perhaps they also feared what she might say. She had been less afraid than they themselves.

They stood around her corpse, watching the blood pour out and mix with the water of the river. One of them turned her over on her back, and her nakedness under the diaphanous white robe startled them. The way her breasts stood up drew their attention and appalled them even more. Averting their eyes, they looked at one another. One of them squatted down and used his hand to splash some water on her neck and front, which made the cloth of the robe cling to her skin, making her breasts even more visible. He almost reached out his hand to touch them, but he hesitated at the last moment and turned her body back onto its stomach. He released her bonds and, holding one wrist in each of his hands, picked her up. One of the others came forward to lift her by the ankles. They waded into the water until it came up to their knees, then stopped. They swung her body several times back and forth before throwing her with all their strength towards the centre of the river. For an instant she looked like a large seagull as her black abaya opened up and fluttered on both sides of her white body like wings, the ragged red wound that was her neck resembling a beak. They watched her body land in the water with a resounding splash, then sink, leaving behind a rippling circle of red. They kept watching in silence until the last trace of her – a corner of her black abaya at the centre of the red ripples – disappeared. When the water was calm once more, they carried the head away with them, leaving behind the cries of the gulls over the river.

On the outskirts of their village, Rahib and his brother Bara were arriving at the resting place of the Father of Lights. Rahib enjoyed watching his brother circle the dome and examine it with keen interest. It was as though Bara were searching for something he had lost. He took a few steps backward, stopped, adjusted his glasses, and then stared over the field they had crossed towards the village, towards his family's house. He was thinking. Then he took several steps in the other direction, fixing his gaze on the villagers' orchards. He put a hand to his chin, his brow furrowed in thought.

"What's wrong, Bara?" Rahib asked.

"Did you and I come here once to play when we were little?"

"Yes."

"Right here, exactly where the dome is now, there was a patch of clayey earth. We brought water here, kneaded it into mud, and shaped it into little animals and cars and other things."

"Yes, yes. I remember."

"We would put them in that nearby thicket until they dried and hardened. Then we would paint them. We'd bring them back to this patch of earth, draw streets and houses, and play with them till nightfall."

"Ah, yes! Those were wonderful days, Bara. You ought to think about coming back to the village."

Bara burst out in sudden laughter. He was laughing so hard he gripped his belly and fell to the ground before the astonished eyes of Rahib, who was struggling to understand what had provoked such an outburst. But Bara was unable to speak, overcome by another wave of laughter. Nothing passed his lips but truncated words amid his gasps and chuckles. "Do you remember? You remember?"

"Yes! Yes, I remember."

"No, no! Do you remember that fart?"

"What fart? Take it easy. Don't go farting now! Please – explain! Help me understand."

"The fart! The fart! *My* fart!"

Rahib squatted down by Bara's head, trying to hear better or else to calm him down, while Bara went on kicking the air like a cockroach flipped over on its back. He held his belly, which was still shaking from the force of his laughter.

"My fart. You piled dirt up where it happened in order to make a small grave, you bastard."

At that, Rahib slapped a hand against his forehead. He did remember. He burst into laughter even louder than his brother's, and he too fell onto his back, kicking the air with his short legs. He did remember that incident, one that he had completely forgotten after promising his brother that he would do so. Bara had farted so lustily it scattered the dust beneath him. Rahib had laughed aloud, which had made Bara quickly forget his embarrassment as he caught Rahib's contagious laughter – just as was happening now, all those years later – and the fart became a running joke between them until the sun went down and it was time for them to go home. Bara had asked Rahib not to mention the fart to any of the other boys, offering in exchange to teach him how to ride the bicycle that their father had given him as a reward for his success in school. Bara promised he would let Rahib ride it whenever he wanted to. Rahib agreed, and Bara had said to him several times, "This will be our buried secret."

In order to reassure his brother, Rahib had said, "I'll bury it now in front of you and forget it forever." He began gathering the earth and placing it in the area of the fart until there was a mound the size of a child's grave. He found two small stones, which he set there as gravestones, and then they left.

"The Father of Lights, the Father of Lights!" was what Rahib was now repeating between his cackles. "Our master, the Father of Lights!" he said amid gales of laughter, while Bara said over and over, "My fart! My blessed fart!" They struck the ground and rolled around as though they were swimming in the river.

"My God! What is this madness? How can we explain to these backward people that their master, whose blessings they have sought and paid for sometimes with their blood, is my fart?"

"Please don't! I beg you not to do that, lest they kill you. It's not possible to speak rationally about things that people consider sacred. They believe in superstition more than they believe in science."

Fresh bouts of laughter punctuated their conversation as they lay stretched out on their backs with their heads close together.

"My God! I can't possibly move back here again."

"Yes, you can! On condition that you respect the beliefs of others, no matter what they are. Better still if you were able to go along with them and join in with their beliefs."

Bara's laughter returned, scaling new heights, as he said, "How? How? How can I join their ceremonies venerating my fart?"

"Silence and respect are the only option. Otherwise, they'll kill you. Believe me. Sheikh Tafir would kill you himself if you opened your mouth."

"Do you really expect me to worship my own fart, you idiot?"

"It's the sensible thing to do. Trust me."

"I have to say something. I've agreed with Wafa that I will conduct a campaign to raise people's awareness of their conditions in order to change them."

"Change them?" Rahib laughed. "Impossible. Believe me,

you'll watch your children and grandchildren as they fearfully approach this dome of the Father of Lights and light candles to him, because that's what they've seen their elders doing."

Bara just laughed and kicked out at the air all the more, which set Rahib off again too. Their howls of laughter were louder even than the dawn crowing of the village cockerel, and they were surprised by the approach of women in black abayas who launched stones and curses at them as punishment for the way they were behaving in the vicinity of the dome of the Father of Lights. They got up and fled, returning to their spot beside the river, still laughing, and infecting with their laughter everyone they passed. This went on until the entire village had been imbued with cheer and good humour, without anyone knowing the reason why.

The other village, meanwhile, woke to find a banana crate containing the severed head of its daughter Qisma. The first person to notice it alongside the main street was the dull-witted herdsman Isma'il. It was where he had found the head of Qisma's father, Ibrahim, along with those belonging to eight other sons of the village, on the dawn of that third morning of Ramadan in that land without bananas.

One village woke to laughter, the other to tears, both of them on the banks of the Tigris. The villages there do not know what tomorrow will bring, laughter or tears, but they know they must go on living with both. And in another village, between the first two, on the banks of the same river, the imam was reciting the Qur'an from the pulpit of the mosque:

And how many villages have we destroyed, when our might comes upon them in the night or when they are dozing?

And are there villages safe from our might that comes in the night when they are sleeping? Or villages safe from our might that comes in the forenoon when they play?

And if we want to destroy a village, we command its rich, but they sin gravely there, and so the word against it is justified, and we destroy it utterly.

Those present cried aloud in admiration at the beauty of his voice without paying any heed to the meaning of what had been said. "God is great!" they shouted. All but one: a bearded Tajik who had slipped in with those arriving for the dawn prayer as they wiped the sleep from their eyes. He sat in among them, caressing the vest of explosives tied around his waist under his robe. He was waiting for the moment when the mosque was at its fullest, crammed with worshippers at prayer, when he would blow himself up, crying, "God is great!"

MUHSIN AL-RAMLI is an Iraqi writer, poet, academic and the translator from Spanish to Arabic of many literary classics. He was born in northern Iraq in 1967 and has lived in Madrid since 1995. He obtained his Ph.D. in Philosophy and Letters from the Autonomous University of Madrid in 2003 with his thesis *The Traces of Islamic Culture in Don Quixote*. Now he works as a professor at Saint Louis University, Madrid Campus. He writes in both Arabic and Spanish, and is a well-known figure in the world of Arabic literature.

His novels *Dates on my Fingers* and *The President's Gardens* were longlisted for the I.P.A.F., known as the "Arabic Booker", in 2010 and 2013, and he was a finalist for the Sheikh Zayed Book Award in 2016 with his novel *The She-Wolf of Love and Books*.

Much of his writing is based on his own personal experiences, including his service as a tank commander in the Iraqi army during the Gulf War. His brother, the writer Hassan Mutlak, was hanged in 1990 at the age of twenty-nine for an attempted coup d'état; he is considered by many in his country to be the Lorca of Iraq.

LUKE LEAFGREN is an Assistant Dean of Harvard College, where he teaches Arabic and translation. He has published five translations, including *The President's Gardens*, also by Al-Ramli, which won the 2018 Saif Ghobash Banipal Prize for Arabic Literary Translation. He is an avid sailor and the inventor of the Stand-Stand portable standing desk.